FOOL ME ONCE & THE INEVITABLE

USA TODAY BESTSELLING AUTHOR

NIKKI ASH

I'll be damned if I'm fooled again.

Fool me once, shame on you; fool me twice, shame on me.

CHAPTER ONE

"Hey, can you talk for a minute?" my sister, Sierra, asks from the doorway of the bedroom we share.

I lower the book I'm reading to give her my attention, confused as to why she wants to talk to me. She never does. No matter how much I beg.

"I was wondering if you have any plans for spring break," she says, causing my heart to expand slightly in hope.

Is it possible? Does she want us to go away together? Is she finally letting me back in?

But then she adds, "Some friends are going to Cocoa Beach, and Jordan said I can't go unless you go because I'm still underage," and my expanded heart—and hope—shatters in my chest.

I should've known better. Of course the only reason she would ask if I have any plans is because Jordan's forcing her into a corner. And of all places, she wants me to go with her to the same beach our parents used to take us to, so she can party with her stoner, loser friends. Create new, shitty memories to replace the meaningful ones. She knows how much that place means to me. *To us.* Is she really that far gone? *Yes,* I remind myself.

Yes, she is. And there's nothing I can do. I've begged and pleaded. I've gotten mad and thrown things. But nothing I've done has gotten through to her. I keep telling myself all she needs is time, but it's been two years and she's still shutting me out.

"No," I say, choking the two letters out.

"No, you don't have plans?"

"No, I'm not going to Cocoa Beach with you," I clarify, raising my book back up so she can no longer see my face, and I don't have to see hers.

"You seriously can't do me this one damn favor?" When I don't answer, pretending to be engrossed in my story, her footsteps stomp across the room. Just as my eyes lift to see what she's doing, she yanks my hardback copy of *Wuthering Heights* out of my hands and flings it across the room. It lands on the wood floor with a thud with the spine pointing up. The pages most likely now bent.

Standing, I step into her space, so close our noses are almost touching. I put up with a lot of shit from her, but I will not tolerate her touching my things. "One, not getting your way doesn't mean you get to lash out and mess with other people's stuff." Shoving her shoulder, I stalk past her to grab my book off the ground. When I open it, just as I suspected, several worn pages are now bent. With my back to her, I run my fingers along them to smooth out the corners before I close the book. I shouldn't have taken it off my shelf. It's too fragile. When Mrs. Barnes assigned it as the required reading over spring break, I should've checked out one of her copies, instead of telling her I have my own at home. If anything happened to this book, I don't know what I'd do. I make a mental note to go by her class tomorrow to grab a copy.

"And two." I swivel around and glare at my sister, who at least has the decency to look sorry over throwing the book, now that she sees which book it is. "If you ever touch any of my damn books again, I'm going to destroy everything of yours that means anything to you." I take a deep breath, holding back the tears, which are burning my lids and begging to surface. "You want to push me away and pretend you have no family left? I can't stop you! We both know I've tried. But don't mess with all I have left of our mother."

Sierra steps toward me, and for a split second I see the sister I used to know. Her caramel-colored eyes, the same ones as mine, go soft, and her pink, heart-shaped lips, which are almost identical to mine—except mine are a bit puffier—turn down into a frown.

"I'm sorry," she says softly, reminding me momentarily of the old version of my sister. The one who wore her heart on her sleeve and loved with every ounce of her being. "I didn't realize it was one of Mom's books. Is it okay?"

"It's fine." I swallow the lump in my throat. Sierra might've let her guard down for a moment, but I know all too well it won't stay that way. She just feels bad because these books are all I have left of our mother. *Of our old life.* In a minute, her guilt will pass, and she'll raise her wall back up to protect her heart. "You better go let your *friends* know you won't be going to Cocoa Beach."

"B, please!" she begs. "I'll do whatever you want. It's the last trip before everyone graduates!"

I halt at her nickname for me as my heart fissures, remembering the day we came up with our nicknames—or I guess I should say, the day we stole them.

We were in our early teens and watching *Gossip Girl,* one of our favorite shows to watch reruns of on Netflix. Sierra pointed out that our first names started with the same letters as Serena and Blaire, the main characters in the show.

"They're best friends just like we are. We should totally call each other S and B just like they do," she said.

"We're more than best friends," I pointed out. "We're sisters."

"Best friends and sisters."

We spent the next ten minutes trying out our new nicknames, as if calling each other a single letter was the best thing in the world. At dinner that night, Sierra called out my new nickname when she asked me to pass the rolls. When Mom asked where that came from, Sierra explained they were our new nicknames.

"Should we start calling you S and B as well?" Mom asked with a smile, while Dad chuckled, shaking his head.

"Nope," Sierra told her. "They're only for Blakely and me. It's a sister-best friend thing."

"Blakely!" Sierra yells, bringing me back to the present. "I'll clean our room and bathroom, and do the dishes for a month."

"Why would I agree to go to the beach with you for a week? For what? So you can party every night until you pass out with your loser friends? No, thank you." My response is a mixture of anger, hurt, and jealousy. Anger because I hate what she's doing to her life. Hurt because she either doesn't see or care how much she's hurting me. And jealousy because I miss my sister something fierce.

"Two months," she counters, ignoring my comment. "I'll do both of our chores until you leave for college." Until *you* leave for college. That one statement has me feeling as if my chest is caving in and crushing what's left of my heart. Until now, she hadn't verbally confirmed that she's not planning to move with me. That would mean actually speaking to me. Something she avoids doing at all costs. Unless she needs something, like right now.

Sierra never planned to go to college. Her dream is—or I guess *was*—to one day open a restaurant or a bar—she loves food and music and having a good time—and since she can do that just about anywhere, and we couldn't stand the thought of being away from each other for four years, we always said wherever I went, she would go too. But that was before the accident. Now, she can't stand being in the same room as me. *She's just trying to protect her heart*, I remind myself. *She still loves you.* The bond we share is stronger than what tore us apart. It will get us through these hard times, and one day I'll have my sister back.

My eyes meet hers, and a silent plea crosses from her to me, and I know I'm going to give in. Not because I condone her partying and wasting her life away, but because at the end of the day, she's still my sister and I love her. And deep down, I keep hoping she'll stop pushing me away and let me back in.

"Okay, I'll go." Maybe being at the same beach where we spent every spring break during our childhood will help her to remember all the good times we had before our world was destroyed. Maybe time at the beach will be what brings my sister back to me.

"Thank you," she says, not even questioning why I changed my mind. She doesn't care. She just wants to get her way, so she can continue to spiral downward.

"What hotel are we going to?" I ask, hoping it's near where we used to stay with our parents.

She darts her eyes all over the room and clears her throat, suddenly looking uncomfortable. "It's not the hotel *they* used to bring us to." She can't even say 'our parents.' It's too hard for her. I read online that everyone handles grief differently. Some people cling to their loved ones, while others push them away. I tried to cling, but Sierra pushed.

"But it's on the beach," she continues, "and you can bring your book and spend the week reading. I promise everyone will leave you alone. We have to share a bed, since I didn't have enough money to get a separate room, but you can have it. I'll sleep on the couch or floor."

I nod robotically, biting down on my bottom lip to stifle the sob that's threatening to release as I listen to Sierra promise that everyone will leave me alone. Meaning *she'll* leave me alone. At one time, we would've been planning our week together, making a list of everything we wanted to do. We would've been ecstatic to share a bed so we could talk all night.

"That's fine," I choke out. "Whatever you want to do is fine." My voice cracks on the last word, my emotions getting the best of me. It's been a while since I've let Sierra see my hurt. When I realized my emotions would only push her farther away, I started to hold it all in.

Sierra's brows furrow in what looks like concern, and for a moment I wonder if maybe she does still care. But then her phone rings, breaking the moment. She pulls it out of her back pocket and checks the screen. Her eyes flit from the phone to me like she's warring with herself. I hold my breath, waiting to see what happens next.

"It's Imani. She's picking me up to go to a party." Imani is her best friend. She's also the biggest slut at school, and is known to do drugs and drink until she passes out every weekend. Therefore, she's the perfect friend for Sierra because she doesn't have to actually be a friend. She doesn't have to open her heart up to her. Their friendship is fake and superficial, exactly what Sierra wants because it's safe.

"Okay." I nod once and walk out of the room.

When I get to the kitchen, Jordan is standing at the sink, peeling potatoes. "Do you need any help?" I ask her. The door slams closed, indicating Sierra left, but neither of us acknowledges it. Jordan knows we're not speaking, but she doesn't get involved. It's not her job. She also doesn't know how hard Sierra likes to party. I considered telling her, but was afraid instead of getting her help, she'd kick us out.

"That would be great, thanks." She hands me the knife, so I can cut once she peels. "Did Sierra ask you about the beach?"

"Yeah, I told her I'd go."

"I'm sorry to put you in that position." Jordan glances over at me, her lips curving into an apologetic smile. "It's just that she's only seventeen…"

"I know… I get it." Jordan is our foster parent. She's not the most nurturing, but when everyone else only had room for one teenager, she was willing to take us together.

Because I'm eighteen, I'm no longer the state's problem. But since Sierra and I are only ten months apart, and both graduating in less than two months, Jordan agreed to let me stay here until graduation.

"If you need some money…"

"No, it's okay. I'm good, but thank you." Because of me being eighteen, Jordan no longer gets any checks from the state to help support me. She insists on still covering all my living expenses, including food, which is more than she has to do. Not wanting to take advantage, I work at the local bookstore for anything extra I might need. In May, when we graduate, I'll be heading to South Carolina to go to college. I was accepted for early admission, so I'll be starting my summer classes the same week we graduate.

Between my academic scholarship and financial aid, I'll have everything covered, including my food and housing. I'll even have a little extra left over, which will allow me to focus on school and not have to work.

I'm assuming since Sierra is no longer planning to move with me, she'll continue to live with Jordan until she turns eighteen in August and then I'm not sure what she's going to do. I don't even think she knows what she's going to do.

After we finish the potatoes, I excuse myself back to my room to read, and Jordan tells me she'll let me know when dinner is ready. While I'm lost in the love triangle between Catherine, Heathcliff, and Edgar, my cell phone dings with an incoming text. Since I tend to keep to myself, I know without looking it's Sierra. Setting my book down next to me, I grab my phone from the nightstand and read the text.

> **S: We're leaving early Saturday morning, and Imani is driving. She said it's cool if you ride with us.**

I roll my eyes at her text. Being that neither of us has a car, and I'm *only* going for her, it's kind of a given I would have to ride with her friends. I mean, how else would I get there? By cab? By foot?

Not wanting to fight with her, I reply with an **okay**, then drop my phone back onto the nightstand. I pick my book back up, but I'm no longer in the mood to read. The thing I've learned about *Wuthering Heights* is that you have to be able to focus when you're reading it. It was written in the eighteen hundreds and the language is hard to understand. It's my first time reading it, so I'm finding I have to read each chapter a couple times to fully grasp what's happening.

When I flip through the pages to make sure they're all intact from the earlier tumble, a small piece of paper falls out of one of the pages and onto my chest. My heart thumps against my ribcage as I open the paper to find my mom's handwriting. When I read over it, I recognize it as a grocery list. Milk, eggs, chicken, juice, tomatoes… I scan down the list, stopping on the last item: almond soy milk.

She must've used it as a bookmark, and based on the last item on her list, it had to have been just before the accident. Sierra was going through a dieting phase and insisted on only drinking almond soy milk. Nobody in the house liked it but her. Hell, I don't even think she liked it, since the diet—and almond soy milk—only lasted a couple weeks. Wow! She must've been reading *Wuthering Heights*.

Lying down, I bring the book to my chest, wishing for it to help me feel closer to my mom. God, I miss her so much. Every second of every day. It's so unfair. She was this beautiful, vibrant woman, who didn't deserve to have her life stolen from her. Especially by her selfish, lying, drunk of a husband.

As the tears escape my eyelids, I hold the book tightly, allowing the small comfort of knowing this was possibly the last book she read before she left this earth, to lull me to sleep.

CHAPTER TWO

Blakely

"Hey, Blakely."

The voice comes from behind me, so I turn to find Brenton Davis walking over to me. Like me, he's fairly new to the school, has only been here a few months, but unlike me—and more like my sister—he's already found his place, which is at the top of the food chain. Football is over, but if it were still in full swing, he'd fit in perfectly with the jocks. Athletic, cocky, good-looking. Yet he also seems to fit in with the book nerds. He's smart and takes his academics seriously. We have a couple AP classes together.

"I heard you're heading to the beach with everyone." He stops in front of me and his lips curve into a million-megawatt smile.

"Yep, I'll be there." I grab my books from my locker and slam it closed since it likes to stick. Today is the last day of school before spring break, so I'm bringing some stuff home with me to work on while we're at the beach all week—including the copy of *Wuthering Heights* that Mrs. Barnes loaned me so I wouldn't have to chance my mom's copy at the beach.

"I was wondering if maybe you'd want to ride with me." He shrugs his shoulders and his hands go into his pockets as if he's… nervous? Internally, I groan. If this were a couple years ago, I would be all over it: hot guy, a hotel, the beach for a week. But now, my priorities have changed.

"I'm sorry, but you're wasting your time," I say, trying to let him down easy.

"Excuse me?" He raises a brow, confused.

"I'm not going to sleep with you," I tell him, figuring just coming out and saying it will push this conversation forward quicker and then we can pretend it never happened. "I'm only going to the beach as Sierra's allocated babysitter."

"Oh… no." He winces. "I wasn't trying to… I don't want to hook up with you." He sighs. "I mean, you're hot…"

A giggle escapes past my lips at his uneasiness, and I slap my hand over my mouth to hide it, but I'm not fast enough and he catches it.

"Jesus, this is all coming out wrong." He runs his fingers through his dirty blonde hair. "I actually just got out of a bad relationship before moving here, so I'm not looking for anything like that. I just thought maybe we could ride together as friends. I heard your sister talking shit about you having to ride with her and her friends." He flinches. "Shit."

"No, it's okay. It's not exactly a secret that my sister wants nothing to do with me," I say softly, my voice cracking with emotion. She's the only person I have left in the world, and yet I don't even have her.

"Well, if you want to ride with me…" He lifts a shoulder.

"That would actually be really great," I tell him, figuring riding with him will be better than being stuck in the car with Sierra and her druggy friends.

"Yeah?"

"Yeah."

"All right. I'll pick you up at eight, so we can miss the morning traffic on 95." His words remind me of something I've been thinking about lately.

"Hey, Brenton, would you mind making one stop along the way? It's right off 95."

"Sure," he says with a smile.

"Thank you. See you tomorrow."

"Is it true?" Sierra drops onto her bed, her backpack hitting the floor with a thud. "Are you going to the beach with Brenton Davis?"

Throwing the last of my clothes into the small suitcase, I zip it up, then sit on my bed, which is parallel to Sierra's. "Yep."

"Thought you were all 'I'm focusing on school, not boys'?" She tilts her head to the side and her chin juts out, something she always does when she's in confrontation mode. These days, Sierra has two modes when it comes to me: She's either mad at me, or she's ignoring me. Both allow her to keep me at arm's length.

"I'm riding up with him. That's it." I roll my eyes and stand, grabbing my suitcase and setting it next to the door. "And I only agreed to ride with him after he mentioned how much shit my sister was talking about me having to ride with her and her friends." I glare at her briefly before I grab my book and drop to my bed to read.

When she doesn't say anything, I glance up. Her face appears pained. I wonder if maybe she'll apologize, tell me she was wrong and then cuddle up next to me like we used to do when we were little after we got into one of our stupid fights. But she schools her expression and shrugs. "Imani was annoyed Tashia wouldn't be able to ride with us. I wasn't talking shit…"

"Yeah, okay," I say, knowing she's full of shit. "Well, now she can." I open my book to the page I left off on and lie back against the pillows on my bed.

"So, you're not going to hook up with Brenton?" she asks.

"Nope," I say, without giving her my attention even though I'm not really reading. Her bed squeaks and then her feet pad across the floor, and when I chance a glance, I notice she's gone. Groaning, I drop the book to my chest and close my eyes, wishing for the millionth time I could figure out how to get her back. Maybe Mom will have an answer…

"Here?" Brenton asks, stopping his vehicle in front of the wrought iron gate.

"Yes. I'll only be a few minutes." Giving him a small smile, I get out of his car and meander through the rows of headstones until I get to the one I'm looking for.

RACHEL JACOBS
LOVING MOTHER AND WIFE

She only has two titles because my sister and I, and our father was all she had in this life. She didn't know much about her family, but what she did know, what foster care told her, was that she was created out of wedlock and her mother was a part of the Catholic Church. Her family forced her to give up my mother, who proceeded to spend her next seventeen years in group homes. She met our dad when she was seventeen. He was older, already in his thirties. He offered her a home and she took it. I'm not sure if she loved my father or if she loved the idea of being taken care of.

What I do know is that my father loved her deeply. So deeply it turned into an obsession. An obsession that ultimately killed her…

"We're leaving," my mom says with tears pouring down her face. "Pack your bags. We don't have much time. Just take whatever clothes you need and anything that's important to you."

"Mom, what's wrong?" Sierra jumps up from her bed and runs over to our mom. "What's going on?"

"Your father," Mom chokes out through her sobs. "He's a liar! He's lost all our money. Lost our house. He's lost everything. We have nothing left."

Sierra and I have heard our parents arguing the last few months more and more, but we just assumed they were going through a rough patch.

"Can't he get it back?" I ask, confused. "Dad's the best at what he does."

"No, he can't. Because he made deals with the wrong people and they took it all. And now they're going to come for us."

"What about Grandma?" Sierra asks. "Can't she help?"

"Sure, she could, but you know she hates that your father is with me. She'll never give him a penny to help. She'd rather watch him fall. Now, please. Pack your bags."

Ten minutes later, Sierra and I are sitting in the back seat with our bags in the trunk, waiting for Mom to come out. Dad's BMW pulls up, just as Mom walks out.

"What the hell do you think you're doing?" Dad demands.

"I'm leaving! I'm taking the girls and getting out of here! I'm not going to just sit here and wait for them to come and kill us."

"I told you I'd protect you!" When Mom doesn't stop in her haste toward the car, Dad reaches behind him, pulling out a gun.

"Oh my God!" Sierra gasps. "Dad has a gun!"

"Greg, please!" Mom begs. "Don't do this. Just let us go."

"You're not taking them! You're not leaving me. We're in this together. Now get in the damn car!"

Mom complies, and then Dad takes off down the road. We drive for several miles as Mom begs our father to let us go, and he argues he's never letting us go.

"Greg," Mom says, her tone eerily calm. "You need to slow down."

When Dad doesn't answer her, she begins to sob. "Greg, what are you doing? That bend is dangerous! Slow down."

"I can't let you leave me," Dad says. "We agreed in our vows until death do us part. I'm sorry, Rachel, I know I messed up. I know I made bad deals. Please forgive me."

"Okay," Mom says, "I forgive you. Now slow down. We can run away together."

"There's no running from them." Dad's face turns toward Mom. "They won't stop looking until they find me. This is the only way."

"Greg… Greg, have you been drinking?" Mom cries. "Are you drunk?"

The tires squeal and the car jerks to the side, flipping several times. There are screams and cries and then everything goes black.

Dad was killed on impact, and Mom died on her way to the hospital. By some miracle, Sierra and I both lived. She had a broken arm and needed stitches on her forehead. I had three cracked ribs and a broken wrist. But we were alive. Without our parents.

Because our father's death was determined a suicide by the life insurance company, and Mom didn't have any life insurance, they refused to give us any of the money. Sierra and I didn't care about the money. All we cared about was that our parents were both gone.

The day our parents died was the day Sierra flipped her switch. I was discharged first, so I went to her hospital room where she was waiting for her arm to be casted.

"Oh, S!" I cry, running into the room to give her a hug. "How are you?"

When I realize she isn't returning the hug, I pull back, eyeing her wearily. "S, what's wrong?"

"Nothing," Sierra says, refusing to look at me.

"Is it your arm? They gave me pain meds. Does yours hurt?"

"No."

"S, look at me," I demand. When her eyes meet mine, they look dead inside. "What's going on?"

"I already said nothing. Can you just back off? I need some time."

A few hours later, we were on our way to our dad's mom's house, who grudgingly took us in. She refused to continue to pay for the private school we were attending, so we were switched to a public school. Every day, for the first couple months, I would ask Sierra if she was okay, but she wouldn't speak to me. At first, I thought maybe she was mad at me. But a few months later, when our grandma died—of course, leaving us nothing as a way to stick it to our parents—and the CPS person came to place us, I learned Sierra wasn't mad at me. She was afraid to love me.

"It looks like we're going to have to separate you both," Darlene, the CPS worker says. "We can't find anyone who's willing to take on two teenagers."

"It's okay," Sierra says softly.

"What?" I shriek, hurt and confused. "I get you're mad at me or whatever, but you're okay with them placing us in different homes? We still have over a year until I turn eighteen, almost two until you do. What if we have to go to different schools? Or live in a different city?"

"We were bound to be separated eventually," Sierra says, zero emotion in her tone. "Might as well get it over with now."

"You don't mean that!" I shout, and then it all clicks into place. Her not talking to me, pushing me away. We lost both of our parents, and we almost died. "You're just afraid you're going to lose me," I accuse. Her eyes go wide for a split second, but she quickly schools her features. "I'm not going anywhere," I tell her, dropping to my knees in front of her. "All we have is each other, S. Don't push me away."

"All Mom had was Dad and look where that got her." Sierra stands and, without looking at me, says to Darlene, "I don't care where you place me." Then she walks out of the room without looking back.

Luckily, despite Sierra not caring, Darlene found Jordan, who agreed to take us both in.

I swat a tear that's slipped out and down my cheek, clearing my throat. "Mom, I'm not sure if you can hear me, but I need you. Sierra needs you. I miss her so much, but she won't let me in. In two months I'm going to be leaving for college and I'm afraid I'll never see my sister again. If you're up there and listening, I just need some kind of sign. Some sort of guidance. I don't want to give up, Mom, but it's been two years and I'm not sure if she's ever going to come around."

I drop to my knees in the thick grass. "Every day she pushes me away, I think her heart forgets the bond we share. What if she never lets me back in?" Tears fly down my face, disappearing into the grass. "It's so crazy. She'd rather not have me now, in case she might lose me, instead of living every day, loving me. She's all I have left, Mom. Please, if there's anything you can do from up there, do it."

"Blakely? Are you okay?" Brenton asks. "I'm sorry. I didn't want to disturb you, but you've been out here for a while."

"I'm sorry." I stand and wipe the lingering liquid from my cheeks. "I'm okay. I just needed to talk to my mom for a few minutes."

CHAPTER THREE

THE SUN IS BLAZING DOWN FROM ABOVE, WARMING THE TIPS OF MY toes, which are the only part of my body that's exposed to the heat. The rest of me is in the shade, thanks to the gigantic rainbow-colored umbrella Brenton's jammed into the sand—before he left to go hang out with his friends—and is doing a fabulous job of covering my entire body while I cry my eyes out over the loss of Catherine Earnshaw. Not because I like her so much—oh no, she was a major bitch. I'm crying because poor Heathcliff. He loved her so much, and now she's gone, and it explains why he's the way he is. Why he's so bitter and lonely—he's heartbroken.

We've been here for four days, and so far, I've spent every single one, right here in this spot, switching from *Wuthering Heights* to my own personal romance novel I brought to read. The only time I leave is to walk to the restaurant to get something to eat, or to go to the room to get some sleep. The first couple days I was hoping to lure Sierra away from her friends so we could maybe go for a walk and talk, but I've kind of given up on that hope, since I've yet to see her awake. I'm asleep before she and her friends stumble in, and then they spend most of the day sleeping off their hangover so they can do it all over again.

Just as I'm turning the page in my book, someone yells, "Watch out!" Unsure of where the voice is coming from, I look to the left and then to the right, but before I can grasp what's happening, the circular object hits my hand, and my book flies out of my grasp and into the water.

"Shit! I'm so sorry." A half-naked guy comes running over, sand kicking up around him as his strong legs pound into the ground. The closer he gets, the more of him I'm able to see, and holy shit, do I like what I see. Messy brown hair I could picture running my fingers through, tanned, smooth skin I would enjoy kissing and licking, and if I'm feeling frisky, biting.

My eyes rake over his tattooed, sculpted chest and down to his abs. Two-four-sex… I mean six. God damn! Look at that six-pack. He must work out, probably several times a day. Damn, I'd love for him to work me out…

As he jogs over, his corded arm muscles flex, making it appear as if the ink on his arms is coming alive, and I briefly imagine holding on to those arms while he fucks me good and hard. He runs past me, and I follow his every move. When he bends over, I check out his butt that's hidden under his low-hanging board shorts as I fantasize about my legs wrapped around his waist and my heels digging into that butt…

But then he turns around, and in his hands is the now sopping wet copy of *Wuthering Heights*, and I instantly snap out of my lust-filled thoughts.

"Here you go," he says sheepishly, the soaking wet book dangling from his fingers. Drops of saltwater fall and land on my knee. My eyes meet his, and just as I'm about to snap at him, the corner of his mouth lifts into a nervous smile, and a single dimple pops out on his cheek, and once again, I'm momentarily distracted by just how good-looking he is.

"Thanks so much." My reply drips with sarcasm. Taking the book from him, I examine the saturated, ruined pages, and mumble, "At least it wasn't my mom's copy."

"I'm Keegan." His half-smile turns into a cocky grin. Oh, hell, no… "I'm not interested."

He throws his head back with the most beautiful laugh I've ever heard. It's raspy and deep and sexy. My eyes land on his Adam's apple, and my tongue darts out, wanting to lick down his throat.

"Fair enough." He nods. "I really am sorry about the book." His gorgeous forest green eyes meet mine. "Can I do something to make it up to you?"

"Like sleep with me?" I give him a playful smirk. I haven't slept with many guys, but I've had a couple one-night stands over the last few years. My way of lashing out over my mom's death.

"No." He shakes his head. "We've already established you're not interested. Although, I think, based on the way you were eye-fucking me on my way over here, I could probably convince you otherwise."

"I was…" I begin to argue, but when he raises one of his brows in a *Really? You're going to try to lie* gesture, I snap my mouth closed. He's right, after all. I was totally eye-fucking him.

"I meant, how about I take you to dinner? But if the dinner leads to…" He shrugs a shoulder and grins, this time both dimples popping out. Jesus H. Christ, no man should be allowed to look this gorgeous and be equipped with not one, but two dimples.

"I stand by my earlier statement," I say, chanting *I'm off dick* over and over again in my head to remind myself I'm focused on school and my future. A decision I made after my dad's mom died and left us with nothing, and I quickly realized if I don't make a future for myself, no one will. "I'm not interested."

"All right." He bends down to grab the football. "Enjoy your day." And with a flirty wink over his shoulder, he runs back over to where he came from.

Giving my book a once-over and concluding there's no saving it, I toss it into the sand next to my bag to throw it away later. Moving my chair to the side, I throw my blanket across the ground and lie on my stomach for a little cat nap. I might not have wanted to go on this trip, but I can admit that so far, despite my book getting drowned, and not being able to spend any time with Sierra, it's been nice to relax and reminisce on the good times we had as a family here. In a couple short months, I'm going to be heading to college and I don't know when I'll have the time or the money to take a week-long vacation again.

I don't remember my eyes closing, and I have no clue how long I'm asleep for. But when I wake up, it's to a shitload of sand hitting my body and face. "What the hell!" I screech, sitting up and spluttering in an attempt to get the sand out of my mouth. It takes a second for my eyes to focus—for me to remember I fell asleep under my umbrella—and when they do, they land directly on the two-dimpled culprit.

"Seriously?" I grab the football that landed next to me and cock my arm back to throw it at him. His eyes widen comically, like he's afraid the ball is going to hit him. But when I release it, and it lands short, several feet in front of him, his eyes twinkle, and his body shakes with silent laughter.

"Uh!" I huff, standing, so I can wipe all the sand off me. When I notice my blanket is half in the water, I let out a loud groan. The tide must've risen while I was asleep. "Damn it, my blanket is soaked!" I bend over and drag the blanket out of the water and up the beach a few feet.

"You are aware you're at a *beach*, right?" He laughs, this time out loud. "It's made up of sand and saltwater."

"Thank you for pointing that out, Captain Obvious." I roll my eyes. With the sun now pounding on my body, the saltwater and sand quickly sticks to my flesh. "Ugh!" I groan. "It's everywhere." I glare at Keegan.

"Here, let me help you rinse all that sand off." He moves toward me so fast, I don't even see it coming. Before my brain can put the pieces together, he throws me over his shoulder like I'm a freaking ragdoll and darts up the beach.

"Put me down!" I squeal, my fist pounding on his ass, while tilting my head slightly to the side so I can watch the ocean getting farther away. "What are you doing?" I yell, and he just laughs. Laughs!

I try to figure out where he's taking me, but my upside down view doesn't really tell me much. When his feet hit the solid ground, my body is no longer bouncing. He's jogging along a wood planked sidewalk that quickly turns into concrete. And then the concrete disappears and… we're both in the air.

Before I can scream again for him to put me down, my body hits the cool chlorinated water. The asshole just threw me into the pool! Paddling my arms, I swim to the surface and find him right in front of me. He grips my hips to hold me up since I can't reach the bottom of the deep end.

"You… you…" I splutter.

"You're no longer sandy." He winks.

I back out of his reach and then swim toward him. I don't even know what I'm thinking when my hands land on his shoulders, and I attempt to dunk him under the water. The guy is all muscle and doesn't even move under my touch. But he does laugh, and that pisses me off.

"Screw you!" I hiss, giving up and swimming away.

"Oh, c'mon!" he yells through a laugh. "Don't be mad."

When my feet can finally reach, I wade through the water toward the steps, but before I make it out, hands land on my hips and spin me around.

"I'm sorry. It was all in good fun." He smiles apologetically, and my anger immediately subsides. "You're at the beach, for what I'm assuming is spring break. It's okay to have a little fun." His words don't seem to be said out of malice, but they still rub me the wrong way. I spent most of my life having fun. Being carefree. Before my parents died, Sierra and I had the world at our fingertips. To do with as we pleased. But everything is different now, and having fun isn't going to help me graduate from high school or college, create a future for myself.

"And who said I wasn't having fun?" Even I can hear how defensive my tone is, but he's struck a nerve. "Because I'm choosing to lounge around and read a good book that means I'm not having fun? Does having fun have to be getting drunk and high? Hooking up at parties?" *Holy word vomit...*

His eyes go wide in shock. Bet he wishes he'd picked another girl to hit on, someone not as emotionally tainted as me. Then he speaks, and with every word, I feel like the biggest piece of shit. "Actually, getting high is the last thing I find fun. Being as my brother nearly overdosed last year. And getting drunk? Sorry, my grandfather was an alcoholic. Died from liver failure. So nope, I don't exactly find that fun either. Don't get me wrong, I'm down for the occasional beer when hanging out, but I'm not really looking to get drunk. And as far as hooking up goes, I'm a man with a working dick. Do I like sex? Sure..." He lifts a single shoulder and quirks one side of his mouth up into a sexy smirk. "But I prefer to know who I'm fucking."

He steps closer to me, until he's so close I can almost feel the heat radiating off him, and in a voice so smooth it drips like the sweetest honey, he says, "Hooking up is a one-time thing. It's fast and over way too quickly. It's simply about getting off. And most times, unless the guy cares enough, the woman doesn't even get off. I'd rather get to know the woman I'm fucking. Find out what turns her on…" His eyes drag down my body, and even though I'm in a somewhat modest bikini—one I've worn several times—I've never felt as exposed as I feel in this moment. It's as if he's stripping me bare without even touching me. "I prefer to get to know every inch of her body, find all the areas that will work her up until she's wound so tightly, she's squirming in pleasure and screaming out my name." The apex of my thighs clench at his words, my chest rising and falling a little faster. Who the hell is this guy? Nope! Not going there…

"Well, I'm sorry about your grandfather and brother, but I have no desire to allow you to… get to know me in that way. So, while this"—I flick my hand between us—"has been fun, I need to get going."

Keegan nods once. "All right. If you change your mind…"

"About what?"

"Having fun," he replies. "If you change your mind about having fun, I'll be here until the end of the week."

Our conversation is clearly over, yet neither of us moves, facing each other in the water. I'm the one who said I need to go, so why aren't I leaving? *Because you're attracted to him and it's been almost a year since you've had any type of fun.*

"You could be a rapist or a murderer," I point out. "You could be luring me in and plotting how to rape and kill me. This is the shit Lifetime makes movies about."

Keegan doesn't laugh. Instead he says, "You're right, I could be, and good for you for even thinking like that. Most women don't. I'm staying at this hotel with some friends of mine for spring break. I've never been to jail or even been given a speeding ticket." He smirks playfully. "I live and go to school in Carterville." Carterville is the city next to ours, only about thirty minutes from here.

When I don't say anything, he adds, "This is where you either tell me a little about you, so I know you aren't going to rape or murder me either, or you tell me to get lost." His lips curl into a huge flirty grin, and my insides turn to mush.

I have less than two months until I graduate. My book for school is ruined, and I'm not about to hang out with Sierra and her loser friends for the rest of the week. I can either spend the rest of my trip alone, or I can take him up on his offer to have some fun, get it out of my system, and when I return home, I go back to focusing on my future. Four days of fun isn't going to ruin everything I've busted my ass to accomplish.

"My name is Blakely, and I'm staying at the hotel next door."

When he realizes that's all I'm going to give him, he says, "At least confirm whether you've been to jail. I gotta know if I need to be worried for my life."

A groan escapes me when I think about what I'm about to say. "Three times," I admit, and he cackles.

"Seriously?"

"My sister and I got caught stealing." Definitely not my finest moment. The sad thing is we got caught while our parents were alive, which means we had more than enough money to pay for the items we chose to steal.

"Damn, should I hide my wallet?" He teases.

"Ha-ha," I say dryly. "It was clothes."

"Keep any of my sexy clothes away from you. Noted." He nods with an almost straight face. The only indication he's joking is a slight twinge to the corner of his mouth. "The other times?"

"A house party gone bad. There were drugs and underage drinking. We all got arrested." I shrug, embarrassed even though I shouldn't be. I don't even know this guy, and those days are behind me.

"Wow." He crosses his arms over his chest. "Didn't see that coming. The third time?"

"I was skipping school and a cop caught me. Brought me in for truancy." I roll my eyes.

Keegan barks out a laugh. "Wow, you've been busy."

"Hey, Keeg!" someone yells. "We're going down to the pier. You wanna go?"

"Nah!" he yells back. "Go without me." Then he says to me, "So, are you down to have some fun?"

"Fine," I say, dragging out the word. "Bring on the fun." I fake fist pump, and he laughs.

"On one condition."

"Oh, now you're giving me conditions? Really?" I scoff.

"One condition," he repeats.

"What?" I huff.

"No negativity. I have three more days before I have to deal with life. I came here to have fun, escape reality."

"Okay, agreed."

We get out of the pool, and Keegan throws his arm over the back of my shoulders like we're old friends. "C'mon, my little jailbird, let's go have some fun… legally."

CHAPTER FOUR

Blakely

"WHEN YOU SAID FUN, YOU DIDN'T MENTION THE POSSIBILITY OF death!" I yell over the sound of the waves crashing against each other as the jet ski flies across the deep blue ocean. My arms are wrapped around Keegan, my fingers threaded together so I don't risk letting go. Between his life vest and mine, I can barely reach around him. The wind whips my hair every which way, and the warm air smacks me in the face.

"No negativity!" he yells through a laugh.

"I won't be able to be positive if I die!" I yell back, humor laced in my words. I've never been jet skiing before, but I have to admit, it's actually a lot of fun—when Keegan isn't going a hundred miles an hour.

Keegan slows the jet ski down a bit as we get closer to the shore. The waves are still splashing around us, but the wind has calmed since he's no longer going as fast. "That was so much fun," he says, sounding like a little boy. "I've always wanted to do that."

He glances over his shoulder. "Admit that was fun." My lips twitch. "Admit it or I'll throw you off."

This time I laugh out loud. "Yes, it was fun!"

When we return to the shore and get off the jet ski, Keegan helps me unsnap my life vest and hands both over to the guy in charge.

"So, what's next?" My body is drumming with adrenaline, and I'm excited to see what else Keegan has planned.

"I was thinking I could take you to dinner."

"Oh." I pout, and he chuckles.

"Hey now, my little jailbird, it won't be anything as wild as a house party, but it will be fun, I promise." He throws his arm around my shoulders with a light laugh and pulls me into his side.

"You're not going to let it go, are you?"

"Nope." His shoulders shake with laughter. "I can't get over that underneath all that cuteness and innocence is a very naughty girl."

"Funny," I sass.

"So, dinner?"

I want to say yes, but at the same time I don't know this guy. It's one thing to hang out outside with him, but to get in a car and leave? I'm not sure that's the best thing to do. "I don't think that's a good idea," I admit. When he raises a single brow, I add, "I barely know you. I'm not sure I'm comfortable going out with you."

His lips curl into a wide smile. "That's okay, because I'm not taking you out. We're staying in."

"I'm not sure your room is any better!" I squeak out.

"Not my room." He shakes his head, clearly trying not to laugh at me. "Just in my hotel. There are a few different restaurants." He points over his shoulder.

"Oh, okay. That sounds good," I tell him, slightly embarrassed that I jumped to conclusions.

We walk back to his hotel and enter the lobby. We're both still in our dripping wet suits, and that's when I remember I left all my stuff at the beach.

"Shoot! I need to go grab my stuff. My phone and everything is in my bag. Someone probably stole it all."

"All right, how about you grab your stuff and get changed, and then meet me back here?"

"Okay, deal."

We part ways, and I head back to the beach where I left everything when Keegan threw me over his shoulder earlier. Luckily, it's all still there, untouched. I shake out my blanket, gather the rest of my things, and rush to the room. When I enter, Sierra and her friends are nowhere to be found. After showering and blow drying my hair so it's not soaked, I throw on a black and white bandeau dress and some sandals.

When I exit the bathroom, I find Sierra and some guy I've never seen before making out on her bed. When she hears the door creak open, she pulls back and looks at me inquisitively. "I haven't seen you all day," she says, almost sounding as if she cares.

"You haven't seen me since we got here," I point out.

"Are you having fun?" She eyes my dress.

"Yeah." I don't tell her the specifics, though. The last thing I need is her throwing it in my face that I'm hanging out with a guy when I've said a million times I'm off dick. It's not really like that, but she won't believe me. "But if you wanted to maybe go for a walk down to the pier Mom and Dad used to bring us to, I could cancel my plans…"

Sierra's eyes go soft for a quick moment, but then she shakes her head. "You need to stop living in the past, Blakely. There's nothing there for us." Then, without waiting for me to respond, she says to her guy friend, "I could really use a beer. Let's go." Getting up from the bed, she drags him out the door.

My mood instantly sours and I slam the door closed harder than intended on my way out. There was a time when Sierra and I told each other everything. When we would've spent this entire trip together. Once when I tripped over a kickball at school and scraped my knee, she refused to leave my side. The teacher told her she needed to go back to class, but she argued and told her she wouldn't go anywhere until she knew I was okay. Now, she knows I'm in pain, but instead of being by my side, she's running in the opposite direction. I'm terrified that once I move over five hundred miles away to go to school, it's going to make it that much easier for her to push me away, and one day we're both going to wake up and realize we have no family left. Not even each other.

"What's the frown for?" Keegan asks when he sees me approach him.

"Just thinking about reality," I tell him, using his words from earlier today.

"Well, then let me help you escape." He smiles a boyish grin, and it's then I notice he's no longer in his suit. Like me, he must've showered. His hair is still wet and messy, but it's shiny now. He's sporting a pair of khaki shorts and a Billabong T-shirt. His feet are donning a pair of brown sandals. He looks like your typical surfer.

"You surf?"

"I do. I've lived near the beach my entire life. I was thinking I could teach you tomorrow." He waggles his eyebrows.

"So sure I'm going to want to spend tomorrow with you, huh?" I joke.

Keegan laughs. "You came willingly just now, didn't you?" His eyes twinkle with humor. "Didn't even have to throw you over my shoulder."

As we walk past the lobby and through the main area, I take in how gorgeous his hotel is compared to the one I'm staying in. Marble floors, restaurants peeking out of several corners. I even spot a Starbucks. My heart aches at the bit of nostalgia this place awakens. There was a time when staying at a luxurious hotel was the norm for my family. Dad would never stay anywhere but a five-star hotel, and even then, it had to be the Presidential Suite. Sierra and I grew up flying first class and traveling all over the world. Dad traveled for business, but Mom always brought us along to teach us about the world. And when we couldn't go with them because of school, she would bring back books about the country and spend hours reading to us.

We stop in front of the hostess stand and Keegan hands her something. Maybe a reservation slip? I'm not sure what restaurant it is, but when we follow her down the hall and through a set of double doors, I have my answer.

"The movies?" I question, getting a good look at the massive screen in the front of the large room that's filled with rows of reclining chairs and bar tables, so people can eat their food while they watch the movie. There aren't a ton of people in the theater, but there's still quite a few.

"You said you didn't want to go out to dinner, so I figured I would take you *in*. Now I get dinner *and* a movie." He winks then follows the hostess to where our seats are—directly in the center of the theater.

"What movie are we watching?" I ask, once we get situated.

"There were only three options," he admits. "A kid's movie, a newer adult movie, or a classic. Since you were reading *Wuthering Heights*, I went with the classic." He shrugs sheepishly.

The lights drop and the commercials start. When the opening scene begins, I know right away what movie it is. "*Armageddon* is not a classic!" I whisper-yell through a giggle, and Keegan grins.

"Really?" he questions. "Well, I know it's old. My dad took my mom to see it before I was born."

I roll my eyes. "It's still not a classic."

We enjoy the movie while we eat our food—both ordering a burger and a shake. When we're done eating, and the server has taken our trash, Keegan reclines in his chair, so I do the same. His hand rests on the arm-rest, and I notice little by little it gets closer to mine. Biting down on my bottom lip, I hide the smile that's trying to break free, focusing on the movie. Eventually, Keegan's fingers reach mine, and he links his hand with mine. The moment our skin touches, butterflies flutter in my belly. Then he faces me, and he grins the most gorgeous shy grin, and the butterflies go into attack mode.

Until our parents died, Sierra and I attended private school. One would think the wealthier you are, the higher class and more respectable you are, but the truth is quite the opposite. The kids we hung out with smoked, drank, did drugs, and had sex like it was going out of style. Guys didn't date since they could easily find girls to fuck. Sierra and I both lost our virginity our freshman year of high school. We'd never even been on a date. We all just hung out. I guess if it's all you've ever known, you don't know what you're missing out on. But sitting here with Keegan, on what feels a lot like a date, I feel like I've missed out. There's something about actually spending time with a guy, wondering if he's going to hold my hand, lean over, and kiss me. He's actually trying to get to know me, woo me, in-stead of diving right into my pants.

The movie ends, and we exit the theater, our hands still threaded to-gether. When we get outside, the resort looks like it's been transformed into a college students' party oasis. Music is pumping from somewhere. Several people are in the pool horsing around with beach balls and inner tubes. There's a table set up in the corner where college-age kids are play-ing beer pong.

"Hey, Keegan!" someone yells, and we both turn to see where the voice is coming from. "Get over here, man."

I spot the guy from earlier standing in the shallow end of the pool with a girl tucked under his arm. Without a shirt on, I can tell he's fit like Keegan but without all the tattoos.

"Those are the friends I came with," Keegan tells me.

"Oh, well, you can go hang out with them." I pull my hand out of his. "I should probably get back to my hotel anyway."

"You could invite your friends over here," he suggests.

"I'm not exactly on speaking terms with the person I'm here with," I admit. When he gives me a confused look, I shake my head. "It's a long story."

"You're here with someone you're not speaking to?" he clarifies, not letting it go. "So why do you have to go back to your hotel room then?"

Reaching back, I scratch the back of my neck, unsure of how to answer him. "I guess I don't have to go back," I tell him. "I just figured you'd want to hang out with your friends. I've kind of monopolized your entire day."

"Only because I made you." He smirks playfully.

Taking my hand in his, he leads me away from the music, yelling to his friend that he'll be back soon. "Why don't you grab your suit and we can hang out for a little while?"

Not wanting to push it, I shake my head. "I think I'm going to head back."

Keegan tries to hide his disappointment, but I can still see it when he nods and says, "Okay. Can I at least walk you back?"

"It's just right next door. I promise I'll be okay."

"All right." He leans down, and his lips brush against my cheek. "Thank you for today," he murmurs, and it takes everything in me not to beg him to take me back to his hotel.

"Thank you," I whisper before bolting away from Keegan—and temptation.

CHAPTER FIVE

"Watch out!" a deep voice hollers. It's nearly 2:00 p.m., and since I haven't seen or heard from Keegan all day, I assumed I wouldn't be seeing him again. So I'm slightly shocked when I find the man the voice belongs to is, indeed, Keegan, and he's running toward me.

Only this time, unlike the other times, there's no ball headed in my direction. "Very funny." I laugh, closing my book and setting it back into my bag.

"I figured throwing a ball at you for a third time may not be the best way to go about getting your attention." He drops onto the sand next to me. "How's it going?"

"Good… relaxing." I don't admit that the entire day I've been glancing around, hoping to see him again.

"My friend Mitch and I are going surfing. His girlfriend wants to learn. I was thinking I could give you those lessons we talked about yesterday, if you're interested."

Not even bothering to play hard to get, I nod. "That sounds like fun."

I have no intention of going back to the room any time soon anyway.

This morning, when I woke up, to my surprise, Sierra was awake and sitting on the nasty balcony overlooking the greenish-blue pool. When I asked her if I could join her, she told me she wasn't in the mood to reminisce over a life we'd never get back, then stood up and walked back inside. I hadn't planned to reminisce, but her saying that leads me to believe it's what she was doing. I wanted to follow her inside and beg her to let me in, but I was afraid of pushing too hard, so instead I grabbed my beach stuff and came out here.

"Cool." Keegan helps me gather my things.

I tell him the umbrella is the hotel's, so he can leave it there. Just as I'm slipping on my sandals, someone calls my name, and I notice Brenton's heading my way.

"Who's this?" Brenton asks, eyeing Keegan, who has my beach bag over his shoulder.

"Brenton, this is Keegan." When I look over at Keegan, his brows are knitted together. He must think this is who I came with. "Brenton is here with my sister and their friends," I explain to Keegan. To Brenton, I say, "Keegan just offered to teach me how to surf."

Brenton's one brow rises. "You work here?"

"Nah." Keegan shakes his head. "I live near here. Surf a lot."

When an awkward silence blankets us, I speak up. "Did you need something?" I ask Brenton.

"Oh," he says, remembering why he came over in the first place. "We're going to drive into town for a late lunch. I was going to see if you wanted to join."

"That's okay. I'm not really hungry." Then, before I can stop myself, I ask, "Is Sierra okay? She seemed kind of off this morning."

"You know her. She's always in her own head. Nothing a beer and a joint can't fix." Brenton's gaze flickers between Keegan and me. "You sure you don't want to go?"

"Yeah, but thank you."

Brenton looks like he wants to say more, but doesn't. Instead, he nods once then takes off up to the hotel.

"You ready to go watch me make a fool of myself?" I ask Keegan.

He laughs. "Absolutely."

***

We've spent the day surfing—or I guess I should say, Keegan and Mitch have spent the day surfing, while Holly, Mitch's girlfriend, and I have spent the day falling off the board. Unless of course Keegan was on the board with me. Then I was able to stay on.

We've swum and lain out, talked a lot, and laughed even more—just all around had a great time. I can't remember the last time I spent time with people my age and enjoyed myself. We ate dinner on the pier, and now we're heading back to their hotel to hang out. Holly begged me not to leave her alone with the guys, and I couldn't say no—although, if I'm honest, the real reason I'm not leaving is because I want to spend some more time with Keegan. The guy is seriously growing on me. Oh, who am I kidding? He's already planted and rooted himself.

"You sure you're okay hanging out?" Keegan asks me once Mitch and Holly excuse themselves to go grab some drinks from the bar.

"Yeah." But then his question has me wondering if maybe I'm over-staying my welcome. Holly is the one who asked me, not him. "But if you don't want to hang out with me…"

"No," he says quickly. "It's just that last night you didn't want to, so I hope you don't feel like you have to. Holly can be a bit… demanding." He laughs.

"I'm okay. I want to."

"Good." He hits me with a two-dimpled smile. "Because I want you to."

Mitch and Holly return with a platter of shots, setting them down on the table near the pool. Holly hands me one, and Mitch hands one to Keegan.

"Cheers!" they yell at the same time, throwing their drinks back. Keegan is about to follow suit, but when he notices me not drinking mine, he lowers his glass.

"Girl, drink up!" Holly yells, grabbing another shot and downing it.

"Babe, come swim with me." Mitch pulls Holly away and throws her into the pool. Just like last night, the outside of the hotel is filled with loud music and louder people partying.

I'm eyeing the shots, unsure if I should drink, when Keegan says, "You okay?"

"I'm not sure," I admit with a humorless laugh.

"You don't have to drink, Blakely."

Sighing, I set the shot down and tell him something I haven't told anyone else. "The person I'm not on speaking terms with… it's my sister." When he looks at me confused, I continue. "She's always high or drunk— partying with her loser friends." It's become her way to avoid dealing with her life.

"And you're afraid if you drink you'll turn into her?"

"Yes and no. I used to be like her." Before our parents died, when their fighting became unbearable, Sierra and I resorted to acting out for attention. That included drinking and smoking—and getting arrested. After they died, there was no reason to act out anymore. They were both gone. I haven't picked up a drink or a joint since then.

Unable to look at Keegan, I focus on the shot in front of me. "I'm afraid if I drink, I'll go back to the way I was. The way she is now." I'm not sure why I'm baring my inner secrets to him, but with every word I speak, it feels like another weight has been lifted off my chest. "Since our parents died, I've been focused on my future, but my sister, she won't focus on anything but chasing her next high. I'm going away to school, and the thought of leaving her, it makes me feel sick. I haven't said it to anyone, but I'm so mad at her. Mad at the decisions she's making. We've barely even spoken in months."

"Looks like we have something in common," Keegan says, and I look up at him.

"You're mad at your sister too?"

He chuckles. "My brother… and no. I meant your sister and I have something in common. My brother is mad at me for my decisions too."

When he doesn't explain further, I ask, "Do you want to talk about it?" Even though I don't think he does. Otherwise, he would've told me.

"Not really," he says. "The reason I let Mitch drag me here is to let it all go. In less than a month, I have to make a pretty big decision, and right now, I don't even want to think about it."

"Then we don't." I pick the shot back up and raise it.

"You sure?" He lifts a single brow in question.

"One night of drinking isn't going to change who I am—who I've become," I say, unsure if my words are more for Keegan or myself. "I know what I want for my future, and one night of having fun is okay."

He gives me a hard stare, as if he's about to argue, but instead shrugs. "Here's to drinking our problems away." We clink our glasses.

"Or at least drinking until we forget what our problems are," I add, then throw my shot back at the same time Keegan does. He hands me another shot, and we both down them.

"Dammit!" I yell as the ball bounces off the side of the table and hits the ground. Holly laughs, and Mitch grabs the ball before it rolls too far. Reaching over, I grab my cup and down the entire contents.

Keegan and I are playing beer pong with Holly and Mitch, except instead of beer in the cups, there are shots of liquor. It's official, I suck at this game. My ball never makes it inside the cup, and you would think that would mean I wouldn't be drunk. The problem is Holly changed up the rules since she too sucks at the game. If you miss, you have to take a shot. If you make it, the other side takes the shot.

"C'mere, Jailbird." Keegan laughs, gripping the curve of my hip. With every shot we take, the more flirtatious we become with each other. At first, it was friendly and fun. But the drunker we get, the more sensual the touches get. The peck on the cheek turns into a kiss on the lips. The hand holding turns into our bodies grinding against one another.

When Keegan pulls me toward him, our bodies collide, and the bulge in his pants rubs against the crack of my ass. His arms wrap around my body, and his hand glides down my forearm until he gets to my hand. His fingers lace with mine, so he can help me throw the ball. I'm hot and sweaty from the warm night mixed with the shots of alcohol, and when he whispers, "Let me help you," into my ear, his cool breath against my hot flesh causes my body to ignite.

"I don't want to play anymore," I tell him, turning around so my body is flush against his. His eyes widen at my sudden brazenness, but he doesn't pull away.

"What do you want to do?" he asks, his eyes landing on my lips. I lick them, knowing full well doing so will turn him on. I don't doubt for a second, the alcohol running through my bloodstream isn't helping me along, but even if I weren't drunk, I'd still want Keegan. He's sexy and sweet. He's fun to hang out with, nice to talk to. Since the moment I took my first shot, I accepted that I'm going to allow myself to have fun. Because once I leave from this vacation, I'm going to be focusing on my education for the next four years. Six if I decide to become a psychologist like I'm considering. I'm going to have a good time, get it all out of my system one last time, and when I walk away, I'll leave everything behind me and look toward my future—with or without my sister.

"Let's go swimming," I suggest.

He nods, and without telling his friends we're done playing, takes me by the hand and guides us to a dark area of the pool. There's a huge rock area with a waterfall, and underneath is a grotto. We step into the warm water and swim to where the grotto is. There's one other couple under there, but they're on the other side, and with the water falling loudly into the pool, you can't hear them.

Pushing Keegan against the rocks, I wrap my arms around his neck and my legs circle his torso. He reaches down and grabs two handfuls of my ass at the same time my mouth slams down on his. His lips are soft yet strong, and when our tongues enter each other's mouths, they move in perfect sync. The longer we kiss, the more turned on I become. My fingers twist into his hair, deepening the kiss, and his hands massage circles into my flesh, pulling me into him. My center rubs friction against the ridges of his abs, hitting my clit in a way that makes my entire body feel the effects. I'm drunk, I realize, not just tipsy. The alcohol is catching up to me, and every touch has me wanting more.

Without thinking, I reach under me and pull Keegan's dick out of his shorts, and pushing my bikini bottoms to the side, I guide him along the center of my pussy lips. He groans into my mouth as I glide up and down, using his hard dick for my pleasure. He doesn't move, doesn't take over. He just continues to kiss me, letting me have all the control. And it feels so damn good to be in control of something, of someone. Years of feeling helpless, feeling out of place as we moved from home to home, school to school. Feeling lost as I try to navigate my way through this life without my sister by my side has me craving control and power, and in this moment, Keegan's giving it to me.

Without breaking our kiss, I grind up and down, my clit rubbing friction against his smooth shaft. With every up and down motion, I work myself closer and closer to the edge. I don't know if he's close, and I don't even really care. I'm horny, and I need this orgasm badly. It's been way too long, and it feels so damn good.

And with one final rub to my clit, my orgasm rips right through me. My pussy spasms, my body shakes, and my legs become jelly under the water. My lips stop functioning, ending our kiss, and my head drops onto Keegan's shoulder. We stay like this for several seconds, my orgasmic bliss wearing off and my head clearing. And when I've finally come down and my thoughts are no longer fuzzy, I realize what I've just done.

Pushing off Keegan, he lets me go. My body hits the water, and I sink to the bottom like dead weight—thankfully it's shallow. And then hands grip my biceps, pulling me back up.

"Are you okay?" Keegan pushes my wet hair out of my face.

"Yeah," I splutter. "Oh my God! I can't believe I just attacked you!" Keegan's eyes widen with laughter. "I'm clean, I swear. I know that's kind of stupid to point out now, and I'm not really sure anyone would ever seriously admit it if they weren't…" I'm fully aware I'm rambling, but I can't stop myself. "I haven't had sex in a while. I mean, I know we didn't technically have sex, but your dick was all up in my…" Oh my God! Someone shut me up now.

"Whoa, calm down," Keegan says with a smile. "I'm clean too."

His words help calm my nerves, and I take a few deep breaths. "I don't know what got into me. I've never attacked anyone like that before."

Keegan smirks. "You're more than welcome to attack me anytime." When he pulls me close to him, I feel his dick, still hard.

"Wow, aren't you quite the overachiever. Ready to go again?" I joke.

He laughs softly. "Umm… I…" He traps his bottom lip between his teeth then drags it out slowly.

"You what?" I prompt.

"I didn't finish."

Well, damn, we can't have that now, can we? After the orgasm I just had, I can't go leaving him hanging. Plus, it would mean getting more of him, and maybe even another orgasm.

Wrapping my arms around his neck, I bring my lips to the corner of his jaw and kiss along his stubbled jawline. "What do you say we go up to your room"—I kiss the corner of his mouth—"and finish what we started?" I run my tongue along his lower lip, then his upper lip before I press a soft kiss to his mouth.

"I would say you've had too much to drink and I'm not about to take advantage of you."

"I'm barely even drunk." I pout. "Plus, I'm pretty sure I'm the one who took advantage of you."

Keegan laughs. "How about we go up to my room, order some snacks, and see where things go?"

"I like the way you think."

When we get out of the pool, we don't see Holly or Mitch anywhere, but Keegan says the three of them are sharing a room, so they're probably up there. Keegan wraps a towel around me, and I grab my beach bag. I consider sending a text to Sierra to let her know I won't be coming back to the room, but stop myself. She doesn't care where I am or what I'm doing, and texting her will only give her another reason to remind me of that.

When we get up to Keegan's room, I notice it's not just a room, but a suite. There's a kitchen and living room. Off to one side, there's a door, but it's closed, and on the other side is another door, which is open. Keegan guides me toward the open door.

"Order us some food," he says. "I'm just going to make sure Mitch and Holly are back." He gives the tip of my nose a kiss then heads over to their room.

After I order us some chocolate cake and brownies with vanilla ice cream—because every girl craves sweets after her body has been rocked to the core—I go inside the bathroom and turn the shower on so I can rinse off. Between the salt water and chlorine, my skin feels like sandpaper.

I leave the door open, hoping Keegan will take it as an invitation to join, then strip out of my bathing suit and slip into the shower. I'm no longer drunk, back to tipsy, but I'm still horny as hell. I've always been a horny drunk, though. Sierra, she's a mean drunk. A couple drinks in her and she'll be starting fights with everyone in sight.

"Hey, Jailbird, the food is here," Keegan yells. I roll my eyes at his nickname for me.

When I don't answer, he appears in the doorway. "J.B., you hear me?"

Oh, so now we're shortening it? Fabulous.

"My name is Blakely," I call out, and Keegan laughs. Then I add, "Come join me." When he doesn't respond, I peek out of the shower curtain to find him standing in place. "I'm not drunk." I shoot him a wink. "Not much anyway."

He inhales deeply then lets out a harsh exhale, obviously warring with himself.

"C'mon, you said you need to rinse off. If you're worried about me attacking you again, just leave your shorts on."

"Oh, like that would stop you." He rolls his eyes. "I'm pretty damn sure my shorts were on in the pool."

"Okay then, suit yourself." I shrug nonchalantly. "It's not like I need you to get myself off. The shower head will work just fine." I slam the curtain closed. "I was just hoping to get you off!" I yell through a giggle.

A few seconds later, the curtain is flying open, and a naked Keegan is entering the shower. "I'm not joining you in the hope of getting off," he states matter-of-factly.

"Oh, yeah?" I smirk playfully. "Then why are you joining me?"

Pulling me by the curves of my hips, he brings me so close, our bodies are flush. My breasts are pressed against his solid chest, and his hard dick is nestled between my thighs. "I'm joining you because I'll be fucking damned if I don't either contribute to, or at least get to watch you get off." He pushes my wet hair off my neck, and leaning down, sucks on my pulse point. "You using my dick to get off in the pool was the hottest fucking thing I've ever seen."

"You thought that was hot?" I back up slightly and take his dick in my hand. "Wait until you see me get you off."

CHAPTER SIX

Blakely

"**W**HAT DAY DO YOU LEAVE?" KEEGAN ASKS. BASED ON THE sunlight shining in through the window, I know it's morning, but I'm not sure how early or late it is. We're both lying in his bed, still naked—the way we fell asleep last night after we successfully got each other off several more times before we both passed out. More than once, we came close to having sex, but he stopped it from happening, saying he wanted to make sure if we did have sex, neither of us was intoxicated. I give him a lot of credit, because if it were up to me, we would've been fucking like jackrabbits all night.

"Saturday morning. Check-out is at noon."

His fingers run through my hair, and he pushes a wayward strand behind my ear. "I leave Friday morning." He frowns. "That means we only have today left."

"Then we better make the most of it," I tell him with a smile, refusing to let the idea of our time coming to an end ruin the time we have left together. As much as I'm enjoying his company, I have no intention of seeing him again after this trip. In less than two months I'll be graduating and moving to South Carolina. I'm not about to start something I know I can't finish.

Pulling the covers off our bodies, I run into the bathroom so I can get ready for the day. After going pee, I put my now dry bathing suit back on, then steal Keegan's toothbrush. I don't have any toiletries here, and there's no way I'm not brushing my teeth. Not when I plan to have Keegan's mouth on mine as much as possible over the next twenty-four hours. He laughs when he follows me in a few minutes later and catches me rinsing it off.

Hopping onto the counter, I watch as he goes about getting ready, pulling his board shorts on and brushing his teeth. He lifts his arms up to put deodorant on, and the corded muscles of his biceps flex. When he catches me watching him, he smirks but doesn't call me out on it. Instead, he moves in front of me and, spreading my thighs, stands between my legs. His hands land on the tops of my thighs, and he runs his palms along my flesh, eliciting goose bumps along my skin.

My fingers entwine in his hair, and I pull his face to me, our mouths fusing. His tongue finds mine, and we explore each other's mouths. I've kissed him so many times in the last twenty-four hours, but I can't seem to get enough. Soft. Hard. Rough. Demanding. Every kiss with Keegan is different. An experience.

One of his hands comes up and pulls my bikini top to the side, exposing my breast. With his thumb and forefinger, he tweaks my nipple, and my pussy clenches in response. His other hand delves into my bottoms, pushing the thin material aside and thrusting his thick fingers inside of me. Not a single word is spoken as Keegan expertly brings me closer and closer to my orgasm.

Just before I allow myself to fall off the edge, I reach down and grip his dick, silently telling him what I want. Keegan breaks our kiss, and reaching over to where he left his wallet on the counter, grabs a condom, bites the edge, and rips it open. In a quick, deft motion, he rolls the condom onto his long, hard length. I think he's going to fuck me right here, on the counter, so I'm shocked when he lifts and carries me back into the room, throwing me onto the center of the bed. After pulling my bikini bottoms down my legs and tossing them to the side, he pushes my legs apart and then crawls up my body, his hands and arms caging me in on either side of my head. His mouth dips down and covers mine at the same time he enters me. The kissing and fucking starts off slow and tender as we learn each other's bodies. But with each thrust, we become more ravenous. Our bodies connecting on a level I've never felt before.

Keegan's mouth leaves mine and lands on my breast, his tongue licking and sucking, his teeth biting my nipple until it becomes deliciously sensitive. Then he moves to the other one, giving it the same attention. My body becomes enflamed by his touch, and my hips rise to meet his, thrust for thrust, needing him deeper, harder. He understands my wordless demand and picks up his speed, pounding into me with abandon until we both come completely undone.

Keegan stills, and I can feel his throbbing dick inside me, the warmth of his release through the latex. His head drops, and he nuzzles his face into the crook of my neck, raining kisses along my damp skin.

"That was…" I trail off, unable to even begin to describe what that was: amazing, incredible, remarkable… None of those adjectives properly convey what I just experienced with Keegan.

"Mind-blowing," Keegan says, finishing my sentence. "That was fucking mind-blowing, and I have half a mind to tie you to this bed and never let you go, so we can do it over and over again in every goddamn position."

I know he's only joking, but the thought of Keegan never letting me go makes me feel all warm and fuzzy inside. It's been a long time since I've felt wanted or needed. Even if what he's feeling is strictly sexual, my body and mind and heart don't seem to know the difference. Which means it's time to get up and put some distance between us. The last thing I need is to fall for a guy I can't possibly ever have a future with. My future is five hundred miles away in South Carolina.

Placing my palms against his chest, I push him back slightly. When he backs up, he slides out of me, taking his warmth with him. My body craves it, and I almost pull him back to me, but instead I stay strong and push the craving away. I can't afford to be sidetracked.

"Hey," he says, picking up on my sudden mood shift. "It…" He clears his throat. "It was good for you too, wasn't it?" His brows furrow, and he stares into my eyes, waiting for my answer.

"Yes, it was really good."

"Then what's wrong?"

I barely know this man, but I can hear the vulnerability in his every word, and the last thing I want to do is make him feel like he did something wrong, when the fact is, how I'm feeling is because he did everything right. But I also can't tell him that, because if I do, I'm putting him in the awkward position of making him think I want more, which even if I did, can't happen. We're both at a crossroads in our lives. Keegan said he has an important decision to make, and I need to graduate and head off to college. We're not at a place in our lives to even consider something more than what we're doing right here, right now.

"Nothing is wrong, I promise," I tell him, keeping it vague. Sitting up, I swing my feet over the side of the bed. "What's on the agenda for today?" I ask, trying to sound as nonchalant as possible.

Keegan studies me for a brief moment, then says, "I was thinking we could do some snorkeling, then get some lunch down by the pier. Maybe hang out by the pool. There's a pretty sweet lazy river that circles around the back of the hotel." He shrugs. "What do you think?"

I situate my top so my breasts are no longer exposed, then grab my bottoms from the floor and put them back on. "I think that sounds absolutely perfect."

CHAPTER SEVEN

KEEGAN AND I HAVE SPENT THE ENTIRE DAY TOGETHER, FOLLOWING his itinerary to a T. After renting snorkeling gear, we met Mitch and Holly, and spent the morning experiencing the ocean from under the water. Once we all agreed we needed a break from the sun, we went to lunch down at the pier. And after Keegan and Mitch paid the bill, Mitch and Holly insisted they were exhausted and needed to take a nap. By the look in Holly's eyes, I think it's safe to assume the last thing they'll be doing in their bed is sleeping.

While I wouldn't mind taking a *nap* with Keegan, I don't want to waste a single moment I have with him. I can't remember the last time I had as much fun as I've had these past few days. Everything we do feels like an adventure, an experience, and I'm afraid once the metaphorical clock strikes midnight—and Keegan and I go our separate ways—my fun will cease. Actually, I know it will. Because I'll make sure it does. I'll focus on school and working at the bookstore, and come May, I'll graduate and go to college and do the same thing I've been doing—focus on my future.

"C'mere!" Keegan grants me a flirty smirk, both of his dimples popping out in the corners of his cheeks. He's lying across the neon yellow inner tube, his tanned, chiseled body on display for everyone to see. We've spent the afternoon and well into the evening between the pool, hot tub, and lazy river, only leaving once for dinner.

When I shake my head at his request, he laughs good-naturedly and reaches for my tube. Raising my hands above me, I drop down the center of the inner tube and swim out from under it in an attempt to get away from him. The last time I fell for that shit, he flipped my inner tube over and knocked me into the water. Sure, I'm still in the water this way, but at least it's not his doing.

A hand grabs my ankle, and I let out a shriek even though I know it's Keegan. Yanking me back, his hands splay across my stomach as he pulls me into a standing position so his front is flush with my back. Then he moves us until we're back under the grotto, the same spot where we *wet* humped each other the other night—when I got myself off using his dick. It's late now, probably close to ten o'clock, and everyone around us is either drunk or well on their way to being drunk.

Keeping my back to him, Keegan nudges my hair to the side and brings his mouth down to the skin that covers my pulse point, licking and suckling on my sensitive flesh. Even in the warmth of the pool, I shiver, and Keegan chuckles.

"I love the way your body responds to mine," he whispers into my ear. His hands move at the same time, one ascending to my breast, and the other descending to the apex of my thighs. His lips go back to trailing kisses all over my shoulder and neck and collarbone. His fingers pinch my hardened nipple through my bikini top, and his other hand enters my bottoms. He wastes no time pushing his thick fingers into me, his thumb gliding across my swollen clit. Even over the blaring music, I can hear myself panting as Keegan skillfully brings me to an orgasm, continuing his delicious onslaught until I've completely come down from my high.

Turning around, I wrap my arms around his neck and pull his mouth down to mine. My legs wrap around his torso, and my center rubs against his hard dick that's clearly standing at attention. His tongue enters my mouth, and every swipe is frenzied, frantic.

"Take me up to your room," I murmur against his lips. He doesn't have to be told twice. Refusing to put me down, Keegan carries me through the lobby, into the elevator, and through his hotel room. Mitch and Holly are in the main area when we crash through the door. They both laugh, but Keegan pays them no mind. He's on a mission and won't be deterred.

The second he lays my wet body on his bed, he pushes his shorts down and flings them into the corner, exposing his perfect dick. It's smooth and thick. The head is slightly pink and looks swollen. There's a single vein that runs from root to tip, and he's neatly trimmed everywhere. He grabs a condom and rips it open. I watch with reverence and awe as he rolls it on, remembering when I had my mouth wrapped around it. It tastes as good as it looks.

Once he's completely sheathed, he pulls my bikini bottoms down and spreads my legs. When he enters me, his hands land on either side of my head, his mouth next to my ear. "This is without a doubt my favorite spot in the entire world," he whispers. "I could stay right here, inside of you for the rest of my life."

I refuse to read too much into his words. It's his dick talking, not his heart. We've only known each other for a few days, and tomorrow he's going home. The next day I'll be gone as well. And this week will be nothing more than a distant memory.

"Come for me, Jailbird," he murmurs. "Come all over my dick, baby."

Closing my eyes, I push away everything except Keegan and me. I can think about everything else later. Right now, it's just the two of us, our bodies connected in the most intimate way possible. And with that thought, I release a cleansing breath and allow myself to let go.

"Where have you been all week?" my sister asks, zipping up her luggage. She almost sounds like she actually cares.

"Just enjoying the sights," I say, not completely lying. This morning, after Keegan and I had the most amazing morning sex, followed by breakfast in bed, we said our goodbyes. We didn't exchange numbers or make any ridiculous promises to keep in touch. He kissed me goodbye and thanked me for making his trip memorable. A part of me wishes he would've at least asked for my number, but a bigger part of me is glad he didn't. I would've told him no, and it would've ended our week on a bad note. Instead, it ended perfectly.

"Why are you packing?" I ask, realizing she's not just zipping her luggage, but actually packing up as if she's leaving when we don't leave until tomorrow.

"Imani and I got into a fight. She's staying and I'm leaving."

"Why?"

Sierra glances warily at me for a long moment, as if she's warring with herself, trying to decide if she should let me in or push me away.

"You can talk to me," I prompt.

She drops onto the bed and sighs. "I slept with Grant."

"Her ex-boyfriend?"

Sierra glares. "I don't need your judgement."

"I'm not judging, S." I raise my hands, silently waving the white flag. "But she's your best friend. Why would you do that?" I make sure my tone comes across as concerned, which I am. Doesn't she see that she's pushing someone else away? Sierra isn't the kind of person to just go around sleeping with random guys, and I doubt she likes Grant. She did it to push Imani away. This is what she does—keep the people who have a possibility of getting close to her at arm's length.

"I was drunk," she says, averting her eyes.

"Sierra." I sit next to her luggage. "You know I love you, right?"

"Can we not do this right now? I just want to go home."

Speaking of which… "How are you getting home?"

"Brenton agreed to leave early," she says.

"Oh." I guess that means I'm leaving early too. "Okay. When are we leaving?"

"As soon as you're ready." She grabs the handle of her suitcase and lifts it off the bed and drops it onto the ground. "We'll meet you at the car."

After packing my stuff, I roll my suitcase out the door. I take the elevator down to the main floor and head out to the front. I'm just through the doors when I hear my name being called. I look around, trying to find the voice, when I see Keegan running toward me.

"You're leaving?" he asks, eyeing the luggage in my hand.

"Umm… yeah?" I'm shocked to see him. We already said goodbye. He already left. Why is he here?

"I want your number," he blurts out, and my body stiffens.

"No," I say back, not even thinking about it for a second. Why would he do this? We ended things on a good note.

"Please." He steps closer to me, and I back up a step. He can't do this. That's not how this was supposed to end. "I left and got halfway home and made Mitch turn back around. I know you said you're moving, but I can't walk away without knowing I can talk to you again. I can't let this be the end."

Not wanting our time together to end on a bad note, I say the first thing I can think of. "Fine, then give me yours, and I'll text you my number."

Keegan laughs. "Yeah, right, Jailbird. I'm not falling for that." He takes another step toward me, but this time I don't back up. His hands land on my hips, and he bends his head down, kissing me softly on the lips. "You won't text me. You'll chicken out. I know you." He grins. "Give me your number, and I'll text you, and if you really don't want to talk to me, you can block me."

"I'm moving to South Carolina. It's pointless."

"We can be pen pals."

"Nobody writes letters anymore." I roll my eyes.

"Texting pals." He smiles that beautiful, sexy grin. The one that shows both of his dimples.

Seeing Brenton's car pulling around, I give in, not wanting my sister to know about Keegan. "Fine." I grab Keegan's phone and, pulling up his notepad, since it's the first thing I spot, I type in my number. I hand it back to him, then standing on my tiptoes, give his cheek a chaste kiss.

"I gotta go. It was fun," I say before I walk away, refusing to look back at the handsome man I know, if given the chance, I could easily fall in love with.

CHAPTER EIGHT

Blakely

Two Months Later

"I**T'S POSITIVE,"** DR. PETERSON SAYS WITH A SMALL SMILE.

"Positive… meaning you're positive I'm not pregnant?"

"No." She shakes her head. "The *test* was positive. You're pregnant."

"Maybe there's something else that can cause a false positive. Like… an STD? Maybe I have Chlamydia or Herpes…"

Sierra snorts from her chair. When she caught me throwing up for the hundredth time, she insisted I go to the doctor.

"B, please. What if something is seriously wrong with you?"

"I probably have a bug," I argue, not even believing my own words.

"What if you're pregnant, or worse, what if you have cancer or something?" Tears pool in her lids, and my heart expands. This is the first time since before our parents died that I've seen her show any type of emotion.

Sierra steps toward me and takes my hands in hers. "I-I can't lose you, B. Please, for me, go."

There was no way I could say no to her after that. So, she made me an appointment—at our gynecologist office, because even though I told her there was no way I could be pregnant, she didn't believe me—and here we are…

"You're wishing for an STD?" Sierra laughs.

"Well, it would be better than being pregnant!" I shout, my voice cracking at the end. "An STD is curable! Pregnancy is… not." Tears prick my eyes, and my sister cuts across the room and pulls me into her arms.

"Shh… it's okay," she coos. Her words are meant to soothe me, but having my sister hug me for the first time in almost two years does the opposite. The wall I've been building to protect my heart from her crumbles, and every emotion I've been holding in flows out of me as I cry in my sister's arms.

"I can't be pregnant," I sob. "I can't be."

"We'll figure it out," Sierra says, pulling back. Her hands cup the sides of my cheeks. "You're my sister, and I'll be right by your side." These are the words I've been waiting to hear for years, but not under these circumstances. Oh, the irony…

"No, you don't get it," I say exasperated. "I *can't* be pregnant." I glance over at the doctor. "The guy I slept with… We used protection every single time."

Sierra gives me a curious look. She'll definitely be asking me later who this guy is.

"Any form of birth control is never one hundred percent effective," Dr. Peterson says softly. I know she's right, but we used one every damn time. I would've known it if something went wrong, right?

"I've put an order in for an ultrasound," she says. "I'm just waiting for the room to become available. We'll be able to confirm it then." She takes a deep breath, then adds, "If you're not in a place to have a baby, please know you have options." Her eyes meet mine, and my stomach drops at the look of pity she's giving me. "Once we confirm it, one way or another, we'll go from there."

The nurse pops her head in and lets the doctor know the room is available, and Sierra and I follow her into the dark room. I lie on the bed and spread my thighs, and Dr. Peterson walks me through what she's doing as she pushes a dildo-looking thing into me. The screen lights up, and a loud whooshing sound comes over the speakers. It reminds me of the beach on a windy day.

"That's the heartbeat," Dr. Peterson says. The breath I didn't know I was holding releases, turning into a choked sob. Tears stream down my face, the warm drops of devastation landing in my ears. She probes around inside of me, clicking and freezing the screen a few times. "You appear to be roughly eight weeks along, due December 14. This can change over time. It's hard to be exact this early in the pregnancy. But everything looks good." She pulls the dildo out of me, then hands me a couple black and white images—my baby.

"I'm going to give you a few minutes," Dr. Peterson says. "Once you're ready, you can go get dressed and then meet me in my office, so we can talk."

Once the doctor leaves, closing the door behind her, Sierra grabs my hand and entwines our fingers together as I stare at the tiny blob through my blurred vision. "Don't cry, B, please," she begs. "It's going to be okay."

"No, it's not," I tell her. "No matter what decision I make, it will never be okay."

I begin to play out every possible scenario for Sierra. "I keep the baby, and I have to drop out of school. I'll have to raise it by myself. Keegan never texted. I gave—"

"Who's Keegan?" Sierra asks, cutting me off.

"The guy I slept with," I admit sheepishly.

"Where? When?" Her brows come together in confusion.

"Cocoa Beach during spring break."

Sierra frowns. "You slept with someone two months ago and never told me…" It's not a question, but more of an observation. The way her eyes widen and her brows furrow, it's as if she's finally realizing what she's done. I hold my breath, hoping and praying she doesn't push me away and run out the door. I'm not sure I can handle her stepping halfway through the door only to walk back out. Leaving me to deal with my future alone.

"You haven't spoken to me in two years," I say nervously. "I didn't really think to confide in you about my sex life."

"No." She shakes her head. "I know." Tears brim her lids. "I just can't believe how long we've gone without talking." Her light brown eyes meet mine. "I pushed you away and you kept begging me to let you in. Our mom has been gone for two years. Two years." She throws her arms around me, and I wrap mine around her as she cries into my shoulder, finally opening up and letting her grief surface. "You're my best friend," she says through her cries. "I'm so sorry. I'm such a horrible sister. Things are going to be different, starting right now."

"It's okay," I tell her. And it is. She's my sister. Of course I'm going to forgive her. "Everybody handles grief in their own way."

Sierra pulls back, and we both wipe our eyes. "I'm such a mess," Sierra says through a sobbing laugh. "Thank you for being so patient. I promise I'm never going to push you away again."

"Good, I'm holding you to that. I love you, S."

"I love you more, B."

We sit in silence for a long beat and then Sierra says, "So, this guy… Keegan…"

"We spent some time together… ended up hooking up." I shrug. "I was okay leaving without exchanging numbers, but after he left, he came back and practically begged me to give him my number. So, I did."

"And, he what? Never called?"

"Nope, not a single call or text."

"Okay," she says with a nod. "First things first. We have to figure out where to go from here, and then, once you make a decision, we'll figure out how to find him. We live in a technology-obsessed world. How hard can it be to find someone? What's his last name?"

When I don't say anything, instead chewing on my bottom lip, Sierra groans. "Don't tell me you don't know it."

I shake my head. "I don't know it." How could I not have gotten his last name?

"Do you know where he lives?"

"Yes!" I exclaim, happy I at least know that. "Carterville. He said he lives and goes to school there."

"All right, well, that's a start. Let's go talk to Dr. Peterson."

Sierra grabs a few tissues out of the holder and hands them to me. "I'll wait for you in her office, so you can get cleaned up."

"Okay."

She walks away, but before she opens the door, I call out her name. She turns around, and it's in this moment, I've never been more grateful to have my sister by my side.

"I know these last few years have been rough, but thank you for coming with me today. For coming back to me. I really missed you."

"You're my sister, B," she says, every word filled with emotion. "All we have is each other. I'm just sorry it took you getting knocked up for me to snap out of my shit."

Sierra and I leave the doctor's office with three pamphlets, each one stating a different option: abortion, adoption, and what to expect when becoming a mother. The ride home on the bus is quiet, both of us lost in thought. I might be the one who has to make the decision, but the thing with my sister and me is when one of us is faced with a hard choice, it's as if we both are. And she proved it today in the doctor's office. Once she found out I wasn't dying, she could've easily pushed me away. Locking her heart back up to keep it safe like she's been doing since our parents died. But she didn't do that. She held my hand and told me we would figure it out together. And I know that no matter what choice I make, she'll support me. I finally have my sister back.

We get home and Jordan is in the kitchen chopping vegetables for lunch. She cooks every meal. She takes one look at Sierra's and my tear-stricken faces, and stops what she's doing. "What happened?"

"I'm pregnant," I blurt out, and her eyes widen. Sierra's hand finds mine, and I take a breath of relief. It feels so good to have my sister by my side again.

"Oh, no, Blakely." Jordan envelops me in a hug. "How far along are you?"

"Eight weeks."

"And the father?"

"I have no clue how to find him."

She pulls back and guides me over to the table. Sierra and I sit quietly, while Jordan goes about making us each a hot cup of tea. Once she's done, she joins us, and getting right to the matter at hand, asks, "What are you going to do?"

"I don't know," I say truthfully.

Jordan sighs heavily. "Listen, Blakely, I care about you. I care about both of you, but—"

"I know," I tell her, not needing to hear what she's about to say. She's in her late sixties. She's been fostering children her entire adult life, but isn't looking to adopt, let alone take on a teenager with a newborn.

"If I were younger…"

"I promise you, I get it." I place my hand over hers. "You've done enough. You took Sierra and me in together when no one else would. You've allowed me to stay here until graduation even though I'm eighteen. I would never ask you to take me and my baby on."

Jordan nods. "Speaking of graduation… Nothing will get figured out before tomorrow. So, I say you try to set this news aside…" When I give her a *yeah, okay* look, she continues. "I know it will be hard, but you two deserve to enjoy your big day. You're about to be high school graduates. And afterward, you can take a look at all your options and decide what's best. If you need to stay a little longer, until you figure out what you're doing, you can stay."

"Thank you," I say with a forced smile.

Three months later

"How are you feeling?" Sierra asks when I walk into our room and drop onto my bed, my hand instinctually going to my protruding baby bump. These last few months I've experienced a myriad of emotions.

Sadness—when I found out the college I'm planning to attend can't accommodate me with a baby in tow. There's a waiting list a mile long, and by the time I would get in, I would lose my entire scholarship. Which means the only way I can go to South Carolina is without my baby.

Anger—both, at myself, and Keegan—when I searched for him online, I couldn't find him anywhere. I know it's because I have no damn last name to search, and that thought made me even more mad. How could I be so reckless that I spent days with a man, having sex and getting to know him on a personal level, yet I never took the time to find out his last name?

Anxiousness—when I hit my lowest point and decided my only option was to go to the clinic and get an abortion.

Relief—when Sierra refused to allow me to go until we talked through it, and I recognized I was just scared and couldn't really go through with it.

Sadness—again—when I came to the conclusion that my only other option was adoption, and in less than five months, I'm going to have to hand my baby over to someone who is able to care for him like he deserves. And yes, I say *him* because I'm now twenty weeks along and found out today that I'm having a little boy.

When the doctor handed me the ultrasound pictures, my first thought was if he'll have Keegan's dimples, and then I lost it. I told Sierra I needed some time alone. She was hesitant to let me go, but we agreed to meet back at home.

If you can even call it that. Ever since I've made the choice not to abort my baby, Jordan has grown distant. I don't blame her, though. This isn't what she signed up for.

And then when I put off starting classes at Columbia until the fall, the distance grew considerably wider. I explained I just needed time to figure out what I'm going to do, but I think she's worried I'm not going to college anymore. I'm supposed to be leaving in less than two weeks for orientation, and I haven't said what I'm doing one way or another.

While Jordan hasn't come right out and said anything, Sierra turning eighteen last week means we're both eighteen and now adults. It's time for us to figure out our next step. Plus, it's not fair to continue to live off Jordan, especially when she could be using our room to foster a child in need.

During my long walk home, I did a lot of thinking and I've come to a decision.

"B," Sierra prompts. "Are you okay?" She moves from her bed to mine.

"If I can't go to college, I can't support my baby," I whisper, the lump in my throat preventing me from speaking louder. "I-I…" I close my eyes, not wanting to see the look she gives me when I tell her what I've decided. "I'm going to give the baby up for adoption." My head drops to my chest and sobs rack my entire body at the thought of giving him up. But what other choice do I have?

"Look at me," Sierra says, her fingers tapping my chin, so I'll lift my head back up. When I open my eyes, she says, "Is that really what you want? Because if it is, I'll support you one hundred percent. I'll be there for you any way I can. But we both know I can't move to South Carolina with you because I'll have nowhere to live." She's right. When we were younger and planned to live together wherever I went to college, we thought our parents would pay for our apartment. Obviously things have changed.

"But listen…" she continues, scooting closer and taking my hands in hers. "We lost everyone. It's just us. This baby you're carrying is a part of us. He has your blood running through his veins. If you want to keep him, I will do whatever I have to do to help you. Columbia wasn't the only college you were accepted to. It's the college you chose to go to. If you pick one in the area, we can get a place together, and I'll work full-time while you go to school."

"You'd do that?" I choke out. It's crazy how much my sister has changed back to her old self since I found out I was pregnant. She never hangs out with her 'friends' anymore. She got a full-time job working as a waitress at a popular restaurant in town. And every dime she makes, she says she's stowing away for our future.

"Of course I would. This baby is my family—our family. I'm not trying to sway you one way or the other. I know how important Columbia is to you, and if that's what you want, I've got your back. But I need you to know that's not your only option. You're not alone in this."

And then it hits me. "Carterville accepted me on a full scholarship." I run over to my dresser and grab the acceptance letters, finding the one I'm looking for. "I can call them and see if maybe they have a family dorm available. I can ask if you would be able to live with me."

"Okay." She nods. "Call. But if it's not possible, we can still get a place. The most important thing is that your college is paid for."

I give them a call and, after explaining my situation, the person in charge tells me there's a waiting list for this August, but if I wanted to defer a year, they could get me in for next August.

"Would I lose my scholarship?" I ask.

The lady looks up my information and says, "You are allowed to defer one year for medical purposes. Having a baby would fall under that category. You could start next August. Also, your scholarship doesn't require you to live on campus. It states that we'll pay a set amount toward your living expenses, which means you can actually live anywhere and with anyone you'd like, and if your expenses are more, you would just have to pay the difference." I give Sierra a look, asking if she's okay with all of this, and when she nods, I tell the lady that's what I'm going to do.

"This is crazy," I tell Sierra when I get off the phone. "How am I going to raise a baby and go to school?"

"*We're* going to raise a baby," Sierra tells me. "We've both been saving all summer, so we can afford a place in Carterville. We'll spend the next year getting situated, and once the baby is…" We both do the math in our heads.

"He'll be eight months old," I tell her.

"When he's eight months old, you'll start school. We got this."

"And what if we don't?" My head is spinning. It feels like I only just found out I was pregnant. Now I'm making plans for well after he's born.

"That's not an option."

And just like that, my future has been paved. Only this time, it in-cludes my sister—my best friend—by my side.

As Sierra pulls me into a hug, telling me everything will be okay, I wonder if somehow, in this clusterfuck of a situation, maybe our mom heard my prayers from above the day I spoke to her at her grave, and helped guide Sierra back to me.

I'd like to think she did.

CHAPTER NINE

Blakely

Three and a half years later

"**Z**ANE KEEGAN JACOBS, IF YOU DON'T GET UP RIGHT THIS SECOND, Mommy is going to be late for her first day, and you're going to be late for school." When my three-year-old doesn't budge, I add, "Don't you want to go to school and see Melissa?" This gets a bit of movement out of him. "You have to give her the Christmas gift you bought her." And now he's up.

"I can give her the doll?" His thick brown hair is all over the place from rolling around in his sleep, and he has pillow creases across half his face. My child is a mess.

"You can. She'll be there today," I tell him, thankful that his best friend Melissa was out of town over Christmas break, which means I can use the gift he bought and is excited to give her as a bargaining chip to get him out of bed.

Zane's tiny lips curve in a huge grin, and both of his dimples pop out—just like his daddy. If I hadn't been the one to carry him for nine months and push him out of me after forty hours of labor, I would think

Keegan, himself, rolled over and created Zane on his own. They look that much alike. And just like every time I think about Keegan, my heart constricts in my chest over the man who is somewhere in this world and has no idea he has a son.

Once Sierra and I found the perfect three-bedroom apartment, walking distance from the school, we moved to Carterville, so we could get ready for Zane's arrival. He was born in December, and we spent the next year learning how to juggle raising a baby while working. I worked part-time, and Sierra worked full-time.

When I wasn't working, I would take Zane for walks around campus. Since Keegan had mentioned he went to Carterville, I had hoped to find him. I asked several people if they knew anyone named Keegan, but most just looked at me like I was crazy. I even tried to ask the admissions office, but they refused to give me any information. Without a court order, student files are off-limits.

When Zane was eight months old, I started school as planned. To make up for my year off, I took extra classes, and I'm proud to say I'm about to begin my last semester of my senior year. I'm majoring in behavioral science, and once I graduate, I'm planning to get my master's degree in school counseling so I can become a school guidance counselor. It's been a long, hard road, and I couldn't have done it without Sierra by my side.

She's been so supportive every step of the way. She hasn't opened her own bar-slash-restaurant yet, obviously, since we're kind of low on funds, but she's now a manager at Orange Sunrise, an upscale bar and club downtown, and she loves it. When she's not working, she helps me with Zane, especially at night when I have to attend study sessions or labs.

I hate that her life revolves around Zane and me. She works so hard, and most of her money goes to our apartment and living expenses. I offered to take out loans when I realized I would never be able to work and go to school, but she wouldn't let me. She said she didn't want me to graduate in debt and promised we would make it work. And we have—because of her. Every time I lost it over not knowing where Keegan was, she was there. When I'd insist we go for walks for hours, hoping to find him, she would tag along without complaint. And when I'd cry for hours afterward, scared of being a single mom because I couldn't find him, she would hold me and promise I would never do it alone.

"Hurry and get ready," I tell Zane, forcing a smile on my face so he doesn't know my mood just plummeted. "And don't forget to brush your teeth," I add as he scrambles out of bed with excitement to give his friend her belated Christmas gift.

"Morning," Sierra says, stretching her arms over her head as she walks into the kitchen.

"What are you doing up so early?" I grab my thermos of coffee from under the Keurig and place her cup under it for her.

She leans against the counter and groans. "I lost two waitresses this week, so I'm doing interviews."

"If you need someone…" I begin, but Sierra shakes her head. I've filled in a few times over the years, but she'll never let me work there full-time.

"Not happening. You have one semester left, and you've applied for the master's program. You need to focus on that," she says, and I nod, once again grateful to have my sister in my corner.

Zane comes running down the hall, his shirt on backward, and his shoes on the wrong feet, just as the front door squeaks open, and in walks Brenton.

When Sierra and I moved here, we found out Brenton was also attending Carterville. He lives on the floor below us, and over the years has become one of my best friends. Sierra swears he's in love with me, but I think she's just trying to play matchmaker. While I've dated on occasion, my focus is on my son and my future. I'll have plenty of time to date once I have a career and can contribute to the bills.

"Brent!" Zane yells, as he runs to the door to grab the bag holding the gift. "I gotta go now to give Melissa my gift. You take me, please?"

Brenton laughs with a shake of his head. "Thank God he's going to finally give that girl his gift. If she doesn't like it, it will probably shatter his heart," he whispers so Zane doesn't hear him.

"Hey, if more men were as thoughtful as Zane and cared about giving their women gifts, more women would be happy," Sierra sasses. Brenton laughs, but doesn't dare argue with my sister. Smart man.

"Zane, you have to eat your breakfast first," I tell him. Grabbing a yogurt and a banana, I set them on the table, then pour him a glass of orange juice. Zane sighs in annoyance, wanting to get to school, while I think of ways to get him out of bed tomorrow. The kid would sleep until noon every day if I let him, and after any break he's even worse, since his schedule has been disrupted.

After he's eaten, we head out. Since Brenton's morning class is the same as mine—actually, all of them are the same—he walks with us to campus. Brenton's major is also the same as mine, which is how I came to the decision. I was helping him study for a test one day and was fascinated by the content.

We're talking about what we think the professor will be like when I spot a man walking toward us and halt in my spot. Unlike the last time I saw him, his hair is no longer messy, but instead neatly combed over. He's not wearing board shorts and a surfing shirt, either. He's dressed in a navy blue, button-down, collared shirt and a pair of khaki dress slacks. His sandals have been replaced with shiny dress shoes. But the man who is quickly approaching us is most definitely the same man I never thought I'd see again. His eyes briefly meet mine, but they hold zero recognition. Could he have forgotten me? It's been almost four years, but wouldn't he still remember who I was?

Just as he's about to walk past us, I move to the left just enough that he has no choice but to stop or step into the grass. When he looks at me confused, it's confirmed.

"You don't remember me." It's not a question. I can see it in his features, in the way his brows are knitted together, curious and confused as to why I'm stopping him from walking by.

Keegan has no clue who I am.

"No, I'm sorry, I don't." His eyes descend to my lips, and I must be frowning because he adds, "Would it help if I said I wished I did?" His lips quirk into the dimpled smile he shares with my son, and I freeze. I should tell him he has a son, remind him who I am. But I'm frozen in my spot. Every time I imagined finally finding Keegan, our conversation always went so differently in my head. For one, he remembered me. I always fantasized him being so excited to learn we somehow created a baby together. Oh my God. I was… am… so stupid.

"Sorry, you're right," I lie. "You're not the guy I thought you were." He has no idea I mean that in more ways than one.

Grabbing Zane's hand, I step around Keegan and speed walk away, not slowing down until I'm at the door to Zane's school. It's on campus, for students and professors to use, and Zane has been attending since last year. It's not cheap, but it's convenient. Before that, Sierra and I made sure our schedules were opposite, so one of us could always be home with him.

Brenton stays quiet while I walk Zane in, who runs straight for Melissa. I smile when he gives her the gift and she squeals excitedly over the doll he picked out. And I laugh when she hugs him and he hugs her back.

"I'll be back in a few hours," I promise him just like I always do when I drop him off.

"Bye," he says, giving me a kiss on my cheek. "I love you." The words out of his mouth right now stir something inside me, and I about lose it. But I hold it all in until I'm out of the building and on the sidewalk.

"That was him," Brenton says, and I nod. He's the only one who has ever seen Keegan.

"Yeah," I say, throwing myself into Brenton's arms. "And he didn't remember me."

"There's no way someone could ever forget you," Brenton says softly. "He didn't want to remember you."

I pull back and meet Brenton's gaze. "You think?"

"C'mon, Blakely, I only met the guy once, but I remember him. You spent damn near a week with the guy." His words squeeze my heart, the blood draining from the organ and leaving me feeling broken. He's right. If Brenton could remember Keegan after all this time, Keegan would surely remember me.

And then a thought hits me. "What if he was in an accident and lost his memory?"

"Blakely, this isn't a Lifetime movie." He's right, but Keegan not remembering me due to a medical condition would make it a lot easier to accept than him just simply *not* remembering me.

We walk to class, hand in hand, but Brenton doesn't say anything else, leaving me to my thoughts. If what Brenton said is true, and Keegan is only pretending not to remember me, then that would mean he doesn't want me in his life. He had to have seen Zane with me. Did he recognize him right away and not want to claim his son? Or maybe he didn't see him, and he just didn't want to rekindle an old flame. It would make sense, since he never called or texted after getting my number.

We walk into class and, like always, head straight for the middle. Not too close to the front but not in the back. Because we're running late from my meltdown, we have to push past several students who are sitting on the edge. A few minutes later, a man who looks to be in his early sixties, steps up to the podium and introduces himself. "My name is Professor Finnigan, and this is Psychology of Inequality. If that's not on your schedule, now is the time to run… run for your life." He winks and everyone laughs.

I'm still laughing when another gentleman makes his presence known, immediately ceasing my laughter. My eyes dart from the guy standing next to the professor, to Brenton, who looks as shocked as I do.

"This is my TA, Kolton Reynolds. He's working on getting his master's degree and will be helping to teach a few of my courses this semester."

My head whips around to look at Brenton, my eyes widening. "Did he… just say…" I can't even finish my sentence.

"Yeah," Brenton says. "His name is Kolton."

Because it's the first day of class, the professor discusses the syllabus, how the grading will work, and what his expectations are. I barely hear a word he says as I focus my attention on Keegan—no, Kolton, as he stands next to Professor Finnigan. When he excuses himself, I consider running after him, but don't want to make a scene.

The rest of the morning goes by in a blur. I'm taking four classes total—two on Mondays and Wednesdays and the other two on Tuesdays and Thursdays. When my second, and last, class of the day is done, Brenton asks if I want to go to lunch, but I tell him I need some time alone. I can tell he doesn't like it, but he at least doesn't argue.

After picking up Zane from school, who's upset that I'm picking him up early and making him miss playground time, we go home and I lay him down for a nap. Sierra is at work and texts me she'll be home late. She's staying straight through to handle the evening shift. Not wanting to tell her what happened through a text or over the phone, I tell her I'll see her tomorrow after class. Then I pull my social media up on my laptop and type in Kolton Reynolds. I know it's a K instead of a C because it's written on my syllabus. A profile pops up, and I click to view it. And sure enough, it's him. Same dimples, same brown hair, same gorgeous green eyes. Every feature matching our son's.

Unfortunately, since his profile is set to private, I can't see anything except his main picture, which is only a headshot. I search Instagram, but nothing comes up. Then I decide to search for Keegan Reynolds. Nothing comes up. I click back onto Kolton's page, but it doesn't show any friends, and I've hit a wall. None of this makes any sense. Why would he lie about his name? Lie about not remembering me? I pull his picture up on my phone and screenshot it so I can show Sierra when she gets home.

CHAPTER TEN

Blakely

"SO, LET ME GET THIS STRAIGHT," BRENTON SAYS, "HE HAS A PROFILE under Kolton, but it's as if Keegan doesn't exist?"

"Yeah," I say as we walk Zane to daycare before we head to class. "I think you should stay away from him. Something is off with this guy."

"He's…" I don't finish my sentence, not wanting Zane to know what we're talking about, but I nod my head toward my son, who is skipping along the sidewalk and purposely jumping over each crack, since he learned at school yesterday from some kids that if he steps on one, my back might break. When he told me, I laughed, but quickly stopped when he glared and told me he was serious.

"So what?" Brenton argues. "If he wanted to be a dad, he wouldn't have acted like you didn't exist. I say screw him."

I glance over at Brenton and notice his fists are clenched together, and his knuckles are almost completely white. Brenton is one of the most laidback guys I know, so it's weird to see him so worked up.

"Jailbird?" I hear being called out, and my body stiffens. There's only one guy who has ever called me that. I look over and spot him, and my heart palpitates. Today, *his* hair is covered by a gray beanie, and he's no longer in a suit, but instead in a pair of ripped blue jeans and a long-sleeved black shirt with a large Billabong logo across the front. A pair of all black shoes with the letters DC in white across the sides.

And he's not walking. Nope, he's skateboarding. He looks nothing like the guy from yesterday, and everything like the guy from our week in Cocoa Beach, and *he* apparently remembers me. What the hell is going on?

I watch for a few seconds as he rolls closer on his board, but I can't do this. Not with Zane here. I don't know what's going on, but I can't have this conversation in front of my—*our*—son.

Picking Zane up, I walk quickly past him, not stopping when he continues to call out my name. I'll deal with this tomorrow. He's my TA all semester, so it's not as if I won't see him again. After kissing my son goodbye, I step outside. A part of me is hoping to see him waiting, but at the same time, I'm glad he isn't. But Brenton is, and he looks as confused as I feel.

"I stopped him when you walked away."

"What?" I shriek, now realizing he wasn't with me when I walked Zane inside. "What did you say? What did he say?"

"I told him to quit playing games with you or I would fuck him up, then I walked away." Brenton shrugs, but his posture is anything but nonchalant. "Why the hell was he calling you Jailbird?"

"It's…" I don't want to lie, but at the same time, I don't want to tell him. That nickname was something between Keegan and me, and it feels like it's all I have left from our week together—well, that and our son. "It's nothing. Let's get to class."

When we find our seats, I decide I can't wait to tell Sierra about Keegan/Kolton. She texted me earlier that she's off tonight but has a date. With our schedules being crazy, it could be next year before we're both home at the same time. I send her the picture I saved with a long text explaining the best I can. And when she replies, I about have a heart attack.

S: That's the guy I have a date with tonight!

Not even sure how to respond, I wait until class ends, then without waiting for Brenton, fly outside and call my sister.

"That's him, B," she says when she answers the phone. "I met him at

Orange Sunrise last week, and he's come in several times since then to ask me out. Last night I finally gave in and said okay. He called himself Kolton."

"This doesn't make any sense."

"I'm supposed to meet him at the restaurant. I'm going to text him to pick me up instead and then we'll get to the bottom of it. If this guy is fucking with you… with us… we'll find out, and then we'll make him wish he never existed."

Despite being so upset over what's going on, I still let out a loud laugh at my sister's words. Those who don't know her would think she's joking or that it's an empty threat, but I know my sister and she's being damn serious.

After picking up Zane, I tell Brenton about tonight. He offers to watch Zane in his room, so we won't risk him hearing anything being said, and Brenton will be close by in case we need him. I'm seriously so blessed to have the people I have in my life. I learned a long time ago, it's all about quality over quantity. I may not have a million friends or a large family, but the people I do have are everything.

When I get home, I busy myself with my schoolwork to distract myself from thinking about tonight. Brenton works at his brother's cell phone shop occasionally, so he told me he'd be back later before he took off. I make Zane his favorite dinner, a hot dog and mac and cheese, then give him a bath. Brenton has barely walked through the door, and is sitting down with Zane to play a game with him, when the doorbell rings.

Sierra opens the door, and standing there is another version of Keegan/Kolton. This guy is dressed in jeans and a white collared shirt with a Lacoste alligator in the corner. He's wearing a pair of brown leather Sperry boat shoes.

"Wow," Sierra says, "I didn't see it before because I wasn't looking for it, but damn, you look just like my nephew."

Keegan/Kolton gives her a confused look, but when he notices me, his lips turn down into a frown. "Am I missing something here?"

"Who are you?" Sierra asks, ignoring his question. "Keegan or Kolton."

His eyes widen, and then his lips curl into a grin. "I'm Kolton."

My stomach fills with lead. He lied to me. "Why did you lie to me?" I ask, needing to know why he wouldn't just give me his real name.

"About what? When?" His gaze flickers from Sierra to me.

"When you slept with my sister!" Sierra bellows. "And don't try to act like you don't remember her. You tried to get her attention earlier."

"I didn't sleep with her," he says, his eyes locking with Sierra's. "I don't even know her."

"Is this a game to you?" I ask, my voice filled with confusion and sadness. Did he know Sierra and I are sisters? I don't get it.

"You think you slept with me?" he asks.

"I think I slept with *Keegan*," I volley.

"And you think… I'm Keegan?"

"Do you have a split personality disorder?" I ask in frustration. He only laughs, which pisses me off.

"I think I know what the problem is," he says, "but it would probably be best if I show you." He pulls out his phone and dials a number. Sierra and I stand in the doorway, neither of us inviting this guy in, while he asks whoever he called to come over and then gives him, or her, our address.

Not wanting Zane to hear anything, I tell Sierra we should close the door so we don't let the air out. She understands what I'm implying and steps outside, closing the door behind us. I have no clue what to expect, but it's obvious this guy in front of me has some issues. He hasn't brought up my son, and I'm not about to expose him to some crazy person.

We all stand in awkward silence while we wait for whoever he called to arrive. And then a few minutes later, I hear it before I see it. The sound of wheels rolling along the concrete. We're on the second floor, so I have to look down, and I see him… dressed the same as earlier. He pops the front of his board up and takes it in his hand as he runs up the stairs, and my breath catches in my throat as I put the pieces together.

Holy. Shit. My gaze goes from Kolton to Keegan and back again. That's right. There's two of them. Both with brown hair and green eyes. Both with the perfect set of dimples. But that's where the similarities stop.

"Jailbird," Keegan says, a huge smile on his face. "I knew that was you earlier."

"Keegan?" I question in shock.

"I see you've met my brother, Kolton." *His brother…*

"You didn't tell me you had a twin brother," I say dumbly.

"There's a lot we didn't tell each other," he says back.

"You never called," I point out. "I… I waited… but you never called or texted."

Tears prick my eyes, my emotions in overload. Keegan is here in front of me. He has a twin brother. He remembers me, which means he chose not to call me.

Keegan steps toward me and says, "I wanted to. I swear I did." He shakes his head. "You wouldn't even believe me if I told you what happened, though."

It doesn't really matter now what happened. It's years later. Our son is here, and too much time has passed to think we would ever be together, like the happy little family I used to envision. But a piece of me still wants to know what happened. Why Keegan never called.

"Tell me, please."

CHAPTER ELEVEN

Keegan

Four Years Ago

"ALL RIGHT, MAN, WE'RE ALL CHECKED OUT," MITCH SAYS, clasping a hand on my shoulder. I'm standing outside by the pool, watching Blakely walk down the wooden path and across the beach back over to her hotel. "Keegan," Mitch says, and I nod so he knows I heard him. But my eyes can't seem to leave the woman walking away from me, her perfect body disappearing the farther away she gets, until she's no longer visible.

"I should've asked her for her number… demanded it." It doesn't matter where she's going to be in a couple months. I need more time with her even if it's long distance.

"You had a good time, and she was a great distraction, but you have a lot of decisions to make when you get home," he reminds me. "Do you really think right now is the best time to start something you can't give your full attention to?" Damn it, I know he's right, but it doesn't stop me from wanting to try. Maybe nothing will come of it, but what if something does?

"You're right," I say, reluctantly turning around and heading back through the lobby. Holly is waiting for us next to the vehicle with our luggage. Mitch clicks the fob and the trunk door rises. We throw our bags inside, then get in. Mitch is driving, and Holly is riding shotgun.

I'm listening to them talk about what they're planning to do when we get home. We've all been living in the dorms, but Mitch and Holly will be getting their own place next month. It makes me wonder where Blakely lives—where she'll be living. Does she know anyone where she's planning to go to school? She seemed so alone this week. Not a single person texted or called her from what I could see—aside from that one time that guy asked her to join them for lunch and she looked like she'd rather eat nails than go.

Mitch says something to Holly, and she laughs, leaning over and kissing his cheek, and it hits me that I'll never be able to feel Blakely's lips on me again. I'll never be able to run my hands along her soft skin.

Closing my eyes, I recall her every feature, what she wore… didn't wear. How she felt in my arms. What her laughter sounded like. Holly laughs again, and I want to tell her to shut the hell up. She's fucking up my memory. In a week, in a month, she'll be nothing more than a distant memory. Every day it will become harder to remember the details. My eyes open, and I breathe out a panicky breath. This can't be the end.

"Turn around," I tell Mitch.

His eyes meet mine in the rearview mirror, and he sighs, not even bothering to ask why. He knows.

Holly looks back at me sympathetically. "Are you sure, Keegan? You said you didn't want anything serious." She's right. I did say that. But that was before I met Blakely. There has to be a reason she's come into my life when she did, and I'm not ready to let her go yet.

"I'm sure."

Mitch turns the vehicle around, and we drive back to our hotel. I should've told him to go to hers, but that's okay, I can walk over. "I'll only be a few minutes," I tell them, jumping out and running across the parking lot to Blakely's hotel. I have no clue which room she's in, but if I have to, I'll knock on every door. It's an older, smaller hotel with only maybe two dozen rooms.

When I step up to the door, though, I realize I won't have to knock on any doors. Because she's walking out of the hotel with her luggage rolling behind her. She wasn't supposed to leave until tomorrow…

When I learn she's leaving early, I know it's fate that I returned when I did. Another two minutes and she wouldn't have been here. It takes some begging and convincing, but Blakely finally gives in and types her number into my phone.

I watch her until she's in that guy's SUV and they're driving away. Then I start my walk back to where Mitch and Holly are waiting for me. I pull up the notepad where she typed her number, and copy and paste it into a text, so she can have mine. I'm not watching where I'm going, so when something hard hits my arm, I'm thrown off. I lose my hold on my phone, and it crashes against the side of the fountain. I dive for it, but I'm too late, and the phone lands in the water with a loud plop.

"I'm so sorry," a woman apologizes. "I told my boys not to throw the football! Is your phone okay?"

Without acknowledging her, I pluck my phone from the water and hit the home button. Nothing happens. I've had this phone for who the hell knows how long. It's been dropped dozens of times, has been thrown across the car, across the room in anger just as many times, but it's never fallen into water. I hold down the top button, hoping something will happen, but it stays black. It's not waterproof. Fuck!

"Sir," the woman says, "is it okay?"

I glance her way, but don't bother to answer. What is she going to do for me? Will it to turn on?

"We need to find an Apple store," I tell Mitch when I open the back door.

"Huh?"

"My phone! It fell in the damn fountain!"

"And you need to get a new one right now?"

"It has her number in it." I sigh.

This time it's Holly who speaks. "You have an iPhone. Everything backs up into the cloud."

"Let's just find an Apple store," I insist.

Holly locates one between Cocoa Beach and Carterville, and we head straight there. After an hour of waiting to be helped, three hours of waiting for them to run diagnostics on my phone, and another hour of them setting up my new phone, I learn that my last backup was done a week prior. Everything saved after that backup is lost—including Blakely's number. If my account would've been linked to another device, it would've synced, but because I have no other Apple products, I'm fucked.

Isn't fate a bitch?

Present

"Is everything okay out here?" Another guy's voice, which isn't my twin's, brings me back to the present. I recognize him from earlier today when I saw Blakely and attempted to approach her. She took off, and he stayed behind to threaten me to stay away from her. I vaguely remember him from when I met Blakely on the beach. She said they were only friends back then, but based on the predatory look he was giving me earlier, and the glare he's shooting my way now, I'm going to assume that friendship is now more.

"Umm… yeah," Blakely says nervously. "It turns out Keegan and Kolton are twins."

Her boyfriend glances from Kolton to me. Not wanting him to think I mean any harm, and not wanting any trouble on campus, I extend my hand. "I'm Keegan. I'm sorry about approaching Blakely earlier. I didn't know she had a boyfriend. I didn't mean any disrespect."

As he places his hand in mine, making it a point to squeeze hard, because apparently he needs to show me he's a tough guy, Blakely says, "Oh, no, Brenton and I aren't dating. We're just friends." Blakely laughs awkwardly.

Brenton's grip on my hand tightens before he drops it, and I notice his jaw clenches. Interesting… Doesn't look like Brenton is too thrilled about Blakely referring to them as just friends, which means they've either dated and broken up, and he wants her back, or she's stuck his ass in the friend zone.

Then I remember seeing a little kid with them. "Was… is that kid yours?" I look between Brenton and Blakely. Yeah, I'm being nosy as fuck, but I need to know what I'm working with here. Four years ago, I thought fate was on my side when I returned in time to get Blakely's number, only to have that fickle bitch laugh in my face when my phone was destroyed and I lost it. Now, here we are, at the same place, at the same time, and I'm not about to let her get away again.

Blakely's eyes go wide, trapping her bottom lip between her teeth. Her eyes leave mine, and she glances down at her feet, shuffling them like she's nervous. When she glances back up, I expect her to answer, but she doesn't. Instead, she turns to Brenton and says, "Is Zane okay in his room?"

"Yeah," Brenton replies. "He's playing with his Legos. I came out here to make sure everything is okay. You were out here for a while."

"Can you go check on him?" she asks softly. "I think I should talk to Keegan alone."

Brenton opens his mouth to argue, but Blakely speaks first. "Please."

"What about them?" he asks, pointing to my brother and the woman who is clearly Blakely's sister—they're identical in almost every way, from their brown hair and eyes, to their heart-shaped lips, to their body type. The only major differences between them are that Blakely's face is a tad rounder and her lips are a bit fuller than her sister's.

"Sierra," Blakely says, turning to her sister.

"We're actually late for our date," Kolton says. "I can probably get us in for a later time, though." He grins at Sierra.

"That's not happening." Sierra scoffs, and Kolton's brows furrow in confusion. "We're practically family." She cackles, and Blakely smacks her arm.

"Really?" Blakely glares.

"Sorry." Her sister shrugs.

And now I'm confused. How the hell are they practically family? That would mean Blakely and I are family… and there's no way we're family.

"Can someone explain what the hell's going on?" I ask, starting to freak out. Are we distant cousins or some shit? My parents are happily married, so there's no way she's my fucking sister, right? Fuck! Did I fuck my sister?

"I'll watch Zane," Sierra says to Blakely, "and you can go talk to Keegan."

"Do you really think it's wise for her to be alone with him?" Brenton asks as if I'm not standing right fucking here.

"They've been alone before," Sierra points out.

"Blakely," Brenton says, ignoring Sierra.

"She's right, Brent. We spent plenty of time together—alone. His brother is my TA. I'm pretty sure neither of them are serial killers."

"That was a long time ago," Brenton hisses, ignoring Blakely's joke.

I'm about to tell this fool it's time he closes his mouth about me, when Blakely's eyes meet mine, and with her lips curled up in a beautiful smile, says, "You haven't murdered anyone in the last four years, have you? Gone to jail for anything?"

I can't help the laugh that escapes as I remember our conversation from years ago. "Nah, Jailbird," I say, and her lips curve into an even bigger smile. "No murders, no arrests. How about you? Have you kept yourself out of jail? Paying for everything at the store? Attending all your classes…"

Sierra laughs. "You told him about the time we shoplifted, and when you got caught skipping?"

Blakely rolls her eyes. "I was making sure he wasn't going to rape and murder me, and it backfired."

"You've been arrested?" Kolton asks, and Sierra and Blakely both laugh.

"We were bad teenagers," Sierra says with a shoulder shrug and a smirk. "Now we're responsible law-abiding adults."

"That's good to know," I tell them both. "So, you wanted to talk?" I say to Blakely to get back on track.

"Yeah." She nods, and her smile disappears. "Brenton, you can go," she tells him. "I'll call you later."

I stifle my grin at his scowl. The entire time we've been talking, anger has been practically radiating off him. I wonder if Blakely knows how badly her *friend* wants her.

"You sure?" he asks, his voice taking on a bit of a whine to it.

Kolton's gaze meets mine, and I catch the laughter in his eyes. He's thinking the same thing I am. Guy has it bad. It's a shame I'm about to step in and make shit even harder for him.

"Yes," Blakely says, patting his shoulder.

With one final glare my way, Brenton stalks off.

"Keegan, want to go for a walk?" Blakely asks me once he's gone, and I nod in agreement.

"Sounds good."

"I better get inside with my nephew," Sierra tells my brother, who looks like he wants to argue but agrees.

"All right, but this isn't over," he tells her. "I'll catch you later, bro." He lifts his chin to me, then takes off in the same direction Brenton went.

Just as Blakely and I are about to take off, a tiny voice yells out, "Mommy!" and the little boy from earlier appears. He has messy brown hair, and he's in a cute pair of pajamas that have Lego men all over them. "Can I have some ice cream, please?" The L in please comes out sounding like a W, and I find myself grinning.

"Hey, sweetie," Blakely says, kneeling down. "I'm going to go for a walk with a friend of mine, and Auntie Sierra is going to watch you. You can have one scoop."

The little boy grins, then looks up at me, and I just about lose my footing. He's sporting two huge dimples in his cheeks, identical to my dad, my brother, and me. I try to do the math in my head, but I don't know how old he is. There's no way.

"Blakely," I say, my voice raspy from shock. "Is he…" I can't even finish my sentence. This doesn't make any sense. It's just a coincidence. But then I remember she never did tell me who the dad was. If it were Brenton, he would've said something. That would've been the perfect way to stake his claim.

Blakely stands, her face showing no emotion. "Let's go for that walk." Then she turns back to her son. "I'll be home in a little while. I love you."

"Love you too!" he yells, already running back inside, probably going straight to the kitchen to get his ice cream.

The front door closes, and we head down the hallway and stairs in silence. I let Blakely guide us across the parking lot and down the sidewalk, in the opposite direction of campus toward the park that's adjacent to the complex she lives in. My intention is to let her lead the conversation, but my anxiousness gets the best of me, my mind going crazy with different scenarios, and before we make it to the park, I grip her shoulder and spin her around.

"Is he mine?" I blurt out.

Blakely's gaze meets mine. Tears glisten in her eyes, and she chews on that damn bottom lip. Her eyelids flutter shut, and several drops of liquid fall. And with her eyes still closed, she nods once. "Yes," she whispers, "he's yours."

CHAPTER TWELVE

Blakely

WITHOUT WAITING FOR KEEGAN TO SAY ANYTHING, I PICK UP MY pace, speed walking to the park I've been taking Zane to since he was born. It first started out as walks in his stroller, but as he got older, it turned into picnics in the grass, and now he plays on all of the equipment.

We sit on a bench a little ways away from the playground, in between the empty field where Zane loves to kick the ball, and the basketball court where he'll spend hours drawing with chalk on the blacktop.

We sit in silence for several minutes. I remember the shock I felt when I found out I was pregnant, so I can imagine what's going through Keegan's head. Only he's not finding out I'm pregnant, but that he has a three-year-old son.

"This doesn't make any sense," he finally says. "We were careful. We used condoms." He sighs loudly, and I turn my body to face him, so he knows he has my attention. "We used condoms every time." His tone isn't malicious. It's confused. And I don't blame him. I had the same reaction when I found out.

"I guess you'll have to ask your condoms what happened," I say, trying to lighten the mood. "I wouldn't have believed it myself, if it wasn't for my protruding belly, the ultrasound pictures, and at the end of the nine months, me pushing a watermelon-sized baby out of my tomato-sized hole."

Keegan flinches. "Sorry, kind of graphic, huh?" I say through a laugh, remembering the ridiculousness of my labor and delivery. "You should've been there. For a minute, I wasn't sure he was coming out. At one point, I think I even begged the doctor to just keep him inside me so I wouldn't have to push anymore. But of course, eventually he came out. All eight pounds, four ounces of him."

Keegan's brows furrow together and his lips curve into a frown. "I wasn't there," he murmurs with a shake of his head. "We used condoms," he says again, and I worry he's in shock.

"We did," I say gently. "But they're not one hundred percent effective."

Keegan nods slowly, still in some kind of shocked trance, and I worry that maybe he doesn't think Zane is his. "We could do a paternity test," I say, and his frown morphs into a scowl.

"I know he's mine. He looks just like Kolton and me. He even looks like Keith."

"Who's Keith?"

Keegan's eyes wince as if he's in pain. "He is… was… my older brother. He died a few years ago." He shakes his head. "I don't want to talk about him, though. I just meant that Zane—that's his name, right?"

"Yeah." I swallow thickly. "It's Zane Keegan Jacobs." His features soften at hearing Zane's full name. "I wanted him to have a part of you, especially since I didn't think I'd ever find you."

Keegan nods in understanding. "That means a lot to me. I just meant that Zane looks identical to my brothers and me when we were little. I'll have to show you some pictures one day."

"I would like that."

We're both quiet for a few minutes, and I imagine it's because neither of us knows where to go from here. So, I decide to tell him a truth in hope of breaking the ice, and also, maybe to find out some things about him. "Sierra and I moved here when I was seven months pregnant, and every day I would go for a walk around campus. I didn't start school until Zane was eight months old, but we still went for walks every day. You said you went to school here, so I searched for you every day for months.

I even asked students and professors if they knew a Keegan, but no one knew who you were."

Keegan breathes out a deep sigh, but doesn't say anything for another minute. "I did go here… but I…" He speaks slowly, and I'm not sure why he's choosing his words carefully, but I listen with patience. "I left school at the end of the year. The spring break we met was my last year here."

When he doesn't give me any more, I ask, "And you're back now?"

He clears his throat. "Yeah."

"What year are you?"

"A junior."

Jeez, it's like pulling teeth. "When did you return?"

"This semester."

I stare at him for a moment, trying to figure out why he just clammed up on me. If he were a random guy I just met, I'd let it go, but he's the father of my child, which means I need to learn about him. "Why did you leave for over three years and then return?"

He sucks in a breath then exhales harshly, averting his eyes.

"Keegan?" I prompt. "What's going on?"

"I got my AA and figured I was done," he finally says. "I'm taking a few classes while I figure out my next step."

"What's your major?"

"I'm not sure," he admits.

"Well, what classes are you taking?"

"Umm… a psych class, U.S. Government, and a criminal justice class."

The awkward silence is now back in full force, and I can't help but wonder how this is all going to work. Will Keegan want joint custody? Do we go to court and let a judge decide? He hasn't even said if he wants to meet Zane at all. Although, he did say he would show me pictures one day, so he must want him in his life in some way, right?

I breathe out a frustrated sigh, and Keegan smiles nervously at me, giving me the confidence I need to ask him my question. "Do you want to meet Zane? I mean, do you want him in your life?"

"What?" He scowls. "Of course I do."

I let out a sigh of relief. "Okay, good." Then another thought crosses my mind. "Are you dating someone?" When he smirks, I realize that came out wrong. "I mean, is there someone you need to talk to? Let her know you're now a dad?"

"No," Keegan says. "I'm not dating anyone. You?"

"No. I'm focusing on school and my future. No guys. No dating. No hooking up." I cringe when I blurt out the last part, and Keegan laughs.

"Got it. So, where do we go from here?"

"I guess we just take it one day at a time." I shrug. "You can get to know Zane, and once everyone is comfortable, we can tell him you're his dad."

"My mom is going to freak out when she finds out," he says with a chuckle, and my heart sinks. I didn't think about Keegan having family, since Sierra and I don't have one. It's always just been the three of us with a side of Brenton. He has a brother he occasionally talks about, but he isn't close to his parents. Actually, now that I think about it, I don't think he's ever mentioned either of his parents. Hmm… I'll have to ask him about them one day.

"Will she be upset?" I ask, already feeling the need to go mama bear on anyone who doesn't like my son—family or not.

"No way." He laughs, and for a second it reminds me of the Keegan I spent time with on the beach. It's light and sweet and masculine, and goes straight into my chest and slides down to the apex of my thighs. "She's going to be ecstatic. She was a kindergarten teacher, so she loves little kids. She retired last year and is always complaining how much she misses being around all the kids."

"Oh, good. How about we start with introducing you to him first and then we can go from there?"

"Sounds good." He gives me the first real smile since we've started talking.

"What about dinner tomorrow night at our place?"

"Dinner at your place sounds perfect." Keegan's grin widens. "It's a date."

CHAPTER THIRTEEN

Blakely

"**P**LEASE, CAN I BRING MY BOOK TO SCHOOL?" ZANE BEGS. HE always wants to bring his stuff to share, but then he gets upset when someone doesn't treat it as they should. And he's very protective of his books. He takes after my mom and me in that way.

"And what if someone draws on it?" I ask, shooting him my best mom look.

His brows furrow. "I won't draw on them this time, I promise."

I stifle my laugh. When Zane let his friend borrow his book, the little boy drew on it, so my son decided he would draw on him to show him how it feels. His mother was not happy about marker being all over her son's clothes and arms, but she couldn't say much when she was told her son drew all over Zane's book. It's a dog-eat-dog world in preschool.

"Fine." I give in. I'm a mom. I pick my battles. "If anyone ruins your book, I will not be buying you a new one."

Zane is already stuffing the book into his backpack and then heading to the front door.

The entire walk to his school, he skips and hops and plays I spy. I have no clue where he gets his energy from, but I'd love to bottle it up and use it on myself.

When we get to his school, Zane runs straight over to Melissa, who is holding the doll Zane bought for her in her arms.

"Have fun, and I'll be back to get you soon," I say to him.

"Bye, Mommy. Love you!" he yells back, already taking his book out of his backpack to show Melissa.

"Thank you so much for the doll," Tarah says. "Christmas was hard," she admits softly. "Melissa loves that doll so much." Tarah, not only goes to school full-time, but works part-time at the college daycare. We've had a few playdates over the last year since she started college, and from what I've gathered, Melissa's dad is a deadbeat who decided one day he didn't want to be a husband or a dad anymore, leaving her on her own. When she went after him for child support, he showed zero income because he's getting paid under the table. Most of her school is paid for thanks to financial aid, but she still has to pay for her living expenses and care for Melissa.

When I listened to her story, it made me that much more thankful for my sister. When I found out I was pregnant, she could've pushed me away, but she didn't. She stepped up, and it's because of her in four months I'll be graduating with my bachelor's degree and moving on to the graduate program—as long as I get in.

"You're welcome. Zane was so happy she loved it."

"The daycare is doing a 'bring your parents to school' day next week." She hands me a flyer. "The kids have been practicing some songs, and they're going to perform."

"I bet this will be adorable." I imagine Zane and his little friends singing and performing. "I'll be there. Do you need me to bring anything?"

"Nope. Just yourself."

"Sounds good. I better get to class so I'm not late, but we should do coffee this week."

"For sure!" She smiles. "Have a good day!"

When I step outside, Brenton is waiting for me. When he didn't show up this morning to walk with us, I texted him to ask if everything was okay. He didn't text back.

"What's up?" I ask as we fall in step together, walking toward our first class of the day.

"You tell me," he demands.

I stop in my tracks, not liking his tone. "Is this about Keegan?"

"Did you tell him he's Zane's dad?"

"Of course I did… because he is."

"You don't even know this guy!" Brenton fumes. I've never seen him this mad before, and it has me feeling uneasy. Subconsciously, I take a step back, needing some space, but he steps forward. I put my hand out to stop him from advancing, and thankfully he gives me space, not stepping any closer.

"I knew him enough to sleep with him," I say honestly. "We created a baby, and you know how long I've waited to find him. So, I don't understand why you're acting all mad and shocked that the moment I actually do find him, I tell him he's Zane's dad."

Brenton's glare hits me hard. "So, what? You're all just going to be some perfectly happy instant family?" His question burns like a slap to the face. He's not asking because he cares, but rather because he thinks the idea is ludicrous.

"What is your damn problem?" I hiss. "You're one of my best friends. You should be happy for me, for Zane. You know how much this means to me. I have zero family aside from Sierra. I never wanted that for Zane, and you know it!" I scream the last part as hot, angry tears spill down my cheeks. "No, I'm not planning to become some *instant family*, but at least my son won't grow up without a dad! And Keegan said he has a mom and a dad. Plus, there's his brother Kolton. Zane will have grandparents and an uncle. Sierra and I don't have any of that. When our parents, and then grandmother, died, we were left as foster kids. At least if something happens to me, he'll have a family."

I didn't realize until this moment, the relief I suddenly feel at knowing if something happens to Sierra and me, Zane won't be forced into foster care. He'll have family, who will love and take care of him. Real blood relatives he can turn to.

As the salty liquid flows down like a waterfall, the sound of a board draws my attention. Keegan is standing a few feet away. And based on the way his jaw is ticking, he heard Brenton's and my conversation. How much, I'm not sure.

"You okay?" Keegan asks, stepping forward and wiping the lingering wetness from under my eyes. The act feels so intimate, but it shouldn't. We created a baby. You can't get any more intimate than that.

"She's fine," Brenton grunts. "I'm sorry, Blakely," he says to me. "I'm just worried."

"About me?" Keegan asks incredulously. "Because I'm pretty sure you're the one making her cry."

"This is between Blakely and me," Brenton volleys back.

"And it's about Blakely, our son, and me," Keegan states. It shouldn't be what I focus on in this moment, but my thoughts linger on *our son*. He's only known about Zane for less than twenty-four hours and he's already accepted Zane as *our son*. My heart thumps against my ribcage. *Zane has a family.*

Brenton starts to argue, but I cut him off. "Stop, please. I appreciate you looking out for me, and I know this is all going to take some time, but what I need is for you to be supportive. Zane looks up to you, and he's going to observe how you react to his dad. If you can't be on board, then…" I let my words linger, not wanting to make threats, but also needing Brenton to understand that Keegan isn't going anywhere.

"Fine," Brenton says, throwing his hands in the air. "We need to get to class."

"I'll be right there," I tell him. His eyes bug out in annoyance. It's just going to take time, I tell myself. Brenton has been the only guy in our lives for the last three years. This is a lot for everyone to deal with.

He stomps away like an angry child, and Keegan snorts. "You sure you don't have two kids?"

I whirl around to face him, my hand going to my hip. "Don't be like that. Brenton has been there for me since Sierra and I moved here. He's been the only male figure in Zane's life, and he's been a damn good friend to me."

"He wants in your pants," Keegan states dryly.

"No, he doesn't," I argue. "He's just protective."

"He wants in your pants," he repeats.

"We'll just have to agree to disagree. Were you looking for me?"

"I was on my way to class." Keegan looks around. "Where's Zane?"

"I already dropped him off." When I point to the building, I remember the flyer I'm holding. "His school is having a 'take your parents to school' day next week. Maybe after you meet him and we tell him you're his dad, you can come?"

I extend my hand, and Keegan takes the piece of paper from me. After a few seconds of reading the details, he says, "I would really like that."

"Cool. I better get to class. Your brother is teaching the lecture today."

"I can't even imagine what was going through your head when you saw him." Keegan chuckles good-naturedly.

"I know I only knew you for a few days, but when I saw him and we spoke, in some weird way, I knew he wasn't you."

Keegan steps closer to me, encroaching on my personal space. "Because you knew deep down I could never forget you." He runs his fingers down the side of my cheek, stopping at my chin, and a shiver breaks out throughout my body. "Everything about that time we spent together was unforgettable."

My eyes close of their own accord, and my cheek leans into his hand that's still lingering on the side of my face. It would be so easy to get lost in this man. To pick up where we left off. But that's not what Zane needs. That's not what I need. He needs a dad. I need a degree.

When I open my eyes, Keegan's face is millimeters from mine. His lips are so close—too close. His gaze is fixed on my lips. He wants to kiss me, but he's waiting for permission.

"Keegan," I whisper, my voice coming out breathless. "We can't do this." I back away from his touch, and his hand falls. "What we had… It was fun and reckless, and I'll never regret it because it gave me Zane, and he's my entire world. But it wasn't the beginning of something. I have Zane and my degree I need to think about. My sister has been busting her ass to help me so I can get a degree and provide for my son. I'm not about to risk that to date someone—even if that someone is the father of my son. Hell, *especially* because you're the father of my son."

"Our son," he corrects. "Are you telling me for the last four years you haven't dated at all?"

"Yep." I nod vehemently. "That's exactly what I'm telling you. I'm not going out and hooking up with guys while my sister works fifty to sixty hours a week to pay our bills so I can get a college education like I wanted. If it weren't for her, I would've either given Zane up for adoption or been living somewhere shitty working full-time to barely make ends meet. I couldn't have done these last four years without her."

Keegan frowns but nods. "Okay, I get it. For now, we'll focus on Zane, but in a few months, you're graduating…"

"And then I'm going for my graduate degree."

"Great, sounds like a plan, but I'm only giving you until you get your bachelor's degree," he says, "and then all bets are off. I came back for your number that day because I wanted more, and four years later, I still do. I'm not giving up on getting to know you."

"And what about Zane?" I point out, dumbfounded by how blunt he's being.

"What about him?"

"What if we date and break up?"

"Then he's no worse off than he was with two parents who aren't together." He shrugs. "But if our chemistry now is anything like it was back then, there's a chance we could give him a family."

A family—his words remind me of what Brenton mentioned earlier. *An instant family.*

"So, you're doing this to give him a family?" I accuse.

"No, I'm doing this because four years ago my phone fell into a goddamn fountain and I lost your number. I have a second chance, one I never thought I'd ever have, and I'd be a fool if I didn't try to see if there's something more with us. And if that means we get to be a family, then that's even better." He steps toward me. "But, Jailbird, even if we don't end up together, we share a son. We're always going to be family." His words crawl under my skin and flow through my veins. I can feel them in every part of my being.

My phone buzzes in my back pocket, reminding me I need to get to class. "Can we talk about this later? I'm late."

"Sure." He nods. "We're still on for dinner tonight, right?"

Shit, I'm already behind on my reading because of yesterday. But I can't not let him meet his son.

"Yeah, tonight's still fine."

"What's wrong? You sound like tonight is anything but fine."

"I was just hoping to get caught up on homework. I didn't get anything done yesterday. But it's okay. You can come over and I'll cook something."

"How about I come over and bring dinner, and if everything goes okay, I can hang out with Zane and get to know him while you work on your homework?"

"Don't you have homework?"

"I've got it handled." He drops his board to the ground and steps on it, then pulls out his phone. "What's your number?"

I rattle off my digits, and a second later, my phone buzzes.

"Now you have my number," he says, looking up from his phone. "And this time, I know where you live in case our phones fall in the water." He winks playfully. "Text me later what time I should come over and what Zane likes to eat."

He pushes the skateboard toward me and leans in, kissing my cheek. "Have a good day at school, Jailbird." Then he takes off, rolling around me and in the opposite direction of where he was heading. Hmm…

CHAPTER FOURTEEN

Keegan

"**M**om, Dad!" I yell, walking into my childhood home. I was born and raised in the small town of Carterville. My mom taught for years, until she had my brothers and me, then she took some time off to be home with us until we were all in school. She retired last year and has been bugging my dad to retire as well. She says she wants to spend some time traveling. Of course, I imagine once she finds out about her grandson, she's going to rethink that.

"In here, honey," she calls out. "Your dad is in the garage, finally putting all the Christmas decorations away." She playfully rolls her eyes, and I laugh.

"Dad, get in here," I holler, knowing he'll hear me since the door is open.

"What's going on, Keegan?" Mom asks. "Is everything okay?"

"Yeah, I think so." I'm suddenly nervous about telling them. Mom and Dad have been married since two months after they graduated high school. They did everything in the proper order, and I hope they don't judge me for Zane not coming into this world the same way. If I have it my way, Blakely, Zane, and I *will* be a family soon enough. I just need to give her some time. Her reasons for not wanting to date are valid, to a certain extent. It's her way of being a good mom. And I'm thankful for it because it means she's single.

"What's going on, Son?" Dad walks inside, wiping the sweat from his forehead with a rag. "Is it something about—"

I cut him off. "This isn't about work." Then it hits me… will this affect my job? I didn't even think about that until right now. I shake the thoughts away. I'll deal with all that later. Right now, I have news. "I have a son."

Dad's brows rise to his forehead, and Mom gasps.

"You got a girl pregnant?" Mom asks. "I didn't know you were dating anyone."

"Tell me it wasn't a girl at Carterville," Dad says. I know what he's thinking, so I shake my head.

"She does go to Carterville…" Dad opens his mouth, but I stop him. "But I didn't meet her there."

"Let's sit down," Mom suggests, so we do.

"I met her four years ago," I tell them. "Right after Keith died and Kolton left."

I explain to them about my time with her and how I got her number and then lost it. They both listen without interrupting while I tell them how Blakely ended up in the class Kolton is TAing for, and how she ran into both of us. Mom giggles a little at her not knowing we're twins. For years, we would play tricks on everyone, including our teachers. Once, my girlfriend made out with my brother, not knowing it was him and not me.

"His name is Zane Keegan Jacobs, and he just turned three in December. I don't know the date, though. There's a lot I don't know, actually."

"Wow," Mom says through a smile. "When can we meet him?"

I grin, happy she's willing to accept him so easily.

"Blakely wants to take things slowly. She's going to introduce us tonight. I was actually hoping maybe we could go shopping. I would like to bring him a small gift or something." I shrug, completely out of my element here.

"I'm very glad you're going to get to know your son," my dad says. "You said she goes to Carterville?"

Always in work mode. "Yeah, and I know what you're thinking—maybe it would be best if someone else…"

"You're already in too deep," he says matter-of-factly. "We'll talk about this later. Go shopping with your mom, go meet your son, take some pictures, and give him a hug from us. I'll see you in the morning."

CHAPTER FIFTEEN

Blakely

"I CAN ALREADY TELL PSYCHOLOGY OF INEQUALITY IS GOING TO BE the death of me," I tell Brenton as we walk to our next class, Child Psychology.

"It was only the second class," he says.

"Exactly, and did you see what the requirements are?"

"You do this every semester, Blakely." Brenton laughs. "We'll get a study group together, and we'll be fine."

"Okay."

"Want to study tonight? I can bring over some pizza, and we can get ahead after Zane goes to bed."

"Umm…" Shit, I was hoping not to bring up Keegan so soon. Brenton seems to be back to normal. "Keegan's actually coming over to meet Zane tonight."

Brenton's shoulders tighten, and his back straightens, but he doesn't say anything. He's quiet the rest of the way to class, and the entire time we're in there. After the professor dismisses us, he tells me he has some things to take care of and will see me tomorrow. It's not unusual for Brenton to take off after class since he works at his brother's cell phone shop, but we usually study together first, and once it's time for me to pick up Zane, he takes off.

After picking up Zane from daycare, I bring him home and give him a bath, so he won't have to take one later. I get some studying in while he naps, and once he's awake, we spend the afternoon playing with his Legos until Keegan arrives. He texted me earlier asking what we would like to eat. Since Sierra is working, it will be just the three of us. I suggested the BBQ place down the street. Zane loves their mac n cheese, and I love their chicken pasta.

When I open the door, Keegan is sporting a gray beanie, a shirt with a brand I recognize as one all the skateboarders wear, and a pair of ripped jeans and Vans. He looks every bit the skateboarder-slash-surfer I know him to be, and looking back, it's comical to think I thought for even a second he was his twin brother, Kolton. Aside from their faces being identical, everything else about them is different. Including the various tattoos Keegan is sporting. Some I recognize from our time together all those years ago, and some are new.

"Like what you see?" he asks with a smirk. His green eyes sparkle, and I roll my mine, even though I know damn well I was checking him out. He might be off-limits, but I'm not blind. Keegan was hot four years ago. Now, he's freaking gorgeous. The little bit of boy that lingered back then has turned into all man. The muscles that were developing are now *fully* developed. He's sporting a short-sleeve shirt, and his biceps and forearms are on display. The guy clearly works out.

"The BBQ?" I joke, taking the takeout bag out of his hands and setting it on the table. "Definitely."

Keegan laughs. "Fight it all you want, Jailbird, but you and me… it's inevitable."

Ignoring his comment and refusing to admit the way his words go straight to my heart then slide down to my belly, ending at the neglected part between my legs, I call Zane out.

"Wait!" Keegan whisper-yells. "How are we going to do this? Shouldn't we come up with a game plan or something?"

I stifle my laugh at seeing his cockiness disappear so quickly. "He's three. It'll be okay. He likes Legos and thinks SpongeBob is God."

"What the hell is a SpongeBob?" he asks, and this time I do laugh.

"It's a cartoon character on a show he watches."

"Mommy, can we have ice cream for—" Zane stops in his tracks when he spots Keegan standing in the doorway. "Is that for me?" His face lights up. When I look back over at Keegan, confused, I notice he has two more bags in his other hand. One of them with the infamous Build-A-Bear logo on it.

"Zane, that's not nice," I tell my son, who's practically bouncing on his feet in excitement. I call it only child syndrome. Anytime anyone comes over and they have a toy, it's always for Zane because he's the only kid around, so now he expects it.

"I'm sorry." He pouts. "But… is it?"

Keegan laughs at his excitement, but looks to me to guide him as to what to do. I give him a small nod.

"This is my friend Keegan," I tell Zane. "Keegan, this is Zane."

Zane stops in his place, his brows furrowing in confusion. I'm not sure what's going through his head until he says, "That's my name! Zane Keegan. Mommy yells it when she's mad. You're my daddy!"

Oh, shit. How could I have overlooked that? How many times have I mentioned where he got his middle name from, wanting him to know that he has a daddy, even if I didn't think I'd ever find Keegan. I didn't think he'd put two and two together, though.

Keegan fake-coughs, his eyes wide in a *say something* expression. So, I do. "Yes, sweetie, Keegan is your daddy."

Zane grins and looks down at the bag. "Can I have the gift now?"

Keegan laughs, relieved at how well that went. I shouldn't be surprised, though. Zane is only three years old, and as easygoing as they come. He's at an age where he knows who everyone is, but he's still too young to really understand what's happening, or to be upset over his dad missing the last several years of his life. Had he been a few years older, this conversation would probably be totally different.

"I wasn't sure what you would like," Keegan says nervously, handing Zane the bag. "My mom went with me to the mall. I had no idea how many different things you could buy for a kid his age," he tells me.

"Look, Mommy!" Zane squeals. "It's a bear riding a skateboard." He pulls the bear out of the cardboard house and sets it on the ground, rolling it across the rug.

"What do you say?" I prompt.

Zane yells, "Thanks, Dad!"

With glossy eyes, Keegan stands and, without looking at me, says, "I, uh…Where's your bathroom?"

"Down the hall. Second door on the right."

"Thanks."

While he's in the bathroom, I set out all the food he bought. "Zane, come eat."

When Keegan comes out, he's composed and calm. He sits at the table and gives me one of his signature smiles. "Sorry about that…"

"You don't have to apologize. Zane's too young to understand the significance of the word, but I remember the first time he said 'Mama.' I cried for ten minutes, then begged him to do it again so I could get it on video. Of course he didn't." I laugh. "Not for another week at least."

Keegan chuckles, and I'm glad the mood has been lightened.

"I got something for you as well," Keegan says, grabbing the white bag he left on the table when he excused himself to the bathroom.

"You didn't have to do that." I open the bag and find a copy of *Wuthering Heights* in there. *Oh, dear God.*

"I owed you a copy." He grins. "For making you drop yours into the Atlantic."

"Thank you." I flip through the pages, excited to have my own copy of *Wuthering Heights*. I haven't read it since high school, and I wouldn't dare touch my mom's copy.

"Mommy, that's just like Grandma's!" Zane hops off his chair and runs to the bookshelf that's filled with all our books, including my mom's. He stops in front of it and points to it. He knows he's not allowed to touch those. "See!"

"It is," I tell him. "This is the same book, only this copy, we can touch." I give Zane a playful wink.

"Grandma left Mommy all her books, and when I get older, I'm going to get to read all of them," Zane tells Keegan, sitting back in his seat. "I'm not big enough yet, but when I'm this many"—he holds up both hands, splaying his fingers out wide—"I'm going to read them all!"

While we eat, Keegan listens to Zane tell him all about his books that he can read now by himself. He listens intently and asks questions to keep

Zane talking. I eat quietly, soaking in this first moment between Zane and his father. A moment I didn't think would ever come.

When we're done, Zane shows Keegan his room, and they spend a few hours playing with his toys and watching SpongeBob while I get some studying in.

When it's time for Zane to go to bed, Keegan helps tuck him in, and Zane insists Keegan reads him his bedtime story, which of course turns into five stories since Keegan can't say no, and I don't have the heart to cut them off. During the fifth story, though, Zane finally falls asleep. I listen as Keegan keeps reading to the end anyway. Then he leans over and kisses him on his forehead, telling him he loves him, and I swear, my heart just imploded in my chest.

I tiptoe back to the couch so he won't know I was watching and listening. When he walks out, he implies hanging out, and I want so badly to ask him to stay. To hang out with him and get to know him. But I tell myself it can't happen. The last time I was with Keegan, all it took was a look and some smooth words and the guy had me under his spell. I have goals and dreams. I have a son who needs his mom to take care of him. I need to give Sierra a damn break. It would be selfish of me to find time to date while she's working her ass off to support us.

So, instead, I thank him for dinner and the book, and tell him we'll make plans for him to see Zane again soon before showing him out.

I'm finishing up my reading for tomorrow when Sierra comes through the door and plops onto the couch next to me. "How'd it go?"

"You're home early."

"Nope, you're studying late," she points out. I glance at the clock and see it's already two in the morning. Shit, I'm going to be hating life tomorrow.

"It went well. Zane heard Keegan's name and *told* him he's his dad." I laugh, falling back against the couch and laying my head next to my sister's.

"He's my nephew," Sierra points out. "So, he's smart and observant like me." She giggles.

"Yeah, yeah. You should've seen Keegan when he called him dad. He started to cry."

Sierra's gaze bores into my cheek. "Are you and Keegan going to…"

"No." I shake my head. "You know I don't date."

"Yeah, because you were hoping Keegan would come back." She sits up and faces me. "Now he's back."

"I don't date because I'm focusing on school."

"Bullshit. You're a straight-A student and mom of the damn year. Hell, you took extra classes to get caught up. You're going to graduate in three years. Give me a break."

"Yeah, because you've worked your ass off to make sure I could do that," I point out.

"Oh no." She straightens her back, telling me she's about to go into fight mode. "Don't you dare blame your lack of dating on me. You don't see me acting like a nun."

"And you deserve to date—to have a life."

"And so do you," she says. "If you're not dating because you feel bad I pay the bills, I'm telling you right now that excuse isn't going to fly. You've never mentioned that, and if you had, I would've told you to stop your shit. We're a team." Sierra takes my hands in hers. "You getting pregnant saved me, B. I was on a bad path, and we both know it. I was drinking and doing drugs. Sleeping around. I had no future, no goals. Zane changed all that. I love our home. I love my job. And I love my life. It's time you start living yours.

"You're going to graduate in May and get accepted into a graduate program. And soon enough you'll have a job as a guidance counselor just like you want. But, B, there's more to life than that. Since our grandmother died, you became the adult. You have all these goals, and those are great, but you deserve to have some fun and fall in love."

"I don't see you falling in love."

"And that's not because I'm not trying," she says with a frown. "I'm not purposely pushing love away. I go on dates. I've had my fair share of relationships. They just haven't worked out. But if I found the right guy, I wouldn't push him away." She lifts a brow at me. "Has Keegan said anything?"

I can't lie to my sister. "He might've mentioned wanting to get to know me…"

"I knew it!" She claps her hands together. "You've been dreaming about this for the last four years, B! Do not push that man away. I gave up a date with his sexy-as-sin brother for you."

"Hey," I say, "I didn't say you had to do that. If you want to date him, go for it." I shrug.

"You sure?" she asks with a grin that tells me she really wants to go for it.

"I mean, if you guys don't work out, it'll make for awkward Thanksgivings…"

Sierra laughs. "Only you would worry about us not working out before we even go on our first date."

"It's called being responsible."

"It's called being a worrywart." She sticks her tongue out. "Life's too short to worry over what-ifs," she says, standing. "If you decide to give Keegan a chance, I can watch Zane for you." She winks saucily. "Maybe if you finally get laid again, you will be less uptight."

"Oh, yeah, because the last time I got laid worked out really well for me," I joke.

"Actually it did," she says seriously. "It gave us Zane, and we both know you wouldn't trade him for anything in the world."

Damn my sister for being right.

CHAPTER SIXTEEN

Keegan

"AND TO WHAT DO I OWE THIS PLEASURE?" SIERRA LEANS AGAINST the doorframe with her arms crossed over her chest and a smirk on her lips. She's dressed in a pair of sweats and a tank top, her hair pulled on top of her head. This is the first time I'm seeing her since the day I found out I was a dad, and that day I was too preoccupied by Blakely to pay any real attention to her sister. But looking at her now, it's obvious they're sisters. Their features are similar, except where Sierra has a look to her that screams *I'm trouble with a capital T*, Blakely has a more innocent look to her. I wouldn't doubt that, even though Sierra was the younger of the two, she was the leader when they were growing up.

"I'm here to see Blakely and—"

Before I can get his name out, Zane shrieks, "Daddy!" as he runs around his aunt and straight into my lower body. He collides with my crotch, and I stifle a groan. "Daddy, you're here!" He grins up at me, and his tiny dimples, which match mine, pop out.

I've only hung out with him a few times now, but since the first day he found out I'm his dad, he's called me Daddy, as if it's the most natural thing, and fuck if it isn't the best feeling in the world. I knew one day I'd get married and have kids, but because I hadn't reached that point in my life yet, I never thought about what it would feel like to have a kid. No thoughts could even do it justice. The way he smiles at me like I'm his whole world is indescribable. I've only known about him for less than a week, but it's safe to say this kid is my entire universe.

"What'd you bring me?" Zane asks, when he spots the bag in my hand. Every time I've come over, I've brought him something. Blakely says I'm forming a bad habit, but I don't care. I plan to do everything in my power to make up for the years lost and to show him every day, month, and year to come how much I love him. Sure, gifts aren't how you show a kid you love him, but I can't help myself. My son loves Legos and reading. I view it as helping to educate him.

I laugh at Zane's question, but Sierra frowns, chiding him. "Don't be rude."

"Sorry," he grumbles.

"It's all right, bud. Here ya go." I hand him the bag and he opens it, pulling out a new book. Like I said, my kid enjoys Legos and reading. I hardly consider bringing him books spoiling him.

"Wow! An animal book! Thank you!" He flies back into my body to give me a hug, and this time I lift him into my arms.

"You're welcome."

"Blakely's not here," Sierra says. I go to set Zane down, but he grips his hand that's not holding his book tightly around my neck.

"I must've gotten the days confused," I tell her. "Hey, bud, I didn't realize your mom wasn't home," I tell Zane, who frowns.

"I want to watch SpongeBob and play with my Legos and read my new book with Daddy," he says to his aunt.

She smiles at the two of us. "You're more than welcome to hang out with him. Blakely is with her study group. I think it was last minute." She waves her hand, indicating for me to go inside.

"Thanks. If I'm cramping your style, just let me know."

"No style to cramp," she jokes. "I'm as boring as they come. Just painting my nails and getting caught up on SpongeBob with this little man." If it weren't for her sincere smile, I would think she resents her life being boring, but the way she glances at Zane tells me she's okay with her life the way it is because he's her nephew.

"I got to paint her nails!" Zane giggles.

"You did? Did you paint yours too?" I dramatically check out his nails, and he laughs harder.

"No! That's for girls. Melissa paints her nails pink."

"Melissa, huh?" I give Zane a knowing look that he's too young to get. This isn't the first time he's mentioned his friend Melissa. Is it possible for a three-year-old to have a crush? Because I'm pretty sure my son is sweet for this Melissa chick.

"She goes to school with Zane," Sierra says, filling me in. "They're best friends." Her lips upturn into a sly smile, and I know she's thinking the same thing I am. My boy's got game.

Zane drops the book between us, and his hands come up to my cheeks, squeezing the sides of my face to get my attention. "C'mon, Daddy, let's go to my room and read my book."

"You got it, bud."

When I place my skateboard against the wall by the door, Zane notices and asks, "Can I ride it?"

"Sure." I shrug nonchalantly, but inside I'm excited that my boy is interested in boarding. I was about his age when my uncle Sean bought me my first board. He was a pro skater and has taught me just about everything I know. He's retired now and lives in Miami with his wife. I can't wait to introduce Zane to him.

Zane wriggles his body so I'll let him down, then walks over to the board, laying the book on the end table along the way. Setting the board down, he kneels next to it, putting his tiny hands on the top, and rolls it back and forth.

"I'm going to jump in the shower," Sierra says. "Make sure he doesn't bust his head on that thing. Blakely would kill us both." When my eyes widen, she laughs. "Just watch him. It will be fine."

She disappears down the hall, and I sit next to Zane on the ground. "Want to sit on it?" His eyes light up, and he nods quickly. "Go ahead, then."

He wastes no time climbing onto the board, while I hold it so it doesn't move. "I wanna stand," he says, already getting up onto his knees. I hold the board tight, and he gets on his feet. When he shifts his body in an attempt to make the board go, I chuckle, but he frowns. "Let go."

"You're going to fall," I warn him.

"No, I'm not." He pouts. "Let go. I wanna go."

"All right, but don't bust your head. Your aunt said your mommy will kill me." Quickly standing, I put my hands out, ready to catch him when he falls.

"Now?" he asks, ignoring my warning.

"Go for it."

With his feet planted on the board, he extends his arms out, and his body sways forward. The board moves a couple inches before he loses his balance. Grabbing underneath his arms, I lift him over my head and, holding him like he's a plane, walk him down the hall to his room, grabbing his new book as I go.

"I'm flying!" he squeals.

I drop him carefully onto his bed, and he laughs. "I rode the board so good, right?"

"Yeah, you did, bud. You rode it like a pro."

"What's a pro?" he asks curiously.

"Someone who is really good."

"I'm a pro!" He points to himself with pride.

"Yep, you sure are."

Grabbing the book out of my hand, he settles onto his bed and I join him. The first time, I read the book to him, and the next time, he helps me. I'm not sure if he really knows the words or if he's just good at memorizing what he hears, but it's safe to say, either way my kid's a genius. After the third time, he tells me he's ready to play Legos.

"What are we building today?" I ask him, nodding toward the mess of Legos all over his floor.

Zane scampers off the bed and over to his Legos. "I'm making SpongeBob's house. He lives in a pineapple." He hands me an orange Lego, and we get to work building the strange sponge guy a house made out of fruit—while I wonder what the hell happened to Sesame Street.

CHAPTER SEVENTEEN

Blakely

"I JUST NEED TO STOP BY THE SHOP AND THEN WE'LL HEAD TO THE coffee shop," Brenton says, as we drive down Main Street. With my backpack between my legs, I grab my cell phone and make sure it's on loud in case Sierra needs to get ahold of me. She's watching Zane while Brenton and I meet our study group for Psychology of Inequality.

A few minutes later we arrive at U Break I Fix, a cell phone shop, Brenton's brother, Travis, owns. Brenton works at his shop occasionally, and that sometimes includes making deliveries. I wait in the car while Brenton runs in. While he's in there, my phone goes off—it's Keegan. The last few days he's been coming by in the evenings to have dinner with Zane and me, and hang out with Zane. I completely forgot to tell him I wouldn't be home tonight.

> Keegan: I'm here, but you're not.

> Me: I'm sorry! I forgot to tell you I have study group.

> Keegan: No worries. Sierra said I can hang out with Zane still.

A second later a picture of a smiling Zane and Keegan hits my screen, and I take in a sharp breath at how identical the two of them look. From their messy brown hair to their perfect dimples. My finger glides over their faces, and I think about my conversation with Sierra—what it would be like for that picture to be the three of us instead of just the two of them. I click to save the image and then make it Keegan's contact photo before I send him back a text.

Me: Give him a kiss for me, please. Have fun.

Keegan: Will do! Maybe I'll see you when you get home?

Me: I might be late. Tomorrow?

Keegan: Okay, I was thinking we could introduce Zane to my parents this weekend. What do you think?

My heart stutters at the word *we*. It shouldn't affect me the way it does. The thought of me and Keegan being a *we*.

Brenton swings the car door open and folds himself into his sport's vehicle. I'll never understand why big guys choose to drive small cars just because they think they're cool. The guy barely fits inside. The thought has me wondering what kind of car Keegan drives. So far all I've ever seen is him on a skateboard or a surfboard. I giggle on the inside, imagining him taking a woman out on a date and telling her to hop on his board. Then I frown when I realize I just imagined him with another woman. Ever since my talk with Sierra, I've been thinking *a lot* about Keegan and me. He hasn't brought us up again, but I think if he did, I wouldn't be opposed to maybe seeing where things go.

Keegan: Jailbird, you there?

"Who you talking to?" Brenton asks, throwing whatever he has to deliver into the glovebox.

"Oh, Keegan. He wants Zane to meet his parents this weekend."

Keegan: Hello?

Me: Sorry, I was talking to Brenton.

Keegan: You're with him?

Me: He's driving us to the study group.

> **Me:** To answer your question, yes, this weekend sounds good. I'm excited for Zane to have more family.

I wait a few minutes for Keegan to reply, and when he doesn't, I put my phone away. I probably shouldn't have mentioned I was out with Brenton, but oh well, I can't deal with these men and their egos.

After stopping at two houses so Brenton can drop off their phones, we arrive at the coffee shop. We spend the next couple hours going over our notes on our reading. Since we have our first quiz next class, we go over the points we all think are critical.

"J.C. is having a party at his place," Lauren says to everyone. "You're going, right?" She looks at Brenton, who looks over at me.

J.C. is the quarterback of Carterville's football team, and the 'it' guy on campus. I only know this because the girls are always gossiping about him, and Brenton is good friends with him. Every once in a while Brenton will drag me out, and it's usually for one of J.C.'s parties since he lives just off campus. He has a huge two-story house his parents apparently pay for, and shares it with several of his friends and teammates.

"Would you mind if we stopped by?" Brenton asks. "We don't have to stay long."

I check my phone, and when I see there's still no reply from Keegan, I assume he hasn't responded because he's upset about me being out with Brenton, which is ridiculous. We're nothing more than friends.

"I'm not sure…"

"C'mon, please," he begs. "Just for a few minutes."

"Fine," I say, giving in, "but not too long. I have to get up with Zane in the morning." Friday through Sunday I have no class, and they're mine and Zane's days to spend time together. We always get up and hit the park first thing, since the weekend is always packed. Fridays are less busy, which means Zane gets more time on the swings.

CHAPTER EIGHTEEN

"**C**OME, BOY, SIT DOWN. SIT DOWN AND REST." I TURN THE PAGE AND notice Zane's eyes are shut and his face is nuzzled into my side. "And the tree was happy," I continue to read, even though he's no longer listening. "The end."

I close the bright green book my son asked me to read five times in a row and set it on his nightstand. I should probably move him off me, so he can sleep in a more comfortable position, but I can't find it in me to move. As I look around his room at all the drawings he's created that Blakely's framed and hung up, at the stuffed animals in the corner, my heart feels like it's being squeezed. Every drawing he's made, every toy he's fallen in love with, I wasn't there for. I don't know what any of it means. I don't know the backstory to anything. I don't know why he loves *The Giving Tree* more than any other book, or why he insists on picking a different stuffed animal to take to bed every night. I don't know where he was when he drew any of those pictures, or why Blakely chose those to hang up.

One picture catches my attention. It's a picture of three stick figures with ineligible writing above and below the people. Writing in sharpie—that has to be from an adult—above the messy writing plays as the caption: Mommy, Aunt Sierra, and Zane. I love you. Happy Mother's Day!

My heart sinks at the thought that every year Blakely didn't have someone to spoil her for Mother's Day. She deserves to be pampered and given recognition. Growing up, every year my dad would take my brothers and me to the store so we could pick out presents for our mom. Then we would wrap them and give them to her in the morning along with a homemade breakfast we would make while she slept in. Dad would always buy her a gift card to the spa she loves, and the following weekend, he would take us to the park to skateboard and play while she would spend the day at the spa. The following month, when it was Father's Day, Mom would take us to buy Dad new fishing gear.

A lump forms in my throat when I think about Father's Day. Does Zane know what that day means? Did he wonder where his dad was and why he wasn't with him? Or did Blakely ignore the holiday and pretend it didn't exist, so Zane wouldn't know what he was missing?

My phone goes off, and I swallow down the huge lump in my throat, shaking away my thoughts. I'm here now, and not another holiday will go by that I'm not with my son—or Blakely—for that matter.

When I pull my phone out of my front pocket, Zane snuggles in closer, and I gently move his head onto his pillow, so he doesn't get a stiff neck. I read the text from my dad, then type out a quick reply and hit send. As I'm about to put my phone away, my eyes land on the locator app. My finger hovers above it for several seconds before I give in and click on it.

I shouldn't have done it, but I did. I couldn't help it, though. While Blakely was in the shower the other day, I saw her phone on the table and made a rash decision. It's not like I had to download the app—it's already there, part of the phone. All I had to do was request to follow her and approve it. And how did I justify it? By convincing myself that because Blakely's the mother of my son, I need to make sure she's safe. In my defense, that's the truth. But if what I was doing was okay, then I would've just asked her. But I didn't.

I feel guilty about it—sort of. But that doesn't stop me from checking up on her. I'm not doing it to be a creep, though. I just want to make sure she's okay. I don't trust that Brenton guy as far as I can throw him. I've been asking around campus, and I don't like the shit I'm hearing—at all.

When I click on Blakely's name, it shows she left the coffee shop a few minutes ago. She must be on her way home. Since it's not too late, I decide to hang out and wait for her, but twenty minutes later, when she should've already arrived at home, I pull back up the app to see where she is and notice she's a mile away from here. Clicking on her location, I zoom in and immediately recognize the house as Jeffrey Corbin Frederick's—also known as J.C., the biggest douche on campus. I know this is his house because the guy's been on my radar for some time now.

What the hell is she doing there? Blakely doesn't seem like the type to party with J.C. Then I remember she was with Brenton. Well, shit… things are starting to make sense now.

After kissing my son good night and tucking him in, I say good night to Sierra, who's on the couch, watching a movie.

Grabbing my board, I head over to J.C.'s place. When I arrive, it's a madhouse. Music is thundering out of the house and spilling into the front yard, where several drunken students are practically having a damn orgy on the front lawn. A few people are making out on the porch. I search the area and spot Brenton's Mercedes. Yeah, the dickhead actually drives a Mercedes. How he can afford one, I have no clue.

Going around back, I tell myself I just want to make sure Blakely is okay and then I'll leave. But when I'm about to step onto the porch, I hear Brenton's voice, so I back up slightly to remain in the shadows and listen to what he has to say. And what I hear come out of his mouth confirms my suspicions: Blakely and my son most definitely aren't safe around this guy.

CHAPTER NINETEEN

Blakely

’M SITTING ON THE COUCH IN THE LIVING ROOM, NURSING MY WARM
beer and searching for Brenton. He told me he was going to find J.C. to
say hi and would be right back. It’s been a while now and I’m ready to go
home. I don’t know anyone here, and I realize it was dumb to come here
in the first place. This isn’t who I am. I don’t go to frat parties, when I can
be home, spending time with my son or studying.

My phone goes off and I pull it out, hoping it’s Keegan. But it’s not.
It’s Sierra.

I click on the text and a picture of Keegan reading Zane a bedtime
story pops up. By the way it’s taken, it’s obvious she snuck the picture, and
that has me grinning. Keegan’s holding *The Giving Tree*, and Zane is look-
ing up at his daddy like he hung the moon.

The book is old, given to me by my aunt when I was little. She shared
my mom’s and my love of reading. She wrote a note in the front and signed
it. She died a few years later from cancer. It was part of the book collec-
tion I was allowed to grab when we were forced to leave our home after
our parents died and the state’s attorney’s office would only let us take our
personal belongings.

Over the years, when we moved from our grandmother's home, to Jordyn's, and then here, I've lost several items along the way, but I made it a point to keep the book collection. *The Giving Tree* is the only book in the collection that's meant for kids, and Zane cherishes it as much as I did when I was his age.

While I'm staring at the picture, my sister sends another. This one is of Zane with his head on Keegan's shoulder and his eyes closed. Keegan is still holding the book, but he's looking at Zane, his eyes filled with parental love.

Wait a second… is he still there? Maybe he didn't respond to my text because he was busy with our son. Have I been sitting at this stupid party while he's at my house waiting for me?

Me: Is Keegan still there?

"No," a husky voice says in my ear from behind. "He's right here." When I whip my head around, I find Keegan leaning over the back of the couch.

"Hey," I say in shock. "What are you doing here?"

"J.C.'s a popular guy." He shrugs. "Doesn't everyone attend his parties?"

"I guess." I lift a shoulder and turn my body to face him.

"Thought you were studying," he says, only curiosity in his tone.

"We finished and Brenton asked to come by here."

"You don't look like you're really enjoying yourself."

"It's not really my scene," I admit. "Did you have a good night with Zane?"

Keegan's face lights up. "The best. You're raising one amazing kid." His words fill me up like helium.

"Thanks."

"What the hell are you doing here?" a menacing voice booms. When I look over Keegan's shoulder, I spot Brenton standing right behind him.

Keegan stands and turns around to give Brenton his attention. "Just hanging out, man." I can't see his face, but I can hear the overly happy tone in his voice.

"You following Blakely and me?" Brenton accuses.

Before Keegan can answer, I say, "I'm ready to go." Both guys glance at me.

"All right, I'll take you home," Brenton says first. Keegan's jaw ticks, but he doesn't argue with Brenton.

"I rode my board," he says, which explains why he didn't offer to take me home. The truth is, I would rather walk home with Keegan than ride with Brenton, but that would make me look stupid, and it would be ridiculous for Keegan to walk me all the way home and then have to go back to his place—speaking of which, I have no clue where he lives. Maybe he lives near me and is going in the same direction.

Not wanting to cause an unnecessary fight between the two guys, I decide to just go with Brenton. He lives right below me, so it only makes sense. Plus, my backpack is in his car anyway. "Okay, I'll text you later," I tell Keegan.

"Yeah," he says back. Then he adds, "Text me when you're home, please."

I nod, then stand, and that's when Brenton steps around the couch and grabs my wrist, pulling me away from Keegan. "Let's go, Blakely."

"Don't fucking touch her," Keegan barks.

"Don't fucking tell me what to do," Brenton threatens.

"Brenton, let go of me, please." I glance up at him, confused as hell why my best friend, who has always been nothing but kind and sweet, is suddenly acting like such a raging asshole.

He inhales a deep breath, obviously to calm his temper. A temper I've never seen until Keegan showed up. "Sorry." He sighs. "I didn't mean to grab you that hard."

"You okay?" Keegan asks, his hands fisted at his sides. I can tell it's taking everything in him not to lose his shit.

"I'm fine. I'll text you when I get home."

Keegan opens his mouth to argue but thankfully doesn't. Instead, he gives me one curt nod and then shoots Brenton a threatening glare.

Brenton's quiet as we walk to his car and during the short drive to my house. I'm expecting him to say something, anything, but he remains silent when he parks in his assigned spot and gets out of his car.

"Are you doing anything this weekend?" I ask to make conversation. He shakes his head. "Okay, well, I guess I'll see you later…"

"Yeah, maybe," he says, heading straight to his apartment and not giving me another glance.

I take the stairs up to my place, thinking about how everything is suddenly changing. I can't even remember a weekend where Brenton hasn't spent time at my place. I know he's upset about Keegan suddenly appearing, but I just don't understand why he's letting it affect our friendship. Unless, Sierra was right…

When I get inside, Sierra is still awake, but barely. She glances over at me, and when she sees I'm frowning, she sits up.

"What's wrong?"

I drop my backpack onto the chair, kick my sandals off, and sit next to her. "I think you were right."

"I usually am." She grins. "You're going to have to be more specific."

I roll my eyes. "I think Brenton might like me… as more than friends."

Sierra laughs, and I glare. "Sorry." She covers her mouth to stifle her laughter, but it still seeps through. "It's just that… well… duh."

"I really didn't know," I tell her. "And now he's mad at me because of Keegan."

"What happened with Keegan?" Her eyes widen in anticipation.

"Nothing. He's just mad at him being around, I guess." I fall backward on the couch and sigh. "I don't know."

"Do you like him?"

"Who?"

"Brenton?"

"As a friend."

"Nothing more?" She pushes.

I turn my head to face her. "Nothing more."

"Then you're going to need to make that clear."

"How the heck do I do that?" I whine. "I've never done anything to lead him on. I don't get it." I huff in annoyance. "Why must men be so complex?"

Sierra laughs. "I'm pretty sure they feel the same way about us… and you just tell him."

"Right." I scoff. "So, the next time I see him, I should just go up to him and say, 'Even though you haven't actually said you like me, I think you do, and you should know I don't like you like that, so can we please stay friends?' That sounds so stuck-up. Like I'm full of myself."

"No, but you can bring up how he's been acting and ask him why. And when he mentions it's because he likes you, you can tell him you're sorry, but you don't feel the same."

"Ugh!"

My phone dings, reminding me I never texted Keegan. When I pull it out, sure enough, there's a text from him asking if I made it home okay.

> Me: Sorry! Yes, I'm home and hanging out with my sister.

> Keegan: Would it be too much to ask if I can come by tomorrow to see Zane? No classes on Fridays for me.

I pause for a moment. Friday has always been Zane's and my day. Then again, so is Saturday and Sunday and every day and night I don't have to be at school or studying. Things are changing, and I'm going to have to get used to sharing my son. This is what I wanted… and if I'm honest, I'm okay with that. Plus, spending time together with our son would be a good way to figure out if we still have the chemistry we had before. Who am I kidding? Every time the guy looks at or speaks to me, I can feel the chemistry sizzling between us.

> Me: I don't have class on Fridays either. Zane and I go to the park. Wanna join us?

> Keegan: That sounds good. I'll pick you guys up in the morning.

> Me: It's the park we walked to.

> Keegan: I'll still pick you up. 9:00?

> Me: Perfect

"Keegan or Brenton?" Sierra asks.

"Maybe neither…" I smart.

"Yeah, okay." She rolls her eyes. "You don't talk to anybody else."

"Am I really that much of a recluse?"

"No… well, yes. You're just so busy being super-student and super-mom."

"I'm neither of those."

"You are." She lays her head down on my shoulder, and I lay my head against hers.

"Yeah, well, if I'm super-student and super-mom, you're super-sister and super-aunt."

CHAPTER TWENTY

Blakely

"ALL RIGHT, BUD," Keegan says through a smile, "you got this." I follow behind Keegan and Zane, snapping pictures of Zane on his first skateboard.

When Keegan showed up this morning, with a long, rectangular box in his hand, telling Zane he got him a skateboard, I thought he'd lost his mind and proceeded to tell him so. He laughed and told me to trust him. So, I took a deep calming breath, making him think I was doing as he asked, all the while imagining every worst-case scenario—my son falling and cracking his head open, breaking an arm, scraping his tiny knees on the asphalt. But then I saw the skateboard put together—an adorable SpongeBob design with three blue wheels and matching colored handlebars—and I felt like shit for not trusting him. He even made sure to include a matching helmet and pads.

I run to get ahead of Zane, so I can get pictures of his face. Keegan is speed walking next to him, staying close just in case Zane somehow tips over. As I snap the picture of the two of them, grins wide and dimples sticking out, my heart swells, and I get choked up. Keegan's eyes meet mine, and his head tilts slightly to the side, silently asking what's wrong. I shake my head, willing the tears to not fall.

When we get to the park, Zane sees one of his friends from school, and after taking off his helmet and pads, takes off to play with him, leaving Keegan and me to follow behind.

"Everything okay?" he asks.

I could lie and tell him everything is fine, downplay what I'm feeling, but I go with the truth. "When I was pregnant with Zane, I'd imagine what it would be like if I found you. To take our son to the park together. To take family vacations, walk him into school together on his first day." I get choked up once again and have to take a deep breath before I continue. "Seeing the pictures of you and Zane last night, and watching you two this week playing together. You buying him his own skateboard. It's just… it's everything I ever wanted for him."

I turn to face him, no longer caring that the tears are now falling freely. "I want to try. You and me and Zane. I want us to try to be a family." I was expecting Keegan to smile since he told me this is what he wanted, so I'm confused when his lips turn down into a frown.

He looks at me for a long moment, and then his eyes leave mine to check on Zane. He's only a few feet away from us, playing in the sand, but I love that Keegan makes it a point to keep checking on him. He's a natural dad.

"I want that too," he says, but I can hear the silent *but* before he voices it.

"But," I prompt, my nerves getting the best of me. I put myself out there, on the line, like Sierra told me to do, and now I'm freaking out on the inside, scared Keegan no longer wants to try.

"You said you want to try to be a family. Everything you mentioned involved us with Zane."

"Right…" I don't understand. Zane is the glue that holds us together. Of course he's included.

"What about you and me? If Zane weren't in the picture, would you still want to try?"

"What… I don't…" I don't know what he's asking. "Why wouldn't Zane be in the picture?"

"If you never got pregnant during our time together, and then four years later we ran into each other, would you want to date me? Every example you gave was about us being a family, and I know you lost your family… and you can have that. The family. My mom and dad can't wait to meet Zane. Kolton is just as excited. Regardless of what happens between us, we're a family, Jailbird. We'll always have a son together."

Keegan's gaze flickers from me to Zane and back to me again. "I don't know much about relationships. I've only been in a couple short-term ones. But I can't imagine that us getting together for the sake of our son can make for a sturdy foundation for a long-lasting relationship." He stops speaking and smiles. Then he raises his hand and cups the side of my face. "If you want us to try for us, then I'm down. But if you only want to try because you want to give Zane a family, then I think we should just stay friends. Either way, that boy"—he nods toward our son—"is going to have a family. I promise you that."

Biting down on my bottom lip, I attempt to rein in these foreign emotions that are hitting me full force. Keegan's right. My speech was all about Zane and giving him a family. But that's not all I want. It's just all I know.

"For the last four years my entire world has been about Zane. Making sure he has a roof over his head, that he's healthy and fed. Feels loved. I worry every day that Sierra and I aren't enough. Growing up, Sierra and I were given whatever we wanted, but we lacked the love and attention we craved. Our mom tried, but she was torn between trying to be the perfect wife to our father and a good mother to Sierra and me. She would read to us every night no matter where in the world she was with our dad, but he demanded she be his wife first, and there wasn't a whole lot left of her after she was done giving to our dad.

"When our parents died, they left us broke and with only a few fond memories that we cling to like a lifeline. And because of that, I wake up every day, second guessing every decision I make. I worry that I'm studying too much, feeding Zane too much takeout, so I can get my schoolwork done. I worry that I'm putting school first, and that what I have left to give my son isn't enough. He's my first *and* last thought every day. I never want him to look back and view his childhood the way Sierra and I view ours."

I know I'm rambling, but it feels good to finally get all of this off my chest. For years I've compared myself to my parents. Terrified one move in the wrong direction would make me like them.

"Blakely, I've only seen you with Zane a handful of times, and I already know you're a damn good mom."

"Thank you. I guess my fear is that if I add you to the picture, where does that leave him? Who do I put first? What if there's not enough of me for everyone and everything?"

"How about we take it one day at a time?" Keegan suggests. "You're not doing this alone. You have your sister and now you have me. Take a deep breath, and I think you will find everything will click into place. We're not your parents. We're us."

I do as he says, and Keegan's lips curl into a soft smile, only one dimple appearing.

Butterflies flutter in my belly, telling me what I already know. "I want you," I blurt out, and his smile grows, that gorgeous second dimple making an appearance, and those butterflies attack my insides. "Not just for Zane, but for me. It may not work out, but I want to give it a try. If Zane weren't in the picture, and we ran into each other on campus, I probably would've already hooked up with you." My hands fly to my mouth, and Keegan's entire face breaks out in the most beautiful smile. Even his damn eyes are smiling.

"I mean…" I try to backpedal, but it's pointless. We both know I meant exactly what I said.

"Then we try," he murmurs. Pulling me into him, he throws his arm over my shoulders and tucks me into his side, planting a soft kiss on my temple. "And for the record, I definitely would've already hooked up with you."

I glance up at him, and he peers down, granting me a flirty wink.

We spend the entire morning at the park. Zane's friend eventually leaves, and his attention goes back to Keegan and me. We push him in the swing, chase him around the play equipment, and Keegan even stuffs himself in the slide to go down with him.

When Zane is wiped out and running on E, we head home. He's too tired to ride his skateboard, so I walk it alongside me while Keegan carries him piggyback style. I would like to give him a bath and get the sand and germs off him, but when we arrive, he's passed out on Keegan's back, his arms slinking around his shoulders like a baby koala holding on for dear life.

Peeling him off Keegan, I carry him to his room and tuck him in for a nap. When I come out, Keegan is checking out all the photos. He's stopped at the one of Zane walking toward me. "It was the second time he walked," I tell him, and he raises a brow. "The first time he walked, of course, I didn't have my phone on me, so I insisted Sierra and I both walk around with our cameras open and ready to go all day."

Keegan laughs.

"When Sunday night hit, and he still hadn't walked again, I started to freak out." I laugh, remembering how crazy I was acting.

"He was thirteen months old and in daycare. The next day was Monday, and I was scared he would walk while he was there, and I would miss it. So, I sat down at one end of the rug and made Sierra sit at the other end. We took turns trying to get Zane to walk to us while the other recorded."

Keegan shakes his head, his face split into a full-blown grin. "And he did it?"

"No," I deadpan. "But luckily he didn't do it at daycare either. When we got home from school, I insisted we try again, and even though Sierra totally thought I'd lost my mind, she went along with it, and after like the fourth time of him crawling between us, he stood and walked to me. Of course Sierra wasn't prepared." I roll my eyes. "But she was quick with her phone and snapped a picture before he dropped back down and crawled the rest of the way."

"I hate that I missed it all," Keegan says, taking my hand in his and walking us over to the couch. Since Sierra is working, we have the place to ourselves.

We sit close together, our bodies right up against one another, and it feels comfortable, natural, almost as if no time has passed. "I hate that you missed it all," I tell him back. "I have tons of photo albums and videos I can show you one day."

"I would love that," he says, his thumb massaging circles into the sensitive spot between my thumb and pointer finger. I glance down and watch for a few seconds. When my eyes lift, our gazes lock, and I swipe my tongue along my bottom lip, suddenly nervous. His eyes flicker to my wet lips, and I take in a deep breath, wondering if he's going to kiss me.

I don't have to wonder for long, because the next second, Keegan leans in and our mouths connect. And for several long seconds, we stay like this—his strong lips brushing against my soft ones. I don't realize how nervous I truly was, until I release a hard exhale and a soft moan escapes my lips. Keegan takes it as his cue to deepen the kiss, and his tongue pushes through my lips and into my mouth. His hand leaves mine and comes up to grip the side of my neck, and I move closer, my body sinking into his.

Our mouths tangle, our tongues duel, and before I know what's happening, Keegan is lifting me into his lap so my legs are straddling his. His mouth leaves mine, and he trails open-mouthed kisses along the column of my neck and down my throat. It's been so long since I've been kissed and touched that my body goes haywire, craving more of Keegan.

As if he knows what I'm thinking, he fists my mane, jerking my head to the side. His lips crash against my neck and he suckles on my overheated flesh. My center grinds down on him, and I can feel his bulge through his pants. Remembering what that *bulge* is capable of, I grind down harder, my fingers gripping the back of his neck.

"Jesus, fuck," he murmurs, his lust-filled eyes meeting mine for a second before his lips once again fuse to mine.

And then a raspy sleep-riddled voice speaks out, "Mommy, I'm thirsty," and I'm being thrown backward and onto the floor. My ass hits the ground, hard, and Keegan jumps to help me up.

"Shit, I'm sorry," he whispers, pulling me into a standing position. "I heard his voice and…" When he sees my face split into a smile, he breathes. "You okay?"

"Yeah." I laugh at having been almost caught making out with Keegan by our son.

"You kissed Daddy," Zane says through a giggle, and Keegan snorts out a laugh. Well, I guess we *did* get caught after all.

"Let's go get you a drink and then I'll make you lunch," I tell Zane, taking the coward's way out and not acknowledging what he's said. He's still half asleep. Hopefully he'll forget what he saw.

After we eat lunch, and I give Zane a bath to get all the sand off him, we spend the rest of the day hanging out at the house. Keegan doesn't say he has anywhere else he needs to be, and I don't ask him. We watch TV shows with Zane, play Legos, and Keegan offers to order dinner in. When it's time for Zane to go to bed, he insists Keegan read him his book, so I use the time to clean up around the house.

About twenty minutes later, while I'm wiping down the counters, strong arms snake around my waist, and then I'm being lifted onto the counter I just cleaned. "He's asleep," Keegan says, just before he brushes his lips against mine softly. He parts my legs and steps between them. "My mom texted and asked if tomorrow would work for you. She said she wants to make lunch and invited Sierra to come as well."

"Tomorrow is good," I tell him, running my fingers through his short yet messy hair. "I'm not sure if Sierra has to work, but I'll let her know." Moving my hands down to the sides of Keegan's face, I lean forward to kiss him. He surprises me when he darts his tongue out and licks across my top lip and then my bottom one. My center clenches, my body aching to finish what we started earlier.

"I want you," I tell him. His response is to bite down on my fleshy lip. "Keegan!" I giggle. "That hurt."

"I can't help it," he murmurs. "You taste so fucking good." His mouth moves to my neck and he bites down on the flesh just above my pulse point, eliciting a moan from me. I can't believe we're here. In my kitchen with Keegan touching me. I fantasized about it so many times, but I never thought it would actually happen.

"I've never been addicted to anything, but I imagine this is what it would feel like. To have something you crave and desire and need, and then be forced to give it up cold turkey." He trails his lips downward, landing on my collarbone. He bites hard, and when I let out a groan, he licks the spot. "Now that I have you back, I just want to devour you. I can't get enough. One kiss, one touch was all it took, and I'm addicted all over again. Only this time is better." He lifts his head to look me in the eyes. "This time there's no end. Neither of us has to leave. I get to indulge in my addiction for the rest of my life."

"Keegan," I whisper breathlessly. "You can't say things like that." I shake my head. "We just found each other again. You can decide a week or a month from now I'm not want you want."

"Shh…" he says, kissing me again. "Stop being such a damn pessimist. You are who I want. You want me, too, right?"

I nod.

"Then just let it happen, Jailbird."

His arms cage me in on either side, and his tongue delves between my parted lips. And I do exactly what he's asked of me. I let it happen.

I'm lying on the couch, watching a rerun of *That '70s Show* when Sierra comes through the door. "Hey, what are you still doing up?" she asks, lifting my feet and plopping down on the other end of the couch.

"Waiting for you." I pause the show and roll over onto my back so I can look at her. "Keegan and I talked today."

"Oh yeah?"

"We're going to give us a try."

Sierra stares are me for a long moment before she barks out a laugh. "You totally hooked up with him!" She smacks my thigh, and I wince in pain.

"I did not!"

"You did!"

"We only made out!" I argue.

"About time you got some action." She waggles her eyebrows. "Was he as good of a kisser as you remembered?"

Slowly, I nod up and down several times. "Better."

Sierra throws her head back with a laugh. "Good for you, B." She winks.

"He's picking us up tomorrow morning to go meet his parents. You're invited."

"I can do that," she says. "I don't work until tomorrow night."

"Yeah?"

"Yeah. This is my nephew's family, which means it's yours, and what's yours is mine."

I sit up and pull my sister into a hug. "Thank you. In case I don't say it enough. I couldn't do this without you."

"Yes, you could," she says. "But I'm glad to be the one by your side all these years."

CHAPTER TWENTY-ONE

Blakely

"They're going to think I'm a hussy, aren't they?" I ask on our way to Keegan's parents' house. Kolton laughs, and I turn around and glare at him.

"Jailbird—" Keegan starts, but I cut him off.

"Don't call me that. They're going to ask why, and then you'll have to tell them I was arrested before and they'll think I'm an unfit parent."

This time it's Sierra who laughs.

"Who invited them?" I ask, partially joking, but partially not.

"Umm… you." Keegan chuckles nervously. "Calm down, babe." He places his hand on my thigh, and it momentarily calms me down, until it hits me that he called me babe.

"Don't call me babe. It's too soon. They're going to think it's too soon. You just found out you're Zane's dad. They're going to think I'm trying to trap you." This time all three of them laugh.

"You guys are all assholes," I hiss.

"Who's an asshole, Mommy?" Zane asks, and I gasp.

"Omigod!" I turn around as far as I can in the front seat of Keegan's truck. The cab is so big, it might as well be a damn SUV. "Zane, we don't use words like that. Mommy shouldn't have said that word."

I lock eyes with Keegan, who's still shaking with silent laughter. "He's going to use that word now. He's going to call someone an a-hole and your parents are going to call child services on me. Turn around. Now."

"Blakely," Keegan says slowly. "Nobody is going to think you're trapping me. There are no rules or a speed limit sign telling us how fast we should go. We're both adults. We can go as fast or slow as we want. Okay?" His gaze leaves the road for a split second to make eye contact with me.

"Okay." I nod emphatically, rubbing my palms up and down the tops of my jean-clad thighs.

"Nobody is going to care that you were arrested when you were younger or that our son said a curse word. Trust me when I tell you that my brothers and I were far from perfect. My parents raised three boys. They've seen and heard it all."

"Ain't that the damn truth," Kolton adds in agreement.

"Mom will be so happy to have Zane there, she won't care about anyone else," Keegan says.

"And add to that Blakely and Sierra." Kolton snorts. "She always says she wishes she'd had a daughter. Now she's getting two-for-one."

"It will be fine," Keegan says softly, taking my hand in his and weaving our fingers together. "Promise."

We pull into the driveway of a cute gray and white one-story house. The front porch, which dons several wooden rocking chairs, has a white wraparound railing. And in front of the porch are dozens of multicolored flowers. Everything about it is homey—and nothing like what Sierra and I grew up with.

I love it.

"You ready to meet your grandma and grandpa?" I ask Zane after Sierra takes him out of his car seat and hands him over to me.

"Do they have SpongeBob on their TV?" he asks, dead serious.

"Yeah, bud." Keegan laughs. "They'll have SpongeBob."

The moment we step through the front door, a petite, brown-haired woman, dressed in a cute cardigan and khaki capris comes barreling out from what I assume is the kitchen with a bright smile on her face. Following her is an older version of Keegan—he must be his dad. He has messy brown hair like his sons, but because he's older, it's not as thick. He's wearing a white collared shirt and khaki shorts.

"Come here, sweetheart!" I assume she's talking about Zane, so I'm shocked when her arms open wide and she wraps herself around my body. "My son has told me so much about you. I'm so happy I get to finally meet you." She pulls back slightly to assess me. "You're gorgeous." She smiles sweetly at me then glances over at Sierra. "You both are." Barely releasing me, she says to Sierra, "Come here," and pulls her into our hug. "I hate what happened with you and Keegan. Him losing your number and you girls having to take care of my grandson alone all these years."

Tears prick my eyes. I wasn't expecting the warm welcome, and I wonder if she has any idea just how much it means to me. "It's okay," I tell her, unsure of what else to say.

"Well, I can promise you that you will never be alone again. You have all of us now. I'm so excited to be a grandma," she gushes. "Anything you need, you just let me know."

"Thank you, Mrs. Reynolds."

"Oh no! You call me Larissa, or Mom, whichever." She winks. "And this here is my other half." She waves her husband over.

"I'm Paul," Keegan's dad says with a friendly smile. He has the same dimples as his sons and grandson. "It's very nice to meet you." He looks at Sierra. "Both of you."

"You too."

"Nice to meet you."

"Now where is that adorable grandson of mine?" Larissa asks, and Zane giggles.

"I think she means you, bud," Keegan says.

"I'm right here!" Zane squeals as Keegan tickles his side.

"Oh my word! The picture your daddy showed me didn't do you justice. You really are a spitting image of your daddy."

"I look like my uncle Kolton too!" Zane laughs. "He has the same face as my daddy!"

Everyone in the room cracks up laughing at that.

When Kolton showed up this morning with Keegan, Zane was shocked to learn there were two of his daddies. Keegan explained there wasn't two of him, but that the second one was his twin brother. Zane was hesitant at first, but after Kolton spent some time with him—and totally won him over with the chocolate donuts he brought—Zane came around.

"He does," Larissa says. She puts her hands out and Zane goes into her arms willingly. "You can call me Grandma and this here is your grandpa." She points to Paul.

"My friend Melissa has a grandma and grandpa," Zane says. "She calls them Grammy and Pop Pop. Can I call you that?"

Kolton snorts out a laugh, and Keegan's parents light up like they've just won the lottery. Sierra glances my way, and I can see the tears in her eyes. Zane may not be her son, and these people may not technically be her family, but what's happening here means as much to her as it does to me. She knows how much I wanted this for my son. To have a real family. Even if our parents had been alive, they never would've accepted Zane, and this situation, the way Keegan's parents are. My father would've freaked out that he was conceived out of wedlock, embarrassing him and in turn, our family—even though he had done enough to embarrass himself with his shady dealings. He would've probably disowned me, and my mother would've followed his lead because she was too scared not to. Most likely, she would've snuck over to visit, but she would've never let my father know.

"You can call us whatever you'd like," Paul says, bringing me back to the present.

"Daddy said you have SpongeBob," Zane says, obviously feeling right at home and ready to get back to the important parts of life.

"It's a TV show," Keegan explains to his parents.

"I know who SpongeBob is," Larissa says, putting her hand on her hip. "I did teach kindergarten."

"Do you love SpongeBob too?" Zane asks, jumping up and down in excitement.

"I do. But Sandy is my favorite," she says with a wink. "Why don't we eat lunch, and then we can figure out how to find SpongeBob for you?"

"Yay!" Zane cheers.

When we walk into their dining room, food is laid out across the table. There are a few different types of sandwiches, potato salad, macaroni salad, a bowl of baked beans, a platter of fruit, and some different kinds of chips.

"This all looks delicious," I say out loud, as we all find our seats. Keegan sits on the same side as me with Zane in the middle of us. Kolton, Sierra, and Larissa sit across from us, and Paul sits at the head of the table.

Lunch goes smoothly. The guys discuss taking Zane fishing, and Larissa asks if Sierra and I would like to go shopping with her. She wants to buy Zane a few items to have at her house. I listen while everyone converses and laughs. Larissa asks Sierra about her job, and she tells them funny drunken-customer stories. As I eat my lunch, I think about how worried I was for nothing. Keegan's parents are everything I could ever wish for. My son has grandparents. We have family.

As if he can hear my thoughts, Keegan leans over behind Zane and says, "I told you it would be okay. This is your family now. No matter what happens with us, we're all going to be your family."

CHAPTER TWENTY-TWO

Blakely

"How was your weekend?" I ask Brenton as we walk to class. When he showed up, like always, to walk to class together, I figured it was best to let whatever happened Friday night go.

"It was all right. How about yours?"

I had a great day on Friday with Keegan and Zane at the park. Then on Saturday with Keegan's family, having lunch and then going shopping with Larissa while the guys took Zane fishing. Yesterday, I spent the day getting caught up with my schoolwork, while Keegan hung out with Zane and me all day, but I don't tell Brenton that. Instead, I shrug and say, "It was good," hating how strained Brenton's and my relationship has become. And to top it off, I'm going to have to tell him that Keegan and I are dating now, and I have a feeling that isn't going to go over too well. But I'd rather him hear it from me than see Keegan and me together.

"I have a Grammy and Pop Pop," Zane says. I should've seen this coming. "I went fishing with my daddy and Uncle Kolton, and Pop Pop and caught a big fish." Zane's arms fly out to show how big the fish was, and I laugh at his exaggeration.

"Sounds fun, Z," Brenton says stiffly.

"Yeah, and Mommy and Daddy kissed! It was like when SpongeBob's grandma kissed SpongeBob! So yucky!" Zane cackles. "And Daddy dropped Mommy on the floor." His arm flies across his waist, and he bends over, laughing hysterically. For a second I think how damn adorable my kid is. But then Brenton shoots me a glare, and I draw in my lip to stifle my grin. I should've known Zane saw everything. He's very observant. Keegan and I are definitely going to need to be more careful in the future.

We drop Zane off and haven't even made it halfway across the quad to our class, when Brenton says, "So, what? You and Keegan are together now? You're a thing?"

I stop in my tracks, not wanting to have this conversation near the classroom, where I know Kolton will be. "Yes, we are," I tell him honestly. "And I really don't want it to affect our friendship."

"Friendship." He spits the word out like it's giving him a bad taste in his mouth. "I thought you weren't dating. That you were focusing on school and Zane."

"I am."

"While you're dating Keegan." He hits me with a hard stare, and I have no clue how to make him understand. It's obvious his feelings are hurt, and I hate that. But at the same time, I don't see Brenton as anything more than a friend. Even if Keegan weren't in the picture, I wouldn't have dated Brenton.

"He asked me to give us a chance and I said okay. I really liked him when I met him at the beach, and I still like him now. I'm sorry if that upsets you, but it's the truth."

"What do you even know about this guy, Blakely? How can you like someone you barely know?"

"That's part of getting to know someone. Part of dating."

Brenton stays silent for a long moment and then says, "So where does that leave us?"

"Same place we were before he showed up—friends… at least I hope so. Who I choose to date shouldn't affect our friendship." When he doesn't say anything, I push, "You aren't seriously going to let the fact I'm dating come between our friendship, are you?" I step toward him. "You're one of my best friends and Zane loves you. I've never allowed any of the girls you've taken out to affect our friendship."

"They didn't mean anything to me," Brenton says. "You're the only woman I care about."

"And I care about you too. I don't want what's happening between Keegan and me to ruin our friendship." I sniffle once, hating that I'm hurting Brenton. I never wanted this to happen. He's one of the best people I know. "Please tell me you aren't about to throw away years of friendship over this."

"I like you," he admits, and my heart sinks. "I've liked you for years."

"I didn't know." I hadn't the slightest clue, and I feel so stupid. "I can't help how I feel. I'm sorry." And then it hits me… "Do you not want to be friends with me anymore?" I can't imagine Brenton not being in my life, but if it's too hard on him, or hurts him, then I'll understand.

He shakes his head and sighs. "I'm not going anywhere. If all I can have with you is friendship, then I'll take it."

I throw my arms around his neck for a hug. "Thank you."

CHAPTER TWENTY-THREE

"YOU'VE BEEN QUIET THE LAST FEW DAYS." KEEGAN PULLS ME INTO his lap and I go willingly, my thighs straddling his. He presses his strong lips to mine then sucks on my lower lip, nipping it lightly before he releases it. "Everything okay?"

I lay my head down on his shoulder and listen to his heartbeat. I love being this close to Keegan. It's only been a short time since we found each other again, so you would think it would be awkward between us, getting to know one another, but it's not. The last week we've somehow fallen into a comfortable relationship like we've known each other forever. He came to Zane's show with me at his daycare, and everyone welcomed him. Apparently Zane has been talking nonstop about his daddy. Every night he comes over with dinner and plays with Zane, and after we put him to bed we talk and get to know each other. But I've noticed that we mostly talk about me and Zane. I love that Keegan wants to soak up every memory I have because he feels like he missed out on so much, but at the same time what Brenton said keeps prickling in the back of my head. *What do you know about this guy?*

"We've never been to your place," I blurt out, and Keegan's arms stiffen around me.

"I live with Kolton. There isn't a lot of room there, and he's home more than your sister is, so that's less privacy. Plus, all of Zane's stuff is here."

That makes sense, I think to myself.

"How do you afford the apartment?" He goes to school and doesn't work.

"I have some money saved, and Kolton and I share the bills."

I nod against his shoulder. Makes sense…

"What do you want to do for a living?"

"Something in criminology," he says after a second of silence. Then he lifts my chin so we're looking into each other's eyes. "What's going on with you?"

"Nothing." I shake my head. "I guess I'm just overthinking things."

"With us?"

"Maybe."

His brows furl together. "What are you overthinking?"

"I really like you, but I feel like I don't know you," I admit.

"I think it just takes time." He kisses my forehead. "Every conversation, every time we hang out, we learn more about each other. Just last night I learned that when I kiss you right"—he plants an open-mouthed kiss to just above my collarbone and I wiggle in his lap—"here, you get all squirmy." His lips land on the same spot again, but this time they linger there, suckling and licking the area, and my body ignites.

"Keegan." I moan as if I want him to stop, yet I tilt my head to the side more to give him better access. My center grinds down on the bulge between his legs, and he groans.

"We have to stop," he says, but his tone doesn't convey he wants to stop at all.

"Or we can take this to my bedroom."

His lips still against my flesh for a brief moment before he lifts and carries me to my room. On the way, we both peek in and see Zane is sleeping soundly, snuggled up with his stuffed animal of choice.

"We created that," Keegan whispers in awe, and my heart riots in my chest.

With his elbow, Keegan closes my door and then walks us over to my bed, laying me down in the middle. He climbs up my body and dips his head down to kiss me. "However far you want this to go is up to you," he murmurs against my lips.

"I think we've already crossed that threshold." I giggle. "Hence the little boy sleeping in his bedroom."

Keegan chuckles. "That was four years ago, JB."

I laugh at the shortened nickname he started using after I told him I was scared his parents would think I'm a bad person.

"We're getting to know each other all over again, and if you want to take things slow, I'm okay with that."

When I nod, our lips brush against each other. My hands roam across his shoulders and down his biceps and forearms. "Do you work out?"

"Every morning at five a.m." He kisses the tip of my nose.

My hands find the front of Keegan, and I lift his shirt, exposing a couple of his abs and a happy trail that leads to The Promised Land. The last four years have been damn good to Keegan. He sits up so he can pull his shirt off and I find some new ink along his chest. I kiss his pectoral muscles, and he groans. "I like your new ink." I plant a soft kiss to each of his perfectly rounded nipples.

Keegan smirks, not making a move. He really is leaving how far we go up to me. Wrapping my legs around his torso and my arms around his neck, I lie back down, taking him with me. His hands fall on either side of my head against my pillow, and I pull him to me for a hard kiss. My center grinds against him. "I want you," I beg. "All of you."

"You're just horny," he jokes, sliding one hand down my side and landing on my hip.

I can't argue with him, because he's right, I am horny. It's been too damn long. My hips buck against his erection again and he says, "I'll take care of you."

Starting at my neck, he kisses his way down—only stopping to remove each article of clothing I have on—ending at the apex of my thighs. Once he has me completely naked, he starts back from the top again, this time taking his time, sucking on my pert nipples, licking the center of my belly button, and finally kissing the hood of my pussy. He spreads my legs and then lips apart and does exactly what he said he would do—he takes care of me. With every stroke and lick, he works me up until I'm trembling with pleasure. As my lips part and his name gets called, his hand covers my mouth. Even through my orgasm, I can feel him laughing against me.

When the aftershocks from my orgasm simmer down, Keegan climbs up my body, and without even bothering to wipe myself from his lips, he crashes his lips down on mine, his tongue delving into my mouth and swirling around. The taste of me on him is an aphrodisiac, and I find myself reaching down and palming his dick through his pants. Then I'm unbuttoning and unzipping and yanking them, along with his boxers, down his muscular thighs. Keegan helps me by lifting slightly so I can get them past his knees, and then he kicks them off completely.

I stroke his dick, root to tip, while we continue to kiss, our tongues moving frantically against each other. My thumb glides along his silky crown and I can feel his pre-cum dripping out. I use it to help jack him off. I want him inside me, but I'm not ready yet. Keegan was right. We might've been together before, but this is all new, and knowing we now have the possibility of lasting has me wanting to take things slowly, make sure what we're creating is strong and sturdy and will last through any storm.

I squeeze his shaft, pumping slow yet hard, and his dick swells. He releases a heady groan and then his dick pulsates. He comes, the hot seed landing on both of our stomachs. I stroke him a few more times, until he softens under my touch, and then I release him.

His arms collapse, his elbows hitting my pillow and his face nuzzling my hair. "That was without a doubt the best thing I've felt in years. I can only imagine what it's going to feel like when I'm back inside you again."

"I promise you won't have to imagine for long," I say through a giggle.

Keegan lifts his head and eyes me seriously. "I'll continue to imagine for however long it takes for you to be ready."

After we both use the bathroom to clean up, I get dressed in a long-sleeved pajama shirt and shorts, and Keegan puts back on his boxers and jeans, leaving his shirt off. We find our way back to my bed, and I turn the TV on, leaving it on the first channel I find, just to fill the silence. Keegan wraps his arms around me tight, kissing the top of my forehead and running his fingers through my hair. I don't think either of us is ready for him to go home yet.

"Spend the night," I utter, and his eyes go wide.

He glances down at me. "What about Zane? I know you were concerned…"

"You're his father. I've never had a man spend the night here before. He'll be ecstatic to wake up to you being here." As I say the words, my heart picks up speed—both out of excitement and fear. If we don't work out, how will I explain to Zane that his daddy won't be spending the night in the future? But then again, isn't that what happens when two people divorce? It's not ideal, but it doesn't stop people from getting together. If it did, nobody would try. Keegan was right. I can't think about the what-ifs. I need to live in the right now. And right now, I'm slowly falling in love with Keegan and want to sleep next to him—wake up next to him. Have breakfast with him and our son as a family. There are a million ways this can go wrong. I could be making the stupidest decision of my life. But what if it all goes right?

Keegan's lips curl into a gorgeous grin. "I'd love that," he admits, pulling us both down onto my pillows so we can snuggle closer. His arm encircles my waist, then he glides his hand down to my ass, squeezing my cheek and leaving it there. I laugh as my head finds a comfortable spot in the crook of his shoulder, and my hand finds its place on his hard chest. Closing my eyes, I think about how I could lie like this, in this position with Keegan, for the rest of my life. Maybe we're rushing things. I don't know. But right now, with my body wrapped up in his, I feel like where we are is exactly where we belong.

CHAPTER TWENTY-FOUR

"Mommy, my throat hurts." A tiny hand smacks my back. "You're not my mommy…" Silence and then, "Daddy!"

I chuckle and roll over to face Zane, who is standing next to the bed in his adorable SpongeBob pajamas and holding his Build-a-Bear I bought him. This must be the side of the bed Blakely sleeps on.

"Can I sleep with you?" he asks, his face taking on a sad little puppy dog look with his eyes widening and his bottom lip jutting out slightly. I'm not sure what Blakely allows, but she isn't awake, and as I stare at his adorably sad face, I know I don't stand a chance against this look. I can only hope he doesn't hit me with it when he wants something I can't give him.

"Sure, bud." I pull him over me and lay him between Blakely and me, moving closer to the edge so there's room for him. Sometime in the middle of the night, she rolled over and out of my arms. Her perfect round ass pushed against my crotch, and it took everything in me to simply hold her and not get lost in her.

Zane snuggles into my side, squishing the bear between us. He named it Bear and brings the thing everywhere he goes—except to school because Blakely told him he's too young to go.

As he stares up at me, I remember what he said when he walked in here. "Does your throat still hurt?"

"It itches," he says through a yawn, his eyes already falling closed.

I watch him and Blakely sleep for a few minutes, wondering what I did for karma to be on my side and be given this second chance. A minute later and Blakely might not have run into my brother. A second earlier and I might not have seen her from across the quad. But as fate would have it, we did see each other.

She was hesitant at first, and I couldn't fault her for that. She was only trying to put our son first. But then she came around, giving me us a chance, and like the sparkler she is, she's lit up every dark place in my life. For the last four years, I've been going through the motions, but now I'm ready to start living. And it's all because of her and our son.

My cell phone dings, and I snatch it up so it doesn't wake either of them. I had turned off my alarm earlier. I'm not sure what time Blakely and Zane wake up, but it's seven in the morning and they're both still sleeping.

I read the text from my dad, and my stomach drops. We got the information.

And with that one text, I can already feel the storm brewing. I look over at my son and the woman I want to spend my life with, and I say a silent prayer that what we're building is enough to weather the storm that is on the horizon.

"Zane, sweetie, you have to wake up."

I open my eyes and find Blakely dressed and standing over the bed with a frown on her face as she tries to wake up our son.

"I don't wanna," he whines. "My throat is itchy."

Blakely sighs and her eyes momentarily close.

"He woke up earlier and said that," I tell her. "Then he asked to sleep with us."

"He gets allergies around this time. The pollen in the air messes with him, especially at night." She puts her hand to his forehead. "It could be the beginning of a cold, but he doesn't have a fever."

"Well, good morning," Sierra says, stepping into the room with a wide knowing smile on her face. "So, we've reached the sleepover step. Niicceee. When can we expect a proposal?"

"Hush it," Blakely groans, but I can hear the laughter in her voice.

I sit up, forgetting I'm shirtless, and Sierra smirks. "I have one question: does your twin brother look *exactly* like you?"

I laugh, and Blakely groans again.

"What?" Sierra throws her hands up. "I might not be able to date him, but I can still fantasize about him. And judging by what your man is sporting over there, there's plenty to fantasize about."

"Why can't you date my brother?" I ask.

"Because he's family." Sierra gives me a *duh* look.

"It's hardly incest. I can't speak for Blakely, but if you want to date Kolton, have at it. The guy can use a little fun in his life."

"I agree," Blakely says. "I already told you I don't care who you date."

Sierra's face lights up, but she quickly tampers it down. "Maybe." She shrugs. "I was just coming to say goodbye to the little guy, but it looks like he's still asleep." She glances at her phone. "You're running late this morning."

"I know," Blakely says. "Wait! You're going to work? Didn't you work late last night?"

"I have three interviews to do today."

"Shit," Blakely curses under her breath.

"What's wrong?" Sierra asks.

"Zane is refusing to wake up. He woke up in the middle of the night with a sore throat. Probably just allergies, but you know how cranky he is when he doesn't get a full night of sleep."

"Do you need me to watch him?" I ask, and both women look at me.

"Don't you have class?" Blakely asks.

"So do you," I point out.

"Well, yeah, but I'm his mom."

I know her answer isn't meant as a dig, but it still doesn't sit right with me. Not wanting to wake up Zane, I climb out of the bed and throw my shirt on. The three of us walk out of the room and into the living room.

"I'm Zane's dad."

"No, I know..." she says, trying to backpedal.

"Which means if he's not feeling well, and someone has to stay home, I can do it too. Sierra has to work, and you told me last night you have a test."

"I know, you're right. Are you sure you don't mind watching him?" Her top teeth worry her bottom lip. "It would only be until a little after noon."

"Let's get something straight," I say, stepping toward her. I pull her fleshy lip out from her teeth before she breaks the skin. "I wouldn't be *watching* him. He's my son. You don't watch him, do you? You take care of him. I've missed three years of taking care of him. I'm here now and I want to be a part of his life, part of parenting him. If we had been together when he was born, this wouldn't even be an issue. I'd be just as much of his parent as you are."

Sierra is the first to speak. "And… swoon." She winks. "I've got to get to work." She kisses Blakely's cheek and whispers, "He's right, you know," and then with her purse slung over her shoulder, exits the apartment.

"So, what do you say?" I ask, once it's just the two of us. "It's only for a few hours, and you won't be far away. If I have any problems, I promise to call."

"Okay." She steps into my space and gives me a kiss. "Thank you. I didn't mean anything by what I said. I'm just used to it only being Sierra and me and occasionally Brenton." At his name, I still.

"He watches Zane?"

"Only once in a while," she says, backing away and grabbing her backpack. She heads into the kitchen and I follow her, wanting to find out what once in a while means, but before I can ask, she hands me a small green and white bottle. "This is for Zane's allergies. When he wakes up, after he's eaten breakfast, give him one. I will reassess him when I get home. Don't let him talk you into a million snacks. He can have as much fruit as he wants, but only one snack between meals, and no matter what he says, ice cream is not allowed for breakfast or lunch." She smirks. "Thank you."

And with one final kiss, she's out the door, and it's just Zane and me until she comes home later.

After making myself a cup of coffee, I go check on Zane. He's still lying in Blakely's bed, but his eyes are now open and he's stretching his limbs.

"Hey, bud, how're you feeling?" I sit on the edge of the bed next to him.

"I'm okay. Where's Mommy?"

"She went to school. You wouldn't wake up. Does your throat still itch?"

"A little," he says, grabbing Bear and sitting up. "Are you staying with me?"

"I am."

"Can we go to the park?" His little face lights up at the thought, and his dimples pop out.

"Sorry, bud, but you're home sick." At that, he pouts, and I look away, not allowing his cute puppy dog eyes to sway me. Blakely didn't say we had to stay home, but I remember when I was little and would stay home sick. My mom never let me go anywhere. As Kolton and I got older, if we wanted to fake sick to get out of school, we knew we would be stuck at home, in bed, and that also meant not going out after school. We always made sure never to fake sick on a Friday. That could mean being stuck inside all weekend. Hell, even if we really were sick, we'd pretend to be okay, just so we wouldn't be stuck at home.

"What are we gonna do then?" Zane asks. "Can we watch SpongeBob?"

"Sure."

"And color a picture for Mommy?" He smiles big, and my heart melts. I can't believe I missed the first three years of my son's life.

"That sounds good." And then an idea hits me. "How would you like to make a big surprise for your mom?"

Zane nods, excited, even though he doesn't know what the surprise is yet. "Yes! She loves surprises!"

CHAPTER TWENTY-FIVE

Blakely

"WHERE'S ZANE?" BRENTON ASKS, SIDLING UP NEXT TO ME ON the sidewalk as we walk to our first class of the day. It's been a few days since I've seen Brenton. When he didn't show up to walk with me to class, I texted him and he told me he has some family stuff to deal with. It's not the first time over the years he's vaguely mentioned having to deal with family stuff, but in the back of my mind, in light of our recent conversation, I thought maybe it was just an excuse. But when he didn't show up for class, I figured what he said was true, since Brenton almost never misses class.

"Home sick."

"He okay?" he asks, his voice filled with concern.

"Yeah, I think it's just allergies. Did you get everything worked out with your family stuff?"

Brenton's steps falter slightly. "Yeah, all good."

His action, mixed with his short response, makes me think about the words he threw at me the other day regarding Keegan. *"What do you know about this guy?"* I've been friends with Brenton for the last four years, yet I've never met his family, ever. Even his brother, who owns the cell phone shop on the outskirts of town, has never come around. He's mentioned his mom a few times, but only that she works a lot and they're not close. He's pointing his finger at Keegan, yet what do I really know about Brenton?

"Who was the situation with?" I ask nonchalantly.

"Huh?" He gives me a perplexed look.

"Your family situation. Who was it regarding?"

"Oh, uh… My brother just needed my help." He shrugs then changes the subject, and now my mind is racing. "Who's watching Zane?"

"Keegan."

Brenton's head whips around, and he stops in front of the classroom instead of going in. "You're letting him watch Zane? What do you even know about this guy?"

"What do I even know about you?" I glare, and Brenton's eyes go wide.

"You're not really comparing me to him, are you?" he roars.

"I know you live in the apartment below me and we have the same major, but I've never met your family. I've at least met Keegan's parents and have been to his family home." I give him a pointed look, expecting him to tell me I'm crazy and then offer to introduce me to his family—his mom or his brother.

But instead he twists his lips into a frown and says, "I'm not close with them, and you not knowing them has nothing to do with knowing me. You don't *know* Keegan."

"Your family is an extension of you," I point out.

"What's my favorite food? Favorite song? What's my favorite season?" he asks. "You don't need to answer. You know all my favorites, just like I know yours: Mexican, 'Closer' by the Chainsmokers, and winter because you love the cold." He raises a brow, daring me to argue. "I know you, just like you know me. Not introducing you to my fucked up family doesn't mean shit. Now tell me this…" He steps toward me, encroaching on my space, and because I'm near the wall, my back hits it. "What are Keegan's favorites? If I asked him right now, could he tell me what yours are?"

"What's going on here?" a voice booms, and Brenton steps back. "You okay?" Kolton asks me. I know it's Kolton because he's dressed in a pair of perfectly ironed black dress pants and a button-down white dress shirt, complete with a black and gold striped tie.

"Yeah, I'm okay," I tell him, forcing a smile on my face, not wanting him to know how uncomfortable Brenton's passive aggressiveness is making me feel. He might have said he was okay with us, but his attitude toward Keegan, and now his accusations, are only getting worse, telling me things between Brenton and me are the opposite of okay. And I have no idea how to fix it. Keegan is the father of Zane, the guy I'm dating. He's not going anywhere.

"You sure?" Kolton asks, his jaw ticking.

"She said she's okay," Brenton hisses.

"I wasn't asking you." Kolton steps into Brenton's face. "Blakely, are you sure you're okay?" he asks, his eyes never leaving Brenton's.

"Yeah, I'm sure. We should get to class. It's not going to teach itself," I joke to lighten the mood, but neither guy laughs or even cracks a smile.

"After you." Kolton backs away from Brenton and opens the door for me. I walk through it, and then Kolton follows, making it a point not to hold the door open for Brenton.

The morning flies by. Usually I would study with Brenton until it's time to pick up Zane, but since he's home, and I'm looking forward to getting back to him and Keegan, I use the excuse that I have to check on Zane instead of going to study. I haven't heard from Keegan all morning, so hopefully that's a sign it really was just allergies and Zane is doing okay.

Using my key, I unlock my front door. When I step into the house, I'm shocked by the sight in front of me. There's a huge rectangular sign hanging across the wall that reads: Happy Mother's Days. No, I didn't mean to say day—it actually reads 'days.' There are tons of balloons all over the place, and several vases of flowers and boxes of chocolates on the table. What is going on here? This must be Keegan's doing. Does he know Mother's Day isn't until May?

"Keegan, Zane," I call out, and both guys come running out of Zane's room.

"Mom! You're home early," Zane yells. "Happy Mother's Days!" He runs over to me and wraps his tiny arms around my waist.

Lifting him, I give him a big kiss on his cheek. "Why, thank you." I have no idea why we're apparently celebrating Mother's *Days* right now, but I'm not about to dampen my son's spirits.

"I got you presents." Zane wriggles to get down, so I set him on the floor.

When he runs down the hall, Keegan comes over and presses a soft kiss to my lips. "You usually pick Zane up later."

"I didn't stay to study with Brenton. I wanted to come home to you guys," I admit.

Keegan's grin is wide and makes my belly do somersaults. "I like the sound of that," he says.

"Of what?"

"You coming home to us."

And now my heart feels like it's being squeezed. His words are so simple yet mean so much to me. Brenton may be right, and I may not know all of Keegan's favorites, and he may not know mine, but that's okay. We have plenty of time to learn all there is to know about each other.

"Here, Mommy." Zane runs back over and thrusts several pieces of construction paper at me. "Read them!" He jumps up and down, clearly feeling better.

I sit on the couch, picking Zane up and plopping him next to me. Keegan sits next to him. "Happy Mother's Days, Mommy," I read out loud. "I love you more than I love SpongeBob." Just like Zane's drawings from school, his writing is messy and over it is Keegan's handwriting. Under the writing is a picture of what I think is Zane, me, and SpongeBob.

"I love this," I tell him.

"Read the next one." He bounces in his seat. I read each of them, and they all say something similar.

When I'm done, I give Zane a kiss and thank him.

"Daddy made you a card too!"

"He did?" I ask, giving Keegan a curious look.

"I did," Keegan says, standing. He grabs the card off the counter and brings it over to me. "There are three vases of flowers, three boxes of chocolates, and Zane made you three cards. One for every year I missed celebrating what a wonderful mother you are." He hands me his card, but I can't read it yet because my vision is now blurry from the tears that are falling down my cheeks.

"I only made you one card," he says, "but it's for all three."

I nod absently, staring down at the homemade card my son's father made me.

"Mommy, don't cry," Zane says, crawling into my lap. "Why are you sad?"

"I'm not sad, sweetie." I pull my precious baby boy into a tight hug, nuzzling his neck. He doesn't smell like a baby anymore, but he still smells like my baby. "I'm happy. I'm very happy."

"We made you a cake too!" Zane pulls back and grins. "I put the sprinkles on."

I laugh when the word comes out sounding like *spinkles* instead. "You did?"

"It's chocolate!" Zane exclaims.

"Zane said it was your favorite," Keegan says.

I laugh because chocolate is Zane's favorite, not mine. I actually hate chocolate cake, but since the only time we really have cake is for him, I always get chocolate. And on the occasion we do have cake for my birthday, we buy a half and half cake since Zane hates vanilla.

"Have you had lunch yet?" I ask Zane.

"Yep, Daddy said you have to go to bed."

When I shoot Keegan a confused glance his way, he laughs. "Mother's Day means breakfast in bed. You have to go to bed so we can bring you your meal." He winks, and a fresh batch of tears falls at how much he thought this through. Sure, Sierra always makes sure to recognize Mother's Day, but for some reason Keegan going out of his way to show me how much he appreciates me as Zane's mother means a lot to me.

"Go, Mommy!" Zane shoves my shoulder. "Go to bed now."

I laugh, but stand and head to my room. When I get there, I find a basket full of items: body wash, bubble bath, face masks, the works. There's an envelope addressed to me, so I open it up, and inside is a gift certificate to the local spa for three massages. I can't believe he did all this…

I put the basket on the nightstand, kick off my flip-flops, and crawl into bed, covering myself with my blanket. While I wait for the boys, and whatever they have cooked up, I open the card from Keegan. With every word I read, the tears sail down my face. About his parents' love and their marriage. How he wants that for us one day. About all the time we've missed and how much he wants to get it all back. He promises to spend every day making up for the lost time. He goes on to tell me how amazing of a mother I am, and that even though he hasn't been around for a long time, he can tell by just hanging out with Zane and me that we have a special relationship. The droplets of salty liquid fall onto the blue construction paper, smearing a couple of the words. I read his message twice over before I hear Zane's voice.

"Mommy's crying again," Zane says, not liking my tears.

"Oh, no, sweetie," I say, needing him to know I'm not sad. "They're happy tears. I promise. I'm very happy."

Zane crawls onto the bed next to me, and that's when I notice Keegan is carrying a tray full of food over: pancakes with strawberries and whipped cream, a container of yogurt, a couple strips of bacon, and a cup of orange juice. He pulls the legs of the tray out and sets it on top of my lap.

"Wow, did you make all this?" I ask Zane, who nods in excitement. "Thank you."

While I eat my food, sharing with Zane, Keegan sits on the other side of the bed, and we all talk. Zane tells me about his day. How he went in his daddy's big truck—and he had to show him how to put the car seat in. They went to the stores and then came home and made everything. Zane's favorite part is that while they were at the store, Keegan bought him a SpongeBob coloring book.

When he yawns, I tell him it's time for his nap. He would've already taken one at school. He pouts, but when Keegan tells him he'll read him a story, he jumps off the bed and runs to use the bathroom before getting into his bed.

I finish eating while Keegan reads him a story. I'm walking the now empty tray back to the kitchen when Keegan steps into the hall, shutting the door behind him. I set the tray on the counter, about to do the dishes, when Keegan's arms wrap around me from behind.

"I'll get those in a few minutes," he says, turning me around to face him. "I didn't have a chance to properly kiss you hello." His mouth descends on mine, and his tongue pushes through my parted lips. We kiss for several seconds before Keegan pulls back. "That's what I'm talking about." He waggles his eyebrows, and I laugh.

"Want to sneak a piece of cake?" he asks, and I scrunch my nose. I consider lying to Keegan, telling him I would love to, but instead I go for the truth. The only way we can get to know each other is by being honest.

"I hate chocolate cake," I admit.

He's quiet for a second and then he laughs. "What? But Zane said you love it."

"Zane loves it, so we always get it. It turns out that Zane loves chocolate and hates vanilla, and I'm the opposite."

"That's hilarious." Keegan laughs harder. "I do too. I love chocolate and hate vanilla."

Wrapping my arms around Keegan's neck, I stand on my tippy toes and give him a chaste kiss. "Thank you for all of this. It means everything."

"You're welcome." He dips his head down and catches my mouth. He sucks on my bottom lip, and a low moan escapes my lips. I tug on his neck, bringing him down, and he lifts me at the same time, setting me on the counter.

His hands roam down my back while mine glide across his muscular shoulders and arms, making their way to his chest. My fingers run across the hem of his shirt, and I break our kiss just long enough to lift it over his head, immediately picking back up where we left off as soon as the shirt is out of the way.

"Ahem." The noise startles both of us and Keegan jumps back. "It seems that me walking in on you guys is becoming a thing," my sister— who has the worst timing in the world—says.

Keegan picks his shirt up off the floor and puts it back on, and I sigh in disappointment. Sierra laughs, and Keegan chuckles, and my cheeks heat, realizing I just sighed out loud and they both heard me.

"Sorry to cock block," she says, and the heat spreads to my neck.

"S," I hiss, shaking my head.

"Ohhh… no cock yet?" She quirks her head to the side. "Well, damn, if you don't have the patience of a saint. If I had that man—or the one identical to him"—she winks—"in my bed, there's no way I'd be able to resist."

I groan and jump off the counter. "You're home early," I say, changing the subject.

"Oh, I'm sorry. Should I leave? Were you about to get…" She waggles her eyebrows, thankfully not finishing her highly inappropriate, yet completely like Sierra, question.

She spots the cake on the counter. "Oh, cake!"

"It's chocolate," I point out.

"Oh, boo." She pouts.

"You don't like chocolate either?" Keegan asks, sitting on the couch.

"No way." Sierra shakes her head. "It tastes like dirt."

"You know what dirt tastes like?" He laughs.

"You know what I mean." She rolls her eyes. "What's with all the decorations?" she asks, as we take a seat. I sit next to Keegan on the couch, and Sierra sits across from us in the love seat.

"Keegan and Zane made it all," I explain. "To celebrate all the Mother's Days Keegan missed."

Sierra's head whips over to look at me, and I can see it in her eyes, she's affected almost as much as I was. "Damn it, and I totally ruined your thanking him."

"Oh my God." I groan. "Shut it."

"How's little man feeling?" she asks.

"Fine. Must've been allergies," I tell her as Keegan wraps his arms around me and pulls me into his side. Sierra notices and gives me a knowing grin. "What are you up to tonight?"

"Well, I actually came home early because I have a date tonight, but I wanted to make sure you are okay with it. I know you said you were, but I wanted to double-check."

"You're going on a date with Kolton?" I grin.

"As long as you're sure you're okay with it."

"Totally!" I look at Keegan. "Are you?"

"I don't care as long as you understand that you're family, and if you don't work out, we're still celebrating every holiday together."

"And what if you two don't work out?" Sierra asks.

Keegan pulls me in closer, if that's even possible, and gives me a kiss on my temple. "Then we make it work as Zane's parents," he says, and while I hate that he doesn't insist we will work, I love that he's being realistic. I believe that if we really didn't work out, Keegan would make sure we still co-parented Zane civilly.

Sierra nods. "I like your honesty. Kolton and I talked this afternoon when he came by Orange Sunrise, asking to take me out, and he assured me if it doesn't work out, we will play nice. I made it clear to him that my nephew and sister come first."

"Where are you guys going?" I ask.

"Not sure." She stands. "He said he'll pick me up at six, so I better go get ready."

Keegan laughs. "It's only one."

"Yeah…" Sierra gives him a confused look.

"It takes you five hours to get ready?" he asks.

"Perfection"—Sierra waves her hand down the side of her body—"takes time. Have fun making out!" she calls over her shoulder as she skips down the hall.

Her door isn't even closed all the way before Keegan has me in his lap and his mouth on mine. Does it make me a bad mom that I hope Zane takes an extra-long nap today?

CHAPTER TWENTY-SIX

Keegan

"I s this really necessary?" Blakely asks with a pout splayed across her gorgeous lips.

"Yep," I say, stifling my laughter. I know she's not really upset, but she's still adorably sexy when she pouts, and it's taking everything in me not to pull my truck over, drag her into my lap, and kiss the hell out of her.

She crosses her arms over her chest and falls back into the seat with a huff. "Can I at least get a hint?"

"Nope." I silently laugh.

"I know you're laughing," she says, and I can imagine her giving me the side-eye from under the tie I borrowed from Kolton to use as a makeshift blindfold.

"No, I'm not."

"Yes, you are."

"Zane said you love surprises," I point out.

She snorts. "Yeah, ones that include macaroni glued to a piece of paper."

"I'm not sure if I can top glued macaroni, but I think you will like this surprise."

I entwine our fingers and bring our hands up to my lips, kissing the top of her hand. Does she really need a blindfold? No. But I thought it would be fun anyway. I've learned quickly that having a child means limited adult time, so when Sierra offered to watch Zane for the night, having the weekend off, I wanted to go all out for Blakely. She deserves to be spoiled. Plus, who knows when we'll get this alone time again. Don't get me wrong, I'm not complaining. I love hanging out with Zane and Blakely. We spent the entire day yesterday at the park. Zane rode around on his skateboard, I pushed him in the swing, and Blakely brought a packed lunch. It was a perfect day.

So, yeah, our time as a family isn't lacking. But what is lacking is my alone time with Blakely. Because I've had to work the last several evenings, I haven't gotten to spend any one-on-one time with her. I feel guilty lying to Blakely, so I've kept it vague, saying I have work to do. She assumes it's schoolwork, which isn't a complete lie, but it's also not the complete truth. It will be nice for us to be able to have an adult conversation over dinner. I booked us a room at the same resort we met at and made it clear to everyone who might need to get ahold of me that I won't be available for the next twenty-four hours.

We pull up to the resort, and I remove the blindfold. Blakely blinks a few times, then grins. "You brought me to a hotel?"

"Not just any hotel. The hotel we met at. I booked us a couple's massage, made a reservation for dinner, and confirmed they're playing a chick flick." I shoot her a playful wink, and she beams at me. Fucking beams.

After we check in, we head to our room. I had Sierra pack Blakely an overnight bag, so I know there's a bathing suit in there. Since it's still early, and our couple's massage isn't for a few hours, I figure we can hit the heated pool and hot tub. Since it's approaching February in Central Florida, it's a tad too cold for the beach, at least to go swimming in—we could probably go for a walk, though.

Blakely opens her luggage and finds everything she needs. "Wow, you thought of everything."

"With the help of your sister."

"This is awesome. Thank you." She wraps her arms around my neck and pulls me down to her for a kiss that, if I don't stop, will prevent us from ever leaving this room.

"C'mon," I say, pulling back. "Let's hit the water."

With our suits on and towels in our hands, we find two open lounge chairs. After laying our towels down, we go straight into the heated pool. The hotel is slow because of it still being winter, and we're the only ones in here right now.

Blakely dips her head under the water, and when she comes back up, she pushes the wet strands of hair from her face. I take a moment to admire her. She's grown up since the last time we were here. Her brown hair is longer now and has blond along the bottom. Her body... Jesus, her body has filled out in all the right places. She's all woman. And her eyes: they're no longer shy and nervous. Instead they're filled with confidence and determination. Even with her having to raise a baby at nineteen, she managed to follow her dreams and go to college. I just hate that she wasn't able to go to South Carolina like she planned. Had I not lost her number, I would've known about her being pregnant, and I'd like to think I would've done whatever was needed to get her there.

"What're you thinking about?" Blakely snakes her arms around my neck and wraps her legs around my hips. Her center rubs against my stomach and then downward, waking my dick up.

"I was thinking about how beautiful you are. Even more beautiful than you were four years ago." I kiss her plump lips then suck on her bottom lip. Fuck, I love her mouth. "And how much I hate that you didn't get to go to South Carolina for school."

Blakely frowns. "I'm okay with where I ended up. It meant keeping Zane and eventually finding you."

"What if you apply to colleges in South Carolina for your master's degree?" I blurt out without even thinking about what it would mean for me to move. My dad would be pissed. I would have to find a new job. My mom would hate the idea of her son and grandson living hundreds of miles away. Plus, she can't stop gushing about Blakely and Sierra, asking when she can have them over again for dinner.

"What?" Her brows furrow in confusion.

"You could apply to colleges in South Carolina like you originally wanted. We could move there." I don't care what it will mean for me or my family. Blakely's entire life and future had to change so she could care for our son. I'll follow her anywhere she wants to go if it will make her happy.

I don't think I'll ever be able to make up for the years she's been doing it all without me, but I'll damn well spend my life trying.

"You would do that? Move away from your family, where you go to school?"

"Yes," I tell her honestly. "I know I'm several years too late, but you could still go there."

"You have no idea how much that means to me." She kisses my cheek then trails her lips down my scruffy jawline. She told me once that she loves the feel of my hair against her skin. "But I would never ask you to do that. We have a life here, and I'm happy."

"If you ever change your mind, all you have to do is say the word."

Blakely's legs tighten around me and she crashes her mouth against mine. We kiss for several minutes before she pulls back. "You know," she says, placing soft kisses along my neck, then taking a moment to suck on my skin, "we have an entire hotel room with a king-sized bed all to ourselves." She glides her body down, so her ass purposely hits my hard dick. I grab her ass cheeks to stop her. If she keeps doing that, I'll blow right here in the pool.

"That's not why I brought you here. We don't have to do anything like that. I just wanted some alone time with you."

Blakely sucks and licks across my collarbone before lifting her head to look at me once again. "Your dick is in complete disagreement." She giggles, and my dick swells at the sweet sound. Blakely is always gorgeous, but when she laughs or smiles, she's fucking magnificent.

Reaching into the water, she grabs my shaft through my board shorts and gives it a light squeeze. "I think we need to go back to our room," she whispers into my ear. She licks the bottom of my earlobe then bites down on it softly. "I need you, Keegan."

I let out a low rumble at her words, but quickly compose myself. "We have our massages soon."

"How about we just give each other massages?" Her hands roam down my chest, while her lips roam all over.

"Jailbird." I groan. "Massages, dinner, movie."

"Sex, room service, Netflix," she counters. Her hand dips into the waistband of my shorts and she strokes my shaft. Her eyes meet mine, and she shoots me the sexiest pout. "Please."

Holy shit, I'm pretty sure my woman could cure all world conflict by simply giving them that look and saying please in that voice. There's no way anybody could resist her. I know I sure as hell can't.

"Your wish is my command."

Tightening my grip on her ass, I walk us out of the pool, forgetting the towels, and carry her straight to our room. She holds on to me the entire way, kissing me and giggling when I kiss her back—both of us using each other's bodies to counteract the slight chill in the air.

"Grab my key," I tell her when we get to the door. She reaches in and grabs the card, but not before getting a squeeze in.

"Woman, we're not going to make it inside," I growl, and she giggles some more.

After inserting the card and opening the door, I head straight for the bed, not giving a shit that we're both still dripping wet.

When I drop her onto the center of the bed, her long, wet tresses of dark hair fan out against the white pillow. She's breathing heavily. Her nipples are hard through her thin bikini top, and her legs are bent at her knees. She attempts to squeeze them together to dull the ache between her legs because she's turned on. I could watch this woman forever. I expect her to get shy or nervous at my staring, but she shocks the shit out of me when she smirks and her hands come up to her perfect tits, which are spilling out of her top, and tweaks her nipples. Her back arches slightly, and her lips part in pleasure.

I'm torn between continuing to watch her touch herself or touching her myself. It should be a given that I would want the latter, but you haven't been where I am.

When I make no move to go toward her and take over, her eyes hood over and her head tilts to the side, as if she's considering what to do next. She's still pinching her nipples, but she's also now massaging the entire breast.

"You look so fucking perfect."

Her cheeks flush, and she smiles at my praise. "How about this?" She moves one hand down, stopping at the waistband of her bottoms. "Is this perfect?" Her hand dips under the material, and her legs spread. I can see the outline of where her fingers are—right at the center of her pussy. Her fingers move back and forth, most likely flicking her clit, while she continues to pinch and pull at her nipple.

"Yeah, that's fucking perfect," I tell her, my voice strained.

"You know what I think would make it even more perfect?" she taunts. Her fingers must hit her clit just right because her eyes roll back briefly, and her thighs clench together. It takes every ounce of control I have not to pull her bikini bottoms down, shove her hand out of my way, and thrust into her.

"What's that?"

"You taking your suit off, so I can watch you."

And I'm pretty sure I just came in my pants…

Pushing my board shorts down, I lift my legs to get them all the way off and throw them to the side. My granite-hard dick springs up.

"Watch me do what?" I tease her back.

"Watch you jack off." Her words are so confident, but the blush across her cheeks and neck tells me otherwise.

Taking my dick in my hand, I stroke it up and down, root to tip. When a bit of pre-cum seeps out, I use it to help with the friction. Blakely watches with rapt attention as she plays with her tits and pussy.

"It's just like I remembered it," she says, her voice breathless.

"Take your bathing suit off," I demand. "I want to see you play with your pussy, baby."

Her legs come together again, telling me she's turned the fuck on. Nobody is going to make her come but me.

She does as I say and, pulling her hand out, unties her top and slowly drags it off her body, dropping it onto the floor. Her tits fall slightly, no longer confined. My mouth waters, needing a taste. Leaning forward, I release my dick and take her tits into my hands, massaging them. I dip my head down and lick one and then the other. Blakely moans in pleasure.

"Oh my God. More." Her fingers tangle in my hair, tugging me closer.

I lick each of them again and then focus my attention on one. I suck the entire nipple into my mouth then bite down. Blakely gasps, and her legs, which I'm between, wrap around my body. She's trying to find relief. Not happening.

"Keegan, I need more," she begs.

Sitting up, I go back to stroking my dick. She glares and I stifle my laugh. She started this, and now she no longer wants to play.

"Take off your bottoms," I tell her. "I still haven't seen your pussy."

"You take them off," she challenges.

"Nope." I shake my head. "I want to watch you play with yourself, baby."

I lean forward and take her nipple in my mouth, sucking and licking it for a second before sitting back up to wait for her to do as I said.

And she does. With two fingers hooked onto each side, she pulls her bottoms down. When they get stuck on her ankle, she moves her foot toward me, her toes landing on my chest. "Help me."

Lifting her small foot, I kiss the tip of her toe, then trail kisses up her foot and along the inside of her ankle. I run my hand along her smooth calf and then remove the material, dropping it to the floor. Without letting go of her leg, I kiss my way up the inside of her calf, over her knee, and continue my way along the inside of her thigh. She moans and begs and pleads. Her words are incoherent. She's so turned on, she's not even speaking clearly. When I reach the apex of her thighs, I place one chaste kiss to the hood of her bare pussy, then stop.

When I sit back, she growls. Yes, my woman actually fucking growls.

"Touch your pussy."

She groans but doesn't argue. Her feminine fingers separate her folds, and I can see her pink pussy is glistening with arousal. She dips a single digit inside her instead of going for her clit. With her eyes locked on my hard dick, she pushes in and out of herself. I watch silently, stroking my shaft, as she fucks herself with a single finger. It's the most intimate thing I've ever witnessed.

"Add another finger," I tell her, no clue where this is coming from. It's as if she's released some sexual beast in me. Her eyes widen and she pulls her pointer finger out then inserts it back in, this time adding her middle finger. As she fucks herself with one hand and plays with her tits with the other, I stroke my dick. The room is silent save for our heavy breathing. We're both turned the hell on. My dick is swollen with need, and so is her pussy.

And then she stops and removes her fingers. Her eyes meet mine, and she brings her soaking wet fingers up to her mouth, parting her lips, then closing them around the digits. When she sucks off her arousal and moans, her eyes rolling back in her head, it's my breaking point.

Letting go of my dick, I cage her in my arms, my body covering hers.

My mouth crashes down onto hers, and I push into her tight warmth. She moans into my mouth, and I can taste herself on her tongue. I suck on her tongue as I thrust deep inside her. She tightens around me, and I push in deeper, harder. She feels like everything that is perfect in this life. She feels like home. Our mouths fuck each other while our bodies make love to one another. We're both close. The foreplay already brought us to the precipice. We're dangling off the edge.

Blakely grips my shoulders—her nails digging into my skin—and calls out my name so loud, if we were at her house, she would've woken up her neighbors. Her entire body shakes and her pussy tightens around my dick like a vice grip as she falls right off the edge, taking me with her.

CHAPTER TWENTY-SEVEN

"WHY THE POUT?" KEEGAN ASKS, TRACING MY TURNED DOWN lips that I didn't realize matched my thoughts. We're lying in bed, our bodies entwined in one another, waiting for room service to bring us breakfast. I'm exhausted and slightly sore, of course in the best way possible, from our love making last night. After the first time, we showered to clean off, only to go back to bed and do it all over again, and again. Keegan is like an addiction. I can't get enough of him. So much so that at one point last night, I actually woke up and pulled him on top of me. He made sweet, slow love to me until we both found our release, and then he rolled over and fell asleep still slightly inside of me.

"I don't want this to end, and that makes me feel guilty because our son isn't here."

Keegan pulls me closer and kisses me softly. "There's nothing wrong with taking some time for yourself. He's at home with your sister, who is practically a second mom to him. You're such a good mom, JB. You give that kid every part of you."

"I know you're right. I just can't help it." I shrug. "It's a mother's curse, I guess."

There's a knock at the door, and Keegan gets up to answer it. I can't take my eyes off his muscular form. He's wearing nothing but a pair of basketball shorts, slung low on his hips, and I know there isn't anything underneath. His back is a work of art, chiseled in all the right places. Not overly built, just lean and perfect. He has a tattoo of his last name across his shoulder blades in gray script.

He wheels the cart of food into the room, the door closing behind him, while I grab his shirt from the chair and throw it on. "Want to eat out on the terrace?" I suggest. It's probably in the sixties this morning, and our room overlooks the Atlantic.

"Sure."

I grab the down blanket from our bed since we won't need it anymore—we're checking out after breakfast and heading home—and drag it outside. There are two lounge chairs, and when Keegan plops down onto one, I go to sit on the other, but he grips the curves of my hips and pulls me between his legs. He wraps his arms around my torso and kisses the side of my neck. "Fuck breakfast," he murmurs. "I just want to eat you." He bites down on the side of my neck playfully, and a giggle escapes my lips. I've never felt so wanted and cherished as I do with Keegan. He suckles on my skin, and my body relaxes against him. I don't know how I'm going to go home after last night and be away from him.

"Move in with me," I blurt out, and he stills. I don't even know what's gotten into me. One second I'm *thinking* about what it would be like to get to be with him every night and morning, and the next thing I know, I'm spouting shit out of my mouth. When he doesn't say anything, I consider taking it back, telling him I was just kidding. But then it hits me, I don't want to. I wasn't kidding. So instead, I turn in his arms to face him and explain. "If you lived with me, you could be with Zane and me every day. We could go to bed and wake up together. We could be a family."

When he still doesn't say anything, nerves overtake me, and I start rambling. "If you don't want to, I understand. I know it's probably too soon. I just wanted to throw it out there. I know my place isn't big, and Sierra lives there too. But… I don't know. I just thought it would be nice for the three of us to live under one roof."

Keegan's brows are pinched together in what looks like pain, and I know without him even saying a word, he's going to turn my idea down. "Jailbird." He exhales. "I—" He opens his mouth then closes it. It's as if he's warring with himself, but I don't understand why. Is it because of Kolton? Does he not want to leave his brother to live on his own? I know they're close, but surely they aren't planning to live together forever. Which can only mean he doesn't want to live with me and is trying to figure out how to let me down nicely.

"What?" I ask, needing to hear the words one way or another. My heart is slowly cracking. I shouldn't have put myself out there. "Tell me, please."

"I want to live with you," he begins, but I can tell a 'but' is coming. "I just…" He shakes his head and curses under his breath. I'm so confused right now. He's frustrated and mad, and I don't understand why. But then several reasons come to mind that have me freaking out. Maybe he *is* in a relationship with someone else. Maybe he lied at the time because he was in shock and now he's backed himself into a corner he needs to get out of. Oh God, what if he already lives with someone? He said he lives with Kolton, but I've never been over there. He always comes over to my place because he said his place is small and doesn't have any of Zane's things. He's never even asked to take Zane for the night.

"You just what?" I prompt, needing him to either shoot down my thoughts or put me out of my misery.

"I want to live with you," he repeats. His hands cradle my face lovingly while his words break my heart. "But I can't. Not yet."

"What does that mean?"

He sighs and swallows thickly, his Adam's apple pushing out slightly. "I need time. It's not that I don't want to live with you, I do. I swear to you that I do. I just… I need you to trust me, please." His eyes and words plead with me, but he's said nothing to tamper down the scenarios whirling around in my head.

"I think we should go home," I tell him, not wanting to be this close to him anymore. My heart hurts, and if I'm honest, I'm also embarrassed at his rejection.

"No, please. I'm not saying no. Just not yet." His eyes implore into mine, begging me to understand.

"I understand," I tell him, even though I don't. "But I want to get home to Zane, if that's okay."

His eyes flicker back and forth between mine, and I can tell he wants to argue, but whatever he sees in my eyes stops him, and he nods. "Okay."

Without eating any of the food we ordered, we head inside and get dressed. I don't bother showering, just wanting to pack and get out of here.

The drive home is silent. It's completely different from how things were between us before I was stupid and asked Keegan to move in with me. When we pull up, he asks if he can come in so he can see Zane and, even though the last thing I want is to be around Keegan right now, I agree. I told myself I would never stop him from seeing his son, and I meant it.

He carries my bag upstairs, and when we enter the apartment, Zane comes running out and straight into his daddy's arms. My heart, for the second time today, breaks. I can't quench my jealousy. At one time, it would've been my arms he ran right into. I push down the negative thoughts, glad that Zane now has a father. He deserves this. He deserves the world.

"You're back early?" Sierra asks, walking out of Zane's room with Kolton trailing behind. *Interesting...*

"I didn't spend the night," Kolton says, wrapping his arm around Sierra. "Just brought breakfast over. I hope that's okay."

"This is just as much Sierra's home as it is mine," I tell him. "Of course you're welcome here."

There's a knock at the door and, since Keegan is the closest, he opens it. "Yeah?" he asks, his voice sounding cold and angry.

"I'm here for Zane," I hear the voice say on the other side of the door. It's Brenton.

Keegan's entire body goes rigid. "For what?"

Not wanting them to get into it right here in my front entranceway, especially with Zane here, I lightly push Keegan out of the way and open the door farther.

Brenton smiles when he sees me. "It's the last Sunday of the month." When I give him a look, trying to figure out what he's implying, he adds, "Home Depot day." Oh, shit! I completely forgot.

Zane must hear him, because he yells, "Yes! Home Depot day!" He runs to his room and, a second later, comes out with his bright orange apron. "I'm ready!"

"Ready for what?" Keegan asks, confused.

"The last Sunday of every month, Brenton takes Zane to Home Depot for their craft day. They make stuff out of wood. Sierra and I usually go get our nails done."

"Like hell he is," Keegan hisses, then turns to Brenton. "You're not taking my fucking kid anywhere."

Whoa…

"Daddy, you said a bad word!" Zane giggles, completely unaware of the high tension in the room.

"Sorry, bud," Keegan says. "Why don't you go play in your room while Mommy and I talk?"

Zane frowns, but does as he says.

Once he's gone, I say what I've been thinking since Keegan spoke. "Your kid?" I'm trying to keep calm, but who the hell does he think he is? He might not like Brenton, but that doesn't give him the right to tell me how to make decisions for *our* son.

"You know what I mean." He hits me with a glare that if I were a weaker woman would have me cowering, but I'm not, and I'm not going to let him intimidate me. "He"—he jabs a finger toward Brenton—"isn't taking our son anywhere."

"Yes, he is," I argue, refusing to back down. "He's been taking him every month for who knows how long. Zane looks forward to it."

"Then I'll take him," Keegan says.

"No," I volley back. "Brenton has been in Zane's life for the last three years, since he was born, and I'm not going to just cut him out because you two are at odds. Unless you have some legitimate reason why Brenton shouldn't be allowed to take him, then he is. Do you?"

Keegan's jaw is ticking, his lips pursed together so tightly they're turning white. He glares at me then at Brenton, but doesn't say a word.

"Is there a reason why Brenton shouldn't be allowed to take Zane to Home Depot?" I ask again.

"Fuck this!" Keegan yells. He gets in Brenton's face, and I'm scared he's going to hit him. I glance at Kolton and Sierra, who are both watching silently. I try to tell Kolton to do something, but he's only looking at Keegan and, for some reason, he looks almost as mad as his brother does. His fists are clenched, and his jaw, which identical to Keegan's, is ticking in the same way.

"Anything happens to Zane, and I'm going to hunt you down and kill you," Keegan warns.

"Keegan!" I yell. "Stop it!" This is getting out of hand. He can't seriously be threatening to kill Brenton over taking our son to Home Depot.

Without another word, Keegan pushes past Brenton, knocking his shoulder on his way, and stalks out the door.

I have no clue what the hell just happened here. My first instinct is to chase after Keegan, but before my feet move, Kolton's hand is on my shoulder. "Let him go. He just needs to calm down."

I nod once and then head to Zane's room to let him know he can go with Brenton.

"Daddy was yelling," he says, looking up from his Legos.

"He was mad," I tell him honestly. "Sometimes adults yell when they're mad."

"Is he mad at me?"

Oh my heart. Keegan and I are going to have to have a chat. He's never been around a child before, and this is a learning curve for him, but he's going to need to learn that it's not okay to behave that way in front of our son.

"No, sweetie, he's not mad at you. Do you want to go to Home Depot with Brenton?"

"Yes."

"Then you better get going. He's waiting for you."

Zane runs out of his room and straight to the front door where Brenton is waiting. "I'm ready."

Brenton looks at me. "You sure?"

"Yes, I trust you."

"All right, little man, let's go."

After they leave, Kolton says, "I better go find Keegan." He kisses Sierra's cheek and leaves.

"Was I wrong?" I ask her once we're alone.

She nibbles on her bottom lip, not answering right away.

"S?" I push. "Was I wrong? You're my sister. Talk to me."

"I just think Keegan wouldn't have done that unless there was a reason."

"I asked him if he has a reason, but he couldn't give me one."

"I know." She nods several times. "Maybe it was just jealousy…" She lets her words linger as I fill in the blanks: *but what if it wasn't.*

CHAPTER TWENTY-EIGHT

Keegan

I STAY BEHIND HIS VEHICLE AT A DISTANCE. CLOSE ENOUGH TO NOT lose him, but far enough away that he won't see me tailing him. If he stops anywhere, it's game fucking over. Lucky for him, he doesn't. He goes straight to Home Depot. I watch from a few aisles over while he helps Zane make some wooden car thing. There are about thirty other kids here with their parents, all making the same thing. Zane laughs and runs around, and Brenton stays with him. He shows Zane how to hammer the nails, and Zane is all smiles the entire time. When they're done, Zane gets an award and a pin for finishing, and Brenton takes a picture, telling Zane he's going to send it to his mom.

"Send to Daddy too!" Zane says.

Brenton smiles, but it's now fake. "I don't know his number," he tells him honestly. "But I'm sure your mom will." Fucker. He better eat this all up because there's no way he'll be bringing Zane to the next one. I'm going to make sure of it.

When they leave, I follow them the entire way home, only leaving once I see Blakely open the door and Zane go inside.

As I drive back to Kolton's place, I call my dad. He picks up on the first ring. "Keegan? Everything okay?"

"No, we need to talk."

CHAPTER TWENTY-NINE

Blakely

IT'S BEEN TWO DAYS SINCE KEEGAN STORMED OUT OF HERE. NO TEXTS. No phone calls. He hasn't even stopped by to see Zane. When Brenton brought Zane back, he tried to talk to me about Keegan, but I put a halt to it immediately. The two of them want to participate in some ridiculous pissing contest, fine. Piss away, but neither of them will be doing it on my damn leg. I'm dating Keegan—at least I think I still am. And I'm friends with Brenton. They're both going to have to get used to having each other around. I point blank asked Brenton if he wants to stay friends, and he said he does. So, until he says otherwise, he will be in my life. I made it clear to him that I'm dating Keegan and he said he understood.

And Keegan needs to understand that Brenton has been around for a long time now. He was there when I delivered Zane. He's been my friend and there for Zane his entire life. I'm not going to rip Brenton away just because Keegan is jealous.

"I need to stop by my brother's shop," Brenton says on our way to meet up with our group from our Child Psychology class. We had to create a group of four to complete a project to present to the class. Our topic is nature versus nurture. Since the other two students, Brianne and Willa, live together off campus, we agreed to meet them at their place. Sierra worked the lunch shift, so she's able to watch Zane for me.

"No problem," I tell him, checking my phone for the umpteenth time to see if Keegan has called or texted, even though it's on loud and I would hear it if he did.

"Everything okay?" Brenton asks.

"Yeah," I tell him, not wanting to give him room to talk shit about Keegan. Maybe I should just text him first. He might be worried I'm mad and he's giving us both time to cool down. I type out a text, then backspace it. I type out another one, read it several times, then delete it as well. I'm typing my third text, when my phone dings with a text from the man himself.

> Keegan: I'm sorry for the way I acted. I should've called or texted sooner, but I was being a wuss. Even now I'm texting instead of calling. I'm a wuss. Can I come by so we can talk?

I smile at his text. He was thinking the same thing I was.

> Me: I was being a wuss too ;) I would love for you to come over, but I'm not home. I'm with Brenton. We're going to work on our group project for our Child Psych class. Tomorrow?

> Keegan: See you tomorrow.

I stare at his short text, knowing it's because I mentioned Brenton. I don't really understand what his deal is, but hopefully we can talk it all out tomorrow.

> Me: Okay, miss you xo

I wait for him to text back, but it never comes.

Brenton stops by his brother's shop, and then says he needs to swing by a customer's house real quick since it's on the way. I check a couple emails from my professors and respond to a few online messages on one of the forum boards for a class where the professor requires us to post our written responses online and respond to a minimum of three other students.

Thirty minutes later, we arrive at Brianne and Willa's house. We spend the next few hours planning and outlining our presentation, assigning parts to each member of the group. By the time we leave, we all know what we need to do and have agreed to meet again next week to check in and hopefully tie up any loose ends before we put it all together.

On our way home, Brenton stops by one other customer's house, and then we head home. It's late when I get home, and the house is dark and quiet. I check on Zane, who is sleeping soundly and cuddling with Bear. Since my bedroom is the master with the bathroom—Sierra insisted on it because I had Zane bunking with me for the first several months after he was born and I was breastfeeding—I go straight inside to grab a change of clothes so I can shower. It's dark in my room, so I flip the switch on. And then I let out a loud screech when I spot a sleeping man in my bed.

Keegan—who I now realize is the sleeping man—jumps out of bed. "What's going on?" He flies across the room as if he's going to protect me. "What happened?"

"Nothing." I inhale and exhale. "I thought you were an intruder."

He takes a deep breath. "Jesus, woman. You scared the shit out of me."

"Me? You scared the crap out of me! A little heads-up would've been nice."

Keegan looks at me sheepishly. "I was afraid if I told you, you'd tell me to go home."

"You're the one who was being short with me after I mentioned I was with Brenton." I give him a knowing look.

"I know," he says, taking my hands in his and bringing them up to his lips to kiss the tops of my knuckles. "That's actually why I came over. I didn't want to wait until tomorrow. I hate what's happening between us."

"It doesn't have to be this way. I'm dating you. I'm only friends with Brenton."

"I know," he repeats.

"Do you trust me?"

He closes his eyes briefly then opens them back up. "I do trust you," he says with complete seriousness in his tone. "It's him I don't trust." He swallows roughly.

"Then you need to trust me enough to make my own judgments. I wouldn't bring someone around Zane who is bad."

Keegan nods once and drops my hands, gripping my hips. "Can I stay the night? I really fucking miss you."

Tilting my head to the side and up, I place a finger to my chin and tap dramatically, pretending like I have to think about it for a long moment. Keegan looks nervous for a good second, until my smile cracks, and he realizes I'm only joking.

"You think you're funny," he deadpans. "I'll show you funny." He picks me up and throws me over his shoulder.

"Wait!" I whisper-yell, not wanting to wake up Zane. I'm surprised he slept through my screaming earlier. "I need to take a shower."

"Sounds good to me." He turns around and heads in the direction of the bathroom instead of the bed. "I can't wait to get you all wet." He smacks my ass playfully, and I yelp.

After we're both undressed, we step into my shower. It's not big at all, and there's no way we could have sex in here or do anything like I've read in romance books, but I love being naked and close to Keegan. He washes my body, making it a point to pay extra special attention to my private areas, and in return I wash his. After I shampoo and condition my hair, we get out. I hand him a towel and we both dry off.

"Can you see if I left any clean clothes here?" he asks, wrapping the towel around his waist. "I think I left a couple things."

"You did. For sure some boxers, and I think a shirt too."

Since I never grabbed my clothes, I wrap myself up in my towel and knot it at the front so it stays in place. I walk over to my dresser to search for his clothes, while Keegan goes to my door and closes it.

I'm closing one drawer and about to open another when Keegan's arms circle around my body. Before I can protest, which let's be honest, I wasn't going to do anyway, he tugs at the knot of my towel and it drops to the ground. I turn around and feign shock, and the corner of his lip curls in amusement. When his gaze drops to my breasts, his smirk disappears and his eyes become hooded with lust.

He lifts and carries me over to the bed, playfully throwing me onto the edge. Wanting to tease him, I turn onto my hands and knees and crawl toward the head of the bed, sticking my ass up in the air. When I sneak a peek over my shoulder, his mouth falls open and his towel drops to the floor. I falter slightly when I catch a glimpse of his thick cock standing at attention.

"Stop right there," he commands, and I halt in my place. "Holy fuck," he murmurs.

I watch as he climbs onto the bed behind me. On his knees, he leans forward and runs a hand down the center of my back.

"Is there anything about you that isn't perfect?"

I don't think he's looking for an answer, so I don't reply. But my heart beats against my rib cage. I've never been called perfect before, but Keegan always says it to me. When Sierra and I were growing up, we could never do anything right in our father's eyes, so eventually we embraced it and made it a point to only do wrong. Looking back now, I know it wasn't the way to handle things. Whether we were good or bad, we wouldn't have gotten his attention. All we ended up doing was stressing out our mother, who had to deal with our father.

Keegan leans forward again, but this time he reaches under me to fondle my breasts. He massages them at the same time, then pinches both nipples. A jolt of pleasure runs straight down my spine and hits my core. My body shivers visibly, and Keegan groans.

"Are you wet, Jailbird?" He doesn't wait for me to answer before he glides one of his hands down my side and over and under my hip. He gently taps the inside of my thigh, telling me to spread my legs, and when I do, his fingers enter me just enough for him to check if I am. Spoiler: I'm soaking wet.

"God damn." He groans, pushing his fingers inside me farther. Unable to be in two places at once, he lets go of my breast. "Play with your tits, baby," he says, as he pumps his fingers in and out of me, working me into a frenzy.

With my elbows on the bed, I pluck at and pinch my nipples like he told me to do. Between his fingers and mine, my body is vibrating with pleasure, but I'm greedy and need more. "Keegan, I want you inside me," I beg, not caring how desperate I sound at the moment.

"You don't have to tell me twice," he says, pulling his fingers out of me. I glance back at him, wanting to see him enter me from behind. He strokes his shaft a few times and then edges closer. I can no longer see his dick, but I feel him part my butt cheeks and his dick glide over my ass. The tip grazes my tight ringed hole, and I clench my thighs and ass.

A moan escapes my lips at the thought of Keegan touching the forbidden territory, and he stills. "Have you ever..." He lets his question linger, knowing I know exactly what he's asking.

"No, but I read once in a magazine it can feel good."

"What the fuck kind of magazines are you reading?" He chokes out a laugh.

"Cosmo. It always has articles about sex in it."

"I've never done it either," he admits. I smile to myself that Keegan and I are comfortable with each other enough to discuss sex like this. Our connection and chemistry is like nothing I've ever felt. It was like this four years ago, and it's even better now.

"Maybe we can try it," I suggest. "I read that you're supposed to start small first and use lube so it doesn't hurt. So you probably shouldn't use your dick at first. That's the opposite of small." I waggle my eyebrows and he chuckles.

"You're good for my ego."

"You could start with your finger and then work your way up." Blush creeps up my neck and cheeks. "I mean, if you want to." Maybe it's not his thing since he's never done it before.

"Oh, I *definitely* want to," he says. "Right now?"

I laugh at how eager he sounds. "I don't have lube, but I have coconut oil in my bathroom." I read in the article you can use coconut oil, petroleum jelly, or olive oil. Now I'm glad my preferred oil is coconut. No way do I want olive oil up in my ass.

I come up on my hands, so I can go grab it, but Keegan stops me. "No, you stay right there, just like that. I'll grab it." He's gone for a good minute before he returns. "This?" he confirms.

"Yeah."

He climbs back onto the bed and spreads my cheeks again. I hear the top of the oil pop open and then warm liquid drips down the crack of my ass. "If it hurts, you have to tell me."

"Okay."

He massages the oil around the rim of my hole and then enters me slowly. At first it feels weird—foreign. But the deeper he goes, the better it feels. I can't imagine orgasming from this alone, but it doesn't hurt.

"Spread your legs," Keegan says. I obey, and then he enters me slowly from behind.

"You okay?" he asks, not yet moving.

With his dick deep inside me, and his finger pushing into my ass, I feel full. I can't imagine anything bigger entering me. "Yes, fuck me, please."

Keegan begins to move in and out of me with deep, long strokes, creating a steady rhythm between his finger and dick. With every thrust into me, I can feel his finger hitting deep within me. The two together are a heady combination that has me climaxing in minutes. My head drops onto my pillow and I moan out my release, muffling it so nobody in the house hears me.

As soon as Keegan feels me tighten around him, his thrusts become harder, more erratic. In the quiet room, all I can hear is our skin slapping against each other. He's so deep, his balls are hitting my clit, rubbing friction in a different yet delicious sort of way. For the second time, I find my release, only this time, Keegan follows right behind.

When we both come down from our orgasms, he pulls his finger and dick out at the same time, and I feel empty. Well, aside from his cum dripping out of me. *Thank God for the shot.* The last thing we need is another *oops baby.*

We both clean up then get dressed—me in my pajamas, and Keegan in his boxers that I found in my drawer. Then we get back into bed and Keegan pulls me into his arms.

"I missed this so much," he says softly, giving my temple a kiss. I want to ask him, if he misses it so much then why did he say no to us moving in together, but I don't. I'm not going to be that girl. The one who sounds desperate and needy. If he wanted to move in with me, he would. I just have to accept that I'm a few steps ahead of him and hope that eventually he'll catch up.

"I missed this too," I agree before I close my eyes and fall asleep.

CHAPTER THIRTY

Blakely

"OH, BLAKELY!" LARISSA PULLS ME INTO A WARM, MOTHERLY embrace. "I'm so excited to spend some time with my grandson. Thank you for thinking of me." Her eyes twinkle with excitement, and my heart swells at the thought of my son and me having an entire family of people who love us. Keegan and I only found our way back to each other six short weeks ago, yet it feels like we've been together for years. His family treats Zane, Sierra, and me like we're one of them. His mom even turned Keegan's childhood room into a room for Zane for when he spends the night or needs to take a nap. When she showed him the SpongeBob bedding she purchased, I thought he was going to beg to move into the room. I had to promise to buy him similar bedding to get him to come home.

It's Valentine's Day, and when Keegan asked if he could take me out, I told him I didn't have a sitter. He asked how I'd feel about his parents—more specifically his mom—watching Zane tonight, since Kolton surprised Sierra and took her out of town for the weekend. Of course, I said yes. Larissa and Paul have been so sweet and welcoming since they found out about Zane and me. Just last week when Zane wasn't feeling well—and this time it wasn't allergies—Larissa offered to watch him at my place and refused to take no for an answer. After taking two crazy hard tests, I came home to find all our laundry done and dinner baking in the oven. I might've shed a couple tears and begged her to move in with me.

She laughed, of course, thinking I was joking—and I was… kind of. But then she told me she's always here for me, anytime. It's why she loves being retired. She gets to be there for her family.

"Grammy!" Zane runs through the door with his backpack on and Bear tucked under his arm. He plows into Larissa's legs and she falls to the floor. For a second I think she really fell, but then she lifts Zane while on her back, and her laughter echoes throughout the house.

"Are we going to have fun tonight?" she asks him.

"Yes! I brought Hi Ho Cherry-o and Elefun!" he exclaims excitedly, pulling the backpack off his shoulders, unzipping it, and yanking the board games out. "Wanna play now?"

"Sure," she tells him. "How about you say bye to your mom and dad and then we'll set them up?"

"Bye, Mommy. Bye, Daddy." Zane waves then runs over to the coffee table.

"Wow." Keegan laughs. "My mom doesn't acknowledge I'm here. No hug. Nothing. And my son barely says goodbye. I'm starting to feel a little left out." He pouts, and I laugh at how adorably sexy he is.

"I'm so sorry, sweetie," Larissa says, walking over and pinching his cheeks. She pulls him into a hug. "How about I come by your place and make you dinner? I can clean up and do your laundry. I can't even imagine what a mess the place is."

I snort out a laugh, then cover my mouth because I think she's actually serious.

Keegan grins at me over her shoulder with laughter in his eyes. "That would be awesome, Mom."

This time I can't stop my laughter from bubbling out. Keegan glares, but the laughter in his eyes only shines brighter.

"Grammy!" Zane yells, and Larissa pulls away.

"Duty calls. Have a good time you two." She kisses Keegan's cheek then mine.

"Ready?" Keegan asks, grabbing my hand.

"You're such a mama's boy," I joke.

"Damn right," he agrees proudly.

"So what's on the agenda for the evening, Mr. Valentine?" I waggle my eyebrows. "No blindfold, I see. I'm kind of disappointed." I pout playfully, and Keegan pulls me into his side. The seat belt prevents me from sitting right up against him, but I'm close enough that he can throw his arm over my shoulder and kiss my temple.

A few minutes later, we arrive back at my apartment complex. I don't say anything, but I'm kind of disappointed he doesn't have anything planned. It's not that I was expecting some crazy grand gesture, but it is our first Valentine's Day together, so I guess I was hoping he would put a little more thought into it to make it memorable. Then again, I didn't plan anything either, so...

Keegan unlocks the door with the key I gave him a few weeks ago and swings the door open. And I stop in my place in shock at the sight in front of me. Candles—clearly battery operated—are all over the shelves and counters. Pink and red and white rose petals are spread across the floor leading down the hallway. There is a large bouquet of roses on the table and a bag of takeout next to it from my favorite Japanese restaurant.

"How did you do all this?" I ask in awe.

"Your sister helped me before she left." He grins. "I considered taking you out to dinner, but you've been so tired lately, working yourself to death between studying and being a mom. I thought it would be nice to have a relaxing evening at home." He gestures to the pillows surrounding the coffee table. "So I thought I would bring dinner to you." The pillows look just like the ones at the Japanese restaurant where you have to take your shoes off before sitting down on the floor.

As if he can read my mind, Keegan says, "Shoes off," as he grabs the bag of food and sets it on the coffee table. I laugh, kicking my flip-flops off and sitting down on the comfy pillows. Keegan sits next to me and pulls several boxes out. After handing me a pair of chopsticks, he stands back up and goes into the kitchen. A minute later he returns with a bottle of Sake and two small glasses.

"This all looks delicious." I give him a quick kiss on his cheek and then dig in. I assumed, since we're sitting out here where the TV is, he would put it on, but he doesn't.

"I was thinking for spring break we could take Zane to Disney," he says, taking a bite of his sushi roll.

"That would be fun. We haven't been. I was afraid he was too young before."

"We can spend the night and go to all the parks." He leans over and feeds me a bite of his noodles. I moan over how delicious they are.

"That would be a little expensive," I admit. "By the middle of the semester, my financial aid money has usually run out and I'm counting down the weeks until the next semester. Only this one is my last, and unfortunately they don't offer financial help to get your master's, which means I'll be taking out loans."

Keegan stares at me for a moment. "Your college isn't paid for?"

"Yeah, my tuition and part of housing is, but not Zane's daycare, my books, and food. Plus, Zane's clothes and such. Sierra already pays the difference in the rent the school doesn't cover, along with the household bills. I use my financial aid to pay for Zane and me, and when I can, I try to help with the bills—when Sierra lets me." I shrug. "Next semester we're going to lose all the school's help." I take a bite of my sushi.

"We'll get it all figured out," Keegan says with a small smile. "I don't want to talk about money on Valentine's Day, but the trip is happening. We'll figure everything out soon."

I'm not sure what he means by figuring everything out soon, but I agree about not wanting to talk money tonight.

"What's your favorite color?"

Keegan gives me a confused look. "Is that a thing?"

"Yes!" I laugh. "Mine are black and pink."

"Quite the opposites," he says. "How did you determine what your favorite colors are?"

"I don't know. Pink is pretty and black complements it."

"Hmm… not sure I get that logic, but okay. My favorite color is…" He looks at me for a moment. "Brown."

"Eww! Brown is the color of dirt and poop."

"It's also the color of your eyes."

"Stop!" I smack his arm playfully. "You're going to make me blush."

"You asked." He takes another bite of his food.

"What's your favorite song?" I ask next.

Keegan's brows furrow together. "What's with you and favorites? You expect me to pick one song out of thousands? And who's to say a new song won't pop up and become the one I like the most next week?"

I snort out a laugh. "You're making it hard to get to know you." I glare at him.

"Fine…" He groans. "This week my favorite song is 'Who lives in a pineapple under the sea? SpongeBob Square Pants.'" His head tilts from side to side as he sings the lyrics, and I bark out a laugh at his silliness.

"You know," he says thoughtfully, "where we should really take Zane to is Universal Studios." His eyes go wide. "Can you imagine what he would do if he came face-to-face with a life-size SpongeBob?"

"Oh my God! Yes!" I agree. "It would be the highlight of his life."

After we finish eating, Keegan and I clean up the area and wash the couple of dishes we used. When we're done, I mention I'm going to go change so we can watch a movie or something and Keegan says that sounds good.

"Do you want to change?" I ask him as we walk down the hall to my room. More and more of his clothes have accumulated over the last few weeks.

"Sure."

When I open the door, I'm faced with yet another shock. The roses that were leading down the hallway continued into my bedroom, and in side are several more candles littering the area. On the dresser is a basket of stuff wrapped in a pretty pink bow.

"What's all this?"

"It's oils and lotions and bubble bath. I want to help you relax to-night." He pulls me into him and kisses me softly. "I was thinking we could start with a bubble bath."

"You're going to take one with me?"

"That's the idea. And then when we're done, I'm going to give you a full body massage."

"That sounds really nice."

We get undressed and Keegan fills the tub with bubbles. The one nice thing about this place is that it has a separate bathtub and it's huge. Zane loves to go swimming in it.

Keegan steps in first, then helps me get in. The water is borderline hot, but feels perfect. I relax between his legs with my back against his chest. Keegan doesn't try anything sexual. We talk and laugh and he uses a loofa he purchased to wash my shoulders and arms. Even in the big tub, his legs are still bent slightly. I've never taken a bath with a man before. It's intimate, and I love the connection between us.

"I thought when we got here, tonight wouldn't be memorable because we weren't going out," I tell him, "but I was wrong. Being with you like this. Spending alone time together. Relaxing. It's exactly what I needed." I turn my face and kiss him. "Thank you."

When the bath gets cold, we get out and dry off, and then Keegan hands me a brand-new fluffy robe. I put it on and sigh at how soft and comfortable it is.

"Go lie on the bed."

A minute later, the light from my ceiling fan is turned off, leaving only the candles to create a warm glow around the room. Soft music comes from somewhere, and then the mattress dips slightly, telling me Keegan is on the bed with me.

"I'm going to take this off," he tells me. I help him by moving my arms so he can slip it off my body, leaving me completely naked. I hear the squirt of a bottle and then he's straddling my bottom half. His hands come down to my shoulders and he begins to massage my body with the oil. It smells like lavender and instantly has me relaxing into the bed. My eyes flutter closed as his fingers massage circles into my flesh, down my arms, and across my back.

When he gets to my butt, he scoots off me and massages circles into each cheek, keeping it completely professional. Too bad I have other ideas. When his hands hit my left thigh, I spread my legs, and his movements still. We've had sex a few times since we've come back from the hotel, but this is our first time alone. And there's no way I'm wasting it.

"Keep going," I murmur.

Keegan massages the back of my thigh then my calf. Slowly, I spread my legs little by little. If he notices, he doesn't say anything. When he gets to my other one, he starts at the top like he did the other. I spread my legs even farther, and I know he can see my pussy between my legs, but he pretends like he doesn't. He works his way down my leg, and then massages my feet. It feels so good, I moan softly.

"Okay, turn over."

"But you didn't finish my backside," I tell him, not moving.

"What part did I miss?" he asks.

I stifle my giggle. He knows what part. I can hear it in his raspy voice.

I wiggle my ass back and forth.

"I massaged that."

"Not all of it." I spread my legs more, and Keegan groans.

"Where did I miss?" His finger runs along the crack of my ass. "Here?" He pushes a finger into me, and I squirm in pleasure.

"Yes," I say breathily.

"How about here?" He pushes a fingers into my center. It must be a different hand or finger because the one in my ass is still there. "Did I miss here?"

"Oh, yes," I moan.

Slowly and tenderly, Keegan massages the insides of my pussy and ass, taking his time as if he's in no hurry to get to the end goal. He adds more fingers, pushing deeper, but continues to finger fuck me with languorous strokes, until I'm writhing under his touch, begging for him to make me come. And then he does, and it's as if fireworks have been lit inside of me. My pussy trembles and my body shakes, and I scream out my orgasm. Before I can come down from my high, Keegan lifts my lower body and licks up my center, landing on my clit and biting down. One orgasm rolls into two. When he finally releases me, my body feels completely relaxed.

"Flip over."

I do as he says, and when I see him, his gaze is filled with lust. His dick is bulging out through his boxer briefs. I go to sit up so I can help him relax, but he shakes his head.

"Nope, stay right where you are." He grins mischievously.

I lie back down, and he squirts more oil into his hands. He straddles my lower half again and massages my shoulders then breasts. My eyes close in pleasure when he tweaks my nipples. I've already had two orgasms. There's no way I'm going to have a third.

When I feel the bed dip slightly, my eyes open back up. He leans over me, and his mouth descends on mine, kissing me deeply. His tongue delves between my lips, and I moan at the taste of myself on him.

Too soon, he pulls away and goes back to massaging my body: my arms, the tops of my thighs and calves. When he glances down at the apex of my thighs, I wonder if he's going to take matters into his own hands this time. And once again, it's as if he can hear my thoughts.

He spreads my legs and situates himself between them. He releases his beautiful, hard dick from its confines and drops down onto my body, caging me in with his strong, muscular arms. His hands cradle the back of my head, and he devours my mouth as he enters me in one fluid motion, burying himself to the hilt inside of me. Our bodies are flush against one another in the most intimate way. Keegan makes love to me until we're both sticky and sweaty and screaming out each other's name.

"Wow," I say softly into his ear. He's still on top of and inside me.

"You're a bad influence," he jokes. "I was supposed to relax you, not fuck you."

I giggle. "Oh, trust me. Three orgasms definitely has me relaxing. I'm not even sure I have the strength to get up and get cleaned up."

"So good for my ego." He grins and kisses me hard before he pulls out and gets off me. "Stay here."

He comes back a minute later with a wet washcloth. I'm confused what he plans to do with it, until he spreads my legs. Then it hits me… I said I was too tired to get up, so he's cleaning me.

"Keegan," I say in protest. "No." I try to close my legs. It's one thing for him to be down there in the heat of the moment, but afterward… No way.

When it's clear he's not going to back down, I snatch the washcloth out of his hands and clean myself up, tossing it into the hamper in the corner of my room afterward.

Keegan shakes his head, but doesn't say anything. Instead, he lies down next to me and pulls the covers over us. He wraps me up tight in his arms and pulls me into him.

"Happy Valentine's Day, Jailbird," he murmurs. "I love you."

"Happy Valentine's Day," I say back. And then it hits me what else he said. He told me he loves me. I've never been told that before by anyone but my parents, Sierra, and Zane. I think for a moment, wanting to make sure if I say the words back I'll be telling the truth. My thoughts go to the way my heart flutters every time I'm around Keegan. How much I miss him every time he's not around. I try to imagine what my life would be like without him in it. If Zane wasn't in the equation, would I still feel this way? The answer is yes, I would. Because I have fallen completely in love with Keegan.

I snuggle my face into his firm chest. "I love you too."

CHAPTER THIRTY-ONE

Blakely

"Me, you, Sierra, and Zane at the beach." Brenton holds up a huge pack of sand toys and grins. It's President's Day, which means there's no school. Every year since we moved here, even when Zane was only a few months old and Brenton had to buy an entire pop-up tent to keep Zane in the shade, we've gone to the beach for President's Day. Brenton cooks, Sierra and I lie out, and Zane builds sand castles.

I'm not sure what Keegan is doing today. We spent the majority of the weekend together, and then around five o'clock he said he needed to go home to get some stuff done. I told him he was welcome to study here if that's what he was doing, but he said he really needed to go. He says that a lot—that he needs to get work done. I don't really understand why he's not comfortable studying here. He knows I'm in school as well, so I get it. Sometimes I wonder if maybe he just needs a break from the family life. Maybe that's why he doesn't want to move in with us. He's not ready to do the whole family thing full time. I don't question him, though, afraid I won't like the answer.

"Brenton!" Zane shouts. "Beach! Beach! Beach!" He jumps up and down.

"Go get your swim trunks on, sweetie," I tell him. He doesn't have to be told twice.

"Hey, Sierra?" I call down the hall. She comes out of her room, dressed in her pajamas and sporting a case of bedhead. She got back late last night from her mini-vacation with Kolton. "Want to go to the beach?"

"Sure." She shrugs a shoulder. "I don't have to work till later."

"Cool."

After we're all packed and ready to go, we pile into Brenton's sports car and head to the beach.

"Do you mind if Kolton comes?" Sierra asks as Brenton pulls into the parking lot.

I look over at Brenton since I'm sitting in the front seat. "Can you be on your best behavior?" I can tell he isn't keen on the idea, but he says it's fine anyway.

Which makes me think I should probably text Keegan to let him know where I'm at. I don't imagine he'll want to join us, but maybe if he does, it will give the guys a chance to put all their crap aside. After I shoot him a text, letting him know which beach we're at and that he's more than welcome to join, I get out and grab a few of the bags. Brenton grabs the cooler, and Sierra carries our chairs and umbrella. Zane carries his sand toys. We find an empty spot and set up camp.

"Are we grilling?" I ask Brenton, opening the cooler. He's always in charge of the food, but usually he gets here early to snag a barbeque.

"Nah, I bought stuff to make sandwiches to keep it easy."

"Hey, Brent!" a guy yells, walking over. He's dressed in board shorts, a T-shirt, and flip-flops. He looks familiar—probably goes to school with us—but I'm not completely sure since I usually keep to myself and don't really pay attention to anything or anyone around me.

"He's welcome to join us," I say, but Brenton shakes his head.

"I just need to give him something he left in my car the other night. I'll be right back."

A few minutes later, he returns and helps me finish getting every-thing laid out and situated, including digging a hole for the umbrella and setting up our chairs.

Shortly after, Kolton shows up and joins us. When I ask if he's seen Keegan, he says he hasn't. I send him another text, asking if everything is okay. But after ten minutes, when he still hasn't replied, I throw my phone into my bag and join Zane to build some castles.

The day flies by. It's the perfect beach weather. The water is a little chilly, but none of us really go in aside from dipping our feet in it.

For the most part, Kolton and Brenton get along. They don't say much to each other, but they at least aren't hostile to one another, so I consider that a win. I check my phone a few times, but I don't hear back from Keegan.

Late in the afternoon, when Zane and I are digging a mote for his castle, a pair of hands land on my shoulders, making me jump.

"Daddy!" Zane yells, dropping his shovel and running over to his father.

"Hey, bud." Keegan lifts him to give him a hug. He dressed in a pair of jeans and a shirt and has tennis shoes on.

"Hey," he says to me. I stand, and he pulls me into him for a quick kiss.

"Daddy, you build the river with me?" Zane asks.

"I wish, bud. I have work I have to do, but I wanted to stop by and see how your day is going."

Zane frowns, but accepts Keegan's answer.

"You're behind on your schoolwork?" I've never even seen the guy study. Maybe that's why he took time off in the first place.

"Nothing I can't handle." He wraps his arm around me. "Having fun?"

"Yeah."

"Daddy, look at my big, giant castle!" Zane points to the piles of sand.

"Those look awesome. Does SpongeBob live in one?"

"No, Daddy." Zane giggles. "He lives in a pineapple." Then his eyes widen and he runs up the beach over to Brenton. Keegan and I watch as he says something to Brenton, and Brenton laughs with a nod. He opens the cooler and hands Zane the pineapple he hasn't cut up yet.

"Look!" Zane thrusts the pineapple toward us. "Brenton said I can use it to make SpongeBob's house."

"That's great," Keegan tells him, but his jaw ticks, and I know why he wasn't here today. He still doesn't want to be around Brenton.

Zane drops to his knees and starts digging a hole to set his pineapple in.

"I better get going," Keegan says.

"Are you coming by later?"

"Depends on how much I get done. I'll text or call you." He encircles his arms around my body and kisses me hard. I go to pull back, but he doesn't release me. When Sierra whistles, I realize Keegan is putting on a show, staking his claim in front of Brenton.

"Not cool," I murmur against his lips.

"What?" he asks innocently. "I can't kiss the woman I love?"

"You and I both know what you just did." I raise a knowing brow. He doesn't confirm or deny it. He just grins so wide, his dimples pop out.

"Text you later, Jailbird." He kisses my cheek then calls Zane's name. "Have fun, bud!" And then he's running back up the beach.

We hang out a couple more hours, until an afternoon shower makes its appearance. Then we quickly pack up and head home. Sierra goes with Kolton, even though he's just dropping her off at our place so she can get ready for work. Zane conks out on our way home, and Brenton offers to carry him up for me.

"I had a good day," Brenton says when he comes out of Zane's room.

"I did too."

"Did you see the text from Brianne?"

"No." I pull my phone out of my purse and see a missed text. "They want to meet tomorrow night to finalize everything. Sierra has off, so that should be fine."

"I have my interview tomorrow at the high school, but it's at noon, so it will be done well before our meeting."

"Oh! That reminds me. I have mine as well."

For our Child Psychology class, we have to interview a guidance counselor. We're supposed to pick the age group we're planning to work with, so Brenton is doing high school and I'm doing elementary.

"Cool. I'll see you tomorrow."

I check my phone again to see if Keegan has texted that he's coming by, but he hasn't. I shower and throw in a load of laundry. Still no text. Sierra comes out dressed for work, and I make us each a Cobb salad. After she leaves, I check my phone, but there's still no text from Keegan.

A little while later, Zane wakes up and I give him a bath. We spend the evening playing Legos and watching his new show obsession: Peppa Pig. When it's time for bed, I read him a story and tuck him in. He asks where Keegan is and if he can call him. I let him, but Keegan doesn't answer, and I try to ignore the warning bells ringing loudly in my ear.

I lie on the couch, select a rerun of *Gossip Girl*, and fall asleep with my phone in my hand. Spoiler: Keegan never texts or calls.

CHAPTER THIRTY-TWO

Blakely

"THE NEXT BUS DOESN'T COME UNTIL ONE THIRTY. AND THEN I'LL still have to walk two miles to the school." I close my laptop and sigh in annoyance, taking a sip of the delicious vanilla iced coffee Sierra made for us. We're sitting outside on our balcony, enjoying the warm weather. She has off today, so she's relaxing in her pajamas.

"I should've thought about this ahead of time when I scheduled the meeting with Cocoa Elementary. I was hoping to get a meeting with Carterville, since it's walking distance, but before I could call to schedule, several other students did, and by the time I called, they were full, so I had to choose another school. The next closest elementary school is Cocoa, and I was able to get an appointment for two."

I didn't consider the fact that Sierra and I don't have a vehicle. Something we've never needed since everything is accessible by bus or is walking distance.

"Call Brenton," Sierra says, taking a sip of her own drink.

"He's doing his interview at the high school." I take another sip of my refreshing drink.

"So? You know he'll still take you over there. Or call Keegan."

"He hasn't called or texted since he came by the beach yesterday. I don't want to bug him. He said he has work to do."

"That's part of being someone's boyfriend," Sierra points out. She's right, but Keegan's been acting weird. It's like he suddenly has all this work to do that he never had before. My initial thought is that maybe his schoolwork caught up to him and now he's playing catch-up. But another thought is that something else is going on. And if that's the case, what is it, and why isn't he being honest with me?

I grab my phone and debate who to call. Deciding I'm a chicken, I hit Brenton's name. It rings several times and then goes to voicemail. I don't bother leaving him a message. Instead, I end the call and hit Keegan's name.

He answers on the third ring. "Hey, Jailbird, everything okay?" His tone is sweet, but there's something hidden in his tone… annoyance? Aggravation?

"Yeah, I have to go do an interview for my Child Psychology class this afternoon. I was wondering if there's any way you can give me a ride."

"Shit, I wish I could, but I'm at… I have a lot of work to do. I'm sorry. Umm… you can call my mom. I'm sure she wouldn't mind." She probably wouldn't, but I don't want to make her do that. She's not responsible for me. It's one thing to ask her to watch Zane. It's another to ask her to play taxi.

"That's okay. I'll just take the bus. No worries." I hang up, annoyed that it feels like Keegan is either avoiding me or lying to me. And as much as I really want to ask him, I don't have time to argue with him right now.

Just as I'm accepting I'll have to take the bus and be a little late, my phone rings. It's Brenton.

"Hey, you called?"

"Yeah, are you by any chance done with your interview?"

"Yeah, I'm at home. What's up?"

"I was wondering if you could give me a ride to Cocoa Elementary. My interview is at two, and I didn't realize the bus stops two miles away. I'll never make it in time."

"What about your boyfriend?"

Ignoring his question, I add, "We also have our group project meeting we have to go to tonight, so I want to make sure I'm not late."

Brenton laughs. "That's not until way later. You didn't answer my question. Where's Keegan?" When I sigh into the phone, he adds, "What? He's already over the whole family thing?"

"Never mind." I can't deal with these boys and their shit today.

"I'm just playing," he says. "Yes, I can take you. I was just about to leave anyway."

We hang up, and I get ready to go. Wanting to look professional, I borrow one of Sierra's longer khaki skirts and pair it with a loose pink top and white and tan heeled sandals.

After giving Zane, who's still napping, a kiss, I say bye to Sierra and let her know I'll either be home in a few hours or later tonight if my interview runs long and we have to go straight to our group meeting.

I meet Brenton downstairs and then we take off in his car.

I few minutes into our drive, his phone rings, and he answers it.

"Yeah?"

I'm not sure who's on the other line, but whoever it is sounds angry. I can't understand what he's saying, but I can hear him yelling.

"All right. I'll be right there."

Brenton hangs up and looks over at me with a frown. "I need to make a stop real quick. I'm sorry."

"No worries." I shrug. Thanks to Brenton giving me a ride, I'll be at the school with plenty of time to spare.

I assumed we were stopping by his brother's shop, so when we pull up in front of an older one-story home, I'm confused. "Whose house is this?"

"Um, my mom's ex-boyfriend. I just need to get something from him. I'll be out in a few minutes."

Brenton leaves the car running, and I use the time to go over the questions I've typed up for my interview so it will run smoothly.

When I glance at the time, I realize I've been waiting for a good twenty minutes, and I need to go pee. I should've gone before we left. That iced coffee was yummy, but it went right through me.

I wait another ten minutes, but when Brenton still doesn't come out, I turn his car off and walk up the sidewalk. If I don't use the restroom soon, I'm going to pee myself.

I knock and Brenton opens the door. "I'll be right out. I'm sorry."

"I need to go pee." I squeeze my thighs together and grimace.

"All right." He opens the door and lets me in. It takes a second for my eyes to adjust since there's almost no light in the place—even the blinds are all closed. The house is rather empty, save for one couch and a coffee table. It's an open floorplan, and I can see most of the house. His mom's ex-boyfriend must be in his room because I don't see him anywhere.

"Use this bathroom," Brenton tells me. He opens the door, and it's a tiny half bathroom. "I'm just going to say bye to him and then we'll go when you get out." For some reason Brenton appears to be nervous, which has me feeling nervous. I glance around the house again and notice the walls are completely bare. Not a single photo or wall-hanging in sight.

"Okay." I give him a tight smile.

When I've finished using the bathroom—I never would've made it to the school—and washing my hands, I step out and find Brenton waiting for me.

"Let's go." He opens the door, and his hand finds my lower back, as if he's trying to get me out the door even faster. The bright sun momentarily blinds me, and I squint my eyes, trying to adjust to the brightness, but before they do, I hear, "Carterville Police Department. Put your hands where I can see them."

I screech in shock as several uniformed officers rush into the house—all of them dressed in bulletproof vests and head gear that read: POLICE.

"Hands where we can see them," one officer demands. There are four officers who don't go inside and they have their guns drawn on Brenton and me. I raise my hands, not wanting to give them a reason to shoot me.

One officer approaches Brenton and turns him against the sidewall of the house, while another one asks me to do the same. I cooperate, turning with my back to the street and my face to the wall. I follow Brenton's moves and raise my hands up, placing my shaky palms on the wall. I have no idea what is happening right now.

The officer next to Brenton searches him and pulls out several bags of… oh God, please no. Please don't let that be drugs. My eyes meet Brenton's and he gives me a look that conveys how sorry he is.

"Ma'am, do you have any weapons or drugs on you?"

"No." I shake my head. "I… I didn't know." I don't even know what to say.

"I'm going to search you now. Okay?" the officer asks.

I nod my okay.

His hands pat down the sides of me. Because I'm wearing a skirt, there's not really anywhere for me to store anything.

"Thank you," he says. "You can turn around now."

I do as he says, glancing over at Brenton, who is now in handcuffs and is being read his rights.

I hear a shuffle to the right of me, and when I look over, I see the officers who went into the house are walking out with an older Hispanic man. He must be Brenton's mom's ex-boyfriend.

"He's confirmed his name is Miguel Sanchez," the officer says, dragging the guy down the sidewalk.

"Ma'am, at this time, we're going to need you to come down to the station. Will you come willingly?"

I hear what he's saying, but my eyes are stuck on the man who is opening the door to a police vehicle while another officer pushes the hand-cuffed guy inside.

"Ma'am," the officer pushes, but I'm in shock, frozen in place, as I stare at the man who has worked his way into my heart. The same man I share a child with. He's dressed in a shirt and jeans, but he's wearing a bulletproof vest like everyone else. And then, in the sunlight, a piece of metal hanging on his hip gleams. A badge.

"Keegan," I say breathlessly. "Keegan!" My voice rises.

"Oh, fuck," I faintly hear Brenton say.

Keegan's eyes lock with mine, and he walks over to me, not looking at all surprised to see me. "What are you doing here?" I ask. "What's going on?" My eyes flicker to the gold badge. "Are you... a cop?"

"Motherfucker!" Brenton roars.

Keegan's eyes leave mine, and his lips curl into a vicious smirk. "Get him in the car," he says to the officer who is holding on to Brenton. When he steps forward, I find myself stepping back, and his eyes narrow, not in anger, but in confusion.

"Answer me," I demand. "Are you a cop?"

"Yes," he admits. "I'm a cop, and your *friend* here is under arrest for drug possession with the intent to sell."

CHAPTER THIRTY-THREE

Keegan

One Hour Ago

"I CAN'T KEEP THIS SHIT UP." I SLAM THE DOOR TO MY DAD'S OFFICE closed behind me and fall into the seat on the other side of his desk. "The guilt is fucking with me, and with us getting close to wrapping this all up, I'm having to find more ways to get around the truth."

Dad sets his cell phone down on his desk and leans back in his chair, his arms crossing over his chest. "You need to have patience, son. When it's all over, you'll be able to tell her everything and she'll forgive you."

"Or not," I argue. "She needed a ride today and I had to tell her I couldn't give her one."

"Which you would have had to do even if she knew the truth. You're working."

"No, because if she knew the truth, she and my son would be living in my house with me, and I would've already bought her a fucking car. But I can't do that because she thinks I'm a goddamn broke college student."

I sit forward, with my elbows on my knees, and bury my face in my hands. "Fuck!" I yell. It's muffled, but still helps to alleviate some of the pent-up anger I'm feeling.

When I glance up, Dad is frowning. He hates this almost as much as I do. "We're getting closer. Just stick to the plan, and we're going to snag him, along with whoever he's working for. I take it you saw the last photos caught on surveillance?"

"Yeah, it's why I'm here." I pull my phone out of my pocket and swipe through the photos that were just sent to me by Scott Cronin, my partner. "It's enough to warrant a search of that shop."

"There's no way he's distributing from there," Dad argues. "We need to watch. If we get a warrant now, sure, we'll find some drugs, but then we have to bank on him giving up his connection." My dad gives me a knowing look and continues. "We can pull Brenton over for suspicion, but if he doesn't have anything on him at the time, it's going to raise alarm. And even if he is carrying, again, it's not guaranteed he'll give up the connection. Since you've been following him, we've found out he's making deliveries to some of the wealthiest, most influential men in the city. There's no way Brenton and his brother are running this operation on their own. We have to be patient. What do we know?"

Damn it, I know he's right. I need to calm my ass down, but it's hard when I feel like every time I talk around the truth to Blakely, I'm slowly losing her.

"We've gone over everything." I sigh in frustration. "Maxwell Travers a.k.a. 'Brenton's brother' who isn't really his brother owns the shop. We know they can't be brothers because they're both only children and neither of their moms remarried. Maxwell has no dad on his birth certificate, and Brenton's is an alcoholic living in New York."

Throwing myself back in the seat, I scrub my face with my hands, trying to piece together the last of this fucking puzzle. We're so close. All we need is that final piece for it to all click together and show us the entire picture.

My phone rings, and I grab it. It's Cronin. "Reynolds."

"Maxwell stopped at a new location."

I sit up straight and pull my dad's laptop over to me, ready to type the address into the database. "Go ahead." Corbin relays the address, and the information on the house comes up. "I'll call you back in a minute."

"It says the home is owned by Patricia Sterling." I pull up her information. "She has one daughter, who died five years ago. Paula Sterling." I click on the police file and read what it says out loud. "She was found in the woods just off I-95. Cause of death: internal injuries caused from being beaten. She had drugs in her system, but not enough to kill her. Her boyfriend…" My eyes flit back and forth between the screen and my dad. This can't be right. Fuck! This is too much of a coincidence.

"Her boyfriend, what?" Dad asks.

"Her boyfriend was brought in for questioning but never considered a suspect."

"Okay…" Dad gives me a confused look, but that's only because he doesn't know what her boyfriend's name is.

"His name is Miguel Sanchez."

Dad stands, his chair knocking over backward in the process. "Are you fucking sure?"

"It has his license right here." I turn the laptop so he can see it for himself. "It's him, Dad. It's the asshole who killed my brother."

It takes my dad a minute to compose himself, but once he does, he flips right into police mode. There's a reason he's been Carterville's Police Chief for the last twenty years. He knows how to compartmentalize. "We need to find out if Patricia is living there. My guess is she's renting out her home to her deceased daughter's grieving boyfriend."

I run a search on Patricia, and sure enough, it shows her homestead property is in Daytona. "Why wasn't she questioned when you were looking for Miguel?"

"Because he was never arrested," Dad says with a shake of his head. "It didn't come up. It's only coming up now because you did a direct search of the address. He was only brought in for questioning in hope of finding out some information to help move the case along. We were at a dead end."

Dad scrubs his hands down his face in frustration. "We questioned Miguel's family and not a damn person mentioned the name Paula. I would've followed up."

A text comes through from Scott. "Maxwell left the residence."

"Damn it! They have to be connected. My guess is Miguel is hiding out in that damn house! He's probably been there for years."

"Did Miguel's family mention Maxwell or Brenton?"

"No, whatever connection he has with them was kept under lock." Dad picks up his office phone.

"Who're you calling?"

"Judge Pruett, to give us a warrant. Between Maxwell going there, and Patricia owning the home and being connected to Miguel, it just might be enough to get a warrant."

The phone rings, and I inhale a deep breath. We're so close. This might be over soon. And then, not only will the man who killed my brother be finally brought to justice, but I'll be able to tell Blakely everything.

"Kevin," Dad says, addressing the judge by his first name. "How are you?"

"I'm good, Paul," he says over the speakerphone. "Was just thinking about you, actually. The wife wants to have you guys over for dinner soon."

"Sounds good. I'll let Larissa know."

"So, to what do I owe this pleasure? Business, I'm assuming."

"I think we've found him, Kevin," Dad says, not having to explain any further. The two of them go way back. They've been friends since high school. Kevin and his wife are our godparents. He knows how much it's killed my dad to not be able to lock up Miguel behind bars.

Dad gives Kevin the details of our findings and how we think Miguel might be hiding away in the house we've come across and how he's possibly linked to Brenton and Maxwell. When he's done, he says, "What do you think?"

"I think if you're right, we're going to nail this bastard. I'll sign for both warrants. Keep me updated."

"You got it."

Dad hangs up and then radios a couple officers to head to the cell phone shop. He's hoping if Maxwell goes to the shop, we can nab him at the same time. That way we don't run the risk of him being tipped off.

Twenty minutes later, just as the warrants are coming through, Scott calls. "You are never going to believe who just pulled up and went inside the same house."

I bet I only need one guess, though. But that's only because I have all the motherfucking pieces now; whereas, Scott hasn't been brought up to speed.

"Brenton fucking Davis," I seethe, as I jump from my seat, my dad following right behind me.

"Ding ding ding."

"Stay there. We're on our way." I click end on our call and jump into my dad's truck, since it's an official police vehicle. If everything goes right, we'll be arresting all three of these motherfuckers.

"This is Chief Reynolds," Dad says into his radio, "requesting backup." He spits off the address then gets the men up to speed. "We have reason to believe a man by the name of Miguel Sanchez is hiding out in the residence. He is a known drug dealer and there's a warrant out for his arrest for shooting and killing a police officer. He is to be considered highly armed and dangerous."

Just as Dad turns onto the street, Scott calls me again. "We're almost there," I tell him.

"A brown-haired female just went into the house," he says, and my heart sinks into my chest. Fuck! "I didn't see her in the car," he adds. I want to rip him a new one, but I can hear it in his voice he already knows he's fucked up. "She didn't go in with him initially. She just knocked and he let her in less than a minute ago."

I pull up my GPS tracker for Blakely and sure enough, she's right where we're pulling up. "She said she was going to some school for an interview," I tell my dad. "When I told her I couldn't take her, she must've called him." I slam my fist into the dashboard. "Fuck. I told her to call Mom. Not him."

"Calm down, son."

"I need to get her out of there."

"No, we need to wait out here," he says.

I whip my head around to glare at him. "Like fucking hell."

"It's a conflict of interest if either of us goes in there, and we need everything to be done by the books."

Damn it! I know he's right. And then it hits me…

"Is she being arrested?"

"No. As long as she doesn't have any drugs on her. But if we find who and what we're hoping to find in there, she'll have to be brought in for questioning." He picks up his radio. "The female inside is Blakely Jacobs—Keegan's girlfriend and the mother of his son. We're going to remain outside. You're going to surround the house and knock. If you think she's in danger, you go in. Her protection comes first. Treat her with respect, boys. She needs to be brought in for questioning, but as long as she doesn't have any drugs or weapons on her, she is not to be arrested."

The guys come over the radio to let him know they understand. We pull up and park along the side of the road and watch as the team surrounds the house.

And then the door opens.

Blakely and Brenton walk outside. Brenton's shocked as shit and Blakely's scared and confused. I want to run to her and hug her. Tell her it's okay. But I can't. I watch as Duncan, one of the officers, tells her to cooperate and then searches her.

My eyes flit over to Brenton, who is being handcuffed while another officer handles the drugs they've found on him. And then over to the door where several of our other officers, who went into the house, are now walking out with none other than Miguel fucking Sanchez. *Got you, asshole…*

"It's him," Dad says as Officer Nunez announces, "He's confirmed his name is Miguel Sanchez," while dragging the piece of shit down the sidewalk and over to his vehicle.

Dad's radio goes off. "Maxwell Travers has been taken into custody. Positive for drug possession."

"Fuck yes," I murmur.

Dad nods in agreement. We got all three.

I open the car door so they can put Miguel inside. As I'm closing it, I feel someone watching me—Blakely.

My eyes find her staring right at me. The officer is explaining to her that he needs to bring her in for questioning, only she isn't responding because her eyes are locked on me. He continues to try to get her attention, calling out, "Ma'am," but she doesn't move an inch.

Her eyes drag down my body, and I hold my breath, knowing what she's about to see: my badge.

Her eyes widen, and she screams out my name, getting Brenton's attention.

He curses, realizing who—or I should say *what*—I am. Only he's not shocked like Blakely is. He's pissed.

"What are you doing here?" Blakely asks. "What's going on? Are you… a cop?"

"Motherfucker!" Brenton yells, fuming that he's been had, which makes me deliriously happy.

I shoot him a *you're fucked* look and tell the officer to get him in the car. Then I take a step toward Blakely, who takes a step back. Officer Duncan, who's walking with her, grips her shoulder, mistaking her stepping back for running.

She ignores him, though, completely focused on me.

"Answer me," she says, her voice full of hate and hurt. "Are you a cop?"

"Yes," I tell her, "I'm a cop, and your *friend* here is under arrest for drug possession with the intent to sell." I take another step forward, needing to touch her, to hold her, to tell her everything. But she glares and takes another step back.

"Keegan," my dad says, "we need to get to the station. Now is not the time." He's right. I know he is. But fuck, I don't like having to let her go. Especially when she's looking at me with a mixture of hurt, confusion, and deception.

CHAPTER THIRTY-FOUR

Blakely

"To the station?" Everything hits me at once.

Brenton has been arrested for drug possession.

Another guy has been arrested.

I was inside the house.

I was searched for drugs and weapons.

Oh my God.

"Keegan." My eyes fill with hot liquid, forgetting how mad and hurt I am at him. "Am I in trouble?" My first thought is Zane. My entire world. Are they going to take my son away from me? Put him in foster care, like they did to Sierra and me?

My second thought is my future—*our* future. I'm supposed to graduate in a few months with my degree. I can't work in the school system if I've been arrested. It was different when I was a minor and made stupid choices. Thankfully, when I turned eighteen, the arrests were wiped off my record and I was given a clean slate. But that won't happen if I'm arrested as an adult. The school system will run a background check, and as soon as they see I've been arrested, they won't give me the time of day.

All these years of schooling will be for nothing. I won't be able to support Zane and myself.

"No." Keegan shakes his head, stepping toward me. This time I let him. Because I need him more than I hate him.

"Are they going to take Zane from me? I swear…" A huge lump fills my throat, and I have to swallow hard to make it go down so I can talk again. "I didn't know."

"Blakely, it's okay," Keegan says softly. "Nobody is going to take Zane from you. I promise."

I want to believe him, but I don't think I can trust him. He lied to me. He never once mentioned he was a cop. Who knows what else he's lied about.

"I don't believe you." I wipe the tears out of my eyes so my vision is no longer blurry.

My eyes bounce over to Keegan's dad, who's also wearing a badge. He gives me a sad smile and says, "Blakely, I know right now you're confused, but I can assure you that you are not in any trouble. Officer Duncan is going to bring you to the station for some questioning and once we have everything we need, you'll be free to go home to your son."

"You lied to me too," I tell him, realizing I've been lied to by everybody in Keegan's family: his mom, his dad, Keegan, and Kolton. Does Sierra know? Did Kolton tell her and she's been lying to me too? I finally thought I had a family, only to learn they've all been keeping secrets from me.

Just like my father…

Paul's face falls, but he doesn't argue. "Go ahead and take her in," he tells Officer Duncan. "We'll meet you there."

Officer Duncan gently helps me into the back seat of his police car. He tells me it's protocol and if he could let me ride in the front, he would. I just nod my understanding. The short ride to the station has me thinking about everything that has happened. Every time Keegan told me he had work to do. When he wouldn't come over. The way he acted regarding Brenton. He knew I was hanging out with a drug dealer. Oh my God! I let Brenton take my son to Home Depot! With every thought, I work myself up until I'm fuming with anger—at myself, at Brenton, and at Keegan.

My father's lies led to the destruction of our already broken family. They led to the death of him and my mother, leaving Sierra and me as orphans. And had they not died, we would've been in danger by the bad men my father was doing business with.

Lies are flimsy. The truth is strong. You can't build anything solid using lies. And that's exactly what Keegan did. He built our entire relationship on lies, and now the safe haven I found in him is falling down around us.

By the time we arrive at the station and I'm brought into an interrogation room, I'm crying so hard—out of fear and anger—I'm hiccupping and nearly hyperventilating. Officer Duncan had taken my phone away when he searched me, so I have no way of calling or texting my sister. I'm left alone in the tiny room that totally looks how they're all portrayed in the television shows: rectangle metal table, cheap metal chairs, and a honey-yellow light hanging above. The only thing missing is the one-way mirror. There's a window, but the blinds are closed. The other three walls are all bare.

Keegan's dad steps into the room with two officers I recognize from earlier. "Blakely, this is Scott Cronin. He's Keegan's partner on this case. He's going to ask you some questions and once you're done, you'll be free to go."

I take several deep breaths to calm myself enough to speak. "Where's Keegan?"

"Because it's a conflict of interest, neither of us can be in here with you," Paul says. "Officer Duncan will remain in here while Officer Cronin questions you."

"Am I going to be arrested?"

He's already said I'm not going to be, but I have to ask again just in case he only said that to get me down here.

"No, you won't be arrested…" he begins, but the officer next to him gives him a look that makes me nervous.

"What? Tell me. Please, I need to know. I can't handle any more lies."

This time Officer Cronin speaks. "Our intent is not to arrest you, but I'm going to be honest with you, and it's not to scare you. If we find that you've been involved in any of this, we might not have a choice."

"Which we don't believe you were," Paul adds.

Oh my God! If I've been involved? "Do I need a lawyer?" Not that I can afford one, but based on them arresting Brenton and that other guy, I imagine whatever they've done is pretty big, and I am—was—best friends with Brenton. What if they feel I was too close? Or what if Brenton somehow sets me up to take the fall? I've seen enough of those cop shows to know crazy shit happens.

"If it would make you feel more comfortable, you are definitely allowed to have one."

A fresh set of tears bursts from my lids and falls down my cheeks. "I can't afford one." I look between Paul and Officer Cronin. Officer Duncan is still standing to the side. "I don't know what to do."

"We'll be right back," Paul says.

When they all leave the room, I cross my arms on the table and put my head down, closing my eyes. My head is pounding from all the stress and crying. I concentrate on slowing down my breathing. I've come close to hyperventilating a few times now, and I don't want that to happen.

A little while later, a gentleman in a black three-piece suit walks through the door and approaches me. "My name is Darryl Berkowitz. Are you Blakely Jacobs?"

"I am."

"It's nice to meet you. I hear you're in need of an attorney." He extends his hand to shake mine, but I don't take it.

"As I told Paul, I can't afford one." I can't imagine what this guy costs an hour. Just the watch that shines on his wrist must cost more than our rent for a year.

"I'm friends with Paul and Larissa. You aren't paying anything."

His hand is still extended, so I take it and shake it. "Thank you." Any other circumstance and I wouldn't take his handout, but if it means I get home to my son and don't get arrested, I'm willing to push my pride aside and take what he's offering.

Mr. Berkowitz sits down and we go over everything that happened. He has me walk him through my friendship with Brenton and tell him anything I know about him and his family. When he feels he's caught up, he steps out to let them know we're ready.

Officer Cronin and Officer Duncan come back in with Mr. Berkowitz and begin to question me. I tell them everything I know, which isn't much. I feel so stupid that I had no idea Brenton has been selling drugs right under my nose. I learn that the deliveries he's been making with me in the car weren't cell phone related.

"Have you ever met Miguel Sanchez before?" Officer Cronin asks.

"No, but Brenton told me he's his mom's ex-boyfriend."

He nods. Since they're recording the conversation, he doesn't have to write anything down.

"I think that's all for now," Officer Duncan says. "If we think of anything else, we'll call you." Both officers stand, and when Mr. Berkowitz does as well, I stand with them.

"If any questions arise, you are to contact me directly," Mr. Berkowitz says, shaking each of their hands, and then handing Officer Duncan a business card.

"Will do."

When both officers leave, Mr. Berkowitz tells me I did well and gives me his card. Then he offers to give me a ride home. While I appreciate his offer, at the end of the day, I don't really know him and would rather take the bus. He tries to argue, but gives up when he sees I'm not going to budge.

When we walk down the hall toward the front desk, so I can get my cell phone back, I hear Keegan's voice. I want to find where it's coming from, but my broken heart stops me from looking.

After getting my phone and telling Mr. Berkowitz again that I'm okay taking the bus, I pull up my maps app to find where the closest bus stop is. I consider calling Sierra, but figure it will be better to speak to her in person. I don't know what I'll do if I find out she's been lying to me as well.

There's a stop five blocks south, so I start to head in that direction when I hear my name being called. I will myself not to look back, knowing full well it's Keegan's voice, but he quickly catches up and stops in front of me, forcing me to stop as well.

"We need to talk," he pleads. "Please."

"Our time for talking has passed." I take in a deep breath so I don't lose it again.

"No." He shakes his head. "I need you to let me explain."

"Explain how you and your entire family has been lying to me since we got back in touch? How I thought I was gaining a family, one I never really had growing up because my father was a piece of shit liar, only to learn I'm a damn fool?" My voice cracks on the last word, and I have to close my eyes so I don't cry.

"You're not a fool, Blakely," Keegan says. "And you do have a family.

None of us wanted to keep it from you, I swear. If there were any other way…"

"There's always another way," I argue. "This entire time I thought we were creating a life together, but I was nothing more than part of your investigation."

"That's not true. I know you're upset right now, but you have to know how much you mean to me. I never imagined you'd get caught up in all of this. And once I found out Brenton was selling, I tried to get off the case."

"When did you find out he was selling?"

"The night you went with him to that party."

I think back to that night. I thought it was just a coincidence that Keegan showed up to the same party I was at. "How did you know I was there?"

Keegan's eyes go wide and then he lets out a loud sigh. "I set up the tracker on your phone."

Oh my God! "You bugged my phone?" I screech.

"No, every iPhone has a tracking app. I just turned yours on and followed you. I couldn't see anything else on your phone besides your location. I swear."

Jesus, this is all too much. "I need to go home." I try to walk around Keegan, but he blocks my way, and that pisses me off. "Move."

"Jailbird," he begins, but I cut him off.

"Don't. Don't call me that name. Don't call me anything!" Hot tears hit my eyelids, but I quickly blink them away. "I'm going home. I have nothing to say to you."

"We have a son together," he points out.

"I'm well aware!" I'm now swiping at my eyes, trying to stop the tears from falling. Everything was so perfect and now it's all messed up.

"I know you're mad right now, and you have every right to be. But I meant what I said before. No matter what happens, we're family."

"No." I shake my head. "We're not family. Family doesn't lie to each other, keep important things from each other! You let Brenton take our son by himself when you knew he was selling drugs!" I step toward Keegan and jab my finger into his chest. "We're not family. And right now, I really wish Zane weren't your son."

Keegan's eyes go wide—in hurt, in fear, in disbelief—but I ignore the look. I'm too hurt, too upset, too pissed to care right now.

"Are you going to keep him from me?" he asks, his voice wavering. My heart cracks at the thought of Zane not getting to see Keegan. As mad as I am, I would never keep him from his father.

When I don't answer right away, Keegan says, "Blakely, are you going to let me see him?"

"I would never keep him from you," I tell him honestly. His shoulders sag in relief. "But you and me… we're done. Once I've calmed down, I'll let you know when you can see him."

Keegan doesn't argue. "Can I give you a ride home, please?"

"I'm taking the bus."

"Jail—Blakely, please, let me take you home. I won't say a word, I promise." Suddenly exhausted and wanting to get home to my son and sister, I nod once and follow him to his truck. Keegan does as he said and doesn't speak the entire drive. When he pulls up to my apartment complex, I glance at Brenton's apartment and find crime scene tape across his door with a single officer standing in front of it like he's guarding the place.

"They have to investigate his apartment," Keegan says, answering my unspoken thoughts. "We only have two CSI teams since it's a smaller town. They're at the shop and the house right now."

"Will he get out on bail?"

"Most likely. If he can afford the bond."

I nod once, trying to mask my sudden nervousness. Will Brenton show up at my apartment? Will he be mad at me for telling the truth? I don't care if he's mad, but I'm scared of what he might do. Thoughts of when Sierra and I were younger surface. Of my mom crying and saying we were in danger. Because of our father. Because of his lies.

"I won't let anything happen to you guys," Keegan says.

I look at him, shocked that he's able to know what I'm thinking without out me even speaking.

"What if he comes here?"

"I'm going to have someone on you at all times, but if it'll make you feel safer, you guys can come stay at my place. It's gated and Brenton's never been there."

Gated? His place is with Kolton down the street.

"I don't really live with Kolton," he says. Damn him! Must he know everything I'm thinking? "I own a house. I was staying with Kolton to go with my cover as a college student."

"Great. Another thing you lied about." I swing the truck door open.

"If it will make you feel safer, you guys can stay there," he repeats.

"With you?"

Keegan flinches at the hostile tone in my voice. "No, I'll continue to stay with Kolton."

I step out of the truck. "I'm good."

"Okay, but if you're not… the offer stands."

I nod and then close the door. And without looking back, I run up the stairs to my apartment, only stopping once I'm inside and Zane is in my arms.

"How did the interview go?" Sierra asks.

"It didn't. We need to talk."

CHAPTER THIRTY-FIVE

Blakely

IT'S BEEN TWO DAYS SINCE I FOUND OUT KEEGAN IS A POLICE OFFICER.
When I asked Sierra if she knew, I could tell immediately she had no idea
either. After I got her caught up to speed on everything, she excused
herself to her room. I heard her yelling over the phone for a few minutes
and then she came out, red-eyed and red-faced. She hugged me and told me
she loves me and then she went to work—even though she was scheduled
to be off. Ever since then, she's been at work every waking moment—I'm
assuming to distract herself from the pain. I know she cares a lot about
Kolton, but right now she's almost as hurt as I am.

I went to class yesterday and today and thankfully Brenton wasn't there.
Luckily, our presentation is already done and if I have to, I'll present both
of our parts. I'd rather do that than have to face my ex-drug-dealing-best
friend. While I'm hurt by Keegan hiding who he is from me, I'm enraged
at Brenton for putting my son and me in harm's way. I don't know all the
details, but from what I gathered at the station, his mom's ex-boyfriend
murdered a police officer. And Brenton's been slinging drugs for him. And
brought me to his house. I can't count the number of times Zane has been

in the vehicle with Brenton when he had to "make a delivery." Stupid me for not asking if the deliveries were goddamn drugs.

"I wanna watch SpongeBob," Zane says, sitting on the couch next to me.

"Please," I prompt, already clicking on the remote to select one of the shows I have recorded.

"Pleeeeaaaasssseeeee," Zane says. He smiles at me and his dimples pop out, reminding me of Keegan.

There's a knock on the door, and my stomach flip-flops. It can't be Sierra because she'd just come in. That leaves Brenton or Keegan. Neither one is welcome here at the moment.

I check the peep-hole and see it's a woman. Larissa. Keegan's mom. I take a deep breath and open the door. She smiles warmly, but it's not as bright as her smiles usually are. This one is more reserved.

"May I come in?"

I want to tell her no. Accuse her of being part of the lies that made me look like a fool. I want to ask why she led me to believe I was family, only to hide important information from me. What if Keegan had been killed while on duty? I never would've even known he was a police officer.

And it hits me in this moment, that's why I'm so upset. He could've been hurt—killed even. And I never would've known. I thought he was a college student, only to learn he's a narcotics officer. His job revolves around catching drug dealers. Sure, I'm mad, but more than that, I'm scared. Because if I forgive Keegan, that will mean my boyfriend, possibly my one-day husband—forever the father of my son—has a job where he risks his life every single day. And instead of being honest with me about what he does, he lied. Just like my father lied… and then died.

"Blakely," Larissa says softly, snapping me out of my thoughts. Glancing around, I realize I've been standing at the door, with her still standing outside, having an epiphany of sorts.

"Yes, sorry, please come in." I open the door wider and she steps inside.

"Grammy!" Zane squeals, running over to her. He wraps his arms around her legs and she picks him up.

"Hey, sweetheart."

"You wanna watch SpongeBob with me?"

"Aww, I would love to, but I need to talk to your mom."

"O-kay," he says. She sets him on the floor and he runs back to the couch.

"We can talk at the table." I can't leave the area because of Zane, but as long as we keep our voices down, he shouldn't hear. "Would you like something to drink? Coffee? Tea?"

"No, I'm okay."

We sit at the table, and I wait for her to speak. She's the one who came over after all.

"I need to apologize to you," she says. "I'm sorry for hurting you. Keegan told me everything that transpired, and one of the things he mentioned was how hurt you were by our entire family." Her hand comes out and lands over the top of mine. "I love you, Blakely, and the last thing I ever want to do is hurt you. I hope you can one day forgive me for my part in all of this. You and Zane and Sierra are part of our family, no matter what."

Her apology is so simple yet sincere. I try to think back to my childhood. Every time my parents would miss a recital or show. When they would be out of town and miss a birthday because my father would drag my mother away on a business trip. Not a single time did they even bother to apologize. Dad would make excuses, and Mom would always come home with gifts to make up for it, but neither of them ever looked us in the eyes and apologized. And I realize now it's because they were cowards. It takes a strong person to be able to face someone they hurt and apologize.

"Thank you. That means a lot to me," I tell her honestly.

She smiles and nods. I expect her to then defend Keegan and her family's decision to lie and deceive me, so I'm a bit surprised when instead, she says, "I know it's going to take some time to get through you feeling betrayed, so I won't push, but I want you to know you're welcome at my home anytime."

She must notice the confused look on my face because she says, "Did I say something wrong? If you aren't comfortable coming over, I will understand. I just—"

"No, it's not that." I shake my head. "I guess I expected you to follow up your apology by defending everyone's choice to lie to me and keep the truth from me."

Dad lied and deceived everyone until his dying breath with zero apologies, and my mom, until the day Dad took her life with his own, allowed him to do so.

The corners of her lips turn down. "I can't speak for my family, but I can speak for myself, so that's what I'll do. Keegan and his father are police officers. It's their job to serve and protect. When you came into our lives, he was in the middle of a job that was very important to him. He never imagined his personal and professional life would collide like it did. But they did. When he came to me, all I was told was that nobody could know he and his father were police officers. I've been married to my husband for over thirty years, and the entire time he's been in law enforcement. I've learned over the years not to ask questions. It's not that he doesn't want to tell me; he's not allowed.

"I've become so desensitized over the years, it didn't cross my mind just how hurt and betrayed you would feel. I can't apologize for lying because telling you could've cost them the case, and that case wasn't just important to Keegan, it was important to our entire family. And while you may not understand it now, you are actually how Keegan was able to break the case. So, in a roundabout way, I have you to thank."

"I'm not really understanding. Why was this case so important?"

Her smile is sad. "I think Keegan should be the one to explain it to you, and once you're ready, he will. Just know that nobody's actions were malicious or vindictive."

I nod in understanding. "Thank you for coming by. I don't understand it all, but it means a lot that you would come over and apologize and explain what you can. I was really hurt. I still am. But I would never keep Zane from any of you."

"And I appreciate that," she says, "but my coming over isn't about that. You are our family, Blakely, and you're hurting. My apology was only for you."

We stand, and Larissa envelops her arms around me in a motherly hug. "I love you, sweetie, and I hope to see you soon."

Shortly after she leaves, there's another knock on the door. I half expect it to be Keegan, so I'm surprised when I open the door to a delivery guy holding a large bouquet of flowers.

"Blakely Jacobs?"

"Yes, thank you." I sign for them and bring them inside. I open the card and read it:

Blakely, I would prefer delivering these in person, but I'm giving you your space. Please know that I'm sorry and I love you. Even if you can't ever forgive me, I would appreciate it if you let me explain.

Xo Keegan

I know I'm being a coward, but I'm not ready to talk to him yet. So instead I text him: **Thank you for the flowers, but I'm not ready to talk yet.**

A minute later a text comes through from him: **You're welcome. I'm here when you're ready.**

The next morning, I drop Zane off at daycare and, as I'm walking to my first class of the day, I spot Brenton standing against the sidewall of the building, his foot propped up. I glance around nervously. Why is he here? He must've gotten out on bail. Is he going to hurt me?

Walking quickly, I keep my head down, hoping he won't notice me, but of course he does. "Blakely, wait," he yells. It's loud enough that there's no way I wouldn't hear him, so I stop, figuring it's best to get this over with. My eyes dart around the courtyard, secretly hoping for Keegan to pop out, but he doesn't.

"What?" I ask, making sure he knows just how angry I am.

"I know what I did was fucked up, and I'm sorry." He stops in front of me.

"Fucked up? Yeah, Brenton, it was definitely fucked up! You sold drugs while you were around me and my son."

"You were never in danger," he says, as if that will make it all better. "I'm cooperating with the police, and I probably won't even be serving any jail time. I shouldn't have brought you to Miguel's place, but I didn't know the cops were looking for him."

"Brenton, do you hear yourself?" I exclaim, my hands fisting at my sides. "You can't seriously be defending and justifying what you did. This entire situation is beyond messed up and as far as I'm concerned you're no longer my friend or a part of my life. You lied to me, you—"

"Keegan lied too!" he argues, and it takes everything in me not to smack the stupid out of him.

"And I'm not speaking to Keegan either. But he lied about being a cop. You lied about selling drugs."

"So, what, you're just going to forgive him for lying, but you're forcing me out of your life? I messed up. I know that, but I'm still the same guy I've always been. I know you're mad right now, but you're going to forgive me…"

"No, I'm not going to forgive you," I tell him point blank. "You most definitely are not the man I thought you were, and I never want to see or speak to you again."

I turn to walk away and see Kolton stalking over. His face full of fury. "You need to get the hell away from her right fucking now," he yells at Brenton.

"I was just talking to her," Brenton says.

"And now you're not." Kolton steps between us. "Walk away."

"The only place I'm walking to is class," Brenton points out.

"Actually, you're not. You obviously haven't checked your email. You've been withdrawn from your classes and disenrolled from this university."

"You can't fucking do that!" Brenton roars, and I jump back in fear.

Kolton, on the other hand, doesn't seem the least bit afraid. "It's already been done. If you want to argue about it, speak to the dean."

Kolton takes my hand. "Let's go," he murmurs. I follow behind him, and once we turn the corner, I spot Keegan and a couple of the officers standing there.

"You were here the whole time?" I ask dumbly.

"Of course," Keegan says. "But I know you want your space." He shrugs. "I told you you'd be safe no matter what and that someone would be on you."

"Thank you."

I leave everyone standing outside and enter the classroom, unsure how I feel about everything. Being hurt is such a complicated feeling, especially when I'm hurt over him doing his job. Over him doing something good like catching a drug dealer. I know his lies aren't the same as my dad's. But they still cut deep.

During the lecture, I find my mind wandering to my conversation with Keegan's mom yesterday. She said it was Keegan's story to tell. While I'm hurt by everything that went down, I think I should at least hear Keegan out.

When Zane and I get home, I find Sierra sitting on the couch in her sweatpants and hoodie, reading a book on her iPad. "Off work today?"

"Yeah, I spoke to Kolton. He said Brenton approached you. How are you doing?"

"I'm okay." Before I continue, though, I tell Zane to go potty and get ready for his nap.

"Okay, Mommy!" He runs down the hallway.

"I can't believe he actually thought he'd apologize and I'd forgive him."

"I can't believe he was doing that shit right under our noses." Sierra huffs. "I feel as stupid as you do. You know he used to sell when we were in high school?"

"What? No, I didn't know that."

"Yep, but I just thought it was him being a stupid teenager. I never thought he would continue."

"He thinks I'm going to come around, but it's not happening."

"Kolton mentioned you and Zane moving in with Keegan. He said it would be safer."

"What else did he say?"

"That's it. He wanted to explain the entire story, but he said he can't until Keegan speaks to you. They feel you deserve to know the truth first."

"I was thinking about talking to him. To at least hear him out."

"I'm not going to tell you what to do, but I think that would be a good idea."

"And if we moved into Keegan's place, would you move with us?"

Sierra traps her bottom lip between her teeth.

"S?"

"I was…" She shoots me a guilt-filled half-smile. "I was actually thinking I could move in with Kolton."

"He asked you to move in with him?"

"He did. He said the only reason he couldn't ask sooner was because of everything going on, but now that it's done, he wants me to move in. But I told him I had to speak to you first."

"I would never keep you from moving in with him," I tell her, suddenly feeling a rush of sadness.

"Are you upset?"

"No." I shake my head. "I guess I'm just a little sad. It seems like everything is changing. I just learned Keegan is a cop and now you're talking about moving in with your boyfriend. Brenton was my best friend for years and now he's being cut out of my life. It's just a lot to take in, you know?"

"I know."

"Mommy! I'm ready for bed," Zane yells, and Sierra and I laugh.

"I wonder if all kids love to nap the way Zane does."

"I doubt it," Sierra says. "Watch, you'll have another kid one day, and he or she will despise naptime and you'll never have a moment to yourself."

"Wow, you're not only knocking me up, but you're cursing me. Thanks." I stand to go tuck Zane into bed, and there's a knock on the door.

"I'll grab it while you tuck him in," Sierra offers.

After giving Zane and Bear a kiss, I turn his light off and head back out to the living room. "Who was it?"

"Brenton."

"What? He came here?" My eyes dart around the room as if he's still here.

"Yeah, but he only made it to knock on the door, when a police officer stopped him and made him leave."

Damn Brenton. Something tells me he's not going to stop any time soon. "I think maybe I should take Keegan up on his offer to move in there with Zane." At least living at Keegan's will mean a gated community, plus, Brenton doesn't know where he lives. He could always follow me back, but I think we'd be a lot safer there.

"I think so too," Sierra agrees.

"I'm going to speak to Keegan today. Let him explain. I don't know where we'll stand afterward, but at least that way you and Kolton can move forward."

I head into my room and lie down on my bed. I pull up my text messages and send one to Keegan asking when we can meet to talk. He responds almost instantly that he'll be off in a couple hours and he can come by.

"Hey, S!" I whisper-yell, "Would you mind watching Zane tonight? I don't want to talk with him around."

"Of course."

> Me: Can we meet somewhere else? Sierra can watch Zane. I don't want him to hear anything.

> Keegan: I'll pick you up at 6. Is that okay?

> Me: Yes.

CHAPTER THIRTY-SIX

Keegan

'VE SPENT THE LAST FEW WEEKS GETTING EVERYTHING READY FOR the day when I would be able to tell Blakely the entire truth and be able to ask her to move in with me. When she asked if we could talk somewhere else, I knew this would be the perfect place. A fresh start for us. It's exactly what we need. I purchased this home when I moved here, but I've yet to actually live here. If all goes well, the three of us will be living here together.

When I picked up Blakely, she was quiet, but no longer angry. When my mom said she spoke to her, she could see how hurt she was. And I don't blame her. She doesn't know the entire story. All she knows is that everyone around her kept important details from her. I'm hoping once she knows everything, she'll be more understanding.

We pull up to a guard gate and the gate opens automatically. "There's a sticker on my window," I tell her. "Without one, you can't get in."

She nods in understanding. I drive a few more blocks then make a right onto my street and then a left into my driveway. The house isn't huge, but it's a decent size single family home. Three bedrooms, family room, living room, and two and a half baths. It also has a pool in the backyard. When I purchased it, I didn't know about Blakely and Zane. My only thought was that the market was low and I might as well buy a home instead of renting. Now, I'm really glad I did.

When we enter the home, the aroma of Italian food wafts in the air, and Blakely finally speaks. "Did you cook?"

"I did. I'm not the best cook, but Mom showed me years ago how to make her famous lasagna."

"Your home is beautiful," she says softly, looking around at the minimally furnished living room.

"I've yet to live in it," I admit.

"What? Why?"

"Why don't we eat and then talk, and then afterward I can show you around?"

"Okay."

I get us each a plate of lasagna, a bowl of salad, and a roll, and set them on the table. "Wine?" I ask.

"I'll have water, please. I need to be clear-headed."

While we eat, we keep our conversation in shallow waters, focusing on easy topics like Zane and school. She doesn't mention anything about me not really being a student and therefore no longer pretending to attend classes. After we're done, we work together to clean up and then sit on the couch.

"Before you begin, I think you should know a little background about me," she says. "Growing up, Sierra and I were more often than not left to our own devices. I know my mother loved us, but she came from foster care and felt she owed my father everything. He was very wealthy and traveled a lot, and he would take our mom with him, leaving us with a nanny."

As I listen to her describe her family life, I can't help but compare it to my own. They're like night and day.

"No matter where our mom was, she would read us stories before bed." She smiles, probably recalling a memory.

"That's why you read to Zane."

"Yeah, it was one of the few things my mom passed down." She frowns, and I find myself reaching for her, but I stop myself.

"I don't know how much my mom knew about my dad's work, but the last day they were alive, she implied he had been lying to her for years. He did a bunch of shady business and it led to his destruction, and like always, he couldn't let my mom go on her own. He ran our vehicle off the road, killing them both."

"Jail—Blakely…" This time I do take her hand in mine. "Where were you when this happened?"

"Sierra and I were in the car," she admits. "He was trying to kill us all." A single tear slides down her cheek. "The thing is, the lies he was telling eventually caught up with him, and he turned to drinking. The drinking made him reckless. He was drunk that day."

"I'm so sorry," I tell her, unsure of what else to say. Your parents are supposed to protect you, not be the ones to harm you. I can't even imagine what she and her sister went through.

"When I found out you lied, everything from my past came back," Blakely says. "I can handle anything, but I can't handle being lied to."

When I open my mouth to speak, she raises her palm to stop me. "I get your lies were necessary, but moving forward, if there's something you can't tell me, I need to know that. No more lying, Keegan. I can't be made a fool of again. I believe my mother let my father lie to her because she loved him and depended on him and would rather be happy and ignorant with the lies than be hurt with the truth. I can't become my mother."

Blakely shoots me the most heartbreaking, pleading look. "Promise me… no more lies."

"I promise you. No more lies. I never set out to make you feel like a fool. I swear."

"Thank you." She squeezes my hand. "Now, it's your turn. I'm ready to listen."

My heart soars at how easily Blakely can forgive. She has such a good heart, and I hate that it's probably because of what she dealt with growing up.

"In order for you to understand everything, I have to start from the beginning," I tell her. "I mentioned once that my brother Keith had died, but what I left out was that he was killed during a drug deal gone wrong."

"What?" Blakely gasps and her hands come up to her mouth.

"The worst part was that the drug deal… it involved Kolton."

Her eyes widen in shock then something clicks. "You told me in Cocoa Beach your brother overdosed…"

"I did, but that's not how Keith died. Kolton was taking too many classes and he needed help staying awake to study and then falling asleep when he was done. He heard about a guy who was selling to students and approached him.

"Keith was a police officer and, at the time, he was investigating the man Kolton was buying from. Kolton didn't know, though, because we're not allowed to talk about our investigations." I pause for a second, hoping Blakely will understand what I'm saying. It wasn't personal. When we're investigating, we can't tell anyone, no matter how much we want to. I know it doesn't change the fact we lied, but I'm hoping she'll at least see this wasn't the same as her father lying. "One day Keith was on campus and saw Kolton talking to the drug dealer he was investigating, so he approached. We don't know if he knew what was going down, or suspected. But the guy got spooked and pulled out a gun and shot Keith. He was wearing a vest, but he shot him in the neck. He was dead before he ever made it to the hospital. The guy ran while Kolton was calling for help."

Tears prick Blakely's eyes and the next thing I know, she's throwing her arms around my neck. "I'm so sorry, Keegan." She sniffles. "I can't imagine losing my sister."

I give her a kiss on her forehead, inhaling her sweet scent. Fuck how I've missed her.

"It was hard," I admit truthfully. "But the worst part was that Kolton blamed himself. One, for buying from the guy, and two, because while he was trying to save Keith's life, Miguel disappeared."

"So nobody got any closure," she says, sitting back and wiping her tears. "Wait a second." Her eyes widen. "Miguel… as in Brenton's mom's ex-boyfriend? The guy you guys arrested?"

I nod once. "The very same. He was hiding out the entire time in that house, while Brenton and Maxwell were selling for him."

"I hate him," Blakely seethes. "I can never forgive him for what he's done. And I'm so mad at myself. I let my son around him."

"You didn't know, and in his defense, I really don't think he knew Miguel had a warrant out for his arrest for murdering a cop."

"I don't care. He was selling drugs! What if my son got a hold of them? Brenton is dead to me."

We sit in silence for a few seconds while Blakely calms down. I love that she cares so much about my family that she hates Brenton, but I also know her heart is broken over the fact it was her best friend who was selling.

"So, your brother died and Kolton blamed himself," she prompts.

"Yeah," I say, remembering just how bad Kolton took it. So bad that I found him lying on the ground of the bathroom half-dead. It was the scariest moment of my life finding him. "Kolton took it so hard he overdosed and almost died."

Blakely shakes her head. "Thank God he didn't."

"I'm not even sure how my mom survived it all," I tell her. "Losing her son, almost losing her other son—and then there was me. I was just finishing up getting my AA and about to graduate from the police academy when all of this went down. When Kolton and my mom found out I was still considering joining the force, they ganged up on me. My mom said she'd already lost one son and almost lost another. She couldn't handle losing me too. My brother felt the same way. He was terrified I would end up like Keith."

"You told me you had a big decision to make," she says, and it warms my heart at how much she remembers from our short time together.

"I did. Kolton took off to Europe, saying he needed to get away. He spent a year over there. I had to decide whether to continue with my degree in criminal justice and do something safer like forensics, or become a police officer."

"And you chose to become a police officer." When she says the words, there's zero judgement in them, and I sigh in relief. I can't imagine doing anything other than what I do, but if it means being with Blakely and Zane, I would give it up.

"I did. But with my brother and mom upset with me, and Keith having died while working for this department, I decided to take a job elsewhere. Give everybody some space. I knew my brother would be returning eventually, and I didn't want to throw my decision in his face. So, I moved to Jacksonville to live with my dad's brother. My uncle Frank. He's also a police officer and heads up the Jacksonville Police Department."

"So this whole time you were in Jacksonville?"

"Yeah, I spent the last three years there training to become a narcotics detective. My uncle is one of the best there is."

"You wanted to avenge your brother's death," she says.

"Yes and no. Did I hope to one day catch the asshole who killed him? Of course. But I also want to work to keep the drugs off the streets in the first place. I saw firsthand what drugs can do to someone, and Kolton wasn't even addicted. I knew from the moment Keith died I wanted to be a part of the Narcotics Division. I took all the required tests and was trained by my uncle.

"And then my dad called and told me it was happening again. There was a guy selling drugs to students on campus. Nobody here knew I was a cop, so it would be perfect for me to go undercover. As far as everyone was concerned, I was back to finish my degree."

"And then you ran into me."

I can't help the smile that spreads across my face. "And then I ran into you." Needing to touch her in some way, I pull her back toward me and take her hands in mine. "I wanted to tell you. I swear I did. The minute I found out about Zane, I went to my dad and told him to take me off the case. He asked me to give it a little longer and then we would discuss it. But then I caught Brenton selling at the party he brought you to and we were just too close."

Blakely nods in understanding. "I get it. It really hurt to feel left out, but I understand now."

"I love you so much," I tell her, pulling her into my lap. "When you mentioned us moving in together, it killed me to not be able to say yes, but I had to keep up with appearances. I hated that you thought I wasn't all in." I press my lips to hers and then add, "I'm all in, Blakely. All fucking in."

I turn her around so she's straddling my lap. "Please tell me we can find a way to move past this. To be together and be a family."

"I was so scared," she admits softly. "When I found out you were a police officer, I was so mad at you for lying, but I was also really scared. If something happened to you." Her delicate hands frame my face. "I didn't even know you're a cop and you could've been killed."

"I'm so sorry I couldn't tell you," I tell her. "But I'll keep my promise to you and let you know any time there's something I can't talk to you about. And I swear to you I'll do everything in my power to make it home every day." It's all I can give her. I won't ever lie to her again. And if I promise nothing will ever happen to me, it would be a lie. She needs to go into this knowing the truth. My job is dangerous. Hell, life is dangerous. And anything can happen to any of us.

"I want this," she says. "I want you and me and Zane. I want a life with you." No sweeter words have ever been spoken.

Grabbing her by her ass, I lift her and carry her to the master bedroom, thankful that I thought to at least buy a bed for the place. I lay her on the mattress and she looks up at me with happiness mixed with lust. We shed our clothes within seconds, and our mouths fuse together. Her hands glide across my skin while mine worship her perfect body. Her legs are spread, and I enter her completely, needing to be as connected to her as possible. I make love to Blakely fast and hard at first, and then, when I feel myself getting close to coming, I slow it down. Reaching down, I apply pressure to her swollen clit and her body ignites under my touch. She screams out my name as her tight, warm pussy squeezes my dick, milking every last drop of my seed that I spill into her.

When we both catch our breath, I pull out of her, and Blakely laughs. "What's so funny?"

"I've never had make-up sex before," she says with the most gorgeous smile splayed across her face. "I think I'm a fan."

After we clean up, I give her a proper tour of the house. With every room we enter, she tells me everything she envisions for the place: the colors, the styles, the types of furniture. And I tell her she can have whatever the hell she wants as long as she never stops smiling the way she is while she talks.

When we're done, we agree that she and Zane will be moving in with me as soon as possible. The apartment they live in is now month to month since they've been living there for so long, and Sierra is excited to move in with Kolton. I don't mention that I'm also glad they'll be the hell away from Brenton. The guy has only been out on bail for less than a day and he's approached Blakely once and tried a second time—only Scott was watching and got to him before he could speak to her. Asshole thought he was slick going around back and coming up the side.

"Can we go see Zane?" It's been too long since I've seen him. I wanted to give Blakely some space, but I'm missing my kid like crazy.

"Of course!" She wraps her arms around my neck and pulls me down for a kiss. "I'm so sorry you haven't seen him. He's asked about you."

"It's all past us now." I kiss the tip of her nose. "But I need you to know something." I don't want her to take this the wrong way, but it needs to be said. "I plan to spend my life with you, but if for whatever reason something changes. If you walk away from me…"

"I'm not going to do that."

"I know, but even if it's for a damn day. I can't go without my son again."

Tears fill her eyes, and I immediately feel bad. But then she pulls me back into her. Her lips crash against mine and she kisses me with abandon. Her tongue sweeps through my parted lips and she caresses and strokes her tongue against mine. If I wasn't in such a rush to go see my son before he goes to bed, I'd take her ass back to bed.

"I love you, Keegan," she says, slightly out of breath from the kiss. "And you are a damn good dad. What you said only proves that."

CHAPTER THIRTY-SEVEN

Blakely

"I S IT WEIRD THAT WE'RE SISTERS DATING TWIN BROTHERS?" I ASK Sierra when the guys leave the table to get us drinks from the bar. It's been two weeks since Keegan told me everything. Two weeks since we went to the apartment and told Sierra we'd be moving in together. I wasn't sure on the timeframe, but I learned the next day, the timeframe was… the next day. Keegan and Kolton and a few of their friends—including several police officers—boxed up our stuff and moved us. Sierra's stuff went to Kolton's apartment, and Zane's and my stuff went to Keegan's house. The first night I cried over missing my sister, and the next night Keegan invited them over for dinner.

I've been so busy with school, and Keegan's been so busy with helping to put together the case to send Miguel away for life, that Larissa insisted we go out and have some fun. She showed up and offered to watch Zane, and Sierra suggested we double date.

"I think it's awesome," she says with a mischievous grin that tells me she's about to say something highly inappropriate. "They're identical twins, right?"

"Yeah…"

"I wonder if they're identical in every way." She waggles her brows and glances over at them walking back with our drinks.

"Oh my God!" I shriek when I get what she's implying. "Don't be thinking about my man's dick!" Even with the music blaring, my words travel and Keegan grins at the same time Kolton grimaces.

"I was not thinking about his dick," Sierra explains out loud. "I was simply wondering if everything on you two is identical. I mean, Kolton is well-endowed, so I was just wondering if my sister was getting the same experience."

Keegan and Kolton both burst out laughing, and I groan, grabbing my drink from Keegan and taking a hefty sip.

"Remember that time when we measured our dicks?" Kolton says. My drink flies out of my mouth, and Sierra throws her head back in laughter. Keegan just shakes his head. "My dick was totally a quarter of an inch bigger."

"Bullshit," Keegan argues.

"I'm going to use the restroom," I announce. My hands and face are all sticky from spitting my drink out everywhere.

"I'll go with you," Sierra says, standing.

"Be back in a minute," I whisper into Keegan's ear. "Prepare to dance with me."

The line to the ladies' room is long, but since I only need to wash my hands, I slip inside. Sierra actually has to use the restroom, so she's stuck waiting in line. As I'm walking out, she's finally making her way in. "I'll wait for you out here," I tell her, and she nods.

I step to the side so I'm not in the way and pull my phone out of my back pocket to make sure Larissa hasn't called or texted. No new messages. Just as I'm putting my phone back in my pocket, I hear my name being called from behind me. I turn around, but when I see who it is, instinctually, I back up, prepared to run.

"I just want to talk to you," Brenton says, putting his palms up in a silent gesture to imply he means no harm. I call bullshit.

"Are you following me?"

"You moved out of the apartment," he says, not answering my question, "and in with Keegan."

Oh my God, he has been following me. "I'm not doing this with you."

I'm afraid to turn my back on him, but at the same time, I don't know how else to get away.

"I just want to talk to you." He steps closer, making me extremely nervous.

"Not happening." I turn on my heel to run, but before I even make it a foot away, he grabs me by my hair and drags me down the dark hallway. I saw the exit sign behind him. He's going to kidnap me. I scream and start to kick, but he wraps his strong arms around my body and shoves me out the door before anybody notices.

His car is waiting by the door and he throws me inside. He shuts the door and opens the front one. I try to open the door, but it doesn't budge. He fucking childproofed it!

Before he gets the idea of taking my phone, I grab it from my back pocket and push it down into the seat. He opens the door back up and grabs my wrists. I scream at the top of my lungs, hoping someone will hear me. But he quickly covers my mouth with duct tape before he wraps a thick rope around my wrists.

Shutting the door again, he stalks around the car and is about to jump in, when he must remember something because he walks back around and opens the door. "Where's your phone?" he asks, as if I can actually answer him.

Without waiting for me to answer, he shoves his hand into each of my pockets and then lifts my shirt, exposing my bra. "Where's your phone?" I shake my head and he rips the tape off my mouth. "Where the fuck is it? I saw you using it!"

"It must've dropped in the club," I say quickly, hoping that Keegan is still tracking my phone and will be able to track wherever it is Brenton is taking me.

He grins evilly. "Good." He sticks the tape back over my mouth and slams the door.

I sit quietly while he drives, looking out the window to see where we're going in case I get the opportunity to escape. After several minutes of being on the road, Brenton turns his radio off and begins to speak.

"I didn't want it to come to this, Blakely."

My gaze flickers over to the rearview mirror and for a second our eyes meet before I look back out the window, not wanting to give him any more of my attention.

"I don't get it. For years I was there for you and your fucking kid. You told me you couldn't date. You had to focus on your son. So I waited and waited." He slams his hand against the steering wheel. "I fucking waited! And for what? So that asshole could step right in and take my place?"

Oh. My. God. He's lost his fucking mind.

"I told you, you didn't know him! The entire time he was a fucking cop. Lying to you! I accepted that you were upset over everything that went down, but I knew you'd come around. And then you go and forgive him and move in with him, but you can't give me the fucking time of day?"

He gets on I-95 and heads north and my heart hiccups. He can be taking us anywhere at this point. The highway runs through the entire state of Florida and all the way up the East Coast. My only hope is that Keegan is still tracking my phone and is following behind us. My seat vibrates, and I thank God I had it on silent. If it were on loud, Brenton would know I still have my phone and would throw it out the window.

"I gave you four fucking years and you shit on me the moment that fucker appeared! And now there's a chance I'm going to go to jail all because of him. Fuck that! Do you even care?" he asks. "Huh? Do you even give a shit that your boyfriend is ruining my entire life?"

Out of the corner of my eye, I see him reach back between the seats. I try to move toward the window, afraid he's going to hurt me, but his reach is long. The car swerves as he reaches farther, and a couple cars on the road honk. "Stop moving! I'm trying to take your tape off." Not wanting us to wreck, I lean forward to let him rip the tape off, but it's too late. The car is going too fast and he loses control. It's dark and I can't see much, but I feel the vehicle hit the reflectors, indicating he's driving off the road. The vehicle hits some kind of bump and then slams forward, tilting to the side. Just before we begin to flip, I catch a glimpse of the wide ditch filled with water.

Brenton screams, and I can't do anything. He put my seat belt on to keep me in place. I have no hands and no voice, and as the car flips and lands in the water, and the inside begins to fill with cold liquid, all I can do is pray Keegan is following us. Because otherwise, I know that as soon as the water fills to the top, my life will be over.

CHAPTER THIRTY-EIGHT

Keegan

"She's gone!" Sierra yells. "She told me she'd wait for me right outside of the bathroom and she wasn't there. I called her phone and she didn't answer. Where is she?" The panic in her voice has me jumping to my feet. My first instinct is to call her. When she doesn't answer, I check the GPS I still have on her phone. It shows her traveling away from the club. There's no way she would leave without us.

"Let's go!" I yell, already running for the door to my truck. I don't know how long the GPS is going to work, how long whoever took her will go without realizing she still has her phone, and I'm not going to wait around here to find out. We jump into my truck and I take off in the direction the vehicle is going.

"She's still not answering," Sierra says.

"Don't call her!" I shout a bit too loud. "Don't call her," I repeat again. "If it goes off, even a vibration, whoever took her will get rid of it and then I won't have any way to find her."

"I'll call Dad," Kolton says.

"Tell him to send someone over to Brenton's place. The GPS says she's going north. And tell him to put someone on Mom and Zane. Make sure they're okay."

"Brenton lives south," Kolton states.

"I know, but if he's home, it will rule out him taking her."

"Who else would've taken her?" Sierra asks.

"Miguel Sanchez and Maxwell Travers are both locked up. Either of them could've had someone pick her up to send a message." I slam my fist against the steering wheel. "Fuck! I should've had someone watching her tonight. I thought she'd be okay because she was with me."

"Bro," Kolton says, "don't go there." But it's too late because I've already gone there.

Kolton explains to our dad what's happened and he says he'll call back once he knows anything. With me doing over a hundred, I'm catching up, but whoever has her must be flying as well because I'm not catching up fast enough.

We drive in silence for a few minutes, none of us having a clue what to say, until Kolton's phone rings. He puts it on speaker phone.

"Your mom and Zane are okay. Duncan is with them now. Brenton's apartment is empty, though. The furniture is all there, but it's been completely cleaned out of his possessions."

"He has her," I say out loud. "I'm only about a quarter of a mile behind her phone." And then a thought hits me that if I wasn't sitting, would knock me down. "What if he set up a decoy? What if I'm following her phone but not her?"

"Son…" Dad starts, but his words are cut off by Sierra screaming.

"Oh my God! Look!" Our eyes fly to the side as a small vehicle swerves off the road and hits the ditch. It flips a few times and then lands in the water. It takes a second for my brain to catch up to what I already know.

"That's Brenton's car. Dad! We need an ambulance stat!" I glance down at the GPS and read off our location before tossing the phone to Sierra. "Stay on the phone with him." I pull over on the side of the road, grab my Life Hammer, and jump out of my truck. Kolton and I run straight over to where the car is submerged under the water. We had a bad storm last week and the ditches are all full. Luckily, when it flipped, it landed upright, so even though I can see there's water leaking in, part of the windows are still visible.

We both jump into the water and head to the vehicle. Figuring he more than likely put her in the back, I smash out the back window. Sure enough, she's in the car and in the back seat. Because the car isn't completely submerged yet, her head is bobbing just over the top of the water. Her eyes are wide with fear, and her mouth… holy fuck! Her mouth is taped up.

I rip the tape off her mouth and she lets out a loud cry. "Keegan!"

"I got you, baby." I can't open the door, though, because of how much the car is already filled with water. "Can you climb through the window?"

"My-my hands." She cries. "They're tied up, but I was able to undo my seat belt." Her hair is drenched and matted to her face. "I almost drowned." Her words have me wanting to find Brenton and kill him… which reminds me. "Kolton, you need to get Brenton out."

"What?" he asks like he didn't hear me.

"Go help him," I demand. I took an oath when I became a police officer, and that oath means something to me. Which means, even though I would like nothing more than to see that asshole die, it's not my place to let it happen.

Reaching into the window, I use my Life Hammer to cut the rope on Blakely's wrists so she's free, and then I remove my shirt and place it over the broken window so I can help her climb out. Once she's out, I pick her up and carry her to a dry piece of land, where Sierra is waiting.

"Keegan!" Kolton screams, and I look over at him. "He's not here!"

"What?" I yell back.

"He's not in the car."

"You sure?" I consider going to check for myself, but there's no way I'm leaving Blakely and Sierra.

And then I hear something behind me. I turn slowly, a feeling of dread hitting me like a semi going a hundred in the wrong lane, right at me.

"Don't move!" Brenton yells. He's holding my gun in his hands, pointing it at me. His clothes are drenched, and there's a huge gash on his forehead.

Blakely gasps, and Sierra yells.

And then a gunshot goes off.

Brenton hits the ground, and the gun he was holding flies through the air, landing a few feet away from him.

I run over and grab the gun as Kolton joins me.

"I didn't know you had your gun on you," I tell Kolton.

"Always. My brother taught me that."

I check out where he hit Brenton to see if he's alive and unconscious, or if he's dead. The bullet went straight through his heart. "He's dead."

EPILOGUE

Keegan

One Month Later

"**D**ADDY! IT'S HIM!" ZANE YELLS, POINTING HIS FINGER TO THE massive rectangular yellow sponge-looking thing. We've spent the last week in Orlando, visiting every park at Disney and then making our way through Universal. Of course, the SpongeBob area is the last thing to be seen, so Zane has been asking every thirty seconds all day long if it's time yet. We probably should've walked the other way around the park, but Blakely wanted to make sure we hit all the rides before the wait became too long. Next time, we'll start with the big sponge guy.

"That's him, bud," I agree. Zane stops in his place and Blakely snorts out a laugh. We both thought for sure Zane would run straight for the big guy, but he's not. He's standing in his spot, frozen in place. "You want to get in line to meet him?"

Zane looks up at me with wide eyes and nods slowly. The kid is starstruck. "Yes," he whispers. "Will you go with me?" He raises his hand to hold mine and I take it. Being a father is without a doubt the best job I could ever have.

We get in line and when it's our turn, Zane walks up to SpongeBob and gives him the most adorable hug. Blakely snaps a million pictures while I stand next to Zane, holding his autograph book for him until he's ready for it.

"I love you so much," he tells SpongeBob. Of course, the guy can't talk, so he just pats his back and poses for some pictures.

Zane takes the book from me and SpongeBob stamps his signature on the page. Zane's grin is so bright it could light up the dark sky.

"It's the best day ever!" Zane sings, trying to sound like SpongeBob does when he sings the song, as we walk out of the park and toward the parking garage.

Blakely thinks we're going home, but she doesn't know we're really heading back to where everything began. When we arrive she gives me a curious look. "I thought we could stop here for dinner. Go back to where it all started."

Blakely smiles. "Sounds good." Holding my hand, while Zane runs ahead, we head down to the beach.

"I got into the master's program," Blakely says. I already know this since I saw the papers on her desk. I also already paid for her first semester. I saw the options she requested, such as working on campus and taking out loans. That's not happening.

"Congratulations, Jailbird." I pull her into my side and kiss her temple. "You're going to make a great guidance counselor."

"Look, there's Auntie Sierra and Uncle Kolton!" Zane yells. Blakely moves away from my side to find them since she wasn't aware our family would be here, and I use that moment to take the ring box out of my pocket.

"I didn't know you'd be here!" Blakely hugs her sister. Kolton nods once and walks around the girls to stand beside me. I look around the women to make sure our parents are also here. They are, and my mom is recording on her phone.

Kolton and I each get down on one knee and wait for the girls to notice. Blakely turns around first to look for me, and when she sees what's happening, her hands fly up to her face. Tears trickle down her beautiful cheeks. Sierra hears her sister sniffle and turns around as well, mimicking Blakely's reaction.

"Jailbird," I begin. "I knew from the moment my football knocked your book into the water right here on this beach you were the one for me." She laughs at my words through her cries. "This has been four years in the making. The football, the faulty condom." I wink and everyone laughs. "Losing your number. Running into you on campus. We've been through a lot to get here, but I believe everything we went through brought us to this moment, so I could ask you to become my wife and spend your life with me."

I stop speaking, so Kolton can continue.

"Sierra," he begins. "Unlike my brother, fate wasn't what brought us together. It was you in that sexy outfit, refusing to give me the time of day at Orange Sunrise."

Sierra cracks up laughing.

"I walked in to grab lunch and the moment I saw you I knew I had to have you. You blew me off several times, but I knew if I kept trying, you'd give in." He smiles wide, making everyone laugh. "And you did."

Sierra rolls her eyes, and Blakely giggles.

Kolton continues. "My brother and I are two of the luckiest fucking guys…"

"Ohhh, Uncle Kolton cursed!" Zane yells.

Kolton shakes his head. "Sorry, little man. We're the luckiest guys in the world to have you two by our sides and we'd be fools not to make sure you're ours forever. So, Sierra Jacobs, will you do me the honor of becoming my wife?"

"Blakely Jacobs, will you marry me?" I ask Blakely right after Kolton finishes.

Both girls nod and screech at the same time. We open our ring boxes and stand. I slide Blakely's on her ring finger and Kolton does the same.

"Yes," Blakely whispers. "Yes, I will marry you. And it's a good thing too because I'm pregnant." I don't think she means for everyone to hear, but Sierra gasps.

"You're pregnant?" I glance down at her flat stomach.

"Yep, only a month along."

"I am too!" Sierra admits out loud. "I'm a month along."

The two girls throw themselves at each other, hugging and crying and laughing as my parents walk over and congratulate all of us on our engagements and baby news.

Eventually Blakely makes her way back over to me. She wraps her arms around my neck and presses her lips to mine. "Thank you, Keegan. For loving me and finding your way back to me. For giving me a family. I love you."

"It wasn't me, Jailbird. It was fate."

THE INEVITABLE

CHAPTER ONE

"CHICKEN SALAD, EXTRA EGG, EXTRA TOMATO, AND AN ADDITIONAL ranch dressing on the side and… a refill of your sweet tea, extra lemons." I set the salad and drink down in front of my customer. "Can I get you anything else?" I ask out of habit, immediately regretting my choice of words.

He opens his mouth, a sly smirk quirking at the corner of his lips, but before the words can spill out, I raise my hand because I already know what he's going to say. For the past week, he's shown up here and sat in the same spot, ordering the same drink and salad while making the same request. *Go out on a date with me.*

And every day, despite how badly I want to do just that, I've given him the same answer: *No.*

"Besides me."

His sexy two-dimpled grin splays across his face. "Well, if you're still off the table, then I'm good." He grabs the ranch dressing and pours it over his salad.

"I'm still off the table," I reiterate yet again. Technically, I'm very much available, just not to him. Because when he walked in here on that first day and our eyes met as he sat at the bar, I immediately felt something course through my veins. Like fireworks waiting to be set off on the Fourth of July, they'll all shoot off with one spark, beautiful and dazzling, and explode in the sky. But what happens once they burn out? When the colors fade into ash, and we're left with only the aftermath?

Even though I have no doubt those sparks would be worth chasing, knowing the destruction they'll leave behind means I can't risk it.

The first time Kolton spoke to me, and those damn dimples popped out of his cheeks, I knew he would be bad for my heart. I went into self-preservation mode the best I could, locking away my organ in an attempt to protect it. But Kolton isn't making it easy on me. Every conversation, every joke, and every shared laugh cracks my shield a little more. I know it's only a matter of time until my heart is exposed, and I'll have no choice but to either flee the country—okay, maybe that's a bit dramatic—or give in and say yes to him, risking everything I've worked hard to protect over the past several years.

"Maybe so," he says, mixing his dressing in with the salad. "But I can feel you caving."

I bark out a laugh, refusing to let him know he's right. "How so? I'm pretty sure we had damn near the same conversation yesterday and the day before… and the day before that." Usually, I'm not behind the bar. For the past couple of years, I've managed The Orange Sunrise, an upscale restaurant-slash-bar in downtown Carterville. But last week, I caught two of my employees stealing and was forced to fire them, leaving the bar unattended.

"True," he agrees. "But today, you got my food without me even having to order it… a sign that you're paying attention to my wants and needs. And when you turned me down, you smiled this time instead of glaring at me. Sierra, you're caving, and soon, you're going to give in to what's brewing between us."

Jesus, he's right. I am paying attention. And he is getting to me. That force field protecting my heart simply isn't strong enough to withstand his charm. What about him urges me to let my guard down?

I release a completely unladylike snort because you know… fake it till you make it. "For a man who's been turned down a half dozen times, you seem quite sure of yourself."

"I don't hear you denying there's something between us." He points his fork my way. "I've been turned down five times, but I won't let that stop me. I can feel it…" He leans in, and without thought, as though a rope pulls me toward him, I do as well. "The sexual tension is so thick between us that it'll be worth the effort because when you give in, this thing between us will explode."

His words roll off his tongue like the sweetest yet scariest promise, reminding me of when I was younger and would use drugs as an escape. When I was high, I was on top of the world, but the minute it ended, and I crashed, it left me in a puddle of pain and regret. And that's what he could easily become to me… a drug. The high would be incredible, but the crash… it would no doubt destroy me.

"Besides," he adds, unaware of how my heart pounds behind my rib cage. "It's inevitable." He stabs the greens with his fork and shoves a bite into his mouth.

I count to five, needing to get my feelings under control. Every day he shows up here, he gets more personal, revealing more of himself. And with every word he speaks, he makes it harder for me to resist him.

"Inevitable, huh?" I choke out, grabbing the washcloth to focus my attention on something else other than him.

"As inevitable as the sun rising in the east and setting in the west."

"How very poetic of you. Is that what you teach? Poetry?"

I've seen his university badge, so I know he works there.

He chuckles.

"What?" I glance up from wiping down the already clean counter.

"You just proved my point. You're caving."

"How so?"

"You're asking me questions. Trying to get to know me."

"More like it's slow and I'm making conversation with the only person sitting at the bar," I retort.

"Whatever you have to tell yourself." He takes a sip of his drink. "But to answer your question… No, I don't teach poetry. I teach psychology. I've almost completed my master's in clinical psychology."

"You want to be a psychologist?" After my parents died, the state required my sister, Blakely, and me to see one. I hated her because she was condescending and lacked empathy. It's one of the reasons my sister is in school to become a guidance counselor. She wants to help guide kids in a positive way.

"I'm actually hoping to get a full-time teaching job at the university. But I'd love to volunteer at various mental health facilities. Therapy saved my life, and I want to help others the way it helped me."

Thankfully, a customer sits down at the other end of the bar. I excuse myself to greet her, and from there, the evening picks up. A steady flow of customers keeps me busy—between running the bar with one other person and managing the restaurant—and when I finally get a chance to check on Kolton, he's not there.

"Can you grab a bottle of Johnny Walker black label from the back?" Wilma asks. "We're out of it up here."

"Sure."

I'm halfway down the hall, my eyes trained on my phone, reading a text from my sister, when I run into a… wall? "Oomph." I stumble backward, my feet losing their balance, and am mentally preparing myself for the fall when powerful hands grip my waist and keep me upright.

My vision adjusts to the darkness, and I find the wall isn't a wall at all, but Kolton. He must've been coming out of the men's restroom.

"Shit, are you okay?" he asks, his voice filled with concern. "I was looking at my phone and didn't see you." His eyes lock with mine, and the sudden heat of his stare fills me with liquid lust.

"I was too." My words come out breathy, our proximity messing with my head. Usually, I have the bar to serve as a barrier between us. But now… nothing's between us. It's just Kolton and me in a dark hallway.

His fingers dig into my sides, his front flush with my own. My chest brushes up against his, and I can feel my nipples, sensitive with desire, pushed up against his muscular torso. Our faces are close. Too close. He's a head taller than me, but in my heeled boots, I'm close enough that I can reach up slightly and lay a soft kiss to his chiseled jawline, working my way to the corner of his mouth before giving his lips my attention…

As if he can sense what I'm thinking, he groans softly under his breath. "I want to kiss you so fucking badly."

"Then do it," I whisper. "Kiss me."

"Go out with me."

And just like that, the moment is broken. I back away, sucking in a breath of air that isn't filled with Kolton's scent. "I can't."

Without waiting for his response, I turn my back on him and disappear down the hall into the storage room. In the darkness, I take a moment to get my breathing—and libido—under control, and then I grab the bottle I need and head back out.

When I return to the bar, all that's left of Kolton is his signed receipt. Wilma must've given him his bill.

"He couldn't keep his eyes off you," Wilma says, glancing over my shoulder. "When I brought him his bill, he looked like a sad puppy that I wasn't you."

"It's not happening…" *Then maybe you shouldn't have told him to kiss you…* I'm going to chalk that up to temporary insanity.

I have no intention of giving him a chance to break my heart. Thanks to my sister and my beautiful nephew, I'm on the right path, and I refuse to ever go back down the path of destruction. I prefer to date men who won't destroy me. The ones I'm safe from giving my heart to.

"Have you seen the man?" Wilma waggles her brows. "He's fine as hell."

There's no denying he's a good-looking man. With his floppy brown hair he keeps swept under his gray beanie, his mesmerizing brown eyes look at me as if he can see straight into my soul, and when he gets comfortable and rolls the sleeves of his dress shirt up… Holy shit! Between his muscular forearms and the ink donning them, my insides become a freaking inferno. Nothing is hotter than a man who can wear a suit like it was made for him while hiding the bad boy underneath. Too bad I won't ever get the chance to experience either. My mom had a man like that once—my dad—and it killed her… literally. No way am I following in those footsteps.

CHAPTER TWO

Kolton

"Y ou're home late," my brother says as I walk through the door of my apartment, shedding my coat and suit jacket along the way. "Actually, now that I think about it, you've been getting home late a lot lately." Keegan crosses his arms over his chest and quirks a single brow. "You have a secret nightlife I don't know about?"

I set my briefcase on the coffee table and drop onto the couch. "Wasn't aware that you staying here temporarily meant suddenly becoming my parent. Do I have a curfew, too, Dad? Am I grounded?"

"Ha-ha. Seriously, though, what gives?" He sits across from me on the other couch and props his shoe-clad feet on my table. I eye it in annoyance, and he laughs, removing his feet.

"How much longer are you going to be crashing here?"

"Not sure." He shrugs. "Stop deflecting."

I sigh, knowing he won't give up. My brother knows me too damn well. A downfall to being in each other's lives for almost twenty-five years—you get to see every part of the other person.

"There's this woman…" I begin, barely getting the words out before Keegan hoots.

"Oh, shit! Seriously? Took you long enough to get back in the game."

"Well, I'm not exactly back in." I release a harsh breath. "More like sitting on the sidelines and begging to get put into the game."

Keegan laughs. "She turned you down?"

"Five times."

He scoffs. "What the hell is wrong with you?"

"She told me I'm ugly," I joke.

He cracks up. "That can't be true. I happen to know you're a sexy-ass specimen of a man." He waggles his brows, and I throw my pillow at him. "But that's not what I meant. What the hell is wrong with you that you asked out the same woman five times? You didn't get the hint the first four times she said no?"

"I know… I know I should let her go, but you're not there. You should see the way she looks at me when she doesn't think I'm paying attention."

I lean forward, my elbows landing on my knees, and scrub the sides of my face in frustration. "And the way she smiles when she doesn't know I'm watching her. She has the most beautiful smile, but there's something about it that's just the tiniest bit sad…"

I close my eyes, replaying the way her heart-shaped lips purse when she tries to hold back her smile. "Something about her has me drawn to her, has me wanting to reach inside her and find out everything there is to know about her." And then tonight, when we ran into each other, and I kept her from falling… When she looked at me and told me to kiss her? Fuck! I should've done it. I should've kissed her. But I didn't because I want more from her, and I knew if I kissed her, she would regret it, and then I wouldn't stand a chance.

"Jesus, man," Keegan says. "I haven't heard you sound this passionate about anything since…" He flinches, his words trailing off, not wanting to finish his thought.

"Since I killed Keith," I finish for him, needing to say the words out loud.

"Will you stop that shit?" Keegan hisses. "You didn't kill him. That piece of shit did."

My family loves to baby me, but I refuse to take the coward's way out. I can't change what happened, but I won't pretend my choices and actions weren't what led to the moment that ended our brother's life. The only way to truly move forward is to admit the truth and deal with it.

"We'll agree to disagree." I shrug. "I don't know. Maybe it's for the best that she's not interested. I have a shit ton of baggage and—"

"Stop," Keegan barks. "You want to blame yourself for Keith's death? I can't stop you, even if I don't agree with it, but I refuse to sit here and listen to you be self-deprecating. You've punished yourself for long enough, and you deserve to be happy. So if you think she'll make you happy, I say go for it. Keep at it until she agrees to go out with you." He laughs and stands. "Or until she calls the police and gets a restraining order."

I slowly raise my middle finger, silently expressing how I feel about his comment.

"No, thanks," he quips. "You might be hot, but you're still blood."

"What can I get you?" a raven-haired woman standing on the other side of the bar asks.

"Umm…" I glance around, hoping to locate Sierra. "I was wondering if—"

Before I can finish my sentence, the woman present in all my thoughts and fantasies walks out from the back. She's dressed in her work uniform: tight black dress slacks and a collared shirt with the restaurant's logo in the left corner. Her purse is strewn over her shoulder as she strolls in her black heels toward the door.

"I've changed my mind," I call back to the bartender while I spring from my seat and chase after the gorgeous brunette.

"Hey, Sierra! Wait up," I yell, catching up with her.

Her steps momentarily falter, and her eyes quickly widen, just before that wall she's an expert at erecting flies up.

"I'm off, but Monica is running the bar. She can take your order." She doesn't stop walking.

"Unless you're on the menu, she can't help me." Cheesy as fuck, I know, but at this point, I throw that shit out to get her attention. Like a five-year-old boy who messes with the girl he likes at recess.

I know it works when she snorts under her breath, then covers her mouth and nose to cover it up—too late. "I really have to get going," she says. "The bus will be here in a few minutes, and unless I want to wait an hour for the next one, I need to grab it."

"Get a drink with me." I rush forward and block her path. "Please. Just one drink."

She stops in her place. "I'm not looking for a boyfriend."

"Who said anything about being your boyfriend?" I joke. "I just asked you to get a drink with me. If I buy you food, will you assume I'm going to ask you to move in with me? Oh, shit." I widen my eyes in mock surprise. "If I throw in an appetizer, will you expect me to propose?"

The cutest fucking blush creeps up her neck and cheeks. "I… I didn't…"

"I'm just messing with you." I step toward her. "In all seriousness, I have every intention of becoming your boyfriend one day." Her eyes bug out in shock. "And one day, you will move in with me… Or I can move in with you." I shrug. "And then, when I know you're going to say yes, I will most definitely propose."

"Kolton!" She gasps.

I ignore the beginnings of her freak-out. "You and me… it's inevitable. But don't worry. I'm okay with taking things slow… for now." I playfully wink. "All I want to do is take you somewhere to buy you a drink and have a conversation. So, what do you say? One drink? Anywhere you want."

She sighs, and her face dips, her gaze dropping to the ground. She's thinking, contemplating. I'm wearing her down…

"Please," I murmur, moving into her space.

Her hair is fanned over her face, so I lightly pinch her chin, forcing her to look up at me, so she can no longer hide behind her curtain of hair. "If you really want me to stop pursuing you, I will, Sierra. But I don't think you want me to stop. I think you're scared of what you feel between us, and I get it because I am too. I've never felt the instant connection with anyone the way I feel it with you."

She sucks in a harsh breath, and a wayward strand of hair falls over her eye. I use it as an excuse to touch her by tucking it behind her ear. As my fingers glide down the side of her face, she shivers.

"Kolton," she breathes, leaning her face into my palm and closing her eyes. "I don't know what to do."

"You take a deep breath, you open your eyes, and then you agree to have a drink with me."

She swallows thickly, then does what I say. "Okay. One drink." She steps backward slightly, out of my reach, and my hand drops. I want to pull her back so I can touch her some more, but I can tell just agreeing to have a drink with me was hard for her. I need to remember to take shit slow so she doesn't feel overwhelmed.

"Do you want to walk to someplace close, or do you trust me to drive us somewhere?"

She glances around. "You'll need to give me a ride home anyway, so I guess we can drive somewhere. Just… if you're planning to murder me, can you at least leave my body somewhere the police can find it so my sister will know I'm gone?"

I chuckle at her dry sense of humor. "I promise."

I guide her around back to the parking lot and over to where I parked my bike. I only have one helmet, but we won't be going far, and technically, they're not required here.

"Wait, you drive a motorcycle?" she says, coming to an abrupt halt when we arrive at my bike.

"Is that a problem?" I grab my helmet and hand it to her.

"No… I don't know…" She groans. "It's just…I dated my fair share of bad boys in high school, and it never ended well. And the past couple of years I've tried to become someone better… Someone my sister and nephew can be proud of and—"

"Whoa there. That's a whole lot of stereotyping and assumptions in one breath. Yes, I have tattoos. Yes, I drive a motorcycle, but I'm also in college getting my master's, and I'm a mama's boy through and through. Sometimes riding a bike is just that… the love of riding."

Her face falls. "Shit, I'm sorry. Are you sure you want to get to know me? I can't imagine what you know of me so far is all that amazing."

"So far, the little bit I know about you is enough to make me curious. And I imagine, once you actually let me in, it's only going to lead to me wanting to know even more."

Her lashes flutter, and her caramel-colored eyes meet mine. "You sure you're not a poetry major? Because you definitely know how to spit out some beautiful words."

I snort out a laugh. "I'm not usually this romantic," I admit. "Actually, I'm pretty rusty in that department. But you seem to bring it out in me." I swing my leg over the side of my bike. "Now, how about you throw your purse into the saddlebag, put my helmet on, and we go for a ride, so I can romance you into agreeing to spend your life with me?"

This time, instead of freaking the hell out at my antics, she laughs. After doing as I said, she hops onto the bike behind me and snakes her arms around my waist, pressing her soft breasts into my back.

"All right, Romeo, I'm ready to be romanced."

"Doesn't he commit suicide at the end of that play?"

"Yep, they both did. Isn't that how romance goes, though? You either live happily ever after or you crash and burn."

I take off out of the parking lot, and Sierra's grip on me tightens. This bike was my brother Keith's. He had it custom made and left it to me in his will. At first, after he died, I didn't want to touch it, but after I got my shit together, I figured what better way to remember him than to ride the one thing he loved. Until now, I've never had a woman on the back of the bike, and I can't help but feel like maybe there was a reason for that. Because the way Sierra's body fits against mine, it's as if she was made for riding on the back.

I take us the long way through town, enjoying the cool breeze and her holding me tightly. A couple of times, I glance back and find her eyes bright, glancing around, her brown hair whipping around her face. In all the times I've gone into The Orange Sunrise, I've never seen her look as carefree as she does on the back of my bike.

When we pull up to a coffee shop my mom loves and frequents, Sierra yells over the engine that she loves this place. I turn off the bike, and she hops off. I watch as she pulls the helmet off and shakes her hair out, and I swear to God no woman has ever looked so goddamn beautiful. With her face flush from the cool air and her hair windblown, she's a fucking wet dream.

"What?" she asks when she catches me staring. "Is my hair a mess?"

"It's perfect." I swing my leg over the side and stalk toward her. "You're perfect." I cup her cheek with my palm, needing to touch her yet wishing I could kiss her.

"You barely know me," she mutters, not realizing that even though she's tried to put a wall up, I've spent the past several days slowly chipping away at it, breaking away every bit I can get my hands on.

"I know you have a sister and a nephew who mean the world to you. You would do anything for them, including working too many hours at a restaurant you don't love and that doesn't appreciate you. You have dreams to one day own your own restaurant, but right now, your goal is to help your sister get through college because you feel you owe her that much. Your parents aren't around, and you don't like talking about them. You prefer vanilla cake over chocolate, which is crazy since chocolate blows vanilla away… You love Cherry Coke and french fries with cheese. You had a rough go of it in high school, and you're trying to make up for it in your twenties. Your favorite color is pink and—"

"I *never* told you my favorite color!"

"No, but it's obvious. You've come to work with your nails painted three different colors, and all of them were shades of pink. The necklace you wear every day has a pink heart on it, and your cell phone case is glittery and pink."

"Holy shit!" She shakes her head, eyeing me speculatively. "I can't believe you got all of that out of me. You really are a therapist in training."

"No," I say through a laugh. "I'm a man interested in a woman, which means I listen and pay attention."

Her features soften slightly. "There you go again with all that poetry."

"C'mon, beautiful." I take her hand in mine, loving the way my hand engulfs hers. "Let me buy you a cup of coffee and convince you to let me take you out."

After we order our coffees, I steer us outside and around the back. There's a park that butts up to the coffee shop, complete with a walking trail, picnic tables, and a pond filled with ducks.

We walk along the perimeter, drinking our coffees in silence until we get to the area with the picnic tables. Sierra hops up on one, and I join her, leaning against the side of it.

Her phone goes off, and she pulls it out. Whoever it is makes her sigh in frustration. She types rapidly for several seconds before she clicks her phone back off and shoves it back into her pocket.

"Everything okay?"

"Yeah." She sighs. "Work… You were right. I hate my job… Actually, I don't hate my job. I love it. I love everything about the restaurant business: the menus, the ambiance, the guests. I just don't love the owner. When I first started working there, her father owned the place. He was so passionate and dedicated to making sure it was run right. Then he died of a heart attack, and his daughter took it over. She knows nothing about the restaurant or hospitality industry. She makes horrible choices and refuses to listen to me. The place is going under, and it breaks my heart to see it happen. I wouldn't be surprised if the restaurant closes by the end of this year. And then I'll be out of a job and looking for somewhere else to work… having to start all over again."

"What is it you want to do?"

"My dream is to own my own restaurant."

"Have you thought about buying it from her?"

Sierra laughs humorlessly. "With what money?"

"Take out a loan."

She takes a sip of her coffee and stares out at the pond. "My sister is hoping to get into a master's program, and her financial aid will end. She'll have to take out loans, so I'll be the only one bringing in any money. Even if I could somehow get approved for a loan, now isn't the time to be taking risks."

Her eyes shine with unshed tears, and my heart feels as though it cracks, but I don't say anything because I know this is hard for her. She most likely didn't mean to let all that out, and she's trying to wish away those tears because she thinks they make her appear weak even though she is quite the opposite.

As I suspected, a second later, she blinks several times and takes in a deep breath. "It's for the best," she says with false confidence. "Being a restaurant owner is a lot of responsibility, and most fail. I would probably fai—"

I turn to face her, stepping between her legs, and cover her lips with my fingers. "Do not finish that sentence. You would not fail. Maybe now isn't the right time, but one day it will be, and you will get that loan and buy or open your own restaurant, and it will be a success because I can see your drive when you're working and hear your passion when you talk about it. You want it, and you will stop at nothing until it's a success."

Sierra releases a harsh breath, and the warmth tickles my flesh. She darts her tongue out to lick her lips, and her tongue grazes the pads of my fingers. When she realizes what she's done, her eyes go wide.

I drop my hand but remain close to her.

"Go out with me." I cup her face in my palm. "Please."

CHAPTER THREE

Kolton

"Who are you all dressed up for?" Keegan jibes when I walk out of my room dressed in jeans, a white collared shirt, and a pair of brown leather Sperry boat shoes.

"Sierra agreed to go on a date with me."

"Nice," Keegan says, waggling his brows up and down like an immature high schooler. "Want me to make myself scarce tonight so you have the place to yourself?"

"I don't think that'll be necessary. She's making me meet her at the restaurant instead of picking her up. I think it's her way of taking things slow." Even though I had driven us to the coffee shop and then driven her home, she insisted she meet me at the restaurant. She said if the date doesn't go well, she doesn't want it to be awkward. It was the stupidest thing I've ever heard—and I knew she was just saying it because she's nervous—but I agreed. Honestly, I would agree to almost anything to get her to give me a chance.

My phone dings with a text, and I pull it out to see who it is. The second I see Sierra's name, my heart drops. *Fuck, she's probably getting cold feet and is going to cancel...* It took some serious convincing on my part to get her to go to dinner and even more convincing to get her to give me her number. The woman definitely isn't making it easy on me, but I'm up for the challenge. What's that cliché as fuck saying? Nothing worth having comes easy? She's worth having, so if it takes some hard work, then so be it.

Sierra: Change of plans. Meet me at my place.

"Everything okay?" Keegan asks.

"Yeah, Sierra just texted me to pick her up."

"You sure you don't want the place to yourself?"

"Nah. Even if it were possible, I'm not about to rush it with her. She's skittish about dating as it is. I don't want her to think I'm just trying to get in her pants."

When it's time to pick her up, I drive over to her place. Since both of our apartments are situated right off the university campus, it only takes a couple minutes.

I park and jog up the flights of stairs, knocking when I get to her door.

A second later, the door swings open, and standing there is Sierra dressed in a flowy, low-cut top and skintight jeans. Her pink toes are peeking out of high as hell heels.

"Wow," Sierra says, "I didn't see it before because I wasn't looking for it, but damn, you look just like my nephew."

Her statement takes me by surprise, and I'm unsure how it's relevant to our date. "Am I missing something here?"

"Who are you?" Sierra asks, ignoring my question. "Keegan or Kolton?"

My eyes widen, then my lips curl into a grin, wondering how the hell she knows my brother. There's no way they've slept together. He barely has time for women, and he would've recognized her name. "I'm Kolton."

"Why did you lie to me?" someone asks. I turn my attention to the other woman standing by the door. I didn't notice her because I was completely focused on Sierra. *Why does she look so familiar?* Maybe it's because she and Sierra share similar features: brown hair, caramel eyes, pert nose… This is obviously her sister—but I don't think she's ever mentioned her name.

"About what? When?" I ask, confused as fuck. I came here to go on a date with Sierra, and suddenly, I'm getting grilled with questions.

"When you slept with my sister!" Sierra bellows. "And don't try to act like you don't remember her. You tried to get her attention earlier." *What the hell is going on?*

"I didn't sleep with her," I say, my gaze locking with Sierra's. "I don't even know her."

"Is this a game to you?" her sister asks, hurt and confusion filled in her tone.

"You think you slept with me?"

"I think I slept with *Keegan*," she volleys.

Oh, shit… What has my brother done? "And you think I'm Keegan?"

"Do you have a split personality disorder?" she asks, making me laugh.

"I think I know what the problem is, but it would probably be best if I show you." I doubt she'll believe me unless she sees it for herself.

I pull out my phone and call my brother.

"What's up?"

"I need you to come here."

"Where?"

"To Sierra's place. Don't ask questions. Just come." I rattle off her address and then hang up.

While we wait for Keegan to arrive, the women step outside, then close the door behind them. Sierra refers to her sister as Blakely, and I damn near choke on my own saliva. Holy shit! There's no way this is a coincidence. My brother met a woman years ago on spring break named Blakely. He talked about her for months, upset that his phone got fucked up, and he lost her number.

We stand in awkward silence until Keegan rolls up on his skateboard a few minutes later, then runs up the steps. The second he comes into view, Blakely gasps at the same time Keegan's face splits into a grin.

"Jailbird," Keegan says. "I knew that was you earlier."

"Keegan?" she asks, clearly in shock.

"I see you've met my brother Kolton."

"You didn't tell me you had a twin brother," she mutters.

Yep, that's right. Keegan and I are identical twins. Hence, why he thinks I'm so hot. It's always been an inside joke between us.

Keegan and Blakely chat back and forth, getting caught up, until the door opens and out walks some guy. Blakely makes introductions—Brenton is a friend of hers, who, I have no doubt by the way he's looking at her, has the hots for her. Even if it seems she doesn't feel the same way.

There's an awkward lull in the conversation, and then Keegan says, "Was… is that kid yours?" And that's when I remember her. She was walking across campus with Brenton and a little boy, who must've been her son. She tried to talk to me, but I had no idea who she was. She had assumed I was Keegan.

Blakely's eyes go wide at Keegan's question, and she immediately looks nervous. "Is Zane okay in his room?" she asks Brenton.

"Yeah," he replies. "He's playing with his Legos. I came out here to make sure everything is okay. You've been out here for a while."

"Can you go check on him?" she asks. "I think I should talk to Keegan alone."

Brenton opens his mouth to argue, but Blakely speaks first. "Please."

"What about them?" he asks, pointing at Sierra and me.

"Sierra," Blakely says, turning to her sister.

"We're actually late for our date," I mention, glancing at the time on my phone. I have no idea what's going on, but Keegan will fill me in later. "I can probably get us in for later, though."

"That's not happening." Sierra scoffs, confusing the shit out of me. "We're practically family." She cackles, and Blakely smacks her arm.

Practically family? What the hell is she talking about?

"Really?" Blakely glares at her sister.

"Sorry." Sierra shrugs.

"Can someone explain what the hell's going on?" Keegan asks, obviously as confused as I am.

"I'll watch Zane," Sierra says to Blakely, "and you can go talk to Keegan."

Shit, there goes our date…

"Do you really think it's wise to be alone with him?" Brenton asks Blakely.

I can practically feel the sudden tension rolling off my brother. Locking eyes with him, I give a subtle shake of my head. Whatever is going on, he needs to keep his cool.

Blakely and Brenton go back and forth, arguing over whether she should be alone with my brother. I'm about to speak up when Blakely smiles, and says, "You haven't murdered anyone in the past four years, have you? Gone to jail for anything?"

"Nah, Jailbird," Keegan replies with a laugh. "No murders, no arrests. How about you? Have you kept yourself out of jail? Paying for everything at the store? Attending all your classes?"

Sierra laughs. "You told him about the time we shoplifted and when you got caught skipping?"

Wait, what?

Blakely rolls her eyes. "I was making sure he wasn't going to rape and murder me, and it backfired."

"You've been arrested?" I blurt out.

"We were bad teenagers," Sierra says with a shoulder shrug and a smirk. "Now, we're responsible, law-abiding adults."

"That's good to know," Keegan jokes. "So, you wanted to talk?" he says to Blakely.

"Yeah." She nods, and her smile disappears. "Brenton, you can go," she tells him. "I'll call you later."

"You sure?" he asks, sounding whiny as fuck. Poor guy, he has it bad.

He takes off, leaving the four of us. Blakely suggests to Keegan they go for a walk and talk, and then Sierra says she's going to head in with her nephew.

Before she can open the door, I snag her wrist gently.

"This isn't over," I tell her. There's no way I'm letting her bail on our date.

She doesn't say a word. Instead, she just slips inside.

The second I'm back home, I send her a text: **When am I getting my rain check?**

I wait several minutes, but of course, my text remains unread.

"You're not going to believe this shit," Keegan says a couple of hours later when he walks through the door with a huge grin on his face.

Sierra still hasn't texted me back, so I'm cranky as fuck. "What?"

"Zane, Blakely's son... he's my son."

He drops onto the couch. "I can't believe it, man. I'm a fucking dad."

Well, shit, now it all makes sense. Sierra's earlier comments… *"You look just like my nephew… We're practically family."* Because she knew Keegan was the dad, which makes me Zane's uncle.

Oh. Fucking. Well. If she thinks that's going to stop me from pursuing her, she's got another thing coming.

CHAPTER FOUR

Sierra

D URING MY ENTIRE SHIFT, I KEEP ONE EYE ON THE ENTRANCE, waiting for Kolton to walk in. Yesterday was a shock, to say the least. My sister, who has dreamed of the day when she would find her son's father, has found him. And of course, he's none other than Kolton's identical twin brother. Because apparently having one of those sexy men in the world isn't enough, God graced us with two of them.

I've been avoiding his texts since yesterday, trying to decide what I'm going to do. I always told myself I wasn't running from love. I've just never come across the right guy. But the second it hit me that Kolton could be the one, I did exactly that. I ran. And now I have to figure out if I'm going to continue to run, or if I'm going to give us a chance because it's not fair to keep stringing him along.

As if the thought of Kolton has summoned him, he appears at the door, sauntering my way with purpose. Today, he's dressed in a navy-blue button-down shirt with his sleeves rolled up and a pair of black slacks that fit his muscular thighs. Maybe if I had teachers like him in high school, I would've considered taking the step toward higher education.

"If you want me, you can have me, Sierra. You just have to say the word." His words knock me into reality.

"Excuse me?" I splutter.

"You're practically undressing me on the spot." He smirks playfully, then leans over and runs his thumb along my chin. "And drooling."

"I am not!" I shriek, grabbing a coaster and placing it in front of him.

"Oh, you were, but I'll try to keep my clothes on in front of all these people. What's underneath is for your eyes only."

I groan, hating that I don't hate him at all. "What can I get you?" I ask, making him smirk.

Dammit! I keep setting myself up for this shit.

"Other than me," I add.

He chuckles. "I'm done with these games. I want you to go on a date with me."

"It's not happening. We're family."

I know. I know. Stupid excuse. But it's all I've got to keep him at arm's length while I figure out my feelings toward him.

"We're not family. But I am excited to officially meet my nephew." A genuine smile graces his lips. "Keegan is meeting him today. He and Mom went shopping for Zane earlier. The guy is on cloud nine."

My heart soars for my nephew and sister. This reunion could have gone in so many directions, and I'm thankful it went in the one that means Zane will have a loving, caring father, and my sister will have a partner to parent with.

"He's an amazing kid," I tell him. "Smart and adorable and funny."

"Of course, he is," he quips. "He's a Reynolds."

I roll my eyes. "Salad and iced tea?"

"Yep, with a side of you, please."

"It's not happening."

"Oh, it is. And the sooner you accept that, the sooner we can move forward… together."

He pulls a bunch of papers out of his briefcase and sets them on the bar top. "Do you mind if I grade my papers here?"

"I don't care." I shrug. "But wouldn't you want to do that in peace and quiet at your house?"

He shakes his head. "I'd rather do it with the backdrop of you."

I shake my head and walk over to the computer to place his order, trying not to seem affected by his words, when the truth is, I'm very much affected. For years after my parents died, I kept everyone at arm's length, not wanting to risk my heart getting broken. I watched my mom's heart get torn to shreds little by little, bit by bit, all in the name of love, and I swore I would never allow that to happen to me.

But the second I heard my nephew's heartbeat on the monitor, it was as if my chest was cracked open, and my heart was on display for the world to see. Which was fine since my entire world consisted of Blakely and Zane—and I knew they would never hurt me.

But now Kolton wants in, and I have no doubt, if I give him my heart, he has the capability to destroy it the same way my dad destroyed my mom. And I have to decide if I'm willing to take that risk.

The evening flies by. Kolton hangs around, grading papers, and when I'm not busy, we chat. When the final customer pays his check and leaves, I glance over at Kolton, who's still nursing his iced tea.

"You ready to go?" he asks, standing when I come around the bar to lock up. The staff has all cashed out and shut down their stations, and Kolton and I are the only ones left.

"Yeah."

He hands me his helmet, and I reluctantly put it on my head, knowing it's going to ruin my hair.

"What's wrong?"

"These helmets are clearly not made for women."

He chuckles. "No, probably not, but you still look sexy as hell with it on."

The ride to my apartment complex is quick, and when I get off the bike, I expect him to ask me out, so I'm shocked when he walks me to my door like a gentleman, kisses my cheek, and tells me he'll see me soon.

When I walk inside, Blakely is still awake, studying. She gushes about her evening with Keegan and how well it went telling Zane he's his dad. He also mentioned he wants to get to know her as more than Zane's mom. After we chat for a few minutes, I jump in the shower and drop into bed exhausted. When I plug my phone in to charge it, I notice a text from Kolton.

Kolton: Good night and sweet dreams.

I usually ignore his texts, afraid to open that door, but tonight, I reply: **Good night.**

The rest of the week feels as if it's in fast-forward. I'm working every day—between managing the restaurant, manning the bar, and running interviews. Kolton shows up every day, but he no longer asks me out. He eats and drinks and grades papers. When I'm not busy, we chat about everything and nothing. I have to admit I miss his flirting, but I also enjoy getting to know him without feeling like there's an agenda.

By Friday, I'm convinced Kolton is over asking me out, and the only reason he continues to frequent The Orange Sunrise is for its iced tea and salad.

But then, right after my sister asks me to join her on Saturday to meet Keegan's parents, a text comes in from Kolton, making it clear where he stands.

Heard you're joining us for lunch. If it were up to me, you'd be coming as my girlfriend and not as my brother's baby momma's sister, but I still look forward to spending the day with you nonetheless... Next time, though, you'll be visiting as mine.

Me: I *think* that was romantic... in a creepy sort of way.

Kolton: Are you saying you miss my flirting?

Me: ....

Kolton: I'll take that as a yes.

So, he has been making it a point not to flirt with me.
I set my phone down, but then my curiosity gets the best of me.

Me: Why haven't you been flirting?

Kolton: Wow, so you really do miss it, huh?

Me: That's not what I asked.

My phone suddenly rings, and Kolton's name flashes across the screen. "Hello?"

"You okay?"

"Um… yeah."

"Just checking. It's hard to tell through text. You seemed very distraught over me not flirting with you all week."

"Hardly. I was just wondering what changed."

"I was waiting for you."

"For me?"

"To realize you miss my flirting."

Motherfucker… Of course! He used reverse psychology… because he's a freaking psychology major.

"I'm hanging up now."

"No, wait," he says through a laugh, but I don't. After hanging up, I go one step further and turn my phone off. Let him psychoanalyze that!

It's Saturday morning, and the five of us are piled into Keegan's truck on our way to meet their parents. Blakely is droning on about how nervous she is to meet Keegan's parents while he reassures her everything will be fine. I shouldn't be nervous since I'm only coming along as moral support for my sister, but I can't help the anxiety attacking my belly. I'm about to meet Kolton's parents. I haven't been around any parents in years. After ours died—and shortly after our grandma died—we were put into foster care. One woman was nice, but she was more like a roommate than a mom… From that moment forward, it was Blakely and me against the world.

"Mom will be so happy to have Zane there. She won't care about anyone else," Keegan promises her.

"And add to that Blakely and Sierra." Kolton snorts. "She always says she wishes she'd had a daughter. Now she's getting two-for-one."

He looks over at me and winks, and my heart bottoms out in my stomach. Has Kolton told his parents about me? If he hasn't, will I be disappointed? Will they think I'm good enough for their son?

My thoughts are still running rampant when we pull up to the most adorable gray and white house. It's nothing like the over-the-top home Blakely and I grew up in… and I love it.

I unbuckle Zane from his booster seat and then climb out, taking it all in. In the front of the house there are flower beds containing beautiful multicolored flowers spread out across the front of a cute wraparound porch with cozy-looking rocking chairs. The entire scene in front of me screams homemade apple pies and family dinners, and it warms my icy heart.

Distracted by my thoughts, I don't notice Kolton come up behind me until his lips graze the outer shell of my ear.

"You must be exhausted," he murmurs.

"What?" I ask, snapping my gaze from the house to him. "Why would I be exhausted?"

Kolton smirks devilishly, and I know whatever he says next will be something flirty. "Because you were running through my mind all night."

I can't help the snort-laugh that bubbles out of me. He has got to be the cheesiest guy I know, and somehow it only adds to his charm.

He takes my hand in his and guides me into his house. When we enter the house, the sweetest woman comes rushing over to us. She makes a beeline straight for Blakely and envelops her in the warmest motherly hug.

"My son has told me so much about you. I'm so happy I get to finally meet you." She pulls back slightly to assess Blakely. "You're gorgeous." She smiles sweetly, then glances over at me. "You both are." Barely releasing Blakely, she says to me, "Come here," and pulls me into their hug. My insides melt at her touch, not realizing how much I've craved this. Even when our parents were alive, our mother never hugged us like this.

"I hate what happened with you and Keegan," she murmurs to Blakely. "Him losing your number and you girls having to take care of my grandson alone all these years."

Tears prick my sister's eyes, but I try to remain strong.

"It's okay," Blakely tells her.

"Well, I can promise you that you will never be alone again. You have all of us now. I'm so excited to be a grandma," she gushes. "Anything you need, you just let me know."

"Thank you, Mrs. Reynolds."

"Oh, no! You call me Larissa, or Mom, whichever." She winks. "And this here is my other half." She waves her husband over.

"I'm Paul," Keegan's dad says with a friendly smile. He looks like an older version of Keegan and Kolton, right down to the dimples. "It's very nice to meet you." His eyes meet mine. "Both of you."

The early morning turns into afternoon as we eat and talk and laugh the day away. After lunch, the guys go fishing while Blakely, Larissa, and I go shopping. The entire day I can see the emotions splayed across my sister's features. She doesn't know what to do or how to act. This is new for both of us. But I can see in her eyes that she's so damn happy. Zane not only has a mother and a father, but he now has an entire family, which only solidifies my decision. Kolton and I can never be anything more because if, or when, it doesn't work out, everything would be awkward. My sister and nephew deserve to have this family, and I won't be the reason they risk losing it.

Later, when we get home, I send a text to Kolton before I lose my courage: **I'm sorry, but we can't be anything more than friends. We're family now, and that's the way it has to stay.**

He sends a response back immediately: **If I believed for a second you really felt that way, I would accept that, but I know you're scared. Sorry, Sierra, but I disagree. We can and will be more…It's only a matter of time.**

CHAPTER FIVE

Sierra

"**I**'M RUNNING OUT TO GET COFFEE. WANT ANYTHING?" I ASK MONICA as she throws her apron around her waist, ready for the start of her shift.

"Nope! I'm good."

"All right. I'll be back!"

"Or you can go home and start your weekend early."

That sounds nice… but at the same time, I need to get a bunch of stuff done before I'm off for the next three days.

I rush out of the restaurant, needing my caffeine fix, and run straight into Kolton.

"What are you doing here?" I ask, not confused that he's here—he's been here every night this week—but that he's here this early. He usually arrives in time for dinner and stays until closing, then insists on giving me a ride home.

"I have Fridays off. I usually spend the day doing schoolwork or grading papers. My brother told me you were working this morning… Are you off already?"

"I'm taking a coffee break."

"How long do you have?"

"Technically, however long I want… I'm not on the schedule today. Why, what's up?"

"I want to talk to you." He walks over to his motorcycle and pulls something out of the saddlebag. "For you," he says, handing me a helmet—this one is different from the one I wore the other night. It's lighter and has a cute black and pink design on the back.

My heart swells behind my rib cage, and I know I'm screwed. "Did you buy this for me?"

"Of course. You're going to need your own helmet since I plan to have you on the back of my bike every chance I get." He nods toward the helmet in my hand. "The guy said women prefer that design because it's easier on their hair."

He gets on his bike, leaving me momentarily frozen. I mentioned to him that the helmet ruined my hair, so he went out and bought one that wouldn't. Jesus, this man is something else. How am I supposed to resist him when he says and does all the right things?

After a few seconds, I hop on, pushing my helmet on my head and wrapping my arms around him. We head east, riding in silence and enjoying the view around us. About thirty minutes later, he turns on to Ocean Ave, the road that runs north and south along the Atlantic Ocean. The breeze from the ocean picks up, and I snuggle closer to Kolton, trying to get warm. He smells clean with a hint of sweetness, like laundry detergent mixed with vanilla.

Eventually, he pulls into a deserted parking lot that overlooks the beach and parks his bike, turning the engine off.

"It's beautiful out here." I inhale a deep breath, feeling immediately rejuvenated. Something about being at the beach, smelling the salty air, and listening to the crashing waves instantly calms my nerves, making me feel like a new person.

"Yeah, it is," Kolton agrees. "I like to come out here when I need somewhere to be alone and think."

"About what?" I ask, wanting to know more even though I shouldn't.

He slides off his bike and takes my hand to help me off. With our fingers intertwined, we walk down to the water. It's a cloudy day, the norm here in Florida, but the sun is shining enough that it probably won't rain until later.

Kolton drops to the ground and pulls me down with him so we're sitting side by side. After sitting like this for a few minutes, he finally speaks. "A few years back, my older brother Keith was killed… and it was my fault. I was young and dumb, and my actions led to my brother's death." He releases a shaky breath, and I swallow down my shock, waiting for him to continue.

"Afterward, I took off, left the country to study abroad. I couldn't be around my family, couldn't handle the weight of knowing they all lost someone they loved because of me. I was only gone about a year before my brother convinced me to come back. Our mom was missing me, and he was pissed that my leaving meant she lost two of her sons. So, I returned. It was hard to be back at first and face everyone… When it would get to be too much, I would hop on my bike, which was Keith's, and go for a ride. I ended up here one night and spent hours staring out at the water. It felt as if all that weight I was carrying ran into the water and was washed away."

"I feel the same way. When we were little, our parents used to bring us here every year for vacation. No matter what was going on, once I was at the beach, with my toes in the sand and the sun beating down on my face, it was as if everything else momentarily faded away."

Kolton takes my hand in his and brings it up to his lips, placing a kiss on my knuckles. When he lowers our hands, he keeps our fingers locked together.

"I lost my parents," I admit. "When Blakely and I were teenagers. We were in a car accident, and by some miracle, even though both our parents died, we survived. It's not the same as what you went through, but I just want you to know in my own way, I kind of get it." Kolton squeezes my hand. When I glance over at him, he's staring out at the water, deep in thought.

After a few minutes, he speaks. "Since I've returned, I've been on a mission to prove myself. To prove that my brother's death wasn't in vain… To prove that, even though nothing I do will bring him back, I'm living up to what he would've wanted for me. I'm in school, getting my master's. I've been working hard on my relationships with my parents and Keegan, but somewhere along the way, I didn't focus on me. Maybe it's because I didn't believe I deserved to be happy, or I was directing my attention on other stuff… I don't know."

His eyes meet mine, and at this moment, I've never felt so in sync with another person as I do with Kolton. I feel everything he's saying down to my core. And because of that, without second-guessing myself, I give him a piece of myself I've never given anyone else—not even Blakely.

"My parents were twenty years apart in age," I begin. "My mom was seventeen when she met my dad. She was an orphan, never had any kind of real love, and he offered it to her on a silver platter, so she took it. In his own weird, twisted way, I know he loved my mom, but he also loved to be in power, to control things and people, and my mom was easily controlled.

"Growing up, to someone standing on the outside, Blakely and I had the perfect life. The huge house, expensive clothes…Our father ran a successful company. We went to a prestigious private school. Our mom attended charity brunches while we were in school and followed him around all over the globe when he needed her to. She was the perfect trophy wife while we were raised by nannies.

"But in reality, it was all a façade. Our dad made bad decision after bad decision. He ran up debt and took risks he shouldn't have. He was involved in illegal activity that, we found out later, he would've been sent to jail for. He kept our mom on a short leash, and when she misbehaved, he hurt her…" I shiver, remembering walking out of my room to get a drink and overhearing him yell at her just before he slapped her across the face. That was the first time I saw him lay his hands on her—and it wasn't the last.

"My mom should've left him, but she was so freaking in love with him… or maybe she was in love with the idea of him, I don't know. Either way, in the end, when he knew his life was about to go up in flames, instead of protecting us from the heat, instead of protecting *her*, he threw us straight into the fire. He found out she was going to take us and run, and he drove drunk, flat out saying he wouldn't live without her, right before he plowed us into a pole, killing them both."

Kolton sucks in a sharp breath. "Jesus, Sierra, I don't even know what to say…"

"There's nothing to say. Just like there's nothing I can say about your brother's death. We can say we're sorry, but we both know that word is useless. It doesn't change anything. Horrible things happen that are out of our control, but it's how we react to them that defines us. And how I handled shit after my parents died was horrible. I pushed my sister away and made her feel as if I didn't love her anymore. We were best friends, and I abandoned her. I was so hurt by what happened… afraid to love again… to be vulnerable. My mom gave my dad everything. Every bit of her. She made him her priority even though she had us, and in the end, her love and devotion to him killed her."

"Sierra—" Kolton starts, but I cut him off, needing to get it all out.

"When Blakely found out she was pregnant, she was terrified. And the day we heard Zane's heartbeat, I realized how badly I messed up. I didn't even know about Keegan. She should've been able to come to me, but she didn't. She considered giving Zane up because she didn't think she had any other choice, and my heart broke. I vowed that day to make it up to her. All the years I spent pushing her away, I would make it right."

"And that's why you work at a restaurant you hate, to pay all the bills so your sister could keep Zane and get her degree."

"Yeah," I breathe, staring out at the ocean. "It's more than that, though. Blakely never gave up on me, and now it's my turn to be there for her. And if I date you and we don't work out, I could risk her happiness. Did you see how ecstatic she was to give Zane more family?"

"I understand how important your sister is to you because I feel the same way about my brother, but it doesn't mean you can't find your own slice of happiness."

"True…" I turn my head to look at him. "But it can't be with you. I feel the connection between us, the spark, the chemistry, and I don't want to end up like my mom. She loved my dad with all of her being, and in the end, her love for him killed her."

Kolton reaches over and pulls me onto his lap, so I'm straddling his thighs. With both hands, he cups the sides of my face. "I know firsthand how easily a single choice can affect someone else's life, and I would never purposely put you in danger. If you give me your heart, Sierra, I promise to always protect it, handle it with care, and provide the love it needs to thrive. After my brother died, I didn't think I deserved to find love or be happy, but then I walked into that bar. With just one look at you, I knew I needed you in my life. The way you danced behind the bar reminded me of how carefree my brother was, and when your eyes glittered with mischief, I swear, it was as if he sent you to me."

"Kolton." I gasp. "You can't say that. I can't possibly live up to those expectations…"

"It's the truth, and the only expectation I have is for you to give us a chance. To see if things can be as good as I believe they can be."

"And if it doesn't work out between us?"

"You have my word that no matter what happens, I will make sure our families are never affected." He glides his hands down the curve of my neck and across my shoulder to land on my hip. "Please, just give us one chance. We've both been through hell, and we deserve to find a bit of happiness, especially since your sister and my brother have found it."

Well, hell, how do I say no to that? "Okay, I'll give us a chance. We'll start with one date and see where it goes from there. When?"

Kolton's face splits into the most gorgeous two-dimple grin. "Tonight, so you don't have time to back out."

I laugh. "We're already out." I run my hands up his shoulders and snake them around his neck.

"No way." He shakes his head. "I want a real date. One where I pick you up and take you out."

"Fine. Tonight it is. I'm watching Zane for Keegan tomorrow night. He's taking Blakely away for the night."

"Perfect." He moves his hands around to the globes of my ass and lifts us both into a standing position. "Better get you back to work. You've taken a helluva break."

"Actually, you can take me home." I pull out my phone and text Sonora—the owner of The Orange Sunrise and my boss—to let her know I won't be back in.

The ride home is different than the other rides we've taken, and I know it's because there's been a shift between us. I've given in, and by doing so, I've lowered the wall I had erected. In turn, Kolton feels less tense, as if my agreeing to go out with him has relaxed him.

Like the gentleman he is, he walks me to the door when we arrive at my place. Only, instead of saying goodbye, he gently pushes me against the wall. With one hand next to my head and the other gripping my hip, he leans in and brushes his lips against my cheek.

"You won't regret this," he murmurs into my ear, causing a shiver to race up my spine. "I can feel it. It's going to be so damn good."

He kisses the shell of my ear and then backs up. "I'll see you in a few hours."

CHAPTER SIX

Kolton

"Wʜᴀᴛ's sᴏ ɪᴍᴘᴏʀᴛᴀɴᴛ ᴛʜᴀᴛ ʏᴏᴜ ᴄᴏᴜʟᴅɴ'ᴛ ᴛᴇxᴛ ᴍᴇ ᴏʀ ᴛᴇʟʟ me over the phone?" Keegan asks when I walk through the door. I've been meaning to talk to him about something, but he's been at Blakely's more than he's been home lately.

"We need to talk." I drop my briefcase on the couch and sit at the table where Keegan types away on his laptop.

"Yeah, I gathered that. So, what's up?"

"I ran into Blakely and that asshole Brenton the other day... He had her pinned against the wall."

Keegan's head snaps up, giving me his full attention. "In what way?"

"Like he was threatening her or some shit. I couldn't hear what was being said, but Blakely looked scared. She tried to play it off, but I got a weird vibe. Something isn't right."

"No, it's not," Keegan agrees. "I just need a little more time, and that fucker is going down."

"Good. That guy is bad news."

"I heard about your date tonight." Keegan smirks, changing the subject. "She finally gave in, huh?"

"Yeah, now I just need to find a way to keep her."

"I'll be staying at Blakely's tonight, so you have the place to yourself."

"I already told you I'm not going to rush shit."

"Yeah, yeah. Anyway, it'll be empty. Just make sure she's home by early afternoon tomorrow. She's watching Zane for me so I can take Blakely away." He waggles his brows and stands. "I just came home to handle a couple of things. I'm heading back over to Blakely's. Guess I'll see you later." He winks, and I chuck a pillow at his annoying ass.

I spend the afternoon attempting to grade papers, but eventually, I give up when the only thing I can think about is Sierra and what I'm going to do for our date tonight. I could take her to the same restaurant I had reservations at the night Keegan found out about Zane, and she bailed, but that feels like bad luck.

No, I need something different—special.

And then an idea hits.

CHAPTER SEVEN

Sierra

'M IN THE BATHROOM, APPLYING THE LAST TOUCH OF MAKEUP TO MY face, when the sound of someone knocking reverberates through the small apartment. *Shit! Is it already six o'clock?* A few moments later, Zane squeals in delight. Words are spoken, but they're muffled, and then the pitter-patter of his feet gets louder and louder until he ends up in the bathroom with me.

"Uncle Kolton's here," he says, stopping in front of me. "He said he's taking you on a date." His nose scrunches up in disgust. "Are you going to kiss him like Mommy kisses Daddy?"

"Mayybbbeeee," I taunt.

"Ewww. Kissing is gross! Girls have cooties!"

"What?" I gasp. "Are you saying I'll give you cooties if I kiss you right now?"

I widen my eyes, and Zane shrieks, knowing what's coming. Before he can dart out the door, I pick him up by his waist and pull him into my arms, raining kisses all over his face.

"Auntie Sierra, stop!" he yells through his giggles as I walk us out to the living room, not stopping my assault on his face until we arrive.

When we reach the living room, I drop him to the ground, stifling my laughter at all the lipstick kisses I left all over his face that he doesn't know about.

"Yuck!" Zane complains, wiping his mouth, the only spot I didn't actually kiss. "Uncle Kolton, you better be careful. Girls have cooties."

"Hey," Blakely says, mock hurt in her tone. "I don't have cooties."

"I know that," Zane agrees. "Because you're not a girl. You're a mom."

Kolton and Keegan both chuckle under their breath.

"I'll be careful, bud," Kolton says, "but if she tries to kiss me, I might have to risk getting cooties."

Zane gives him an incredulous look as if he can't believe Kolton would even consider such a thing. "I'm gonna watch the *SpongeBob* movie with my daddy and mommy." He shrugs and heads over to the couch to get comfortable.

"All right," Keegan says, his tone serious. "Curfew is eleven. No drinking and driving, and remember… no glove, no love." He whips a condom out of his pocket and throws it at Kolton.

"Oh my God, Keegan!" Blakely smacks him in the chest. "Go make us some popcorn." She pushes him toward the kitchen. "Have fun, guys!"

"But not too much fun!" Keegan calls back as they disappear.

Once they're gone, my attention turns to Kolton. He's dressed in a forest green, short-sleeved collared shirt that shows off the ink on his forearms and biceps, a pair of nice blue jeans, and black dress shoes. His wrist holds a chunky silver watch. He's shaved since I saw him earlier, leaving only enough to be considered a five o'clock shadow, and when he steps closer, I smell a light scent of vanilla mixed with woods.

"You look beautiful, Sierra. Fucking gorgeous." His words are softly spoken, so Zane can't hear. "That dress…" He rakes his eyes down my body, sending goose bumps along my flesh. "I think I made a mistake."

"What? Why?" I breathe. He asked for this date over and over again, and now he's not sure? I don't understand. Is it what I'm wearing? I glance down at myself. I went with a pale pink floaty dress and a pair of knee-high suede boots since I wasn't sure if he would be picking me up on his motorcycle.

"I wanted you all to myself, so I planned to take you back to my place, but seeing you dressed like this with your makeup and hair done… It feels like it's a damn waste not to take you out and show you off." He runs his fingers along the edge of my dress where it meets my collarbone, and the area between my legs clench in sudden need. It's been a hot minute since I've been looked at and appreciated like Kolton's doing right now.

"C'mon, Romeo." I hook my arm in his. "I promise you this dress will *not* go to waste."

As suspected, Kolton drove his bike over here. He climbs on, and I follow. Because the bottom of my dress is flowy, I'm able to sit behind him without exposing myself to the entire town of Carterville. But when Kolton takes off, and his hand lands on the exposed flesh of my thigh, I couldn't care less about the town or the people or anyone besides Kolton.

With my body up against his, my center rubs against his lower back, causing friction. The sensation causes my nipples to pebble through my thin bra and dress, and I tighten my legs, wondering if Kolton can sense how turned on I am.

All too quickly, we arrive at his place. He places his hand in mine to help me off the bike, and the sparks between us flow like a live electrical current.

"This is it," he says, closing the door behind us. "I made dinner. Are you hungry?" My eyes meet his, and I know he's feeling what I'm feeling. The thick sexual tension. The desire to touch each other. The need to be close to each other. But this is only our first date. You don't have sex on the first date, right?

"I'm starving," I say, my voice breathy.

His brows rise, understanding my double innuendo. "Good. I am too." Lacing our fingers, he walks us to the dining room. The lights are dim, and table is set with beautiful-looking china. In the center, he turns on two electric candles to illuminate the room along with a bottle of wine.

He releases my hand and uncorks the wine, pouring us each a glass. "To our first date," he says with a sexy grin, making my insides turn to mush.

"To us," I agree. We clink our glasses, and he throws his back like a shot, his Adam's apple bobbing as he swallows. A fantasy of me licking down each ridge of his throat and sucking on his flesh hits me hard.

It suddenly feels hot in here, so I down my own glass and grab the bottle to pour myself some more.

"You okay?" he asks, his tone more knowing than concerned.

"Yeah," I breathe. "Just… hot." I lift my hair to emphasize my point, but since the burning ache comes from inside me, it does nothing to put the flames out.

Kolton steps closer, and the air thickens, making it hard to breathe, to function, to think clearly. "I can see the look on your face," he murmurs. "The flush creeping up your neck… I can see the way your squeezing your thighs together… And if I were any less of a gentleman, I would act on it. I would pull that dress up to your waist and pull your underwear down your thighs, and then I would ravish every inch of your body until you begged me to make you come. But I didn't bring you back here to fuck you, and if I do just that, you're going to think I did. And like I told you before, Sierra, I want you long term. Not for the night or the weekend… I want you forever. So, instead of letting my dick call the shots, I'm going to grab our dinner warming in the kitchen, and we're going to eat and talk."

"Okay," I say, swallowing thickly. He turns to leave, but before he does, I grab his arm, making him turn back to look at me. "But let's say I wanted to think with my pussy…"

Kolton groans. "Sierra…"

"Would you fuck me?" I wrap my arms around his neck. I don't know what the hell has gotten into me, and I really don't care. Maybe it's stupid, and maybe it's crazy, but with Kolton, it feels right. I've spent the past five years focused on Blakely and Zane, hooking up with guys I knew I didn't have a future with so I wouldn't have to worry about catching feelings. But with Kolton, I know he's the one. It's the reason I've pushed him away. I was scared. But I'm not anymore. I want him now.

In me, on top of me, all over me.

"Would you take me right here on the table? Make me scream your name?"

Kolton's answer is to lift me into his arms and lay me on top of the table. The china clinks, and some of it might even land on the floor, but neither of us cares enough to look.

His mouth crashes against mine, his tongue plunging past my parted lips, capturing and swirling with my own. My legs wrap around his waist, my center grinding against his already growing erection.

"Fuck," he hisses against my mouth as I reach for his pants, unbuttoning and unzipping them. I push his briefs down and feel his dick spring free.

"Sierra," he moans, breaking our kiss when I wrap my fist around his shaft and stroke it up and down. "It wasn't supposed to happen like this." He runs his thumb along my swollen lips. "I was supposed to wine and dine you. Convince you to go on a second and third date with me."

"Didn't you say what's between us is inevitable? That we're forever?"

"And you said you were scared."

"And I am," I admit. "But I also feel it… what you feel. And I'm done living my life in fear." I latch onto his shirt and tug him toward me so our bodies are flush with only my hand wrapped around his dick between us. "If we crash and burn, then at least I can say it was a hell of a ride."

He stares at me for a long beat, and I wonder if he's going to push me away and tell me we're going too fast. I hold my breath, hoping he does neither.

"It will definitely be a hell of a ride," he growls. "But nobody is getting hurt." His mouth fuses with mine. He bites, sucks, and nibbles on my lips.

We're all teeth and tongue.

Hands touching and caressing.

Needing and wanting.

As if neither of us can get enough.

He pulls my dress up my body and unlatches my bra, exposing my breasts to the cool air. He wraps his lips around my nipple, and his tongue lashes back and forth across the hardened tip. Bolts of electricity spark inside me as if he has a direct line to my clit.

"Kolton," I moan, pumping his cock harder. Squeezing it in desperation.

He kisses his way down my middle, and when he gets to my belly, I lose my connection with his dick. He presses an open-mouthed kiss to the top of my silk-covered mound before he tugs my panties off, dropping them onto the floor.

"I need to taste you," he murmurs, licking his lips as he spreads my thighs wide open.

He drops to his knees, and his eyes glint in the darkness. His thumb and middle finger spread my folds open, and his forefinger strokes my center up and down, teasing my clit. "I bet you taste better than what I made for dinner." He looks up at me. "What do you think?"

I'm not sure if I'm supposed to respond, but it doesn't matter because when the flat of his tongue lands on my center, I'm rendered speechless. My hands fist the edge of the wood table as Kolton devours my pussy like a starved man. He works me up, licking and sucking on my clit, bringing me to the brink of my orgasm before his mouth leaves my pussy.

"What the hell!" I hiss, my chest rising and falling in quick succession.

"I was right. You taste fucking delicious." Standing, he reaches behind him to pull his shirt over his head. As it rises, each of his cut abs makes an appearance until he's displayed his entire upper body. He's all ink and muscle and—

Holy shit! He drops his pants and briefs, and his dick juts out. Thick and veiny with a tiny bead of pre-cum dripping out of the mushroom tip.

"My turn," I breathe, not even caring that I never got my orgasm as I slide off the edge of the table and drop to my knees. I lift his shaft and run my tongue along the velvety smooth flesh. When I get to the top, I lick the saltiness away, swirling my tongue around the angry head, and then take him all the way into my mouth until he bottoms out in the back of my throat. I do this several times, getting his dick nice and wet. He's hard as steel, and I can practically feel him throbbing in need.

Just as I'm taking him back into my mouth, he fists the back of my scalp. I think for a second, he's going to face fuck me, and right now, as turned on as I am, I probably wouldn't mind.

But instead, he gathers my hair and gently pulls my mouth off him, bringing me to a standing position.

"As much as I enjoy your pretty lips wrapped around my dick, I need to be inside you." He lifts me back onto the table, pushes my legs apart, and pulls me to the edge. He reaches down and grabs the condom his brother jokingly gave him and rips it open with his teeth. He rolls it over his shaft and then grabs my thighs, hauling my legs over his forearms.

His lips capture mine as he drives into me hard and deep. We're so close I can feel his heart beating erratically against my own. As if we've become one in every way possible.

His thumb finds my clit, and with a few strokes, I detonate, my climax hitting me hard and fast. Kolton moans into my mouth, and even though he's wearing a condom, I can feel when his orgasm hits him and his warm seed fills the rubber barrier.

Our kiss ends, and he drops his face into the crook of my neck, trying to catch his breath. "You realize what you just did, right?" he asks, lifting his head to look me in the eyes.

"What?"

"You solidified everything I already knew. How good we would be together… How amazing you would feel." He presses his mouth to mine in a quick yet punishing kiss before he pulls back, leaving my head spinning. "You know what this means, right?"

"No… what?"

"You're mine."

CHAPTER EIGHT

"**I**S THAT BOX FROM DUNKY DONUTS?" ZANE ASKS, HIS EYES LIGHTING up.

"Yep." I open the box, just long enough for him to get a peek before I close it. "Go grab some plates."

He rushes into the kitchen, giving me enough time to drop the box on to the table and pull Sierra into my arms for a kiss. "Fuck, I missed you," I mutter against her lips.

"It's only been a few hours." She giggles, peppering me with several quick kisses before stepping back.

"A few hours too many," I whine, fully aware I sound like a child. But in my defense, after spending the night before with Sierra in my bed and me in her all damn night, it was hard to spend last night alone. But she was watching Zane and didn't feel it was appropriate for me to spend the night, so to respect her wishes, after we finished watching *SpongeBob* for the second time, I took off, leaving her to put Zane to bed.

She rolls her eyes. "We spent the night on the phone."

"Yeah, we did." I grin, remembering the phone sex we had. It was hot as fuck, but not the same as the real thing.

"Got 'em!" Zane yells, thrusting the plates at me. "Can I have three?"

"You can have one," Sierra says, opening the box so he can choose the one he wants.

"I'll grab the milk," I offer.

As the three of us sit at the table, eating donuts and drinking our milk, I can't take my eyes off Sierra. She talks and jokes with Zane, laughing and smiling the entire time. She's so attentive and patient with him. My mind goes to what it would be like to have a baby with her, to create a family together.

"What?" she asks when she catches me staring.

"I think I'm falling in love with you." I didn't mean for the words to come out, but fuck it, she already knows I'm obsessed with her.

A blush creeps up her neck. "Kolton…"

"Can I do my puzzle?" Zane asks.

"Yeah," she tells him, her eyes never leaving mine. "Go wash your hands first."

He jumps off the chair and runs down the hallway, leaving us alone.

"I mean it," I say, edging closer into her personal space. "I know it's too soon, but I can't help how I feel."

"I feel it too," she admits. "I'm falling in love with you too. And that should scare the hell out of me, but it doesn't."

"Auntie Sierra! I can't pump the soap," Zane calls out.

Sierra leans over and presses a soft kiss to the corner of my mouth before she gets up to go help Zane. I clean up the mess, and when I go back to check on them, Zane is on the floor in his room, dumping his puzzle out.

"C'mon, Uncle Kolton," he says. "We have to put the million trillion pieces together to make SpongeBob!"

We're putting the last pieces of the pineapple together when the door opens.

"Blakely and Keegan must be back," Sierra says, standing. "I didn't think they were returning until later."

"Go tell them I only have two pieces left," Zane says, his tongue sticking out of the side of his mouth in concentration.

We head out to greet them, and maybe it's brotherly intuition, but something feels off… tense… between them.

"You're back early," Sierra says when we get out to the living room.

Blakely eyes me curiously.

"I didn't spend the night," I tell her, wrapping my arm around Sierra. "Just brought breakfast over. I hope that's okay."

"This is just as much Sierra's home as it is mine," Blakely says with a forced smile plastered on her face. "Of course, you're welcome here."

There's a knock on the door, and Keegan answers it. "Yeah?" he asks, his voice filled with contempt.

"I'm here for Zane," a masculine voice says.

"For what?" Keegan asks.

Brenton steps around him and enters the apartment. "It's the last Sunday of the month." When Blakely looks at him confused, he adds, "Home Depot day."

"Yes! Home Depot day!" Zane yells, running out, fist-pumping the air, and then darting back into his room. A minute later, he comes back out, holding a bright orange apron in his hand. "I'm ready!"

"Ready for what?" Keegan asks, confused.

"On the last Sunday of every month, Brenton takes Zane to Home Depot for their craft day. They make stuff out of wood. Sierra and I usually go get our nails done," Blakely explains.

"Like hell he is," Keegan hisses, turning toward Brenton. "You're not taking my fucking kid anywhere."

Oh shit, this isn't going to end well.

"Daddy, you said a bad word!" Zane giggles, having no idea his dad is about to beat the shit out of his mom's friend.

"Sorry, bud," Keegan says. "Why don't you go play in your room while Mommy and I talk?"

Zane's face falls, but he does as his dad says and goes to his room.

Once he's out of earshot, Keegan and Blakely get into an argument about Brenton taking Zane. Blakely doesn't understand why Keegan isn't okay with it, and Keegan can't explain it to her. I keep my mouth shut the entire time, staying close in case Keegan loses his shit and tries to hit Brenton. I wouldn't blame him, but it would fuck everything up that he's worked his ass off for.

"Fuck this!" Keegan yells, getting into Brenton's face. "Anything happens to Zane, and I'm going to hunt you down and kill you."

"Keegan!" Blakely yells. "Stop it!"

Keegan pushes past Brenton and stalks out the door. Before Blakely can chase after him, I stop her. "Let him go. He just needs to calm down."

I follow him, catching up to him just before he takes off in his truck. "You need to chill the hell out."

"Fuck that!" he barks. "That asshole doesn't belong anywhere near my kid or girlfriend."

"And you're going to make sure that doesn't happen, but in order for you to do that, you need to calm down. Keep that shit up, and you're going to fuck everything up."

He releases a harsh breath. "Dammit, I know you're right, but… fuck!"

"Remember the endgame."

He nods once. "Yeah."

"You going home to calm down?"

"Fuck, no, I'm going to follow his ass."

"Figured." I chuckle, knowing my brother too damn well. "Just don't get caught."

Not wanting to face Sierra right now, I get on my bike and head home. She'll assume I went home with Keegan, which is for the best.

I'm home for about twenty minutes when a text comes in from Sierra: **Blakely is upset. I didn't have a chance to say goodbye. I'm sorry. I know we were planning to hang out today, but I need to be here for my sister. <sad face emoji>**

Me: It's okay. It's a shitty situation.

The next two days are spent with my brother freaking the hell out over the fact that Blakely isn't talking to him. Not wanting to risk being put in a bad position, I keep it neutral when Sierra texts bitching about the situation. It's late, probably ten o'clock, when there's a knock on my door. I'm grading papers and have lost track of time. Having no clue who it could be since Keegan has a key and my parents would call first, I get up to answer the door.

"Who is it?"

"Sierra." Sierra… I swing open the door and find her standing on the other side in a pair of tiny cotton shorts and a matching hoodie. Her hair is up in a messy bun, and her face is free of makeup. She looks gorgeous… and like she just woke up.

"Everything okay?" I open the door wider so she can walk through.

"Yeah," she says, wrapping her arms around me as I close the door behind us. "Keegan showed up tonight. Blakey wasn't home, so he waited for her. They must've made up because the last I heard was her screaming his name before I snuck over here." She leans on her tiptoes and kisses me. "I was thinking we could have a sleepover of our own."

"You sure as hell don't have to tell me twice." I scoop her into my arms bridal style and walk us to my bedroom, dropping her onto the bed. She shrugs out of her hoodie, leaving her in only a tiny tank top and shorts that could be considered underwear.

"Kolton, get over here." She runs her fingers over her belly and lifts her shirt up and over her head, exposing her pert breasts.

I spring into action, pulling my shirt over my head and dropping it onto the floor. I climb onto the bed and spread her legs, situating myself between them. Starting at her feet, I trail kisses along her smooth flesh, inhaling her soft, sweet scent. I make my way up one leg and then switch to the other. The entire time she wriggles in her place, moaning softly. I have no doubt she becomes wetter with each kiss I place on her body. I glance up, and her eyes are hooded over with lust, her hands kneading her breasts, her fingers tugging on her nipples.

When I get to the top of her thigh, I yank her shorts down. She's wearing a thin, light-pink cotton thong, and I can tell she's neatly trimmed through the material. I pull them down as well, so she's completely bared to me, and press an open-mouthed kiss to the top of her pussy, inhaling the sweet signature musk of her arousal.

"Fuck, Sierra. I could live between your legs for the rest of my life and die a happy man."

I spread folds open and insert a single finger to gauge how turned on she is. My digit glides in with ease as her juices coat my skin. I pull it out, then insert two—this time, pushing them in deep until my fingers disappear inside her. Sierra moans in pleasure, squeezing her legs against my shoulders.

"Kolton, I need you," she whines.

"Shh… I'm admiring your perfect pussy." I pull my fingers back out once more, making her huff in annoyance, then insert three fingers, fill-ing her up.

"Oh God, too much." Her head whips from side to side.

I remove my fingers once more and spread her legs wide. Her wetness drips down onto the bed. Which makes me wonder…

"Hey, Sierra."

"What?" she asks, popping her head up slightly.

"Has anyone ever fucked you… here?" I drag her juices downward, circling her puckered hole.

"No," she breathes, a slight blush creeping along her neck.

I wet the area and push my finger past the first ring of her ass, and she groans in pleasure. "More," she begs. "I need… more."

Slowly, I push it all the way in, sending her ass off the bed. I'm fucking entranced by everything that is this woman. I can't take my eyes off her.

With one finger in her ass, I push the other into her pussy. She's tight and wet, and I wish to fucking God my dick was in one of those holes. I finger-fuck both her holes until she's screaming my name, writhing under my touch. Never letting up until she's come down from her orgasm.

"Holy shit," she groans, grabbing my head and tugging me up to her face. My fingers, no doubt covered in her orgasm, slip out of her. "I'm go-ing to need you to fuck me now," she demands, her voice filled with a fi-ery passion.

Her fingers thread through my hair, and she tugs me down to her. My palms land on either side of her head, caging her in, and our mouths collide in a passionate embrace. Our kiss isn't stemmed from want but from need. I need Sierra in every way, the same way I need to breathe. She's quickly become an integral part of my life.

Our kiss heats up, becoming an inferno of lust and desire. Her legs wrap around my backside, and her warm pussy grinds against my erection. I break our kiss, wanting to taste other parts of her—the shell of her ear, the delicate area just underneath. My tongue glides down the curve of her neck, sucking on her pulse point before nipping her collarbone.

I take her breast into my mouth, pulling on her nipple with my teeth. When she gasps, I release it, licking away the sting of the pain and loving the way her body reacts to mine.

While I give her body attention, licking and sucking and laving at her perfect tits, her hands find my shorts, pushing them down and wrapping her fingers around my shaft. The feel of her stroking my dick sends bolts of electricity through my body.

"I need you," she breathes, sitting up and pushing me onto my ass. She climbs onto me so we're both sitting up, our bodies connected in almost every way. She uses my shoulders to lift, and then she lowers herself onto me, sucking my dick into her heat, inch by inch. She's tight as fuck in this position, and I have to count to five in my head so I don't blow my load before she finds her second release.

She continues to use my shoulders as leverage, bouncing up and down on my dick. I grip the curve of her ass with one hand and find her clit with the other. As she rides me, I rub circles against her clit, using her wetness to create friction.

"Oh God, yes!" she screams. "Right. Fucking. There."

Her body tenses like a stretched bow awaiting release, and then she lets go, exploding around my dick. Her body trembles, her clit throbs, and her head gets thrown back as she rides out wave after wave of pleasure—the sight sending me straight over the edge along with her.

Nobody has ever affected me the way Sierra does, and when I'm with her, all common sense flies out the window, leaving only my need for her.

"I love you," I murmur against her lips, "so fucking much."

CHAPTER NINE

Sierra

H E LOVES ME… KOLTON REYNOLDS LOVES ME. BUT DOES IT COUNT when a man says it during sex while he's coming deep inside you?

Oh, shit!

He came inside me.

"Pull out quick!" I screech even though I'm the one on top.

I scramble off him as he looks at me like I'm crazy. "You came inside me."

He tilts his head to the side in confusion. "I'm not on birth control." I had an IUD since the pills make me feel sick, and the shot gives me horrible acne, but I had issues with it, and they had to remove it. Since I wasn't actively having sex, I took a break from all birth control.

It takes Kolton a second to understand what I'm saying, implying, and once he does, I expect him to freak the fuck out. So, I'm taken aback when a huge shit-eating grin spreads across his face. He pushes me onto my back and spreads my thighs.

"Are you telling me that what we just did…" He thrusts a finger into me, making me moan. "Me coming in you…" He leans over me until our faces are only inches apart. "Could lead to you carrying my baby?"

I nod in shock.

His smile grows wider. "I hope it does."

"Kolton!" I smack his shoulder. "Have you lost your damn mind?"

"Maybe," he says, his features sobering. "But for the first time since my brother died, I'm feeling again. You've woken me up, Sierra, and I never want to go back to the shell of a man I was before."

He presses a chaste kiss to my lips. "I meant what I said. I love you. I don't give a shit that it's only been a short time. I know you're the one for me, and if what we've done leads to you being swollen with my baby, then good."

What he's saying should send a signal to my brain, telling me to run fast and far, but the only thought that enters my head is the image of me pregnant with Kolton's baby. Giving birth to our little boy or girl with him by my side. Creating a loving family with him.

It should scare me, but it doesn't. Instead, it leaves me wanting more.

"Where are we going?"

"It's a surprise."

I roll my eyes, acting as though he's annoying even though deep down, I'm excited. It's Valentine's Day weekend, and Kolton surprised me with a long weekend away. He even called my boss and asked her to ensure I was off. I'm shocked she agreed, but it shouldn't surprise me. Kolton is a charmer.

"We're on I-4," I point out, "which means we're going to Orlando."

He chuckles. "You're right, we are, but what are we doing there?" He quirks a brow up and glances over at me.

"Hopefully going somewhere with a bed, so you can fuck me." I run my fingers across his leg and over his crotch, making him chuckle. We've been together for a month now, and the heat between us hasn't cooled at all. When I'm not working, I'm with Kolton, and he's either wooing me or making love to me. I haven't been home much lately, and I haven't spent as much time with Blakely and Zane as I usually do, but I don't feel too bad because I'm with Kolton the same way Blakely's with Keegan.

"That'll definitely happen," Kolton says, scooping up my hand and lacing our fingers together. "But first, I have a little surprise for you that I think you'll enjoy." He gnaws on the corner of his bottom lip, suddenly looking nervous. "At least I hope so."

A little while later, we arrive at the Gaylord Palms, a fancy resort in the heart of Orlando. I've been here before with Blakely and Zane to see their annual Christmas exhibit, but we've never spent the night.

After we get checked in, Kolton asks the woman where the conference is being held. She hands him a sheet of paper and draws some directions for him before giving him our keys.

"We have a few minutes to freshen up, but then we have to head out," he says. "We have somewhere we need to be. Wear something nice." He told me to make sure I included a few nice outfits, but I had assumed it was to go out to dinner—yet it's only ten in the morning.

We step into the room, and it's gorgeous, but what's really cool about it is that the balcony leads to an atrium that makes it feel as though you're outdoors.

I grab a pair of dress pants, a flowy top, and my heels and get dressed in the beautiful bathroom. When I come out, Kolton is wearing a pair of charcoal gray dress slacks that hug his ass, a black long-sleeve button-up, and dress shoes.

With his hand in mine, we walk to the elevator and take it to the first floor. Then we head to the left and walk for a while. The signs point to the convention center, and I remember Kolton asked the woman at the front desk about the conference.

And then I see a sign: The International Restaurant and Foodservice Show.

"Kolt…"

"Surprise."

"What are we doing here?" I pull him to the side. "I'm not a restaurant owner."

"No, but one day you will be. I read about this show. It's where all the top restaurateurs come to discuss the business. Independently owned, franchises… You name it. A guy I know from school who teaches business had some extra tickets. I figured it would be fun. Remind you of what you want, what you can one day have."

Oh, my heart… Tears prick my eyes, making him misunderstand. "We don't have to—"

"No," I choke out, wiping away a tear. "I want to. This is so thoughtful of you." Even if the chance of me ever buying or starting my own restaurant is equivalent to one winning the lottery. It feels good to have someone think about me… to put me first.

We spend the day meeting a plethora of people in the hospitality industry—from liquor vendors to interior decorators. When the conference ends for the day, I walk away with enough contacts and information to have a great start to opening my own restaurant if I had the money. It also made me see and understand all the ways Sonora is messing up with The Orange Sunrise. It's too bad she didn't attend this conference.

"All right, I think I'm switching from psychology to opening a bar," Kolton says as we walk out of the conference and back to our room.

"It's kind of the same thing," I joke. "All those people drinking at the bar tend to tell their life stories once they're drunk."

Kolton chuckles. "Some even end up falling in love with their bartender." He throws his arm around my shoulders and kisses my temple.

When we get inside our room, he says, "We have reservations for dinner at—"

But before he can finish, my mouth closes over his, desperate to show him how much I appreciate his thoughtfulness this weekend. "We can eat dinner later. Right now, the only thing I'm hungry for is you."

CHAPTER TEN

Kolton

"**J**ESUS, THESE KIDS CAN'T WRITE FOR SHIT.**" ON ANOTHER PAPER, I note that the student needs to take time to visit the writing center and then move it to the graded pile. As I'm grabbing the next paper from the pile, my phone rings out in the quiet room. Since Sierra is babysitting Zane today, I'm not expecting it to be her—our nephew is great at keeping whoever he's with busy—so I'm not surprised when Keegan's name appears on my caller ID.

"What's up?" I ask, standing to pour myself another cup of coffee so I can get through the rest of the papers.

"It's over. We found him, and he's behind bars."

"*Him*, as in…"

"Miguel. Turns out he was connected to Brenton. He's been here, right under our nose, the entire time."

I exhale a breath of relief. I've been waiting to hear those words from Keegan for too damn long.

"There was one minor snag," Keegan adds, his tone weary. "Blakely was there when it all went down. She knows I'm an undercover narcotics officer."

Oh, shit… That is not how he wanted to tell her. "How is she?"

"Pissed as fuck. And I don't blame her." He sighs. "I just dropped her off at home. She wants nothing to do with me."

"Just give her time. You were in a shitty position and did the best you could. She'll come around."

"Yeah, I hope so. I need to go back to the station. There's a shit ton of paperwork that needs to get done."

"Does this mean you're moving home now?" Keegan was only living here to play the part of a college student. He actually owns a nice-ass house elsewhere.

"Yeah, I'll be back tonight to pack my shit."

"Hey, Keegan…"

"Yeah?"

"Thank you."

"You're welcome." We're both silent for a beat before he adds, "Blakely doesn't know the whole story… or really any of it. Can you let me tell her, please? I would rather it come from me. I had to keep it all a secret so I didn't compromise the investigation."

"Of course."

We hang up, and I call Sierra, knowing she's going to pissed. She and Blakely are two sides of a coin. And even though I technically never lied to her—and I made sure I didn't—omitting the truth is still lying. When she doesn't answer, I send her a text that I need to talk to her. She doesn't reply.

I consider going to her place, but I don't want to push too hard, so instead, I try to finish grading the papers, which ends up taking twice as long as it normally would since I can't focus for shit. The longer my phone call and text goes unanswered, the deeper the sinking feeling in the pit of my stomach goes.

Just when I'm about to say fuck it and go to Sierra's place to explain my side, my phone rings.

"Please, let me explain," I beg when I answer her call.

"Explain that your brother is an undercover cop who was investigating Brenton, and instead of telling my sister, he let her continue to hang out with him and put her and Zane in harm's way? I already know."

"There's more to it than that."

"You and Keegan lied and kept important shit from us," she says, her voice resigned. "That's exactly what my dad did, and it's exactly what I was afraid of happening to me." No. No. *No, No, No...*

"It is not the same thing."

"My sister could've had Zane taken away!" she yells, her voice filled with heartache. Heartache I inadvertently caused. "And for what? So your brother could catch a drug dealer? He put his job above his family, just like our dad did, and you sat back and watched it all happen!"

"No. Keegan was watching them. He was following them everywhere. He never would've let anything happen to them. Please, you have to trust me."

"It doesn't change the fact that you lied and kept things from me, and now, I can't trust you," she says, her voice cracking with emotion. "I don't know what'll happen between Keegan and my sister, but as for us... we're over."

She hangs up on me, and I want to call her back, beg her to listen, to see reason. I want to go over there and make her understand why he did what he did. But I can't do any of that until Keegan talks to Blakely.

Shit! I slam my phone on the table. Will the domino effect of my choices back then ever come to a stop?

"How are things with you and Sierra?" Keegan asks at breakfast three days later.

"Not good. I can't really do much when I can't tell her the entire story."

Keegan flinches. "Shit, I'm sorry. I didn't even consider that. Look," he says, taking a sip of his coffee. "If you want to tell Sierra, you can, but if you can ask her to please let me tell Blakely, I would appreciate it."

"Thanks," I say, standing and patting him on the shoulder. "I'm not sure if she'll even hear me out, but I appreciate it."

"Brenton got out on bail. I'm going to head over to campus to make sure he doesn't fuck with Blakely."

"He shouldn't even be on campus."

"Doesn't mean he won't be."

Ten minutes later, my brother and I arrive on campus and walk toward the psychology building when I spot none other than Brenton and Blakely in a heated argument in the quad.

"Fuck!" Keegan yells, ready to charge over and lay Brenton out.

"Stop! Let me handle it. You don't want to take a chance of getting into it with Brenton and fucking up the case. Call for backup."

"They're already on campus." He yanks out his phone, no doubt to give them the location of where we are while he steps into the shadows so nobody sees him.

I stalk over to Brenton and Blakely. "You need to get the hell away from her right fucking now," I yell at Brenton, who's now in Blakely's face.

"I was just talking to her," Brenton says.

"And now you're not." I step between them. "Walk away."

"The only place I'm walking to is class," Brenton points out.

"Actually, you're not. You obviously haven't checked your email. You've been withdrawn from your classes and expelled from this university."

"You can't fucking do that!" Brenton roars, making Blakely jump in fear.

"It's already been done. If you want to argue about it, speak to the dean." I take Blakely's hand, needing to get her away from Brenton before Keegan flips his shit. "Let's go," I murmur as we round the corner to where Keegan and two other officers are standing.

"You were here the whole time?" she asks Keegan.

"Of course," Keegan says. "But I know you want your space." He shrugs. "I told you you'd be safe no matter what and that someone would be on you."

"Thank you."

I'm distracted the entire time in class, but I still somehow manage to get through the lecture. Once class is dismissed, I head out to The Orange Sunrise, needing to speak to Sierra since Keegan is okay with me telling her everything.

CHAPTER ELEVEN

Sierra

I FEEL HIM BEFORE I SEE HIM. KOLTON. THE MAN I'VE FALLEN IN LOVE with. I've been thinking about him every second of every minute since I hung up on him. The tiny hairs on the back of my neck rise, and my belly tightens in anticipation as I watch him walk over to where I'm standing at the hostess stand.

"I can't wait any longer," he says. "I've tried to give you your space. I get it. The entire situation sucks, but I can't just let you walk away. Not like this… hell, not ever."

Kolton's jaw tightens, and his eyes shine with unshed tears, and it's then I see how badly he looks. Dark circles under his eyes, his normally tan complexion pasty. He's been suffering right along with me.

"Paula, please make sure you keep all takeout receipts tonight. I'm heading out. If you need anything, Sonora will be in soon."

Like everyone else does when I mention Sonora, she rolls her eyes. "See you tomorrow."

I grab my purse from behind the hostess stand and walk outside with Kolton following. Not wanting to have this conversation on the streets, I walk over to his bike. "Want to go to your place and talk?"

"Yeah," he says, his voice cracking.

The ride to his apartment is quick, but as I sit behind him with my arms wrapped around his torso and my face nestled against his back, I wish we could ride for longer.

We walk inside his place, and it looks different… I can't quite place it.

"Keegan moved out, so his messy ass shit isn't all over the place," Kolton says, answering my unspoken thoughts. "He's planning to ask Blakely to move in with him." He sits on the couch and scrubs his palms over his face.

"I doubt she'll be on board with that." I sit across from him on the loveseat.

"With Brenton out on bail, he's hoping she'll put aside her hurt and do what's best for her and Zane's safety. Brenton's already approached her once, and I had to intervene."

"What?" I shriek. "When? She didn't tell me."

He sighs, exhaustion evident in his features. "This morning… But I don't want to talk about them. I want to talk about us."

"I don't know what there's to talk about. You lied and hid shit, and I can't be with someone like that. You knew about what my father did, yet—"

His eyes lock with mine. "That's such bullshit!" he barks, making me jump. He cuts across the area to where I am, kneels in front of me, and frames my face with his palms. "It's not fair for you to compare what happened to what your dad did. You said it yourself when the fire caught, he threw you guys into it. Keegan, on the other hand, was in that fucking fire doing everything he could to fight it so Blakely and Zane wouldn't be touched. He's been fighting that fire for fucking years."

"Years?" I knew Brenton sold drugs in high school, but why would it have taken Keegan that long to put him away?

Kolton sighed. "There's something you need to know, but I need you to keep it between us until Keegan speaks with Blakely. He wants to be the one to explain it to her."

"Great. More secrets. If you're not supposed to tell me, then don't." I stand, and Kolton stands with me. "I don't know why I even came here." *Liar! You came here because you love him and miss him and need him to make it right because even though what he did was wrong, you can't imagine your life without him.*

"Sierra." He grabs my hips and tugs me toward him. "You came here because you love me, and despite how hurt you are, you know that whatever happened was done to protect you and your sister and Zane. You can try to push me away to protect your heart, but you know I would never do anything to hurt you."

Jesus, it's like he has insight into my head and heart...

One of his hands glides up my side and cups my cheek. "I love you so goddamn much, and even though I hate how you and Blakely found out, I wouldn't change a single thing because what Keegan did was to protect the three of you." He swallows thickly. "And..." Tears well up in his eyes and then tip over, racing down his face. "He did it for me too."

My heart tightens in my chest. I don't understand what he means, but I can feel it in his words and in the way he's touching me. In the way he's looking at me. How upset he is over all of this. He means what he's saying, and he's right. He's not my father. He's nothing like him, and it's not fair to compare Kolton to him.

"I'll tell you everything..."

"No," I breathe. "I... I trust you," I choke out. "I was shocked and scared, and I felt so damn stupid. But you're right, you aren't my father. Neither you nor Keegan are. And yes, I do love you. So, even though I'm upset, I'm not going anywhere. I want to be with you. Whatever the reason Keegan did what he did, and your family supported him, I believe you. That it was done, not to throw us into the fire, but to save us from it."

Kolton sighs a breath of relief, and then shocks the hell out of me with his next words. "Move in with me. I don't want to be without you. I don't want to wake up or go to bed without you. I want to spend my life with you. I wanted to ask you weeks ago, but with Keegan here and everything going on, I didn't want to ask you while hiding shit from you."

"Technically, you're still hiding things from me," I sass.

He nods. "Only because you don't want to lie to your sister. Otherwise, I would tell you everything now."

"I want to move in with you." Kolton's eyes go wide in surprise. "But I need to speak to Blakely first and see how she feels. If she doesn't forgive Keegan—"

"She will," Kolton says. "I know she will. They love each other, and when you love someone like that, you don't throw in the towel that easily."

I nod in agreement. "I can't move out if she isn't taken care of. I pay the bills, so she needs me."

"You can keep paying them." Kolton presses his lips to mine. "I'll take care of everything. In May, I'm graduating, and if all goes as planned, I'll be working at the college full-time. I can afford to pay our bills. I just want you in my bed with me every night."

"I want that too," I murmur against his mouth. "I just need a little time."

"Off work today?" Blakely asks when she and Zane walk through the door. I was technically off, but like always, I had to go in and take care of shit. I considered going back after Kolton and I talked, but instead, I came home so I could wait for Blakely.

"Yeah, I spoke to Kolton. He said Brenton approached you. How are you doing?"

"I'm okay." She pauses and glances at Zane. "Hey, sweetie, go potty and get ready for your nap, please."

"Okay, Mommy!" he says like the good boy he is, before running down the hallway.

"I can't believe he actually thought he'd apologize, and I'd forgive him," Blakely says once Zane is out of earshot, referring to Brenton.

"I can't believe he was doing that shit right under our noses." I huff. "I feel as stupid as you do. You know he used to sell when we were in high school?"

"What? No, I didn't know that."

"Yep, but I just thought it was him being a stupid teenager. I never thought he would continue."

"He thinks I'm going to come around, but it's not happening."

"Kolton mentioned you and Zane moving in with Keegan. He said it would be safer."

"What else did he say?"

"That's it. He wanted to explain the entire story, but he said he can't until Keegan speaks to you. They feel you deserve to know the truth first."

The truth is, he wanted to tell me, but I wanted to wait. Blakely deserves to know the truth first.

"I was thinking about talking to him," Blakely admits. "To at least hear him out."

"I won't tell you what to do, but I think that would be a good idea."

"And if we moved into Keegan's place, would you move with us?"

Shit! I wasn't planning to say anything about Kolton asking me to move in with him yet, but I can't lie to her… I won't.

"S?"

"I was…" I take a deep breath, trying not to appear too excited. I don't want her to base her decisions on me. "I was actually thinking I could move in with Kolton."

Blakely's eyes bug out. "He asked you to move in with him?"

"He did. He said the only reason he didn't ask sooner was because of everything going on, but now that it's done, he wants me to move in. But I told him I had to speak to you first."

"I would never keep you from moving in with him," she says softly.

"Are you upset?" I stand and walk over to her. Blakely and Zane will always come first. If she doesn't want me to move, I won't.

"No… I guess I'm just a little sad. It seems like everything is changing. I just learned Keegan is a cop, and now you're talking about moving in with your boyfriend. Brenton was my best friend for years, and now he's being cut out of my life. It's just a lot to take in, you know?"

"I know."

"Mommy! I'm ready for bed," Zane yells, making Blakely and me laugh.

"I wonder if all kids love to nap the way Zane does."

"I doubt it," I tell her. "Watch, you'll have another kid one day, and he or she will despise naptime, and you'll never have a moment to yourself."

"Wow, you're not only knocking me up, but you're cursing me. Thanks." She stands to go tuck Zane into bed, and there's a knock on the door.

"I'll grab it while you tuck him in," I offer, already heading to the door.

I open it up and find Brenton standing there, only before I can yell at him and tell him to go fuck himself, an officer steps between us. "Sir, there's a restraining order." The officer hands him a piece of paper. "If you come within fifteen hundred feet of Blakely, Sierra, or Zane Jacobs, you will be arrested. This is your one and only warning."

"This is bullshit," Brenton hisses, but does as the officer says and walks away.

"Thank you," I tell him.

He nods once. "Someone will always be here to make sure you're safe."

"Who was it?" Blakely asks as I close the door.

"Brenton."

"What? He came here?"

"Yeah, but he only made it to knock on the door before a police officer stopped him and made him leave."

"I think maybe I should take Keegan up on his offer to move in there with Zane."

"I think so too," I agree. Even if they can't make it work, I know Keegan will keep them safe.

"I'm going to speak to Keegan today. Let him explain. I don't know where we'll stand afterward, but at least that way you and Kolton can move forward."

I wrap my arms around her and give her a hug. "I'm not going anywhere. Not until everything is figured out."

CHAPTER TWELVE

Kolton

K NOCK. KNOCK. KNOCK.

I jump up and sprint to the door, hoping like hell it's Sierra. She texted me earlier that she was watching Zane so Blakely and Keegan could talk. Then, a few minutes ago, Keegan sent me a text that said he told Blakely everything, and they're okay. I was dying to text Sierra to ask her to come over to talk, but I didn't want to appear *too* crazy.

"Hey," she says when I open the door.

"Hey."

"My answer is yes."

"Yes?" I quirk a brow up, confused.

"I'll move in with you." She steps inside, and I close the door. "I needed you to know that before we talk. No matter what you have to say, I need you to know that I'm one hundred percent in."

We sit on the couch, and as much as I want to pull her onto my lap, I refrain, needing to tell her everything. But before I can start, as if she can sense what I really need, she edges closer and then climbs on to me, straddling my thighs.

"Talk to me, Kolton. Tell me everything."

I close my eyes, taking a deep breath, then open them, ready to tell her the entire truth. "When I was nineteen, and in college, I did the stupidest thing someone could do. I was struggling to keep up with my classes, and I went in search of drugs to help."

I search Sierra's face for judgment, but she doesn't give anything away as she waits patiently for me to continue. "A friend of a friend referred me to this guy, Miguel. He sold all types of shit, including pills he swore would help me stay awake and focus. One pill turned into several, and soon, I was addicted, relying on them to help me function. I didn't know it at the time, but my brother Keith was a narcotics officer investigating an influx of drug dealing on campus…"

Sierra's arms snake around my neck, and I grip her hips, needing to feel her to keep going. "I was buying another bottle from Miguel when Keith approached. Miguel took one look at Keith's badge and pulled a gun on him. Shot him dead right there."

Sierra gasps, and her hold on me tightens.

"That's right. I was buying drugs from the man who killed my brother. Everyone went into panic mode, and Miguel got away. Keegan became a narcotics officer, determined to follow in Keith's footsteps. A few months back, there was a whisper that the dealing was happening again. Keegan was brought in undercover as a college student to catch the guy."

"Brenton," she breathes.

"Yep, he was selling. Only, he wasn't doing it on his own. The man running the operation was his ex-stepfather… Miguel Sanchez."

"Oh, my God!" Tears prick Sierra's eyes.

"Keegan not only brought Brenton down, but he also brought down our brother's killer," I choke out. "It won't bring him back, but…"

"But your family will at least have some closure."

I nod. "Yeah. I can't bring him back, but at least I could give them that. I went in and identified it was him."

"Oh, Kolton. I can't imagine that was easy for you. Having to see that piece of shit."

"It was the hardest thing I've ever had to do, but something I deserved because it was my fault…"

"Stop it," Sierra demands. "That man choosing to kill an officer was not your fault."

"If I hadn't been buying from him—"

"You can't live like that. It's unhealthy. But I get it," she says. "When my parents first died, I used to blame myself. I overheard my dad hurting my mom so many times, yet I never told anyone. I used to think, what if I would've told someone: a teacher or another parent. Or what if I would've told my mom I knew. Maybe she would've left him sooner… But eventually, I realized that there was no point in wondering what-if. We all make choices, and many of them are mistakes, and most of the time, we get a chance to right them."

"But sometimes, our choices are deadly."

"Yeah," she agrees. "But in our case, they weren't our choices. My dad chose to put us in the car and drive drunk, and Miguel chose to pull that trigger. They don't deserve to be let off the hook. They made those choices, not us."

I lean forward and nuzzle my face in Sierra's neck, so fucking thankful for her. "You're perfect," I murmur. "Don't ever leave me, please. I need you. Forever."

"I'm not going anywhere," she says, lifting my face and kissing me hard. "It's like you said. You and me… we're inevitable."

EPILOGUE

Sierra

Five Years Later

"**H**OLY SHIT." I STARE DOWN AT THE TEST, THEN LOOK UP AT MY sister. "Tell me I'm reading this wrong."

Blakely laughs. "Sure, you're reading it wrong…and so am I."

My head pops up. "You're…"

She nods. "Yep."

"Babe!" Kolton yells from outside my back office. "Get out here. We need to celebrate! I ordered some apps and drinks."

"I'll be right out," I yell back even though the last place I want to be is out there, in my new restaurant, smelling all that food and not being able to have a single drink.

Blakely giggles. "I can't believe this is happening…again."

"That's what we get for marrying brothers."

We both walk outside to find our families sitting at the table. Kolton and Keegan are each nursing a beer while Zane plays a game on his phone.

"Mom! Can I borrow your phone?" Colby, Kolton's and my four-year-old son, asks. "Mine is dead."

"Mine is too!" Finn, Blakely and Keegan's son, who is also four years old, says.

That's right. A couple of months after I moved in with Kolton, and Blakely moved in with Keegan, we both found out we were pregnant and due the same week. Neither of our guys knew, but they found out at the same time when they both proposed together.

Six months later, we were married on Cocoa Beach alongside each other, and three months after that, we both gave birth to our little boys only three days apart.

"There she is," Kolton says, wrapping his arms around me. "That article in *Foodie* is amazing! And the critique was right on all accounts."

I smile, replaying the article in my head. When I found out a food critic had stopped by anonymously, I freaked out. What he wrote and published could make or break me. But Kolton told me it would be okay. What I've built here is solid, and I had nothing to worry about. The article came out today, and he was right. The critic loved the restaurant and gave it three Michelin stars, the highest compliment a restaurant can receive.

I'm so proud of what I've created, but I'm also scared. It took four years of saving to come up with enough down payment for a loan to open my own restaurant. I decided to buy one that was failing and resurrect it. I couldn't do it with The Orange Sunrise since it closed less than a year after I predicted it would. I had just given birth and wasn't in a position to save it.

I'd busted my ass for almost a year getting the restaurant ready, and for the past six months since it opened, I've been working even harder to make it a success… only to find out tonight that I'm expecting again. I knew it was a possibility, but I kind of thought it would take a little longer than a month for it to happen. Don't get me wrong, I'm excited, but I have no clue how I'm going to juggle running a new restaurant, raising a four-year-old, and being a wife while baking another little one in my oven.

"We have shots," Keegan says, handing one to Blakely and me.

"To Sierra," Kolton says. "For following her dreams." He leans over and kisses my cheek. "I knew you could do it, baby. I'm so damn proud of you."

The guys both throw back their shots and then look at Blakely and me in confusion when neither of us does the same.

"What's wrong?" Keegan asks Blakely.

"I'm pregnant," she blurts out.

"What?" His entire face lights up. "Are you serious?" He stands and pulls her into his arms. "Hell yeah! That's what I'm talking about." He releases her and glances at his brother. "Looks like you owe me a hundred bucks."

"For what?" Blakely asks.

"I knocked you up first." Keegan shrugs.

"You bet on which one of us would get pregnant first?" Blakely laughs, smacking her husband in the chest.

"The other night while we were watching the game, Kolton mentioned they were trying again, and I told him we were too, so we made a friendly wager… Whoever's sperm was stronger wins."

Blakely snorts out a laugh, glancing at me knowingly.

"I'm pregnant too," I announce.

Kolton's eyes go wide before a shit-eating grin spreads across his face. "You're pregnant?" He looks from me to Blakely and back to me again. "You're both pregnant."

"Yeah," I tell him, rolling my eyes playfully. "We're both pregnant."

He fist pumps the air before he pulls me onto his lap. "I'm so fucking excited," he murmurs into my neck, kissing the sensitive spot beneath my ear. "I can't wait to see you growing my baby again."

"I'm a little scared," I admit. "Do you think maybe we're taking on too much?"

Kolton pulls back slightly, his eyes meeting mine. "We've got this, Sierra. You and me together… we can handle anything." The moment his mouth connects with mine, my entire body visibly relaxes. He's right. We've got this. Not a single day has gone by that Kolton hasn't been my partner in all things. Supporting and encouraging, standing by my side.

"So…" Keegan starts, making Kolton and me look his way. "Which one of you is further along?"

ABOUT THE AUTHOR

Nikki Ash is a USA Today Bestselling author of contemporary romance, focusing on single parent, secret baby, and surprise pregnancy romances. She spends her days and nights getting lost in words. When she's not writing, she's reading. From the Boxcar Children, to Wuthering Heights, to the latest single parent romance, she has lived and breathed every type of book.

Nikki resides in South Florida with her husband, two children, and dog that she considers to be one of her kids. When she's not reading or writing, she's traveling the world with her family—in search of inspiration.

www.ingramcontent.com/pod-product-compliance
Lightning Source LLC
Chambersburg PA
CBHW071401300726
48976CB00006B/1948